K L Cox is a young upcoming fantasy writer and author. She has been a lifelong writer as she began to create extensive worlds and detailed characters since her primary school days. Working from her home in East Sussex, she brings to life stunning plotlines and epic adventures and tales born from dreams and idyllic inspirations around her daily life. She regularly splits her life between her writing and her love of her cats.

For my parents and family, who have believed in me since I was a child and have inspired some of my colourful characters throughout the years. It couldn't have been done without you.

K L Cox

Dreamcatcher

Austin Macauley Publishers™
London * Cambridge * New York * Sharjah

This is a work of fiction. Names, characters, businesses, places, events, locales, and incidents are either the products of the author's imagination or used in a fictitious manner. Any resemblance to actual persons, living or dead, or actual events is purely coincidental.

A CIP catalogue record for this title is available from the British Library.

ISBN 9781398459748 (Paperback)
ISBN 9781398459755 (ePub e-book)

www.austinmacauley.com

First Published 2023
Austin Macauley Publishers Ltd®
1 Canada Square
Canary Wharf
London
E14 5AA

My wonderful grandmother, Carole Evans, for always pushing me to go above and beyond with my writing, and believing that I could be a published author.

My mother, Dawn Cox, for nurturing my imagination and gifting me with the ability of creating whole worlds and people.

My friend, Ellie Martell, for always letting me bounce ideas off her when I first began to write, and for letting me annoy her with my writers block.

And to all the people who told me my hobby was just that—a hobby, I thank you. You've inspired quite the few characters throughout my work who would never exist if not for your disbelief in the art of writing.

Chapter One

The world around Galen was a paradise that she could only wish was real. She was utterly alone in her dreams, a place where she knew she was safe, where she could create whatever she wanted. All around her was a picture-perfect scene of autumn. Red, yellow, orange and brown leaves fell in spirals all around her and piled at her feet. The trees towered hundreds of feet high, stretching right through the clouds to the heavens above her. Little rays of sunlight pushed through the thick canopy, illuminating little patches of dry, earthy path that Galen followed happily.

This was a dream that she had often. She fell asleep willing the place to form around her, and tonight was one of the lucky nights where she got her way. Galen followed the same path to the same place watching the same sights happen all around her. The same noises of the bubbling creek, the swoosh of the wind, the creaking of the trees and branches, swelled around her and filled her with warmth and happiness. It was perfect. Anything she wanted was right at her fingertips. She was the creator in this world—she was its god, and she only strived for perfection and happiness in her oasis.

Just as the sun began to shine through more vibrantly, the autumn scenery around Galen tumbled away into that of a beautiful, shining white beach with clear, crystal waters that lapped at the shore. The heavy boots that had been on Galen's feet disappeared as she picked each foot up, her toes sifting through the sand. Her coat and her scarf fell from her shoulders and fell through the sand, and her long hair was scraped up into a loose ponytail. A tight bodysuit strapped itself about her body as sunglasses fell over her eyes, shielding her from the bright sun in the sky.

People lined the beaches on towels of different sizes, shapes, patterns and colours. There were families enjoying the heat and the water, children playing in the rockpools. Men fought with parasols and women baked in the sun's rays, turning an awful shade of beet red. Galen wandered by them all, waving at them and smiling at those that called her name. She knew them all. They had the faces of strangers she had seen wandering the streets, people she'd spoken to at work, the occasional person she knew from school.

But then there was one face she didn't know.

Right there, at the very back of the beach where the sand met the jungles was a woman. She was standing with her arms crossed over her chest, but one hand lifted to her mouth. Atop her head was a giant, floppy sunhat that hid the top half of her face. Galen could only see her lips, painted a shade of scorching hot pink. Those lips curled up into a horrifically beautiful smile once she noticed Galen looking her way and blew her a kiss just for good measure.

Stopped in her tracks, Galen blinked and rubbed at her eyes roughly. She couldn't believe what she was seeing. When her vision cleared, Galen saw no such woman standing in the background. There were only trees, empty sun loungers and families not so keen on the sea. Was she just seeing things? Was that possible in a dream? She wouldn't let it faze her; Galen decided. There was no use in dwelling on something that obviously didn't exist.

Galen wandered into the cold waters, letting them lap about her. She grazed her hands flat against the surface of the water, watching as every single ripple she caused ceased to exist. Still as ever, the sea halted to an everlasting calm. Galen stood at the centre of it, her toes still buried in the sand, watching the fish swim about her in schools. There were goldfish, angelfish, clownfish and butterflyfish alike. They darted back and forth between Galen's legs as she waded deeper and deeper, though those tiny fish grew larger the further in she went.

Sucking in her breath, Galen submerged herself. She plummeted deep into the depths, eyes wide open and limbs perfectly calm. The water soothed her, kept her calm, washed away thoughts of that strange, unrecognisable woman. A smile returned to Galen's face as she swum down to the bottom of the ocean, towards a beam of light. This was never here before. Where could it lead? Galen hesitated, even throwing a look back at her precious beach that she had grown up with. Still, the allure of something new was overbearing, difficult to ignore.

Slowly, Galen dragged herself towards it. It only grew brighter and brighter the closer that Galen got, blinding her. Heat emanated from it that tugged Galen in further. Tendrils of light and warmth unfurled from the mass, beckoning to Galen like an outstretched finger. Its long limbs floated by Galen's sides, brushing against her, and caressing her skin. It waited, and it waited, patient as ever. Galen felt enticed by it, enthralled. She had to get closer, pushing her arm forwards and just gently grazing against the ball of fire. It felt soft, warm, cosy. There was nothing threatening about it at all. If it was a person, it would be a friendly worker in a small, tucked away bookshop that was all smiles and laughs. Just that thought alone brought a smile to Galen's face, though that smile sat pretty for all of two seconds.

Suddenly, those friendly and comforting wisps coiled about Galen's arms and her legs and began to drag her. It burned as hot as hellfire, leaving burns and lesions all over Galen's skin. The more she fought, the tighter they wrapped about her limbs. It bound her, held her, pulled her further to the bottom of the ocean.

No more was the water crystal clear. It was thick and black and viscous. Galen could barely move, barely see. She opened her mouth to scream but her tongue was tainted with a bitter, acidic taste. Clumps of the tainted water stuck in Galen's throat as she wrenched herself free from the fronds. She twisted round, staring up at the surface where she'd be free. Her arms flapped frantically against the current, but she was suspended in mid-air, unable to move. Her screams were muffled as more and more tendrils came shooting out from the ball of light, scathing her skin. One shot from the centre, crawling up the length of Galen's spine until it slithered from one cheek to another, gagging her.

There was no escape now. Galen willed herself to wake up, desperate to get free from her binds. She struggled despite her efforts being futile, not wanting to succumb to the light. She wanted to be up on the beach again, or in her autumn park, or somewhere else. Her teeth grinded down against the cord that gagged her, but it was no use. There was nothing that she could do.

Hundreds more wisps wrapped about Galen and dragged her back. She rocketed backwards, entangled in a snare that she didn't know how to break. The last thing she saw was the surface of her dream, the crystalline skies up above her that were so close yet so, so far away, before she was wrenched into a pit of bright light and sweltering heat.

Galen sat bolt upright in her bed, sweating profusely. She pressed her palms behind her as she fought to catch her breath, her eyes still scarred with the burning light she'd been dragged into. Manically, Galen searched her room. She stared at the posters and pictures on the wall, the little bits scattered across her desk, the sun shining in through the lazily drawn curtains. A sigh left her body as she rubbed at her eyes and pushed her covers back from her body and stood, confused, and frightened.

"You're up early," Galen's mother retorted as her daughter meandered into the kitchen, only roused by the smell of bacon cooking on the hob. "I heard you tossing and turning up there. Something bothering you?"

Nessa, Galen's mother, did everything by herself. She had once been an eclectic scientist who had studied psychology and how the brain worked and knew everything about anything. Now, she slaved away by herself in her house, cooking cakes and loaves of bread for her shop. She kept her two children close in fear of losing them, as she had lost two of her other children. Her husband had taken them in the divorce, claiming that Nessa was too frantic and manic to care for so many kids. Galen had managed to stay with her beloved mother, as had her brother, Cress. Galen hated her father, hated the man he'd become after the fight.

He'd worked with Nessa whilst she'd been a scientist. He was a professor at one of the top universities and taught all the modern world's geniuses what they knew. The man was so smart that there was nothing on earth he didn't know, but he was a jealous man. The success that his wife found was never a treasure of his own. Every breakthrough she had threw shadows on his career, so he did what he thought was right and stole every inch and every word of her work, and then divorced her.

Nessa ignored his existence. She hadn't forgotten the children he'd taken with him, Ava and Loic, but she had forgotten about him. To say his name in her house was a punishable offence, and she often put a penny in a jar for every time she thought about him.

"I had a nightmare."

Galen's mother stopped what she was doing, resting her spatula against the rim of the frying pan. "A nightmare? You haven't had one of those since you were a child. Is there something on your mind?"

"I don't know what happened." Galen ran her fingers through her hair and pinned it back on her scalp, trying to keep her breathing calm and rhythmic. Her heart was still beating out of control, her mind still thinking she was in danger. "It was so normal to begin with and then suddenly it just..."

"What happened?" Nessa took the seat next to her daughter, covering her hand with her own and remaining blissfully unaware that her bacon was burning. "You can talk to me. It's all over now. Nothing is going to hurt you."

Galen found herself wishing that could be true. "I was at the beach," she started shakily, remembering every frame of the dream as if it had been a show she'd watched on television. "I was walking across the sand and then I saw someone I'd never seen before. She was so out of place, lurking on the outskirts. She blew me a kiss…I rubbed my eyes and, when I opened them again, she'd disappeared, so I thought she wasn't real and that I was just seeing things." Galen sighed as her mother squeezed her hand to urge her on, recalling those vivid pink lips and hungry, charming grin. "I walked into the water and I saw this ball of light at the bottom of the ocean. I didn't think it could do me any harm. It was so inviting and warm, and it reached out to me. It felt like a hug, but when I touched it…"

"Go on," her mother pushed.

"It suddenly attacked me," Galen murmured. "It flung all these tendrils at me, like the arms of an octopus, and dragged me towards it. It was drowning me. The sea turned all black and inky, like it had been poisoned. I could taste it and I could feel it choking me as I was being dragged down this hole." The panic began to rise in Galen again. She could feel the sweat beginning to mount on her brow, the warmth rushing back to her cheeks and chest. "I couldn't fight against it. No matter what I did, I went down with it. I tried to scream but it gagged me and got the better of me. It beat me."

Nessa sat closer, scooping both of Galen's hands off the table and into her lap. "What happened when it dragged you through the light?"

"I woke up."

"I see." Her mother went to say something else, something reassuring, but quickly smelled smoke. Her nose twitched for a few seconds before she realised what was happening and rocketed from her seat to fix it. "It's over now, sweetheart. Nothing's going to get you. That woman wasn't real, and that ball of light doesn't exist. You're in the real world now, my love. What happens in your dreams is only in your mind."

Galen slumped against the table. "I know. You're right." She watched her mother frantically try to fix the bacon that she'd sizzled for a little while too long and let her eyes drop to the plate that was pushed in front of her. "Can you dream about people you don't know?"

"Well, the people in your dreams that you don't recognise are often those you see in the street and pay no attention to," Nessa responded. "Perhaps you've seen this woman whilst out and about and you just didn't realise it."

"That can't be. I would've recognised her."

A little scoff emanated from Galen's mother. "That striking, was she?"

"I've never seen a person like her before. She was so ethereal. She felt so real, too. It was like I wasn't dreaming, but I was living, like I encountered her when I was working or something. She was…gorgeous."

"Sounds like you have a little crush." Nessa scooped her charred bacon out of the pan and placed it as delicately as she could on the plate. Next to it she plopped two eggs and a few slices of bread which she fiddled with until they sat perfect. "Your brother hoped you were going to go to work with him today. He said that you'd made some sort of arrangement between yourselves."

Galen perked up. How could she have forgotten? She'd started taking days down at the beach to help her brother with the lifeguard patrol. It was something to make the summer go by quicker, and she'd promised Cress that today would be one of the days they'd go together, and she'd missed it.

Overcome with guilt, Galen simply picked at the food her mother placed in front of her. "I should go."

"You should. He misses spending time with you."

Groaning, Galen scooped everything into her mouth and pushed away from the table.

"If you have any more of those dreams, Galen, you should come to talk to me," Nessa called to her daughter before she lost sight of her. She shoved the frying pan into the sink and let it sit there and sizzle, a little puff of smoke rising from the bubbles. "I may be able to help you. I used to…study these types of things in my spare time."

"Thanks mum, but I don't think I'm going to be sleeping anytime soon."

The beach in reality was not anything like the one in Galen's dreams. The sky wasn't always a piercing blue with not a cloud in sight. It was a dark grey with heavy clouds that choked out every inch of sunlight. The sea wasn't always clear, and the schools of fish weren't always tropical and brightly coloured. It was often a murky green with patches of scum and seaweed floating on the top, and the fish were most often dead. The sand wasn't white and soft, but beige and coarse, rough and abrasive. The place was horrible on the best of days, and downright unbearable on the worst.

"You said you had a nightmare?" Cress stood out on the balcony watching over the towering waves, binoculars held to his eyes. There wasn't a person out in the water, but Cress liked to pretend there was someone out there that needed him to save them. "What happened?"

"Something tried to drown me." Galen simplified it, already tired of having to remember the trauma again and again and again. The truth was she hadn't forgotten it for a second. That woman's face and that ball of light had been haunting her thoughts ever since she'd woken up. "That's why I was late today."

Cress made a noise in the back of his throat. "I figured you'd just decided that you didn't want to spend time with your big brother."

"You are a bit of an asshole when you come back from Dad's."

"Ah, you acknowledged him as your father. That's a rarity."

Galen rolled her eyes. "No matter how hard I pray at night, the man remains my father." She ran her fingertips over the maps that Cress had lain out, wandering to stand by her brother's side and stare out over the raging ocean. "Did he have anything to say?"

"Not really."

"Did he remember I exist?"

Cress lowered his binoculars. "He did."

"And?"

"He wishes you'd come see him," Cress sighed deeply. He pushed a hand through his curly locks and let his fringe stand up on end, his eyes slowly travelling to his younger sister. "I wish you'd come with me to see him. He's not as bad a guy as you think he is."

Galen's shoulders lilted in a shrug. "I'm busy doing other things."

"Other things like daydreaming? Drawing? Writing up your little stories?" Cress laughed at his sister as he hugged her tightly to his chest. "I know you have a strong imagination, sis, but maybe it's time you spend some time in the real world with people that actually exist."

Galen pushed away from Cress. "This world is boring and the one I've made in my head is more entertaining."

"Even if it does give you nightmares."

"That, I believe, was a one off. If it happens again…" Galen scratched at the side of her neck. She hadn't thought of what she would do if it happened again. It couldn't happen again. "I guess I'll just have to find a way to keep myself awake if it does. I'm not going through all of that again."

"I'm sure you're a drama queen." Cress tutted and shook his head. "Think about my offer of coming to Dad's with me. He misses you and so do Ava and

Loic. They don't even remember what you look like. It'd be nice to spend time as a family."

Galen slunk down into a spinning chair and tilted her head as far back as possible. There was nothing worse than the idea of going to spend time with her father. He had never treated her like family, not even when he lived with her. His disdain for her was more than obvious in her eyes. She was too much like his wife, and that only angered him more. No, what she wanted was to sleep, to get some rest without being disturbed. What she wanted was for something to happen, for someone to need saving or for Cress to go on a patrol so she could sketch up her mystery woman.

Deep down, what she wanted was to meet that woman again, to see her again. Galen found herself missing that face, that charisma, that confidence, but her memory of the woman was tainted by the flailing ball of light whose tendrils lashed out towards her.

No, it wasn't real. The woman wasn't real, and neither were the tendrils or the ball of light or any of it. Galen would sleep and she would do so as soon as she went home, as soon as her head hit the pillow, and nothing in this world would stop her.

Sleep was a rarity, a luxury, ever since Galen's dreams had been infiltrated.

That first dream had terrified her so much that she had neglected to go to sleep. Her room was filled to the brim with empty cups of coffee and cans of energy drink that had been drank and then crushed. Junk food littered almost every surface in her bedroom—crumpled crisp packets and bags of chocolate were still piled high upon the duvet.

Galen hadn't been anywhere near her bed. She sat at her desk, a cold cup of coffee by her side and a pencil in her hand. There was a rough sketch in front of her that was outlined with balled-up papers of rough attempts and drawings of different people. Galen was determined to draw this woman's face, to make her real. She had to see her again, had to be certain of what she had seen, but her dreams were now tainted.

With her eyelids drooping, Galen roughly shaded the shadows that were cast across the woman's face. She could barely hold the pencil anymore. It fell from her fingers and rolled across the desk, clattering against the floor. Galen's body slumped forwards and her head hung, strands of her hair falling into her face. She rested her forehead against her arms and closed her eyes for just a moment, just to relax, but she shot bolt upright once the darkness began to creep in.

“No,” she murmured quietly to herself. Her eyes fell to her sketch and her heart fell in her chest. “I can’t let you scare me forever. I have to sleep eventually.” Galen knew it to be true. There was no avoiding sleep. Eventually, it would creep up on her. It would drag her under whether she wanted it to or not, but it was a thought that she didn’t mind.

Once more, her eyes closed. Galen didn’t fight it. In her mind, Galen could see those autumn leaves falling once more, the calming waves, the bright ball of light. She jolted but her eyes didn’t open. The tiredness was starting to sweep in. Sleep was coming in waves that towered high over Galen, ready to fall at any second. It loomed, waiting, threatening, but never fell. Galen urged it over and over again, standing with her arms spread out and her head tilted back. She issued it a challenge and, not to be a weakling, sleep accepted and tumbled down upon Galen.

When Galen opened her eyes, she was standing in the autumn park watching the leaves spin around her. A smile rose on her face, but then she noticed something. There were people wandering through the park with their strollers and their dogs. It was like any other day out in the park, but this was her park. This was her dream and there were strangers invading it. How had they gotten here? This couldn’t be real. It couldn’t be happening.

Then, Galen’s eyes caught something else.

Off in the distance, sitting on a park bench with a wide-brimmed hat atop their head, was that same woman from the beach. Galen knew because of the lipstick, the signature hot pink colour smirched across her plump lips. She was dressed so elegantly in finery the likes of which Galen had never seen before. Her black coat was taut against her body, buttoned right up to under her chin. The fabric of it glittered in the sunlight, shining like diamonds. Leathery jeans were strapped up her legs, cut off by long, black, thigh-high boots that had a heel higher than any other.

Galen didn’t near her. She was frozen to the spot, her mouth agape and her eyes as wide as pits. She couldn’t believe what she was seeing in front of her. Her hands twitched but did not move, staying down by her side as flocks of people passed her by. She knew how they looked at her. Each of them judged her as they passed, holding their children closer or tightening their grips on their partners.

“You look pale as all hell, poppet.”

That voice. Galen almost swooned into the arms of the strange woman. She had flittered from the bench to right by Galen's side, standing so close it was oddly intimate.

"Seen a ghost?"

"No…I…you…" Galen swallowed heavily, staring deep into the eyes of the mysterious woman.

They were so gorgeous. Her eyes were like little gemstones set against a rich, black pupil. Topaz in colour, they glittered like fire in the light of the sun. They shone even brighter as her face stretched and lit up with a grin, much like that she'd shown Galen on the beach.

"I haven't seen you before," Galen managed to squeak. She kept her distance, slowly edging further and further away from the woman. "I've never dreamt of you before."

"You're a powerful dreamer," the woman remarked, offering to walk by Galen's side as close as she could. She kept her smile high even as Galen hesitated, and chuckled softly and warmly as Galen took the first step. "Do you dream lucidly?"

Galen walked side by side with the stranger through her own dream but found it strange how she recognised none of it. "Sometimes. It doesn't happen very often."

"Your imagination is incredible. I can't fathom the things that go on in your mind."

The leaves parted for the woman, clearing her a path. Branches and twigs would bend out of her way, and the sun would only shine on the path made for her. Galen's dream was being manipulated in the stranger's favour, and Galen had no control over it. She watched in awe as every person swooned for the woman. They stared up at her like she was some sort of deity, some sort of god.

"Has anyone ever told you that you have a very unique power?" the stranger asked.

"No…"

A scoff came from the majestic woman. "They don't know what they're missing out on, poppet. They overlook you, but you are more powerful than you'll ever know—than they'll ever know. You're someone incredibly special."

The scenery suddenly changed. The trees tumbled down into nothingness to reveal the beach that Galen had once loved. Once her feet hit the sand, she gasped and jolted. She tore herself away from the perfect stranger and staggered backwards. Galen tripped over her own feet, landing heavily in the sand, and scuttling back to hide beneath an abandoned parasol.

Gentle laughter followed the footsteps of the woman as she ducked down to withdraw Galen from her hiding spot. "You don't have to be afraid of me, my love. I'm not here to hurt you. What is there to be scared of? These are your dreams!"

"They don't feel like my dreams anymore. Something is…wrong."

The woman's perpetual smile died for a split second, and a flash of worry flared in her eyes. "Wrong, poppet? What could possibly be wrong? This place is heaven. You've created a paradise for yourself here." She seemed to falter, hurt crossing her face. "Are you frightened of me?"

"I don't know you." Galen stayed beneath her parasol, clutching her legs to her chest. "You've never appeared here before. I've never seen you before. Who are you?"

"I'm a friend, poppet. You can trust me. I promise you." The woman outstretched her hand for Galen to take—that signature smile returning in full bloom. She didn't falter once as Galen didn't take her palm, but rather withdrew it as Galen clambered to her feet by herself. "I would never hurt you. You're far too precious to me for me to hurt."

Galen drew her brows together. "I'm precious to you?"

"Of course!" the woman cheered. "You're precious to every person here! You are their creator. Without you, they wouldn't have an existence." Her words quietened towards the end of her sentence, a pause in her cheery nature. There was a glassiness to her eyes that appeared from out of nowhere, a sudden realisation of sadness and sorrow. It didn't last long. She quickly backed off a few paces, skipping through the sand cheerfully as if nothing had even happened, as if no doubt had been cast in her mind.

Galen just watched.

The stranger was a beautiful creature, a stunning work of art that surely could only exist in dreams. No one real could ever boast such gorgeous, well-chiselled features, carved so carefully and delicately that it could've only been the work of God. There wasn't a person alive whose smile shone so brightly, whose teeth were so straight and white, whose cheekbones were so high and mighty and jawline so taut and carved. Her hair was long and blonde in colour, sun-bleached and expertly braided in patches. Long plaits were strewn throughout her wavy locks, tied together with little strips of ribbon. They hung down to the middle of her spine, swaying back and forth with every little movement she made.

Everything about her radiated happiness and brightness. She was a ball of light amongst people who just blended into the background. There was no mistaking her in a crowd. Something about her was so attractive, so alluring, so riveting. She was a rush of adrenaline that frightened Galen, shaking her to her core. There was so much energy about her, so much electricity crackled throughout her fingertips. The way her voice travelled through the air was so soothing and tempting. Galen wanted more of her—she wanted every part of her charming, glamorous, enthralling life, but she didn't belong here.

Who was this mysterious creature?

"I have so much to show you!" the woman suddenly erupted. She came skipping back and went to take Galen's hands in hers, but she suddenly yanked her own hands back to her, as if Galen's hands were disgusting. It caused her to falter and turn bright red in the face, embarrassment consuming her whole being. "There's so much in this world I'm sure you've forgotten. Your whole childhood is here—everything you've ever dreamt of! All those imaginary friends and thought-up people still live here, poppet. They miss you dearly."

"How do you know so much about me?"

A softness took over the woman's features. "Now, that's not something to trouble yourself with. Let's just have fun now that you're here!"

"Why don't you answer my questions?" pushed Galen. She could tell her questions were burrowing under the woman's skin, but why? A little rift fluttered between the two as Galen backed away from the stranger, visibly alarmed. "I've never dreamt about you before. How are you here?"

"You should trust me more, poppet. I'm not here to hurt—"

Galen held up her hands as she backed up. "I don't think you're going to hurt me, but I don't understand how you're here."

"You have a powerful imagination, like I said." The stranger was relentless. She took a step forward every time Galen shuffled backward, that smile starting to ooze a certain kind of perverseness. "That type of creation is something to be desired. You attract what you put out into the universe, poppet."

"I'd like…" Galen rubbed her hands together nervously, laughing to herself under her breath. "I'd like to wake up, please."

The stranger's brow arched high on her face, her smile falling in the corners. "Why would you ever want to do that? Isn't it perfect here?"

"I'm not so sure anymore..."

"Poppet, I want you to stay with me. I don't want to scare you."

Galen smiled anxiously. "You don't scare me...whoever you are. I just don't...this can't be real."

"Oh, I assure you. I'm very real." There was a darkness in the woman's tone that Galen hadn't heard yet. It made her voice low and husky, and every word rumbled and vibrated in the back of her throat. "Do you believe I'm real, poppet?"

"Of course, I do. You're stood here in front of me. I could reach out and touch you if I wanted to, I'm sure."

The woman beamed delightfully. "What a treat that would be." She suddenly glowed, but it wasn't from the sunlight. Her skin illuminated and her eyes brightened as she stared holes through Galen. The world transformed around her. The sand was torn away under her feet and replaced with wooden planks—floorboards. Her clothes were ripped from her to reveal an elegant dress that clung to every curve of her body, and her long, swishing hair was coiled up on her head in an elegant updo. She was so much more radiant, glowing in a new light that only made her more and more desirable.

"I can wake you up...if you really want to leave me."

Galen, still trying to gather her surroundings, glanced around herself at the old-style house she found herself stood in. This place had never appeared in her dreams either. She'd never seen it whilst she was awake and had never thought up such an abode.

"I will admit, it'd be a damned shame," the woman moaned, whining. She was pulling on long gloves that stretched all the way up to her mid-bicep, prolonging the movement in a slow, seductive way. "I've grown rather fond of your company. I've been watching you for a while now, and to have you so close to me..." she trailed off, her eyes drinking in Galen's being. A sudden shift in her eyes saw a darkness take hold of her but, within the blink of an eye, it was gone. "Do you trust me?"

Galen's eyes travelled to the woman. "I..."

The woman swept in closer, but still didn't touch Galen, though it showed in her stare that she desperately wanted to. "Do you trust me, poppet? That's all you need to tell me. I'll do all the work, I promise."

"I trust you..." Galen murmured lightly.

Dark chuckling emanated from deep within the back of the woman's throat, coming out as a husky but irresistible growl. "That's good. That's all I need to know." The woman held her palm to her lips and kissed the centre of her hand, blowing it into Galen's face.

Galen was enveloped in a cloud of pleasant smells and inviting warmth that made her feel cosy and held. She could smell vanilla and lavender and roses and strawberries—all the things she loved. Her eyes closed and she felt herself fall backwards into a void of nothingness. As she fell, she didn't move. That air of warmth and cosiness was still wrapped tightly about her like a warm, knitted scarf. She had nothing to fear. She felt safe. She felt taken care of, and she felt loved.

That was until she realised that she was falling.

Galen woke with a tiny scream. Again, she was drenched with sweat and her heart threatened to burst from her chest at any second. She pushed a hand against her racing heartbeat to soothe it, but it did nothing for her. Her head pounded and bile began to crawl up her throat. Everything was too overwhelming, too intense. The scent of vanilla and strawberries still lingered in the room. Galen swore she could still smell it as she dashed from her bed to the bathroom, almost kicking the door down. She bent over the toilet and retched horribly, feeling bile and a horrid burning shoot up the back of her throat.

Violently sick, Galen could only sit back on her haunches and think of the mysterious stranger and her words and her weird habits. She thought of the way she would dance around every question and refuse to answer a thing. She thought of how she always went touch her, but never would. She thought of that smile, that damned smile that remained in her brain.

Her sleep was tormented. Her dreams were infected. Galen hurled more of her stomach contents up, clinging to the toilet bowl for dear life, as all thoughts of that mysterious but desirable woman escaped her mind.

"This is hell. This is hell. This is hell. This is hell. This is hell," Galen chanted over and over and over again, huddled up in her dark room, forcefully holding her eyes open. Still, she sat surrounded by coffee cups and energy drinks, but they were failing her. Her mother brought her a new drink every hour, each one stronger than the last, but it wouldn't work its magic on her anymore. She yearned for sleep, but she couldn't possibly allow herself to drift away—it was too risky.

Knocks at the door made Galen jump out of her skin. “Sweetheart? Are you still awake in there?”

“Yes! Yes, I’m awake.” Galen was almost hysteric. She blamed the amount of coffee and caffeine in her system. She shot from her dark corner, rushing to the door to eagerly collect the cup that her mother held.

“I’m worried about you, dear,” Nessa cooed. She pushed the cup into her daughter’s hands and watched her chug it with a brow arched high on her face. “Why won’t you sleep? Are you still frightened?”

Galen, not realising that she had gulped down a soft tea and not a black coffee, wiped away the remnants from her lips with the back of her hand. “It’s too dangerous. I could lose control. That…thing could get me again.”

“That woman?”

“She’ll be there, I’m sure of it, but no. That…ball of light. I see it every time I close my eyes. It won’t leave me.” Galen handed her teacup back to her mother and slunk slowly back to her hiding place. “I don’t feel like I’m in control of myself anymore. My dreams have become treacherous. Nothing there is my own. I’ve been sabotaged.”

Nessa sighed as she shut the door behind her, sealing herself in with her child. “You’re beginning to worry me. You need to sleep, darling. You can’t stay awake forever.”

“If I stay awake then she can’t get me.”

“She is a figment of your imagination, Galen. There’s nothing real about her. She can’t get you.”

Galen’s eyes shot upwards to meet her mother’s, bloodshot and frantic. “She can get me. If I go to sleep, she can get me. I can’t sleep. I won’t.”

“Come here.” Nessa held out her arms and wiggled her fingers when her daughter didn’t react. She hauled Galen to her feet and hugged her tightly, coiling her fingers in Galen’s unbrushed, matted hair. “You’re scared because you don’t know what’s happening. That’s all. You’re not frightened of that woman. You’re scared because your norm was disrupted. It was just one nightmare, I promise.”

“But I dreamt of her the night after.”

Nessa kissed the top of her daughter. “Was it a nightmare?”

“No.”

“Then what are you so worried about?” Nessa chuckled. She cleared a space on Galen’s bed, pushing off the empty crisp packets and wrappers and sitting her daughter down. “It won’t happen again, and you can trust me. You are scared because you haven't had a nightmare since you were a small child. You haven't had anything to be afraid of, and now you do."

Galen listened to her mother, closing her eyes, and cuddling into her once Nessa sat next to her.

It had been days since she'd slept. There was only so much coffee that Galen could chug until it didn't work on her. She'd drawn so many things, written so many little stories, but a hysteria was setting in. Her movements and her thoughts were frantic, her body constantly covered in sweat. Her hair was matted, and her eyes were encircled with purple bags that hung heavy against her skin. Being awake was driving her insane but being asleep was even worse.

"Tell me that you'll at least try to fall asleep," Nessa asked lightly. She kissed Galen's temple and stood, pushing back the duvet and making the bed look more appealing than it had done it days. "If you try, I'll get off your case. Is that a deal?"

Galen pursed her lips and stared up at her mother, afraid.

"No more coffee. No more energy drinks. Just sleep."

"Fine," Galen agreed. She tucked herself under her duvet and propped herself up against her pillows, watching her mother edge towards the door. "I'll try, but I can't make any promises."

Nessa smiled. "So long as you try, my love. Goodnight."

"Goodnight, mum."

Nessa shut the door and left Galen sitting in the dark. Her footsteps travelled down the corridor and down the stairs, and then disappeared into the abyss.

Galen was alone. She untucked the covers from the bed and piled them up on top of her, flipping them up over her head. She kept her back pressed against the headboard of her bed and her eyes on the door, though they flickered constantly to her open window. The shadows crept in closer and closer, the branches of the trees outside crawling across her walls.

"*I'm safe,*" Galen whispered to herself. She hugged the covers tighter to herself and watched the shadows all suddenly disappear, leaving her with nothing but her thoughts. "*Nothing can get me here. I'm safe. I'm awake.*"

Being awake is an awfully boring misfortune.

Galen jolted at the sound of the woman's voice in her head. She had to be dreaming now. Had she fallen asleep? Was this all a dream? Throwing herself to her feet, Galen ran her hands over everything she could touch, turning cups back and forth in her hands and clinking them against one each other to make sure they were actually real.

"*I'm just crazy,*" Galen reasoned to herself, still whispering. She didn't want her mother to hear her chatting to herself, because then she really would be thought mad. "*I'm just hearing things. She's not here. I'm all alone.*"

You could have my company if you wanted it. All you must do is sleep, poppet.

Galen clamped her hands over her ears and squeezed her eyes closed. "You're not here! You're not here! I'm just hearing things! You can't be here…you're just a dream! You only exist in my dreams!" She moved her hands from her ears to her mouth when she realised how loud she was, and heard footsteps coming back to her room. "*Let me be,*" she hissed, whispering again. "*Let me sleep peacefully.*"

But I can make your dreams much more exciting. You and I could have so many adventures together.

"I just want to sleep! Let me sleep."

Come to me and you can sleep for as long as you want.

Galen swayed around her room, her vision blackening. She kept shaking her head to wake herself up, slapping herself in the face as her eyelids drooped lower and lower. Her feet led her back to her corner where she'd piled up her blankets and some cushions. Dramatically, Galen fell against the wall and slid down into the bundle, ignoring her quickening heartbeat.

Come to me, poppet. You won't regret it.

"I can't…"

Come to mama, sweetheart. Let me take care of you.

Galen couldn't fight it anymore. Her eyes closed and refused to open again. A wave of tiredness and sleep came rushing at her, the gateway to her dream. It flew towards her, desperate to envelop her, to entice her in. Galen was frozen. She didn't bother to struggle, but rather tensed up as the wave slammed into her and knocked her further into a deep sleep than it ever had done before.

Chapter Two

The world was still black when Galen opened her eyes. Her dreams were void of colour and life and substance. All around her was nothingness, an everlasting, vast stretch of darkness that didn't waver once.

Galen turned round and round in circles, glaring into the bleakness as her breathing hurried. Her heart began to beat harder and harder, anticipating the next move. Was this a nightmare? She feared something would jump from the darkness and grab her, or that ball of light would return and unfurl its tendrils towards her.

Just the thought made Galen shudder.

She took a step forward, then another, and then another. Soon enough, she found herself wandering deeper into the abyss. Galen traversed it and explored it as if there were sights to see, but she was just staring at herself. She felt trapped within mirrors, peering back at herself and at little glimmering lights that decorated the darkness like stars.

The further she wandered in; the more Galen saw. The ground underneath her feet turned rocky and earthy, bumpy in places. Her feet bent over tree roots and her knees buckled with strain as she clambered over the uneven terrain. Above her head, a night's sky appeared. The stars twinkled beautifully, each one glimmering brighter than the last. They appeared in the thousands—little clusters decorating every single inch of the dark blue abyss. Some were larger than others, with hundreds upon thousands of smaller ones bunching up around it, hugging it.

Galen's eyes lowered when she saw a brick bridge stretching across a vast river, framed with lampposts that were connected by garlands of littler lights in the shape of stars and crescent moons. A well-trodden dirt path had been carved out in the centre of neatly cropped grass. In the very distance sat an old manor house, traditional and proper. Galen could see, even from as far away as she was, that the building was of incredible stature. There was a wisteria spread across the entire face of the house, stretching from the bottom corner diagonally across to the upper bay window. Cars were lined up around the huge, ornate fountain in the centre of the driveway, each of them sleek and black, expensive, and elegant.

"Impressive building, isn't it?"

Galen almost jumped out of her skin as the woman appeared behind her. She twisted, her eyes instantly connecting with the stranger's and her mouth parting to speak. There were words towered up on the end of her tongue, but she hadn't the strength to say any of them. She just gawked awkwardly at the woman, dressed in all her finery, and backed herself up against the bridge.

She was dressed head to toe in black. The dress that she wore fit her like a glove, hugging all her curves and showing off a gorgeously carved figure. She had wide hips and squared shoulders, with collarbones that stuck up against her taut, ivory skin. The woman looked to be made of porcelain. There wasn't a single flaw in her skin: not a single mark, not a single freckle. The dress clung to her torso and stopped just atop her breasts, wrapped about her biceps, and falling from her shoulders. It split at one of her hips, showing off an elegant, shapely leg and showed off the highest, velvety pumps that must've pinched her toes all together.

Her hair was strewn across one shoulder, trailing down her shoulder and across her breast to hang in a loose plait. There were a few silver shining clips pushed against her scalp to keep the stray strands off her face. The plait was tied with a silver ribbon that caught the light at every angle, glimmering like stardust. It mimicked the glitter that coated her eyelids. There was no silver on her lip. She wouldn't be without her signature hot pink lips that could more than likely stain skin if she were to kiss someone. Still, she looked stunning. She oozed elegance and class, and every movement was graceful and planned.

"I'm glad to see you, poppet. I was frightened you might never sleep again, that I had scared you off."

Catching both her breath and her nerve, Galen wandered further across the bridge. "I'm not scared of you. It wasn't you that frightened me, but whatever dragged me into the ocean…"

"Mm, I know how tumultuous dreams can be and how they turn on a whim," the woman crooned. "Horrid things, really. Sometimes, our own imaginations can get the better of us."

"And sometimes they create houses like that." Galen glanced back at the manor house and watched as guests filed in the huge front doors, let in by two giant men clad in black suits. Each person was of a certain class, a certain wealth. Not one of them looked like Galen—no, they all looked like the stranger at her side.

Slinking up to Galen's side, staring out across the rushing river, the woman let out a deep sigh that stirred the jewels hanging about her throat. "I did say your dreams were powerful. Why, you could create anything you wanted to, and yet this was the scene you painted. And you thought to include me. I'm flattered."

"You look beautiful," Galen commented, though she quickly tightened her lips. Had she just said that? She watched as a stunning blush filled the woman's cheeks, though her timid glance soon turned into a stunned, awe-filled stare. "I didn't mean to come on so strong. I didn't mean to come on to you at all, really."

"I appreciate the comment, poppet."

Together, the two stared across the river and watched the water as it rushed towards them. It slipped underneath the bridge, disturbing the greenery on the riverbanks and pushing down little pebbles that had been polished to look like precious gems and stones. Galen hoisted herself up onto the side of it, whereas the stranger rested her gloved arms against the top of it, sighing gently to herself with a smile written high on her face.

"I envy your willpower, my sweet," the woman said suddenly. "I have been around for as long as people have been able to dream, but I have never seen a sight as beautiful as this. Your mind is something to be jealous of, poppet."

"Who are you?" Galen asked again. This time, she prayed that the woman would answer her. "I don't know what to call you, or who you are, or where you came from. You seem to know everything about me."

Galen's dream was suddenly filled with the most delightful laughter. "On the contrary, poppet! I know nothing of you, just that your mind and your ability to dream is a wonder. I don't even know your name."

"I'll tell you mine if you tell me yours."

"Look at you, striking up deals," the woman laughed again. The expression on her face became more seductive, lustier, incredibly quickly. "They call me the Dreamcatcher," she suddenly said, forcing the words out of her mouth, "but if you want to get formal, then my name is Eve."

Eve. A beautiful name. Galen had always been fond of it. There was a girl she used to work with that had been called Eve. She couldn't even hold a candle to the Dreamcatcher—no one could. There wasn't a soul alive like the Dreamcatcher, whether they existed only in dreams or in reality.

"And yours?" the Dreamcatcher prompted.

"Galen."

There was a momentary pause that was followed by a stunning grin. "Galen," Eve repeated. She made a little noise in the back of her throat, running a gloved fingertip across her painted bottom lip. "I suppose it's only fair that a beautiful girl has a beautiful name."

"You're a charmer," Galen giggled. "Why do they call you the Dreamcatcher?"

"Hmm, that's a long story."

Galen glanced around herself, back at the house and then back at Eve. "I'm sure we have more than enough time, no? I have no intentions of waking up so soon."

Delight painted the Dreamcatcher's face. "I've never had someone take such an interest in me."

"Who wouldn't be interested? You're a mystery, and I'm convinced that you can't have been something my brain invented in one night."

"Think of me like…" Eve trailed off, struggling to find the right words, "an enigma. I am seen by only a chosen few and, when I choose someone, they get my full and undivided attention." She edged closer to Galen, standing in front of her, just between her knees. "You are the lucky one at the moment."

Galen watched Eve as she went gliding off towards the house, as if it was calling to her. "The Dreamcatcher is a pretty nickname. It makes you sound like a story parents tell their kids, like the Tooth Fairy."

"Many people think I'm like a spider," the Dreamcatcher suddenly sung. She beckoned Galen to follow her across the bridge and down the path, curling her finger slowly and rhythmically. "I catch you in a web and I show you all the power of dreams." Her smile widened, though held a certain perverseness to it, as Galen began to follow after her as she wanted. "In return, you show me what you can do. You show me how powerful that brain is, and you show me how you can make things exist. Truly exist."

"How did you get here?"

"Here, poppet?" Eve went to take Galen's hand, but suddenly wrenched hers away and gasped. It was as if she'd been shocked, as if gut-wrenching pain had shot through her when her hand had grown too close. "Where is here?"

Galen gestured around herself, wondering if she should reach for the Dreamcatcher's now curled-up fist. "In my dreams. How did you get here? Did I dream you up, or did you come to me?"

"You practically called my name and begged me to come," Eve replied. She wandered slowly, holding an air of grace and poise about her. "Minds like yours attract me. You need me, and I need you. We can help each other, you, and me. I can nurture you, help you, shape you."

"And what can I do for you?"

Eve beamed pure happiness at Galen and stopped just by the fountain. "You, poppet, can accompany me inside and keep me entertained through this party."

Inside, Galen felt overwhelmed. Her attire changed from her tatty pyjamas into a formal suit without the blazer. Her shirt fit her body perfectly and was overlain by a waistcoat that was light grey in colour. The trousers she wore clung to her legs and made it hard to move. They stuck to her thighs and somehow tightened when she tried to sit. On her feet she wore the finest brown leather shoes that tapped obnoxiously against the polished floors. Everywhere she went, she was accompanied by an orchestra of clicks and taps and clacking. It quickly grew on her nerves. She scratched at her hair that had been scooped from her shoulders, brushed through, and tied in a messy bun on the back of her head. A few strands still hung in her face that she would huff at every now and then but would never move.

Galen fit in perfectly with the guests now. They too wore their finest, clad in suits and ballgowns that were only fit for the most high-fashion runways. Their voices, though grating, travelled through the air accompanied by beautifully played symphonies. Despite the sheer volume of people, Galen could still hear Eve perfectly well.

"Who are all these people?"

The Dreamcatcher weaved in between the crowd, ignoring all of their eyes. "People you've dreamt of. You've seen all these people before. They've been in many of your dreams. You've just never paid them any mind."

"Did you bring them here?"

"No."

Galen paused for a second, staring out into the crowd. Everyone she could see was watching Eve dance about. Not one of them paid attention to their date or to anything else in the room. Even those playing instruments weren't reading their sheet music but staring intensely at Eve. Galen began to recognise fear within their gazes. Some were in awe, as they should be, but there was a worrying amount of terror.

"What's the matter, poppet?" the Dreamcatcher asked. She loomed behind Galen, staring over her shoulder at the people that Galen surveyed. "Is the crowd not to your liking?"

"They look scared of you."

The Dreamcatcher made a small noise in the back of her throat—a noise of displeasure. "Now, don't be silly. They have no reason to be scared of me."

Galen still cast her eye out to the sea of people. Upon realising they had been caught, they had all turned their attention to something different. Their eyes were elsewhere. Not a single person even dared to look in Eve's direction, not even at her feet. They whispered behind their hands and would occasionally let their eyes flicker to Galen, but their stares were sorrowful. Some were desperate, pleading, as if they were all urging Galen to get away.

"Are you in these people's dreams?" Galen asked. She observed people's faces change as she and Eve swept by them. One man almost fainted as the Dreamcatcher glided by him, repelling him backwards, as if he was desperate not to touch her. "Do they see you as I see you?"

"No, I'm not in their dreams and no," the Dreamcatcher laughed, "they definitely do not see me as you do. I'm only here for you. Only you have my attention, my love. Everything I do," Eve's hand lifted, her fingers just millimetres away from Galen's chin, "I do for you." She stared down her thin nose into Galen's eyes, lips parted. Her thumb straightened as if she meant to run it down Galen's lips, but she didn't once touch her.

Galen watched the Dreamcatcher's hands and fingers twitch. They twitched out of want, and they twitched out of irritation. It was as clear to see in her eyes as it was to see across her face. These people feared her, and she knew it, and that fact agitated her. It had irritated her beyond repair, and now her gaze was scathing and tampered with.

"Why do they look at you like that?" quizzed Galen.

"Like what?"

Galen checked all their faces again and, sure enough, the crowd was still too timid to meet the Dreamcatcher's heavy gaze. "Like they know who you are, even though you aren't in their dreams. You can't have singled them all out like you have done me, but yet they're scared to even look at you."

Eve's face boiled a bright red. "What's wrong with you people?" she suddenly shouted above the noise in the room. The Dreamcatcher's booming tone vibrated throughout the entire manor house, shaking everyone to their core. "Aren't you having a good time? Is nothing good enough for you?"

Galen had never heard a voice so deep and earth-shattering. She tumbled back as the whole world shook, falling into a corner and watching as the manor house around her almost fell to the ground. The walls wobbled in and out of view, like they didn't really exist. Parts of the floor fell into a deep, black pit—a void. Some of the guests glitched and didn't return, culling the crowd to a meagre few that all trembled for their lives.

"Poppet?" Eve suddenly said. Her tone became worried and confused as she spun around in circles, trying to find Galen. When her eyes landed on Galen, the Dreamcatcher rushed forwards and went to scoop her up, but her body froze with her arms outstretched and her fingers curled up like gnarled branches. "Are you okay? Are you hurt? Did I hurt you?" She was frantic. Her eyes were filled with concern and unease as Galen pushed herself back to her feet and brushed herself off. "I didn't mean to raise my voice. These people are ungrateful. They don't deserve you being here."

The worry in Eve's eyes and the fear in the crowd's played heavily in Galen's mind. She let her eyes dart between the two, though they weighed heavily upon the partygoers.

One man, stood far at the back of the crowd, was mouthing something to her. She couldn't quite read his lips as they moved too fast, too frantically. Galen brought her brows together in confusion and gently shook her head, not understanding what he was trying to convey.

Glancing at the Dreamcatcher, the man came closer, slipping in between people to stand just a few metres away from Galen. He made sure that Eve didn't notice him moving, that she remain blissfully unaware. His mouth moved again but, this time, a little bit of a voice came with it.

"*Run,*" he whispered painfully quietly. "*Wake up.*"

Galen frowned harder, not sure that she understood the command.

"*Wake up,*" he urged again, whispering still. He was hissing through his teeth, forcing the order out so hard that there were tears in his bloodshot eyes. "*Don't believe. She's not real.*"

"Poppet?" The Dreamcatcher's voice snapped Galen out of her trancelike state and her eyes were so hard to look away from. She blocked Galen's view of the rest of the partygoers but, with a sudden click of her fingers, the room returned to its bustling state. "I'm sorry that I snapped, my love. Why don't we go somewhere where it's just us? We should get to know each other a little more…intimately."

Galen gulped, eyes rolling to the side. She watched the man that had been warning her just a few seconds again, but his demeanour had completely changed. He partied with the people around him, arms in the air and a drink in hand. The look across his face was that of a drunken grin, and his eyes were barely open. He was a drunken mess now, and not a single person in the room had that look of fear plastered in their eyes anymore.

"Come with me," the Dreamcatcher said, eyes filled with wonder. "I know a place that you'll like."

Eve led Galen through the house and out of the back doors to reveal a completely different scene. What lay in front of Galen was a vast lake that was lined with cherry blossom trees, all of which were blooming. Petals and leaves floated down in the faint breeze and rested gently against the surface of the water. The moon, sat high and mighty in the sky, illuminated both the water and a little firepit cleared at the edge of the water, overlooking the dark forests that lay behind the lake. As soon as Galen's eyes rested on the pit, it burst into flames, revealing two wineglasses that slowly filled from the stem with a thick, viscous, crimson liquid.

Galen thought she could feel a hand on her back leading her towards the cosy firepit, but the Dreamcatcher was already pacing in front of her. She walked tentatively, choosing her steps as she took them and lingering on the outskirts of the clearing. She couldn't deny that the place was beautiful. Many times had she dreamt of somewhere like this, somewhere cosy and breath-taking, but she found herself unsettled.

"Do you remember the dream you had when you were here?" Eve asked. She took her seat by the fire and warmed her hands, her elegant evening dress shortening into a woolly coat that made her look like a grizzly bear. "It was so long ago, but you were so peaceful. It was some sort of…lovey-dovey affair. You were dreaming about—"

"I was dreaming about my ex," Galen finished the sentence for the Dreamcatcher. That dream had once been a treasured one, but now it brought her pain. "I wasn't aware you were here that long ago."

Sipping her wine, the Dreamcatcher suddenly stumbled over the rim of her glass, like she was caught in a lie. “Oh, no. I wasn’t here. I can see every dream you’ve ever had. It’s like an archive open to only me. I get to see every beautiful thing that has ever crossed your mind.”

“Those guests…” Galen trailed off, sitting opposite Eve. “They didn’t act like people in my dreams usually do. They didn’t do as I thought they would.”

“Oh?”

“They acted as if they had their own consciousness, their own conscience.”

The Dreamcatcher’s eyes lifted, but she didn’t lift her head. She ran her tongue across her bottom lip and smudged her lipstick, letting out the tiniest of sighs. Her patience was running extremely, treacherously thin.

“They acted like they were real people stuck in my dream,” Galen continued.

Eve forced a smile. “I can assure you they are just figments of your imagination. Refashioned copies of people you’ve seen in the real world. They’re just empty heads, nothing more. They hold no value in this world.”

“One of them tried to talk to me.”

The Dreamcatcher’s pupils shrank to a mere sliver. “Did they?” she asked almost sarcastically, that smile she had on her face becoming carved into her skin. Her teeth sharpened into a drastic point, like little daggers in her mouth, and her ethereality wavered. “What did they try to say to you?”

“They told me to run.”

Eve’s eye twitched.

“They told me not to believe, to wake up.”

A jolt of pain rendered the Dreamcatcher doubled over in her seat. She dropped her wineglass at her feet, smashing it against the cold, hard earth. Her gloved hand flew to her chest where she gripped her heart, a low groaning emanating from the back of her throat.

“Eve?” Galen murmured quietly, worried but afraid.

The Dreamcatcher’s bones crunched as she wrenched her head upwards, so she was looking at Galen. “Don’t worry about me, poppet.” Her voice was low and distorted. She sounded nothing like her usual self.

Galen backed off a little, feeling the nuances of a nightmare begin to take hold. She watched as the pinkness in the petals on the trees melted into a deep red, dripping with blood. The trunks twisted round and round on themselves, turning black and rotted in colour. The wood peeled away from the trees and burned through the ground like acid, tearing apart the earth that had once been so pretty and so green.

Then, as the Dreamcatcher took in a sharp inhale, everything reversed. The holes filled themselves and the bark flew up from nowhere to plaster itself against the trunk that untwisted slowly and painfully. Every petal was sucking up the droplets that it had spilt and blossoming back to its rightful and natural colour. The glass that Eve had broken slowly pieced itself back together, sticking together like magic and flying back into her hand. The only thing left was the Dreamcatcher herself, who sat up slowly and released her heart, only to grip onto the armrest by her side.

"You believe in me, don't you?" Eve asked, her voice as light and as airy as the first time Galen had heard it. "It would break my heart to hear that you didn't, that you'd changed your mind."

Galen took her seat, but she sat with her body all tucked up. "I have no reason not to believe. I don't know what you are, but I believe you are real."

"There are people here that don't want to believe in me, poppet. There are some people that are scared of me because they think that I'm some sort of monster. They believe me capable of harm. Do you think that I could hurt someone?"

"I don't know."

The Dreamcatcher's lips tightened. "My purpose isn't to hurt a single soul. I could never hurt you."

The way Eve spoke made Galen dubious. Lightly, she chewed on the inside of her bottom lip, her mind racing. She could hear the man's whispering in her head, begging her to run, telling her to wake up. Galen thought of the way that his demeanour suddenly changed, as had everyone else's. It had happened in the blink of an eye, and all because they had regarded the Dreamcatcher with fear in their gazes.

"You look confused," Eve pointed out.

"I'm trying to work you out, is all," Galen replied with a wry chuckle. "Why are they scared of you? Why did they tell me to run?"

The Dreamcatcher's shoulders lilted. "They're jealous, I suppose. That's all I can think of."

"It seems like more than that."

"Read into it all you will, but I'm not a monster." The firmness in Eve's tone made Galen lift her eyes. The Dreamcatcher stared into Galen's soul and cracked her jaw, trying her best to put on a brave face and a smile. "You shouldn't waste time dwelling on what other people think. What do you think of me?"

Galen ran her tongue across her bottom lip. "I don't know what to think. I feel as if you are misunderstood, as if people see you differently to what I do. I take you at face value, whereas these people seem to have met a different you."

"I want to show you the real me," Eve said suddenly, loudly. She got to her feet but was still staggering, still clutching at her heart. The pain was still prevalent within her, doubling her over. "I want to show you all the things I can do for you. I can prove to you I'm not a monster, and that you shouldn't believe in those people's toxic lies about me. Let me show you how powerful I am."

Galen slowly climbed to her feet, though she moved a lot more reluctantly than the Dreamcatcher. She watched Eve closely as the Dreamcatcher padded away, standing at the very edge of the water. A little trickle of fear entered her veins as Eve waded in, standing in the water that bubbled up to her waist. Her breath caught in her throat as the Dreamcatcher's hand stretched out towards her, beckoning her to follow.

"Nothing bad will happen to you," Eve promised. "I'll protect you."

Images of the nightmare she'd had rushed back to Galen, hitting her like a ton of bricks. Galen staggered back, shaking her head as the world around her suddenly dimmed. She felt herself quake in her boots, as if she was going to wake up at any second.

The Dreamcatcher sensed that too, an abrupt panic taking over her. She dashed from the centre of the lake, moving so fast that Galen didn't even see her until she was right in front of her. Her very being blurred as she ran to catch Galen, but again the Dreamcatcher couldn't bring herself to make contact. Instead, with a little wave of her hand, Eve changed the scenery around the two, fixing all the breaks in the world and replacing them with a darkness that was somehow soothing and calming.

"Look at me," the Dreamcatcher murmured under her breath, standing so close that her breath hit Galen in the face. "There is no danger here. It's just you and me. There's no need to wake up. I can keep you safe in here."

Horrified, Galen did her best to catch her breath. "I don't feel safe."

"Put all your energy into me," Eve asked. "I can make you feel safe. I can show you everything I can do. Aren't you interested in seeing that? It'll be like magic, and I can conjure up anything you want and need to soothe your mind." She lifted a hand as if to run her fingers down the side of Galen's face, her eyes following her hands downward. There was never a moment when the Dreamcatcher did touch Galen. There was still a fear, and it was starting to drive Galen crazy.

"I don't want to go near water," Galen blurted out. She shook her head as her nightmare came rushing back to her. It loomed over her like towering shadows, beckoning her to go back in. Her mind spun and whirred with the evil that she'd endured, an evil so strong that it started to bleed into her dreams.

A black gunk oozed from the spot where Galen stood, infecting everything and anything all around it. It crawled across the ground like rotting tree roots and turned everything that stood black and gnarled. Once more, everything fell apart in front of Galen's very eyes. The trees melted away. The lake dried up into a jellified pit of blackness, and the fire from the firepit exploded to envelop everything.

Galen heard a gasp and then a whoosh. She squeezed her eyes shut as the wind whipped viciously around her, blowing ferociously through her hair. The cold was biting at her skin, but it was over within seconds. A deafening silence fell over Galen, which prompted her to open her eyes.

At first, Galen wasn't sure what she was looking at. She turned round and round in circles, recognising her own bedroom. Her bed was there, perfectly made with no rubbish all over it. All the mess that had been strewn across the place was gone. The pictures on the wall had been straightened, the chair that sat usually in the middle of the room was tucked under the desk, and the coats that hung over the chair were hung up on the back of her door.

"I figured you would feel safer in your own home," Eve reasoned. The Dreamcatcher was nowhere to be seen, but suddenly appeared. She wandered through the door like a ghost, eyes running all over the room taking in everything there was to see. "Your mind is a fragile place, poppet. I overestimated how much you could take."

Galen sat on the edge of her bed, her breathing finally calmed. "You were there," she murmured under her breath. She stared blankly at her desk, wondering what the papers atop the desk were. Could they be her drawings? "You were there in my nightmare, when I was attacked."

"I was."

"Did you see me go under?" Galen asked. "Did you watch me almost drown?"

Eve stared blankly at Galen, lips pursed and eyes void of all emotion and reaction. "You were already too far under before I realised that anything was wrong."

That sounded like a lie.

"I couldn't get you out of there, poppet. It would've had a much worse effect on you, and you would've been more frightened to come back here. I couldn't have that. You know that, right? I need you here," the Dreamcatcher crooned. She sat by Galen's side, with her back pressed against the wall and her legs curled up underneath her. "I'm sorry that I didn't help you."

"I wouldn't have trusted you anyway," Galen replied. She stared down into her lap, letting strands of her hair fall into her face so her hurt expression was hidden. "You said you were going to show me some magic."

Eve perked up. "I can show you anything you want. I can do anything you want. I'm just as powerful as you are."

"If not more."

The Dreamcatcher laughed. She turned so that she faced Galen, staring empathetically into her eyes. The smile on her face was childlike, innocent. There was so much excitement brewing in her gaze—it was like she had never gotten the chance to show off what she was truly capable of.

Eve held her hands out flat in front of Galen, her fingers twitching ever so slightly. She glanced down at them and, in a heartbeat, little flames appeared. They were blue and green in colour, with the tips flickering between purple and pink. They grew higher and higher as Eve's excitement and amusement rose. The more she laughed, the more out of control the flames became.

"Touch them," the Dreamcatcher said. She lifted her eyes and grinned at Galen, holding her hands closer to Galen.

The flames were awfully enticing. They were pretty to look at, pastel in colours and beautiful in the way that they moved. They coiled around each other, writhing into a mesh of colours that blended perfectly and seamlessly.

Galen reached out tentatively, head cocked to the side and fingers lingering over the flames. They didn't touch the pads of her fingers yet, but they were close. They seemed hungry to reach her, to touch her. Galen's mouth coiled upwards into a small smile, a little smirk that rapidly disappeared when the embers suddenly clung to her hand. She gasped, expecting to be burnt and hurt, but the flames were cooling and ticklish. They trickled up her wrist and up her arm before extinguishing into a little puff of smoke.

"These are just my silly little parlour tricks," Eve explained. "I'm capable of creating worlds, universes. I make dreams feel real. I make them so that people never want to leave."

"Can you create people?"

"People, places, scenes, events, whatever you want. What is it you want to see?"

Galen pondered it. "I want you to take me…to the mountains."

"Easy." Eve went to click her fingers but stopped when she saw Galen hold up a hand. "Oh, there's more?"

"I want to go to the mountains, and I want it to be raining across the peaks, but I want the sun to be shining on us. I want there to be wildlife, and a little nook to sit in. I want a rainbow and cats." Galen paused for a minute. Was that too much to ask for? From the look on Eve's face, it was a piece of cake. "And I want one last thing."

The Dreamcatcher rose to her feet and stood in the centre of Galen's room; arms spread out in a challenge. There was no request too big or too small, it seemed. She was an all-powerful being, but Galen was determined to test her strength and her wit.

"I want you to be dressed in a bright green and orange dress with pink shoes and one of those silly hats that clasps underneath your chin."

The smile on Eve's face wavered, and she winced, but she didn't protest. "If that's what you want."

"It'd prove you're powerful."

The Dreamcatcher gestured for Galen to join her in the middle of the room, smirking still. "The fact I have to prove it to you damages my ego, but I shall do whatever you ask of me, if it keeps you here." She drew in a deep breath and closed her eyes as Galen joined her and, when she exhaled, the bedroom around her shifted into what looked like an abstract painting.

Galen was witness to it all. She was trapped in some sort of vortex with the Dreamcatcher but remained in a bubble floating over meshes of colour and shapes. It was like advanced cloud watching, seeing all sorts of images appear as mountains began to shoot up from the ground. They started as little mounds, like molehills, but slowly rose. Rivers and lakes formed between the cracks and crevices shaped by the towering mountains.

Just when Galen thought they couldn't grow any bigger, they shot up and doubled in height. They exploded out from the top to cover more ground and wrap about a massive lagoon framed with trees and canopies and blossoming with wildlife. Birds of paradise flew over the waters and up to the peaks, where rain was showering down upon the rocky crags.

Ground began to materialise underneath Galen's feet. She stood on flattened stone that had been smoothed down. Behind Galen was a little nook, just as she had asked for, with a little swinging bench tucked against the curve of the rock. The sun was shining just over her little patch of mountain, with a rainbow shooting from the edge of it down into the lagoon.

Just when Galen thought it couldn't get any better, she heard a little meow. She glanced in every direction, trying to find the little kitten. Galen found it sitting on the swinging bench and ran to it instantly, cooing over it and petting its soft head. As it purred at her, Galen didn't even realise that the putrid dress she'd described was clad against Eve's body. Her attention was snatched away from the kitten that was rolling around, flashing its belly, by the Dreamcatcher sauntering up to her wearing the god-awful outfit that Galen had concocted in her mind.

Trying to stifle her laughter, Galen's face was rife with evidence of a smirk. "I didn't think you'd actually wear that."

"I had to prove a point, and so yes, I am actually wearing this. Although, I did make a few tweaks to it."

Galen thought she had made an outfit so ugly that no one would be able to pull it off but, of course, the Dreamcatcher was capable.

It fit her body perfectly, as everything did. The colours were blended together like some sort of psychedelic swirl, made from a velvety fabric that looked wonderful to touch. Her shoes were the pinnacle of the outfit—fluorescent pink with touches of silver on the toes and the straps. Again, they were ridiculously high. How she walked in those things was a mystery. The only thing that looked out of place was the hat on her head. The thing was massive and shrouded the top of her head, almost covering her eyes. She had to keep pushing it up her brow so that she could see, but still wore her signature smile high and mighty on her face. It carved deep into her face, pronouncing her dimples, and producing laugh lines that Galen had never seen before.

"You seem to change every time I look at you," Galen murmured. She placed the little cat on her lap and petted him, her eyes consistently dropping to the purring mammal. "I never noticed you had dimples."

"Do you want to stay here?"

The question took Galen by surprise, stopping her dead in her tracks. "Stay here?" she repeated. "Stay in my dreams? Isn't that…like dying?"

"No, poppet. I would never kill you, but I don't know how I will be able to cope if you're not here. It gets so lonely…"

"Can't you make some people? You said you could create anything, so why not make yourself some friends?"

Eve's smile was a sad one. "I have plenty of friends, but what I need is you."

"Why am I so important?"

"Oh, poppet." The Dreamcatcher wandered over to Galen, walking through the rainbow that she had perfectly placed to be between herself and her prized possession. "One day, you'll understand how much you mean to me. Right now, I just need to keep you close to me."

Galen went silent. The cat in her lap evaporated, leaving her with nothing to distract her hands. She stared vacant holes through the Dreamcatcher. Her thoughts began to cloud over once more, her doubt and her worry rushing back to her. The man had told her to run, and the Dreamcatcher was telling her to stay. The strange man had told her not to believe and to wake up, but Eve kept reaffirming Galen's belief and wanted her to stay asleep, forever. She felt held onto, trapped, kidnapped even.

Galen's gaze fell away from the Dreamcatcher and rested solely on her feet. She shuffled them back and forth across the rocks, scratching nervously at the back of her neck. There were words sitting on the top of her tongue, words that she knew Eve wouldn't like. Galen was already imagining the reaction, but still rose to her feet anyway and put distance between herself and the Dreamcatcher.

"Something not to your liking?" Eve asked, her voice full of hope and belief.

"I think I should go," Galen said quickly. She turned her back to the Dreamcatcher, staring out over the lagoon and watching it in its bubbling glory. "I don't know how long I've been asleep, and people are probably worried about me."

There was a momentary pause. "Go?" Eve cracked her jaw so loud that it made Galen wince. Had she just broken her bones? "Where would you possibly go? Everything you could ever want is right here."

"Eve, I don't mean to upset you—"

"No, no, it's okay," the Dreamcatcher hissed through her gritted teeth. "Why should I expect you to be different than everyone else? The pattern proves strong again. It only makes sense you should follow the path."

Galen turned to Eve, only to see that she had stripped free of the barmy outfit she'd been given and replaced it with a white dress shirt, a black corset over the top and tight-fitting jeans. "I don't want to leave you here, but I can't stay in my dreams forever."

"Why not?"

"This isn't how life works."

Eve's jaw tightened even more, the skin across her jawbone becoming so taut it was almost see-through. "Life isn't always fair, poppet. Sometimes we have to do things we don't want to, and why? Well, because we just have to. There isn't a choice."

Galen backed up. "What's happened to you?"

Again, the Dreamcatcher's jaw tightened, but this time it snapped where it connected to the rest of her skull. It disconnected with a horrible pop, severing almost all of Eve's face. A horrid split formed down the entire right side of Eve's face, spitting and oozing viscous black gunk. Every time she tried to adjust it, the tissue and muscles just snapped so her jaw fell further down. She tried to speak, but her words slurred. It was almost as if she didn't notice that half her face had fallen off.

Eve grabbed hold of her jaw and shoved it back up in place, clicking it back into its socket. Gunk still poured from tears in her skin, but somehow the Dreamcatcher managed a smile. Her teeth were black, as was most of her skin, but still she paid it no mind. She staggered towards Galen, holding out her arms as if she was going in for a hug.

"You can't leave me, poppet. Bad things will happen to the both of us if you leave me. Do you understand why I can't let you go?"

"I want to wake up." Galen rushed the words out of her mouth as she staggered back towards the edge of the mountain range. "You're turning this into a nightmare. I want to wake up."

The Dreamcatcher's jaw fell off again, this time only holding on by a single thread of tissue. "Oh, is my fault?" she stuttered, her words not fully forming. She staggered closer, seemingly dragging one foot behind her. All her usual beauty was starting to drip away from her like water. Her bones cracked and broke underneath her skin, some poking up through it. Inky black liquid spewed from every wound that blistered across her flesh, squirting in all directions and pooling in front of her. She suddenly lashed out, throwing an arm forward to grab hold of Galen, but miraculously missing just by a little bit. "You can't leave, poppet! You have to stay here with me! You have to keep me alive! You don't like to see me like this, do you?"

Galen took step back after step back, arms held out to the side of her. She glanced behind herself, stopping when her foot almost slipped right over the edge. Galen swung her arms back and forth to balance herself, but the Dreamcatcher was relentless. If she didn't take a step back, Eve would snatch her up in her grasp. She had a choice—fall backwards or go forward. Galen stared at the craggy lagoon beneath her, waiting for her, calling her name, and gulped.

"Don't think you can escape me so easily!"

That was the last sentence that Galen heard before she slipped off the edge of the mountains. She didn't jump, but she fell into the abyss, plummeting like a sack of potatoes through the harsh and vicious winds. Her body was battered by the rain which pinged off her skin like thin bullets, stinging and burning. Galen's eyes were still upwards, watching as the Dreamcatcher stood on the edge of the cliff, her body bending and distorting. She watched as huge, spiderlike legs stretched from Eve's pelvis and bent, crooked wings sprouted from her back, beating once against the hard current of the wind.

Galen spun in the air. Expecting to see water and the lagoon, Galen was stricken with fear to see nothing but a void lying beneath her, with a growing ball of light in the centre of it. Those same tendrils she'd seen in her nightmares were flapping towards her, one of them curling in a beckon to usher her in closer.

Galen's arms began to flail. She opened her mouth to scream, but the wind tore away all noise that came from her. Her lungs emptied and her heart flew up to the middle of her throat, choking her. All she could hear around her was the hum of distortion and her own heartbeat thudding harder and harder in her ears. She fell faster, rocketing towards the throbbing orb of light that reached for her desperately. Its tendrils stretched towards her, the tips curling like fingers. It was so close to her, so close to touching her face, so close to grabbing hold of her. She could only anticipate it, knowing that it was coming from her. Galen's fate was looming in front of her, and she watched it unfurl in front of her very eyes.

Out of nowhere, the tendrils seemed to perk up. The ball of light became sentient, aware that prey was just falling into its lap. Like a frog snatching up a fly with its tongue, arms flew towards Galen and wrapped all about her. She felt like she'd been snagged by bungee cords, flung against the light with reckless abandoned and knocked from her deep unconsciousness when, abruptly, everything went black.

"She got away, boss."

Galen could hear voices, but still she could see nothing. She didn't recognise the voice, but its tone and accent were both interesting and exotic.

"That she did. That's no bother though." That was the Dreamcatcher's voice, disappointed but normal. There was no distortion to her tone, no monstrous underlays that played with Galen's ears.

"Shall we find her, boss?"

"I'd say she's woken up now. She won't be back for a while, so we should start getting everything ready. We can't let her get away from us again."

"Yes, boss."

Galen awoke with a thud. Beneath her wasn't the soft carpet of her room, but the coarse roughness of the grass in her back garden. She lay in a heap at the very bottom, stuffed beneath the weeping willow that she'd once been fond of climbing when she was a child. Her clothes and her skin were amuck with mud, coated in such a thick layer that it may never wash out.

Panting, Galen tried her best to find her bearings. She thought she could still hear the Dreamcatcher and that tropical accent that had accompanied her. She thought she could still see her in all her deformed glory. Is that what she really looked like? Was the Eve that Galen had been seeing all an illusion? It was a dream, and anything was possible, but Galen refused to believe it. She refused to think of it anymore as the fear pulsed through her veins like hot lava. Instead, she pushed herself to her feet despite slipping in the mud, clawing her way forwards. Her house was just in the distance, sitting at the top of the grassy knoll it had been built upon in the late sixties, waiting for her.

Galen ran as fast as her feet could take her in as straight of a line as she could manage. The world was still a blur around her. Her only motivation was her fear. Tears streamed down her cheeks and hung from her jaw as she burst onto the back porch and pelted herself into the kitchen door, eager to see someone.

"Mum!" she called out, hoping that her mother was nearby. At first, there wasn't a response. There were a few footsteps sounding from above her head, but they didn't move with any urgency or worry. "Mum!" Galen cried again. This time, a whimper clasped hold of her voice. Her words wobbled and her throat seized up. Pictures of the Dreamcatcher's horrid, malformed face and body kept springing up in her mind at every turn. She saw Eve in every shadow, saw the beasts that were waiting for her. "Mum, please!"

"Galen?" Nessa's voice was quiet and sleepy. How early in the morning was it? "Galen, why are you covered in mud? Where have you been? I haven't seen you in days."

Galen ignored her mother's questions. She didn't even hear them properly as she skidded across the floor and into her mother's arms. The mud from her clothes transplanted onto her mother, making her just as mucky. She squeezed with all her might, her cheek pressed against her mother's chest and her eyes tightly closed.

"What's the matter? What's happened?"

"She's after me!" Galen sobbed. "I can't sleep! I have nightmares every time I close my eyes. She's always there waiting for me. I can't escape her! I'm stuck! She tried to kill me!" Her head suddenly wrenched upwards so that her frantic, bloodshot eyes could meet her mother's timid and worried gaze. "She wanted me to stay in my dreams. She was going to keep me there. I was never going to wake up!" Galen knew how insane she sounded, but the words kept falling from her tongue. "And that ball of light! It follows me. It knows everything I do, everywhere I go! She knows I'm scared of it, and it knows too!"

Nessa clasped hold of her daughter's face, pushing her cheeks together. "Okay! Okay! Calm down! I can barely understand a word you're saying." She took Galen's muddy hand and led her towards the sofa, where she promptly pushed her child into the corner seat. "Tell me again what happened, but this time slowly, so I can understand you."

"I had a dream."

"I gathered."

"I thought it was a dream, but it was just a nightmare in disguise," Galen murmured. She spoke so fast that spit coated her bottom lip and her chin. "That woman is a nightmare in disguise. She was there again."

Nessa's brow arched. "The same woman from the beach?"

"Yes!" Galen roared. She stared dead ahead of her as her mother draped a blanket over her shoulders, doing her utmost best to wipe some of the mud off her. "I know her name now. Her name is Eve, but people call her the Dreamcatcher. She's haunting me, and I don't know why! I don't know what I've done. She keeps…calling me precious and telling me that she'll never hurt me, and I don't—"

“Okay, baby,” her mother soothed. Nessa ran her fingers through Galen’s hair, trying again to brush through clumps of mud and grass. “Why were you outside? I thought you’ve been in your room this entire time.”

Galen’s brows came together. “Entire time?” She drew away from her mother slightly, her frown still sitting heavy on her features. “I’ve only been asleep for a few hours…”

The confusion translated onto Nessa’s face. “No, sweetheart. You’ve been asleep for three days.”

Three days? How could that be?

“I left you alone because I thought you had finally drifted off and that you needed the rest. How did you end up outside? Did you sneak out?”

“No, I passed out on the floor. I heard her voice…”

A hand covered Galen’s and squeezed it tight. “You’re hearing voices?”

“Just hers. She seems to be able to get to me when I’m exhausted…it felt like she dragged me into sleep.”

There was a moment of silence, a moment where Nessa just stared at her child. The worry was rife across her face. Her eyes didn’t glimmer with their usual eccentricity, their usual happiness. Instead, it was just empathy and sympathy, mixed with concern. Nessa ground her jaw as she swiped her thumb over the back of Galen’s palm, trying to think of the best thing to do.

“You sit here, bub, and collect yourself. I’m going to make a phone call.” Nessa rose to her feet and let go of Galen’s hand, but kissed the top of her head in reassurance. “Cress! Can you come down here please?”

Galen drowned out her mother’s voice. She didn’t even notice Cress come barrelling down the stairs. Her eyes and her focus were elsewhere. Though she watched the weeping willow swaying elegantly in the breeze through the back window, she could only think of Eve. Her mind clung to those thoughts that were the most pleasant—the time on the bridge, the time in the park, the time by the cherry blossoms. Still, the image of Eve’s jaw hanging on by a thread, of her back being torn open by massive wings, her legs breaking in their sockets, were stuck at the forefront of her memory, and nothing could shake them free.

“Hey, sis.” Cress landed with an inelegant plop on the sofa next to Galen, draping his arm across the top of the pillows. “Everything okay?” His tone of voice was so friendly and so caring—Galen could tell he was worried.

“I feel like I’m going insane,” Galen replied with no intonation, no passion, no feeling. “I’m losing my mind.”

Cress pursed his lips together. "Happens to the best of us. Would you like some tea?"

"Tea would be lovely."

"You've never spoken to me like that before," giggled her brother. He got back to his feet, bouncing up with the energy of a kitten. "You really must be losing it. I'll make you some toast, too."

Galen just nodded, her eyes still watching the drooping branches of the willow tree sway in the breeze. They were hypnotic in the way that they moved, drifting back and forth with not a care in the world. Galen felt her eyelids droop. She instantly sat herself upwards, unbending her spine in such a way that she felt some of the vertebrae slip and pop. Her body went tumbling over the top of the couch, landing on the hardwood floor behind it with both a thud and a crack.

"Galen?" Nessa slid back into the room; the landline phone held to her ear. She padded slowly and curiously to the living room and glanced behind the sofa with a look of unease on her face. "She's very erratic and paranoid, yes. I know all these signs, doctor. I used to study this type of thing."

Ah, the doctor. Even Nessa thought Galen was crazy. Still, Galen was relieved at the thought of help. What she wanted was for someone to see that she wasn't insane, to see the Dreamcatcher. She was real, and other people needed to know it. They wouldn't, though. Galen could already predict the outcome of the doctor's diagnosis, and it was one that she had received many times in her life—overactive imagination.

"I'll bring her in straight away. I don't think she'll survive another night of this torment. She's lost too many hours of sleep." Nessa paced back and forth like a plotting tiger, though it was anxiety that moved her feet for her. "Yes, thank you. We'll see you in a few hours." She hung up the phone with the beep of a button, tossing it on the vintage armchair with the pattern of a pair of old curtains. "We're going to see Doctor Evergreen. I think it's time that we had you looked over, Galen. I don't like where these dreams are heading."

"Alright," Cress sung as he came dancing back into the room. "I've got your tea and your toast—oh," he suddenly murmured. "Where'd she go?"

Nessa smiled wryly down at her daughter, her eyes ablaze with fear. "She's on the floor."

"Ah," was the noise that came from Cress. He swept through the room—Galen could hear his feet slapping against the hardwood. There was a little clink of a cup being sat down and the clattering of a plate before more footsteps led him to stand in front of Galen. "For some reason, I didn't think you were serious."

"Help me get her up. We have to make sure she's okay for the doctors."

Galen let her family hoist her to her feet, though she stayed absentminded. Her head lolled as she was led back to the sofa that she'd thrown herself from. Slowly, Nessa and Cress positioned her hands so she could hold her teacup and her toast without dropping it, but her mother ended up feeding her little torn-up bits of her food. Words were said, but Galen couldn't hear them. There was a never-ending ringing in her ears, a high-pitched fuzz that sounded like distortion. She was reeling, wanting to sleep but wanting to never close her eyes again. Every blink was a risk, every memory traumatising. Her only sanctuary, somehow, was her brother's restlessness. She found herself watching him dart about the living room, mumbling to himself under his breath and twitching his hands. There was no danger here, not so long as she kept her eyes open and kept her wits about her.

The doctors' office was white. Too white.

The walls were white. The furniture was white. The people were dressed head to toe in white. Even the pictures they had on the walls were white. It was bright and exhilarating in all the worst ways.

Galen felt like her eyes were about to burst in her skull. She sat wedged between Cress, who wouldn't stop bouncing his leg, and her mother, who was chewing her nails off in sheer panic. Opposite her sat a young mum and her bratty child who had been crying for the last twenty minutes. There was an elderly couple sat in the corner who kept muttering insults and comments under their breaths as if no one could hear them, but everyone could. Even the snooty receptionist who sat behind her Plexiglas screen and tapped on her computer, probably pretending to do any work, eyed the screaming child with disdain.

"Last time I was here," Cress began out of nowhere, prompted like an old man who wanted to tell stories about his life, "they told me I had an attention problem and gave me pills that were pink and yellow."

"I don't think you have an attention problem."

Cress's leg-bouncing was starting to get out of control. "No?"

"No," Galen confirmed. "I think you have too much energy."

"Oh." Cress had obviously never thought of it that way. "An interesting view." He crossed his arms over his chest and sniffed in, glancing from the elderly couple to the fish tank that sat on the other side. "Those fish are dead," he said out the blue. He spoke like a toddler that had no self-control.

Galen gave the fish a glance. They didn't move at all. Were they even alive to begin with? They looked wooden, painted, floating on the bottom of the tank.

"They were dead when I came here last time."

"You're very observant."

"Galen Valentine?" a nurse called. She appeared from behind the door marked 'Dr Evergreen' with a surgical mask across her face and a clipboard in hand.

Nessa prompted Galen to her feet. "It'll be okay," she soothed, smiling down at her daughter. "Cress, you stay here. Don't bother these people and don't talk to them about the dead fish," she commanded.

"No promises," was his retaliation.

With a huff, Nessa walked Galen through the door and into a room that was much more pleasant to look at.

The walls weren't white, but a pastel blue. All the frames actually had pictures inside of them, some of them landscapes and some of them pictures of family and faces. The furniture hadn't been coated in an ungodly white varnish, and Dr Evergreen's fish were alive and swimming happily in a much better, much larger tank.

"Ah, Miss Valentine." Dr Evergreen was a man that Galen had seen rarely and did not recognise at all. He was all smiles, standing behind his desk with his arms spread wide, like he was about to envelop her in a hug that old friends would share. "I will say I was taken aback by the urgency in which this appointment was called with."

"Forgive me, Dr Evergreen," Nessa stepped in. "That would be my urgency. I was panicked. I still am panicked."

Dr Evergreen's eyes flickered over to Nessa. "I understand." He gestured to the two chairs placed in front of his desk. "Please, take a seat. Let's get to the bottom of this hysteria, shall we?"

Galen sat, taking a deep breath in, and letting out an even longer sigh.

"So, tell me," Dr Evergreen lent forwards, hands melded together in a thick knot of pudgy fingers, "what seems to be the problem?"

Galen glanced to her mother, finding only a sliver of reassurance in the nod and smile she received. "I've been having incredibly vivid dreams."

Dr Evergreen began typing away furiously on his computer, as if his life was dependent on the sentences he was stringing together.

"I haven't had nightmares since I was a child, because I could just…stop them from happening, but they've been starting to creep up on me out of nowhere."

"How did you stop them before?"

Again, Galen's eyes went over to her mother. "I have lucid dreams," she gulped. "I could stop whatever bad was going on from happening, but now I have no power."

"Okay, continue."

"There's been this persistent figure in my dreams. Eve is her name. I know that the people in your dreams are supposed to be people you've met before or that you've seen, but I've never seen or met this person before in my life. She appeared out of nowhere." Galen felt her heartbeat start to rush in her chest and sweat start to build on her brow. "She is the reason everything is going bad. I know she is. In my first nightmare, I saw her and then I was attacked by this giant ball of light that had tendrils and kept trying to grab me."

Dr Evergreen's typing stopped, and his brows became increasingly tighter knitted together.

"Then I had one last night, or three days ago apparently, and she was there again. She kept urging me to stay there, and that she could keep me from waking up. She transformed into this horrible creature and I fell off the side of a mountain, into that same ball of light that plucked me out of the air this time."

"She woke up in the garden," Nessa interjected. "She'd been asleep for three days straight in her room, and then suddenly she was in the garden."

Dr Evergreen's confusion was clear to see. "Sleepwalking does happen to those with a strong imagination."

"I didn't walk anywhere," Galen butted in, "and I didn't fall asleep willingly. I was dragged into sleep."

"How so?"

"I heard her voice."

Dr Evergreen sat up. "You can hear voices?"

Galen shook her head. "Just hers. I'm not crazy, I swear. I'm just tired."

"Miss Valentine, you are a confusing case," he chuckled wryly to himself. "It was noted on your record that you had an extremely overactive imagination when you were a child. It was also expected that it would die down as you got older, but that doesn't seem to be the case."

"What can you suggest for her?" Nessa asked. "Would something like a sleep aid help?"

Dr Evergreen shook his head. "No, I don't think that's necessary. Her problem isn't getting to sleep or staying asleep. It's what happens whilst she's asleep." He sat back, drumming his fingertips on the edge of his desk, and sucking in his bottom lip repeatedly. "It is a marvel. I don't get to deal with many cases like this. I would say that your mind has taken up a life of its own and has created its own world. There have been cases that I've heard of where people find themselves trapped in their dreams and can't wake up without some sort of nightmare-esque trauma happening. Yours would be that orb of light you mentioned."

Galen stared holes through Dr Evergreen. He was blaming her imagination. Of course, he would. He didn't understand. She felt herself sink into her chair, the life and the energy slowly draining from her body.

"There isn't much that I can prescribe for this," he went on, picking at his nails. "There are obviously tablets available, but I can see from your record that you've been prescribed most of them. Did they work?"

"I didn't take them," Galen admitted freely.

There was a wry laugh. "Well, why not? Did you not want to get better?"

"I'm not ill. I was a kid."

"And now is different?" Dr Evergreen asked. His tone was sharp and bitter, like he was suddenly upset with Galen. "Miss Valentine, tablets are only prescribed to you because your doctor feels like they will help you. In order for them to help you, you must take them. Do you see?"

"I'm also not stupid."

"Galen," Nessa chided under her breath. She turned back to Dr Evergreen, giving him a smile that was both apologetic and embarrassed. "Both my children are…eccentric, in a way. Pills have never helped either of them. Is there not a more…herbal way we can fix this?"

Dr Evergreen wanted to roll his eyes, but he simply threw his hands up in defeat. "I don't know of a herbal remedy for hearing voices that aren't there, Ms Valentine. Your daughter is facing extreme hysteria. She's incredibly paranoid and skittish. There isn't a tea she can drink for that to go away. She'll need tablets or therapy, and we can offer both here."

Galen had taken the tablets before—they never worked. They were all placebos. Doctors just thought people like her were crazy and needed pills to affirm their own belief that there was something wrong with them. Therapy was something she'd also tried before, but she'd felt stupid. The man she'd had as her therapist made her worse. He told her that everything she did was wrong and that she should stop doing it immediately, as if it were her own choice her mind was the way it was. She didn't want to do either of those things. She just wanted to sleep normally again, without the Dreamcatcher coming to seduce her off the path she'd been so happy to walk in the first place.

"Miss Valentine, what say you?"

Galen sat up a little bit, wanting to go home. "I don't have a choice. You think I'm mad."

"Mad is a strong word," Dr Evergreen replied. "I think that your hysteria has led you to severe paranoia and, further down the line, insomnia will start to be your norm. I'm even inclined to think that there is a touch of undiagnosed schizophrenia in your lineage, which would play into this mightily."

Schizophrenia. That was one that Galen hadn't heard before. She could add it to her list.

"The tablets are quite strong, but I think they'll do the trick."

"What do they do exactly?" Nessa asked nervously.

Dr Evergreen scribbled down his prescription on a little pink slip that he slid across the desk to Galen. "No need to worry, Ms Valentine. They won't have any lasting effects on your daughter. The side effects are normal—drowsiness, nausea, dizziness, low motivation. Hopefully, Galen will experience none of them."

Galen hated when he used her name. She took the slip from him and got to her feet, not waiting for her mother. Before Nessa or Dr Evergreen could say anything else to her, she was out of the door and standing in front of Cress.

"What drugs did you get?"

Galen read the little slip she'd been given. "Selesol."

"Oh, I've had those," Cress replied. "Strong things. They make you a couch potato."

Galen let out a sigh and sat next to her brother, reading through the rest of the text on her pink slip. "It says that these are used to subdue FPP..."

"Is that what Doc said you had?"

“Must be what he thinks will help,” Galen said. She took out her phone and searched the term, reading through a website with her eyes squinted and her face scrunched up. “FPP, better known as Fantasy Prone Personality, is a trait in which a person experiences a deep, extensive and lifelong involvement in fantasy.”

“So…like nerds do?”

“This disposition is an attempt, in part, to better describe and overactive imagination.” Galen shut her phone off and sighed deeply. Was this finally an accurate diagnosis? If so, why hadn’t Dr Evergreen just told her that? “I’m not crazy, at least. I just really like fantasy roleplaying.”

Cress laughed at that as the young mum was called in with her snot-nosed brat. “What did he think of your Dreamcatcher lady?”

“He thinks that my brain got bored of the real world and real people and created its own world with its own people.”

“You don’t sound impressed.”

“I’m tired, Cress.” Galen hung her head, pushing the balls of her hands into her eyes and rubbing aggressively. “I’ve drunk so many energy drinks and so much coffee that I don’t think caffeine even works on me anymore. I think my blood is caffeine now.”

Cress looped an arm about his sister’s shoulders as their mother appeared once more, slowly wandering towards them. “But at least you’re not crazy.”

Galen faked a smile as Nessa grew nearer. “At least I’m not crazy.”

Chapter Three

Galen sat with Cress in her room, the tablets she'd been given in front of her, rolling around in their orange bottle. She'd been staring at them for a good half hour whilst Cress had been muttering nonsense and pacing about the room, otherwise busying himself.

"You can go to your own room, you know," Galen murmured. "You don't have to stay with me. The doctor said I wasn't crazy."

"The doctor said someone had to make sure you took your tablets, and mum is squeamish."

Galen sighed. "Don't you have a video game to play or a girl to chat up? Isn't there anything better to do than babysit your eighteen-year-old sister?"

"Mum said I have to."

"Do you listen to everything mum says?"

Cress stopped his pacing, staring straight at Galen. "If you don't want to take them, it's not my problem. I'm just here because I'm worried about you. Usually it's me with the problems."

"I guess it's my turn now." Galen tucked her feet underneath the covers of her bed, letting her heavy duvet weigh her down. She slithered right down against the cold mattress and brought the covers up underneath her chin, letting the warmth seep into her cold bones. "I know what I have to do to make myself better."

"Oh yeah? Is it the tablets?"

Galen chuckled gently to herself, shaking her head. "No, it's not the tablets. You should let me sleep. It's about time I got the rest I need and deserve." She curled herself up into a ball and tucked herself against the wall, turning away from Cress. She could still hear him padding about her room, but his footsteps led towards the door and left shortly after.

Galen knew what she had to do. She'd been planning it since the drive back from Dr Evergreen's office. One way or another, she had to go to sleep. She had to track Eve down, bring the Dreamcatcher to her knees, and kick her out of her dreams. For that, she was prepared to go asleep for as long as she needed to. Galen knew it wouldn't be easy, that she wouldn't wake up for days, or weeks possibly, but that was the price she would pay for comfortable, easy, and restful sleep.

"I'm not going to be scared forever," Galen murmured to herself. She closed her eyes and let all her usual scenarios play in her mind. Visions of the autumn park and the beautiful beaches flashed up but would be wiped out by a burst of light. "I'm going to get rid of you one way or the other. I'm going to get my normal life back. You aren't going to stop me."

Is it a fight that you want, poppet?

Ah, there it was. That ethereal voice travelled back into Galen's head, soothing her further into sleep. Galen didn't mind and didn't bother to let the fear spread through her soul.

"If I have to fight you, then I will," Galen replied calmly. She let her head go heavy with fatigue, that void creeping closer towards her. "I will do anything I have to."

Come and fight me, poppet. I'd love it.

When Galen opened her eyes, she wasn't exactly where she had imagined herself. She had every intention of staying in a place that she knew that she recognised, but this was not such a place.

It was a vast land that looked like it had been created by a child. Bright colours and odd shapes littered the place, with trees that spiralled into the air with blue and pink leaves, and grass that was purple in patches and yellow in others. A well-trodden path cut directly through the centre of a meadow blooming with wildflowers, though the flowers were so beautiful and ornate it made them more than just mere weeds. Some were glasslike in nature—their petals so crystalline and opaque. Others were made from felts and velvets and satins.

Galen was in the middle of nowhere. It seemed like a forgotten land. There were rickety buildings everywhere that were half-complete or abandoned. Some had been burnt to a crisp, charred beyond repair, whereas others were strange effigies like you'd see in the middle of the woods, meant to scare anyone who came across them. They popped up so randomly in the middle of the files and the meadows, some of them even overlapping the path. There was one that ran up the trunk of a tree and then stretched across into the surrounding canopies, creating a way to crawl throughout the trees without being detected. What on earth could that be used for, and who was using it?

The place felt off. The atmosphere was heavy and dense, and breathing was hard. Galen still wandered aimlessly forward, however. She felt as if all her fear had been sapped from her. She had surely seen the worst of the Dreamcatcher. There couldn't have been much else that Eve had to display and, if there was, it couldn't have been as bad as what she'd already seen.

The sky above Galen's head was a baby pink in tone, as if the sun was setting peacefully. It dipped and bobbed between the tops of mountains, casually peeking out from behind the peaks to cast rays on light down onto a tiny village built from all sorts. It was still quite far away, but Galen could see that it was nothing like anything the Dreamcatcher had shown her. There wasn't that touch of elegance to it, that picture-perfectness. There had never been a detail out of place with Eve but this village, if it could be called that, was just thrown together. It barely looked real. Houses were made from wooden block toys that had been painted bright, luminous colours. Some were built from wooden pallets, others of bricks that were shaped strangely, most of tree branches and large rocks farmed from the mountains behind the settlement.

Well disguised against the mountains, with trees and shrubs covering it, Galen wondered if this was strategic. She wondered if it was even a place she had dreamt of before. It couldn't have been. This never would've crossed her mind. The randomness to it all alone made her question its origin. This had to have been created by someone as some sort of cutesy town. Was her mind capable of this franticness? Everything was placed without a purpose, just lying in the dirt where it would fit. Even the way the trees grew stressed Galen out. Their unusualness and sporadic pattern made her mind feel as if it was being squeezed, like it was taking every brain cell to comprehend what she was wandering towards.

It couldn't be a place from her childhood. Galen was too old and too forgetful to remember every dream. Perhaps this had been a place that had come into her mind when she was just a toddler. It looked like a child's drawing, so perhaps it was. Galen clung to any sort of answer she could come up with, though it still didn't seem as if she'd really figured it all out.

"Hold up!" a rough, old English accent called. "Where do you think you're going?"

Galen stopped in her tracks, glancing all around for a face to put to the grainy, harsh voice. There was no one to be seen, however. Not even in the houses afar were there any faces around. No one peeked from their windows or the cracks in their doors. There was no one.

"Are you deaf, love?"

Galen's frown deepened. Was it coming from the ground? She tilted her head down and gasped to see a little duck in front of her, also frowning just as heavily. Her head cocked to the side as she watched it move, not on its feet but on a set of wheels, like a toy.

"What's the matter with you? Never seen a duck before?"

Galen got a little closer.

It *was* a toy! It was her toy! It was a little pull-along toy that she did recognise from her childhood, but that was so long ago. Had she dreamt about him? She'd called him Ducky at the time, and he was a painted wooden duck mounted upon a base that had four wheels attached underneath. She would pull him about the house and garden all day by the frayed rope tied to a metal loop on his chest. His coat of paint looked just how it used to—his head was painted green, his beak a bright yellow, and his body a stunning red and navy blue. His feathers were all outlined in white, though that had faded a long time ago and had never been vibrant. His wheels were each different colour; one red, one yellow, one green and one blue, though they were worn down by the grit and the coarseness he'd been dragged across when Galen had been a child.

"Hold up," Ducky suddenly said. He wheeled backwards with no prompting, like a gust of wind had pushed him. His facial expression changed, no longer the usual painted-on resting glare he always had. He was alive and animate, living a life of his own. "Aren't you…What are you doing here?" he quacked suddenly, darting forwards, and almost running over Galen's toes. "You're supposed to be dreaming, not in the dream!"

"You remember me?"

A scoff. "How could I forget you? You're the kid I used to spend night and day with! You did this to me wheels!" Ducky came forward and showed off his two front wheels, worn down and sad, in dire need of repair. "I'll ask again—what are you doing here?"

"My dreams have been sabotaged," Galen explained. She couldn't put into words how strange it was to be speaking to Ducky, and to have him replying to her with a voice all of his own. "Someone's taken them over, and I decided to put a stop to it."

"Sabotaged?" Ducky scoffed again, shaking his two-dimensional head from side to side. "No one can sabotage your dreams. Your dreams are your own."

Galen crouched. "Not anymore." She glanced about the place again, watching as the sky changed from baby pink to bright purple and then to a hazy yellow. "What is this place? Why does it look like this here?"

"This is the Safe Haven," Ducky explained. He turned somehow and wheeled towards the village, leading Galen along by his rope. This time, he was dragging her around, and it didn't seem like he would have it any other way. "This is the place where dreams go when they want to be safe or forgotten."

"Safe?"

Ducky's wheels creaked incessantly, in need of oil. "Some of us have to keep ourselves safe here. Ain't all fun and games like you would think it is. Nightmares are a lot more…nightmarish when you're in them."

"What could be threatening you?"

"Lots of things." Ducky stopped as the path became a clearing, leading into the village. A lot more of it was on display, showing off the little quirks and oddities of the place. "We're all hunted. Our homes are not what they used to be anymore. That bitch doesn't like us being here because we aren't perfect, and she don't like anything old."

That bitch? Galen perked up suddenly, her mouth falling open. "Eve?"

"Eh?"

"The Dreamcatcher. She's hunting you?"

Ducky rolled back a few paces, brows heavily furrowed and eyes accusing. "How do you know about her? No one is supposed to know about her, especially not you! Ah, that's what you meant, isn't it? Sabotaged…" His accusing glare suddenly went soft and fearful, a loud huff of defeat escaping his wooden lungs. "Well, I shouldn't be surprised. Happens to everyone. Can't have expected you to keep your guard up forever."

"Where is she?" Galen asked frantically. Maybe this would be easier than she thought. Maybe it wouldn't result in a fight.

Ducky laughed. "You think I'd know a thing like that? No, love. I keep myself and everyone here as far away from her as possible. If she knows we're here, then *poof*, just like that, we're gone. Isn't really the kind of fate you'd like to wind up with, is it?" He wheeled circles around Galen, observing only her ankles and feet as that was all he was tall enough to see. "Now, the real question is, how do you know of the wicked witch? Don't let me find out you're in cahoots with the cow."

"No! No, not at all!" Galen responded defensively. "She just…appeared in my dreams one night. There was something so off about her. I'd never seen her before. She gave me nightmares after over ten years over never having one."

"She only came to you once?"

Galen shook her head. "I've seen her a few times. The last time I saw her she tried to convince me to stay, not that I know how that's possible. She got angry with me when I said I should wake up and turned into this…this horrible—"

"Trust me," Ducky interjected. "I've seen what that woman can turn into and I don't need a description of another one of her fucked-up forms." He released a sigh again, this time once that caused him to drift backwards a touch. Only a patch of grass kept him from rolling all the way down the hill. "Seems like she's got her claws in you pretty deep, lovely. Sucks to be you."

"You're a lot meaner and uncaring than I thought you would be."

"I'm a wooden duck," Ducky replied stiffly. "My purpose is to be dragged about all day but snot-nosed kids who don't treat me well. Granted, you were never like that, but that brother of yours can rot in his nightmares for all I care. Took a chunk out of my head, that bastard did." Ducky unfolded his wings from his side, a motion he could never do in the real world, and ran the tips of his feathers across a crater in his skull. "Who bites chunks of wood out of their toys? Not even their toys; their sister's toys!" He dropped his wings and quacked loudly once, surely a curse word in whatever language it was he spoke normally. "Why couldn't it have been him? Why'd she have to get you?"

That was a good question. Cress was just as imaginative as Galen, though he was able to control his more. That was what his pacing was about, and that was why he spoke to himself. He wasn't afraid to look insane, whereas Galen wanted no attention from anybody around her. She kept hers bottled up and contained, whereas Cress was as free as a bird with every single one of his abnormalities.

"I tricked her into dragging me into sleep so I could go after her and stop her," Galen revealed. She figured that anything she'd created in her dreams, or any of the toys she'd played with as a child and had loved fiercely, would be on her side. "I can't go on losing sleep. My family think I'm insane and so does my doctor."

"Stop her?" Ducky cocked his head to the side. "How in fresh hell do you expect to do that? Do you even know what you're up against?"

Galen rubbed at her bottom lip, suddenly worried. "She didn't seem all that bad to deal with. She's taken a liking to me. I reckon I could swindle her pretty easily if need be, but I don't want to have to hurt her."

Ducky was staring holes through Galen, but it wasn't anger or frustration in his gaze. He looked worried. Genuinely worried. His beak parted a little bit as if he had something to say, and he did, but he just didn't know how to go about saying it. There was a secret he was keeping, not on purpose, but the right words just didn't arrive at the right time.

Ducky wheeled forwards slowly, his wheels creaking sadly as he moved. "I think you should come and talk to someone with me, sweetheart. Letting you go out there alone would be a purely irresponsible thing for me to do." He turned. "Come. This won't take long."

Ducky led Galen through the village, but he moved slowly. It was as if he wanted her to see his way of living, the way that everyone else here thrived and survived. He showed off little monuments scattered throughout the town. There were little shrines that he described as being tokens to fallen dreams, those that had been snatched away by the Dreamcatcher. Those types of memorials were mounted on plinths, with random items scattered underneath. They were random to Galen but held all the meaning in the world to the villagers. Somehow, all her dreams had become connected. Everything she had ever thought up or created in her stories or in her sleep or whilst daydreaming or whilst playing as a child had come to life in this place and had bonded with one another. One dream could fall in love with another, and one dream could easily become two.

The place that Ducky stopped was in front of the biggest building in the village. Out of every home or shop or shed, it looked normal. Whoever had built it had just nailed pieces of scrap wood together to build the exterior and had threaded together hay and straw for the roof. It was an old farm outbuilding, taking straight from one of Galen's daydreams and plonked in the centre of her mind. Some tweaks had been made, some repairs along the way, but it still looked like it would house livestock, not dreams.

Inside, Galen was witness to emptiness. It should've been thriving. There were chairs and tables all over, as well as another monument that was in the very centre of the room, stretching from rickety floor to unstable ceiling.

Ducky paid that no mind. He rolled straight past it, gently touching the base of it with his wing as he went before moving away to a door that was open ajar. His wheels came to a screeching stop at the threshold, and his head turned back so he could glance almost pleadingly at Galen.

"What is this place?"

"We use it as the town hall," Ducky explained. "If something goes wrong, or if someone goes missing, we all gather here. Not much we can do about these things, but we can ask the dreams that still hold a little bit of power to help strengthen our defences. The more hidden we are, the better." Ducky knocked on the door and rolled in, not waiting for Galen to follow in his tracks.

"What is it now, Duck?" another voice that Galen didn't recognise spoke up. "You've been in here almost every day now with a new problem. Surely something else can't have gone wrong."

Galen padded towards the voice, a rich crooner's voice, almost the same as Frank Sinatra's. It was incredibly soothing, though it did carry undertones of a mafia boss. That brought fear through Galen's body. She tried her best to recount any dreams she'd had that would include such a man, such a villain, but her mind was empty.

As she rounded the corner, Galen's fear drained away from her. She saw no threat sitting in the back room, but a teddy bear that she recognised within seconds. Gillette. That was his name. Galen hadn't thought of that as a child but had seen the word branded across a packet of razors in her mum's room one night. She'd always called him Gil, and he had been her favourite toy for years. He was still sitting in her room, though now he only collected dust. He watched over her sleep from a shelf mounted across the other side of the room to her bed, where he could keep her safe and free of nightmares.

Gil perked up at the sight of someone new, but he didn't quite see who was looming in his doorway. "Did you find another lost dream, Duck? That doesn't surprise me. That wench is driving more and more of us out of our homes each day." He spat on the ground, a sign of utter disrespect. "I hope she burns alive."

"No, Gil," Ducky laughed nervously. All that attitude he'd had towards Galen was suddenly gone in front of Gil, as if the poor little duck was afraid of the big, purple bear. "Seems to me that we have a bigger problem on our hands. Come in, girl."

Galen did as she asked, stepping further into the room and into a beam of light that shone down upon her.

When he saw her, Gil dropped whatever he was doing. He couldn't help but stare at her in awe, his once sewn-shut mouth opening. The little beads he had for eyes were full of life now, but also filled with fear and anxiety. He hopped up from the table he'd been sitting behind, standing all of two-foot-tall, and swaggered his way up to Galen. His fat little legs rendered him from moving fast, making him plod like an old man with a limp.

"No…" he murmured under his breath, reaching out with a stumpy arm. Galen could see the little patch she'd sewn onto the end of it still intact, still bearing her name. "No, this can't be…tell me this isn't so…"

"We should've guessed, Gil," Ducky said quietly. "Why else would that woman be here if not for our Galen? There's nothing else here for her."

"There was plenty here for her!" Gil roared. His voice was so old, like that of someone's grandfather who had been smoking for fifty years. "There were dreams here for her to consume, to feed on! She could've used us, Duck. She could've just used us and moved on to the next unfortunate bastard." Gil's head hung, and his body slumped so he plopped cutely down against the floor. "As good as it is to see you, to finally meet you, Galen, these aren't the circumstances any of us would've liked."

Galen felt rude towering over her toys so sat, crossing her gangly legs beneath herself. "Is there something that I'm missing?"

Gil glanced to Ducky, but Ducky was quick to avoid that look. "Does she not know?"

"She knows practically nothing, Gil."

"Then that makes this so much worse." The teddy bear pawed at his eyes before dropping his chubby arms back at his sides where they stared. His head lifted, but it wasn't a smile that greeted Galen. "I can understand how a child like you would grow to be naïve. I'm willing to bet that wretched demon showed only the good sides of her to you, came across as a treat, not a trick."

Galen nodded, remembering the way that Eve had been so caring and attentive straight off the bat. There hadn't been a moment where the Dreamcatcher had stopped smiling. There hadn't been a second where there was anything but love and adoration and want in her eyes. She'd been the friendliest person Galen had ever met, but apparently it was all too good to be true.

"Do you know what she is, Galen?" Gil asked. "Do you know why she's here?"

"I know what she's told me, and that's all." Galen fidgeted, picking at a freckle on her ankle. "I knew there was much more to her than what she said, but she wouldn't talk to me. She has a habit of dancing around my questions."

Gil nodded his head and, with the flick of a paw, sent Ducky away so he sat alone with Galen. "The Dreamcatcher is nothing of what she presents herself as. That creature doesn't love you; she doesn't care about you. There isn't a heart inside of that chest." He pushed himself up to his feet, rocking back and forth as he tried to catch his balance on rounded padding in his paws. "The Dreamcatcher is a parasite. Nothing more, nothing less. She feeds off imaginations and dreams and the power to make things that aren't real, real. You see, she doesn't really exist."

Galen arched a brow. Eve didn't exist? How could that be? She felt so realistic, so lifelike. There had to be a person in the living world that was the exact replica of Eve, the original, so that the Dreamcatcher could exist in dreams. There just had to be.

"I don't know how she was created or who thought of her, but she preys on people like you—people who have incredibly powerful minds and can dream things that other people can't even begin to imagine. That power fuels her. It drives her. It makes her that little bit more real. There are only two things that she needs; belief and dreams."

That would explain why the Dreamcatcher was obsessed with Galen believing in her. It would also explain the glowing of her skin that would happen once she heard those magic words. She was rejuvenating, repowering, growing stronger.

"If you don't believe in her, she'll convince you to start believing as soon as she introduces herself to you," Gil went on. He'd given this speech many times, it seemed. Either that or he'd rehearsed it well. "If she catches you saying that you don't believe, she'll kill you. It takes nothing at all for her to consume your very life-force just because you won't believe. She drinks in everything that you are, absorbs your existence, your heart, your love, your dreams, your power, and then leaves you as a pile of dust." Gil began to pace back and forth. He attempted to hold his hands behind his back, but his chubbiness and rotundness wouldn't allow it. "I've seen it happen too many times, Galen. Too many of my friends have refused to tell her what she wants to hear, and they've paid the price for it."

Galen could barely talk over the lump in her throat. "And why does she need my dreams?"

"Dreams make her real," Gil said simply. "The energy and the focus and the power that you put into dreaming are what she's feeding from. When you're asleep, you're giving her power. I presume she's tempted you into staying with her?"

"She said she wanted me to stay."

"And that's precisely why. She is sapping everything she can away from you without you noticing." Gil went to his desk and heaved himself up onto the chair, having to jump a little to reach it. "That's why you're so tired when you eventually wake up. You could be asleep for days, weeks, months, but if she's got hold of you then you will always wake up worse for wear until, one day, you don't wake up at all."

Galen's breath hitched in her throat.

"When you're done, and you have nothing else to give her, she traps you here and she moves on to the next bastard who has an extraordinary mind." Gil managed to stand in his chair, reaching across the desk for papers that he had stacked up neatly. "You'd think that she'd have a little bit of heart, a little bit of sympathy, and let you go, but no. It's where she gets her name from. The Dreamcatcher catches you in her web and never lets you go, not even when you have nothing left to give."

Galen could feel her heart beating out of control. She put a hand against her chest, sealing her lips together to stop herself from panting like a dog. The Dreamcatcher was a villain after all. Galen should've guessed. That man at the party had warned her. He had told her. Eve had made quick work of him, though. Why hadn't she just killed him? Had she wanted to spare Galen of thinking she was a monster? Well, now Galen knew, and now her nightmares were becoming more and more haunting.

"When she started to show up, we thought nothing of it." Gil still went on, sounding wistful and reminiscent. He tugged the papers off his desk and fell from his chair, hitting the floor with a little thud. He soon picked himself up and brushed himself off, acting as if nothing had ever happened. "We weren't here, in this village. We were in the places that you created us in, in those dream worlds. She took them over. One by one, I started to notice that more of our world was being taken away from us. She was killing us left, right and centre. Those that didn't want to die converted and pledged their allegiance and their belief. They gave her the right to possess them any time she wanted, to see through their eyes so she could watch everything that happened inside your mind. We've had to put a few of our own down because of it…"

"Has she ever hurt you?"

Gil's head lifted as he dragged the papers towards Galen, desperate for her to see them. "Let's just say she isn't fond of me." He dumped the papers on Galen's foot, as that was as close as he could get them. "There are a few of us that are still around that have our own strength and power. We are still strong dreams, so we can hold our own against her if we must. Saying that, I bet she'd eat us alive now if we were to go anywhere near her."

"I don't remember dreaming about you…I just remember playing with you as a child," Galen explained. She scooped up the papers, reading the typewritten text that was lain so neatly against the page. It was all information on Eve, all accounts of dealing with her, or deaths. One sheet was just a page of tally marks titled 'Kill Count'. That page made Galen sad. "What does this all mean? Have I made a mistake in coming here?"

"In a way, yes, but in another way it was always inevitable." Gil plopped himself at Galen's feet and stared up at her admirably, his stitched mouth curling up into a gentle smile. "There's no stopping the inevitable, child. She would've dragged you here kicking and screaming eventually. The fact you came on your own accord is good. The fact you aren't infatuated with her is also good."

Galen couldn't help but keep her eyes on the tally sheet. "It's hard not to be infatuated with her. It's hard not to believe in her."

Gil's eyes clouded over with sorrow. "So, you do believe." He sounded so sad, so heartbroken, but so understanding all at the same time. "It's hard not to. If only it was as simple as telling you not to believe in her anymore, I'd be screaming at you. You've seen her. That beast is the closest thing to real I've ever met, and I know what she truly is."

"How many people are here? In this village?"

"Enough," Gil replied coldly. "I take in as many as I can, but not many people come over the horizon anymore. Used to be flocks of them at a time. Poor Duck used to have to get his wheels changed due to the amount of rolling about he'd do. Then, it all just stopped. No one came anymore, so we put up a wall."

"Does she know you're here?"

Gil shrugged his shoulders lightly. "If she does, she's done nothing about us. What my question to you is, does she know you're here, right now?"

Galen didn't know how to respond to that. Every time she'd met Eve, the Dreamcatcher had already been there waiting for her. This was the only time that was different. She'd been all alone when she'd opened her eyes, something she wasn't used to experiencing.

"I don't know," Galen finally said. "She's always just...been there when I've opened my eyes. This is the only time that's different. She's nowhere to be seen."

"Nowhere to be seen but she can't be far." Gil climbed back to his feet and staggered towards the door. He moved the same way Galen's grandfather did—painfully. "Duck!" he called out of the open door. "Duck!"

"I'm coming!" Ducky shouted back. "Impatient old man." He rolled into the room and almost knocked Gil off balance again. "What?"

Gil glanced over his shoulder at Galen again, a remorseful look wearing down his fabric features. "We're going to have to do an awful lot of explaining to the townsfolk."

"You're keeping her here?" Ducky asked.

"I have to."

Ducky had apparently never been more outraged in his life. "You realise that she is going to get us all killed? Whether she means to or not?"

Again, Gil's shoulders lilted. "We've been alive a long time, Duck. If we're going to meet our demise, it might as well be now. Go rally up the people whilst I find a place to hide this lanky creature, will you? And check to see what the patrols have said. It's been too long since I've heard from the boys."

Ducky hesitated for a moment, his painted eyes flickering between Gil and Galen. "I won't die because of her," he quacked. "I will not give my life away just so she can survive the same threat we're avoiding. It's one for all, not all for one."

"Get out, Duck. Do as I've asked!" Gil roared. "I've had enough of your backchat."

Ducky, resentfully, did as he was told. He rolled backwards out of the room, but not without staring holes through Galen's soul. He said not a thing to her, keeping his lips sealed as he disappeared out of sight, squeaking all the way into the town centre.

"It won't be long until she wakes up and senses that you're here," Gil said to Galen. He nudged her arm and then tumbled out of the room into the main hall, heading straight for the door outside. "We have to do everything we can to prolong that period. The longer we have with you without her knowing, the better. I can tell you everything you need to know and hide you away somewhere safe."

"How long will I have to hide?"

"I'll hide you forever if I have to," grumbled Gil. "Ducky may not die for you, but I will. I'm an old dream. I don't need to be here. The others can have their say when they meet you, but I'm sick of fighting this monster. It's not something I should have to do."

Galen agreed with that. "It should be my job, and my task alone."

"You will not face her alone!" Gil suddenly bellowed at the top of his lungs. He whirled around on Galen, pointing a stubby arm in her direction. "You will not leave this town alone; do you understand me? You will stay here until we have a plan, and I will expect nothing else of you."

Galen stood in shock. She watched as Gil hobbled away from her, her mouth wide open and her heart pounding in her chest. This was not the playful teddy bear that she'd played with as a child. His personality was dense and stony, his exterior cold and unemotive. Galen understood his fear and his apprehension, but she didn't want to have to hide. She didn't want to have to keep herself hidden away. Galen wanted a fight, and a fight she would have, whether Gil and Ducky were on her side or not.

Bursting free of the town hall, Galen watched Gil as he dragged himself across the clearing to another little hut. He didn't glance over his shoulder as Galen skittered across the dusty ground, skipping around stray garbage and hiding herself behind a well to watch as Gil knocked at the door. Galen's eyes flickered straight to who answered it; a tall woman dressed in a western outfit with a curved hat sat atop her head. She watched the two of them talk quietly until the cowgirl agreed to step outside, away from the noise in her home.

"I hate to drag you out and away from your family, Peep," Gil sighed under his breath. The old bear was tired, that much was painfully obvious. He rested against an old bench, staring up at the woman named Peep with hope in his glass eyes. "She's here, Peep. Galen. She's here. The Dreamcatcher has begun to show herself to our girl. The danger that we had always feared has finally arrived on our doorstep."

Peep took her hat from her head and held it against her heart. "This was a day we were prepared for. Think of it that way. We're more prepared to face the

Dreamcatcher than we ever have been. Our chances of losing have been lessened."

"Our chances of winning have never been realistic." Gil hung his head and let the sun shine down against his purple fur. It revealed patches that had fallen out and showed off a few stitched that he'd received from Galen's mother. "What we must do is keep Galen protected and safe, away from that woman. We can't risk a fight when we don't know the outcome."

"She's not going to want to stay here, Gil. We ain't going to be able to keep her here if she doesn't want to be here. This is not her place."

Gil's expression darkened. "It's not a case of what she wants anymore, Peep. I know what's best for the girl. I've gone through what she's about to go through and I've never succeeded. What makes you think she'd be able to?"

"Because she's not a teddy bear," Peep replied. "She's not a toy duck. She's not a doll. She's a real person."

"There is too much at stake."

"We have no idea what the Dreamcatcher is capable of anymore," reasoned Peep. She put a reassuring hand on Gil's shoulder and let loose a sigh that rippled through her plastic body. "She's been drained for a long time. There hasn't been anybody for her to leech off of. Life is a thing that has been scarce here, and you should know that."

Gil shrugged off Peep's hand and staggered backwards, staring up at the cowgirl with shock and hurt in his glare. "You would hand her over that easily?" he scoffed, almost laughing in Peep's face. "You care for her that little? When she is the reason that you exist in the first place? Is there no integrity left in you?" He turned his back on the cowgirl and muttered something under his breath as he went, shaking his head. "You will survey this town and you will watch that girl closely. She is not to leave here, and if she does then I will hold each and every resident here responsible for it!"

Galen didn't recognise the toy that was hobbling around, kept up by nothing more than a little matchstick for a walking stick. He was so robust and bossy, selfish in a way. The bear had the hardest exterior that Galen had ever observed, and it showed no signs of cracking at all. It flinched a little when a sudden rumbling over the earth appeared from nowhere, stopping the bear in his tracks.

"Poppet?" Eve's voice crooned over the town, shaking its very core. All the buildings and statues and monuments trembled where they stood, and little cracks and breaks in the hard ground split and ran underneath Galen's feet.

"*How?*" Galen whispered under her breath. She backed away from where she was hiding, turning each and every way and trying her best to find the Dreamcatcher.

Eve could've been anywhere. She could've hidden anywhere. There was no sign of her—no footsteps or tracks in the dirt, no shadows that she could've hidden in. Galen was out in the open with almost anywhere and everywhere to go, but she felt trapped in. The walls were closing in around her, holding her in place as thunder rumbled overhead. Lightning split the sky in two, illuminating the dark tones of blue and green and grey that the sky was choked with. All those beautiful pastel colours were gone now, evaporated, painted over with darkness and evil.

"Poppet, where are you?" the Dreamcatcher asked.

"Everyone get inside and batten down the hatches!" Gil shouted at the top of his lungs. "Let her see none of you! We aren't here!" He ran suddenly, ditching his little walking stick and running straight at Galen. "You! Get inside!" he screamed as loud as he could.

Galen turned on her heel as lightning struck the ground just in front of Gil, throwing him back. The tiny bear went soaring through the air and thudded into a pile of pallets, shattering through some of them.

"Gil!" Galen called after him. She went running after him, sprinting across the dry earth to reach him. Though her feet slipped constantly, Galen pushed forward. She had to dodge gigantic hailstones that fell gracefully from the clouds above, and bolts of lightning sharp enough and strong enough to split her in two. She weaved back and forth, tumbling over a stray bucket, and rolling across the ground. Galen pushed her feet flat against the ground and sprang back up, grabbing hold of Gil and throwing herself underneath one of the rickety houses just as another bolt of lightning ricocheted off the earth, making it sizzle.

"Why aren't you inside?" Gil roared at Galen.

"You expect me to just leave you out there?" Galen roared back. She cuddled him underneath her as the ground split and a low, deep groaning rung out clear for all to hear. It echoed throughout the storm despite the thunder, the howling wind, the hailstones. "You are not sacrificing yourself for me, no matter how much you may want to! I need all the help I can get!"

Gil tried to shove Galen off him, but it didn't work. He clambered to his feet and went to dash from underneath the house but fell back to the ground with a little *poof* as Galen grabbed hold of his leg. His body slid across the dirt as Galen brought him back to safety. Though he fought and wriggled, Gil didn't get his way. He flopped onto his back and stared up at Galen, his expression taut and sour.

"You're doing more harm than you are good, child," Gil warned.

Galen stared right past him. She was watching the earth, the hole that had been created by endless, repetitive lightning strikes. The bolts had torn open the ground to create a chasm that was smoking. Little tufts of smoke billowed against the harsh breeze, but still rose in perfect spirals and swirls. The weather didn't affect it, instead only raging around the site, as if something was deterring it.

Whatever lay within that void was truly evil. An ominous glow radiated upwards from it, as if stars had fallen from the sky and lay at the bottom of the pit. The light was warped and twisted with the smoke, intertwined as one, moving as one. Even the groaning and the growling and the distortion that Galen could hear was emitted from the void. What could possibly be within it? Had the lightning strikes cut deep enough to open up the depths of a nightmare?

"Gil…" Galen's voice drifted off. She kept the teddy bear pinned down against the ground and hidden in the shadows underneath the hut, but her eyes were firmly lodged on the pit. The light grew brighter and the smoke more persistent, and the growling and sputtering much louder. "What's happening? What is that?"

"We need to go," was all that Gil said back. He tried to drag himself across the ground, but he didn't get very far before Galen dragged him back. "What is that? Where did that come from?"

Galen watched as a crooked arm suddenly shot up and out of the hole. Fingers dug into the dirt, clawing through the mud to heave something upwards. Little by little, more of a body was revealed. There was a bicep, muscled but torn to shreds. As it tensed and dragged itself closer to the surface, a shoulder popped up next, then a head. Tufts of hair were stuck to a balding, cut scalp that was turning green and grey. Sharpened teeth hung in decaying gums that overlapped thin, chapped lips barely still attached to a skinny, skeletal face. There was only one eye sunk deep into a socket. The other was just an empty hole in the rotting skull, with skin barely just stretched over the top of it.

More and more of the monstrous little creatures popped up, each of them desperately clawing their way up out of the earth. They groaned and complained as their muscles became taut with the effort their exerted. Still, though it was hard work, the monsters only doubled in number. When one appeared at the surface, three more would be right behind. Each one was louder than the last, complaining like little old men as they lined up around the crevice and then split off into groups to search the town.

"*What are they?*" Galen whispered, keeping herself hidden in the shadows. Every time one of the little gremlins came near her hut, she shimmied further back into the darkness to keep herself from being spotted. "*Where did they come from?*"

"Those, my dear, are the Dreamcatcher's little hunters," Gil explained. He watched them with a beady eye, scowling at them but in no fear of them. "They are braindead, for the most part. They're the dumbest breed of cretin that the Dreamcatcher has thrown into our world. Yet, somehow, they still manage to get their job done, and I would presume that their job is to bring you back to her. We cannot let them find you."

Galen let out an exasperated sigh, sitting back on her haunches. "How do we get around them?"

"We need to outsmart them, that's all."

"How?"

Gil smacked his lips together and paused, watching as the last of the gremlins had crawled out of their grave. "We need to burn them."

Chapter Four

"If we burn them, they go away?" Galen asked. She didn't believe in Gil's plan, but she hadn't told the old bear that. It didn't seem plausible. How could something as simple as fire kill off Eve's henchmen? They didn't look indestructible. In fact, they looked as if they had been through the wars. Just the sight of them made it clear that the Dreamcatcher didn't value them, didn't care for them. They were falling apart at the seams, and fire seemed like a drastic measure for a simple problem.

"If we burn them, they go away forever." Gil was crawling underneath the houses, slipping from hut to hut and following along with a group of the Dreamcatcher's ragtag gremlins. He hadn't been spotted yet, but he was looking for his window of opportunity. "These things are like zombies. Persistent, stupid, and practically invulnerable to everything you throw at them—except for fire."

Galen could see the logic in it, but it made her uncomfortable. How could she bring herself to light those poor beings on fire? She didn't see them as Gil did. They were enslaved. It was obvious to see in their eyes; those that had them. Whatever creatures they used to be had died long ago, and now all that was left were animated carcasses forced to listen to a demon's every command.

Gil and Galen came to a stop at the end of the last house, hidden behind a few barrels, watching the gremlins rip everything apart. For such thin, gangly, dead things, they were awfully strong. They lay a siege upon Gil's little town, ripping down monuments and kicking their way through doors. Anything that lay in their way was abruptly destroyed. They worked in perfect harmony, tearing up boards of wood and stomping their way through weaved fencing, almost humming a song as they went.

That was until lightning struck one of the memorials in the centre of the town and set it ablaze.

Galen had never seen terror like it. She'd never heard shrieking so shrill. Her eyes were wide with awe and fear, emblazoned with the flames, as she watched those monstrous creatures suddenly flee like startled cats. They screamed like children as they desperately sought cover, running around in circles like headless chickens with bits of themselves falling off. Some of them lost arms and legs, some eyes and noses, others lost all their skin. It melted from them like a poorly applied piece of wallpaper, slopping against the ground.

But there was one creature, a smart one, that stared at the fire with its head cocked curiously to the side. He didn't seem scared. He didn't seem at all frightened. The poor thing was entranced by the dancing flames, watching as the colours swirled one by one in front of his eyes. Reds and yellows and oranges. He extended a crooked arm and pointed an even more crooked finger, toying with the idea of touching the flames. The tip of his finger got closer and closer and closer, not stirred by the shouting of his friends behind him, until it did touch the fire.

It took a matter of seconds.

If Galen had blinked, she would've missed it.

It was like a scene from a movie that kept everyone on edge yet happened so fast. If Galen could rewind time, she would have.

In front of her very eyes, Galen watched as the fire leapt upon the creature. It took only seconds before he was entirely engulfed and then consumed. All that remained of him was a little puff of smoke that trailed off a pile of ash and soot. He hadn't even had the time to react. He hadn't screamed or made any noise, but had just stood there.

It silenced all of his friends. Some of them grew the nerve to pad over to the pile of ash that their friend now was, and prod at it. They didn't understand what had happened. Had they been told they were indestructible? Had they been led to believe nothing could kill them? Eve couldn't have been that evil, surely.

They babbled something to themselves, talking as a group. The one that stood over the pile of ash seemed to take charge, suddenly frowning deeply and gesturing aggressively to the debris. He was shouting, but the language made no sense to Galen.

"*Do you know what they're saying?*" Galen whispered to Gil.

"I could hazard a guess," Gil replied, just as quiet. "I don't think they realised that could happen to them."

Galen felt confused. "I thought you knew this was the only way to defeat them?"

“I knew it, but I don’t think they did.” Gil shuffled closer to Galen, so his body was pressed up against her bicep. He watched on carefully, observing the shouting and screaming gremlin as it acted like an outraged ape, throwing everything and anything in reach—even his friends. “You see, when the Dreamcatcher loses enough of these little wretches, she bakes up a new batch. Obviously, she doesn’t expose them to fire wherever she keeps them. They’re fascinated by it, but little do they know it’ll be their demise.” Gil’s attention suddenly flickered to the burning memorial, a split of different emotions blazing in his eyes. “One of us needs to get to that podium and set alight a torch, whilst the other rounds up the little bastards.”

“Neither of those tasks sound ideal,” Galen laughed nervously.

Gil scoffed. “No, and you’re not going to like what I have to say next.” His paw slid across the earth to rest against the back of her palm, his symbol of pity. “We’re going to have to send you out as bait.”

That wasn’t what Galen wanted to hear.

“They’ll go for you more than they will me,” Gil reasoned, trying to explain himself quickly. “They have no reason to chase me other than to dispose of me. You, on the other hand, are their target. You are what their master has asked them to retrieve.”

Galen hung her head, pushing her forehead against the cold dirt. She squeezed her eyes shut as strands of her hair fell into her face, tickling her eyelids. It took all she had to muster up courage. She could do this. Could she? Oh, how she hated nightmares. How she hated where she found herself. How had it all led up to this?

“All you have to do is run, Galen,” Gil assured. “Run and stay out of their grip. They can’t possibly outsmart you.”

“There are more of them than there are me.”

Gil shrugged his shoulders lightly, almost as if he didn’t care. “Think of it this way,” he proposed. “All of them combined do not have the smarts that you do alone. This will either be the easiest thing you’ve ever done, or the hardest, but only if you make it hard on yourself.”

“What will you do?” Galen asked fearfully. That was what she was more afraid of. Her own fate didn’t frighten her so much. Even if those creatures did catch her, she’d end up with someone who would never hurt her. She had escaped Eve before, and she could do it again, but Gil was a different bag of nuts.

“I will go to Peep,” he said gruffly in response, staring at Peep’s house. “She’s the only one strong enough to grasp a torch. Truth be told, she’s the only one with hands.” He chuckled to himself wryly and broke out one of the first smiles Galen had seen from him. “Once she’s lit the torch, you’ll need to meet her and take it from her, and then set those fiends alight.”

Galen’s heart jumped up to the middle of her throat, and she almost choked. “I have to kill them?”

There was a moment of silence from Gil, a moment of sheer aggravation. “This world isn’t as easy as yours is, I’m sure. You’re going to have to kill off a lot more than zombies. This won’t be the first time that you’ll do harm, and it definitely won’t be the first thing you’ll kill. You’re going to have to do a lot of toughening up, young lady. This is where you begin.”

Galen peeled her eyes away from Gil, sick of the sight of his face. How could her dreams be so harsh? She watched as the gremlins resumed tearing at the town with an incensed rage now that one of them had died. They moved so much faster, ripping and shredding anything that they could wrap their bony fingers around. Their repeated failure made them even angrier, and made them work twice as hard, twice as fast.

Taking in a deep breath, Galen pushed herself up onto all fours. She was ready to sprint out from her hiding place but waited. Her eyes travelled slowly back to Gil, and a sigh escaped through her parted lips.

“*Start crawling towards it,*” she whispered to him. “*If I run out now, they’ll know where we’ve been hiding. They’ll see you go.*”

Gil nodded his head and shuffled away from her. He moved so efficiently, rolling across the earth until one of his arms was exposed to the storm. It was as if the Dreamcatcher knew, sending a lightning bolt down to strike his hand. Luckily, the old bear had his wits about him. He wrenched his arm towards him and flopped onto his back, staring up at the bottom of the house.

Galen had to leave him there. She had to go now. Whilst he was contending with the weather, Galen had other things to worry about. Her eyes darted back to her opposition. She could outsmart these creatures easily. It would be no challenge for her. All she had to do was keep them on her tail until Peep had the torch, and then it would be all over. Whilst there was the repeated lightning, the wind, the hailstones, the cracks in the earth to also contend with, Galen felt a surge of confidence drive her forward and send her sprawling out into the open.

"Hey!" she called to the dim-witted miscreants. She waved her arms above her head and jumped from her tiptoes, making herself as big of a spectacle as possible. "Over here! Come get me, you zombie freaks!"

That caught their attention.

They tipped their heads to the side, all of them moving in unison, and suddenly grinned. One looked to the other, who then looked to another, who then peered at Galen and leered. They said something, but Galen couldn't understand it, and suddenly burst into a sprint that was much, much quicker than Galen had been expecting.

"Run, girl!" Galen heard Gil shout from behind her. "Run like your life depends on it!"

Galen took off. She vaulted over an old stall and took off down a twisting and winding alleyway that wasn't wide enough for all those creatures to follow. Her ears pricked up to the sound of crashing and banging behind her. There were groans of pain, grunts of pressure. She couldn't afford to look away from her target—a long beam of wood jutting out from the side of a house, reachable if she launched herself from a pile of unsteady and untrustworthy wooden fruit boxes. If she went up, they'd have to go up too, and there wasn't a chance in hell they could manage that easily.

Galen had never run so fast in her life. Her feet were slipping beneath her with every step that she took. There was nothing planned in the way that she moved. Everything she did was panicked. There was everything on the line and, if it all went wrong, she put the lives of all her dreams in jeopardy.

The boxes were quickly approaching, and Galen could feel hands reaching for her behind her. A few fingers had snagged in the back of her clothes, but nothing had grabbed her. They couldn't quite reach, but they were painstakingly close. She jumped across a fallen tree trunk, clearing it with a leap that was elegant and graceful; not like her at all. Galen went sprawling across the floor, rolling into herself to spring back up and dodge a hanging sack pegged to a washing line. Miscellaneous cloths and clothes snatched up some of the gremlins, wrapping them up like little presents. Still, a large group was left, following her all the way to the boxes where some of them began to skid to a halt.

Galen could hear them chatting, could hear one of them giving orders, but continued onwards. The thrum of their footsteps against the ground lessened, but they still gave chase. Her eyes locked onto the boxes as she pushed herself from the ground, let her feet graze against the lowest box and land atop the tallest tower of them. She almost went through, having to push the edges of the boxes into the centre of her feet painfully before launching from them with arms outstretched and hopes high.

Soaring through the air like a bird, Galen panicked. Would she make it? The beam seemed so far away, and it seemed so fat. Her hands wouldn't wrap around that. No, she'd collide with it then fall. Her panic began to overcome her. She could hear the chattering of the gremlins, watched them pile up beneath the beam. They looked ready to catch her. How kind of them. Their eyes were hungry with hope. If they did this, then they would've pleased their master. The Dreamcatcher would be happy with them. She would have what she wanted, and none of them would be set on fire. Happy days!

Galen was about to rain on all of their parades.

Her hands smacked into the beam and her fingers instantly coiled about it. She could feel the grain of the wood beneath her fingernails as she clung for dear life to it. Galen hoisted her bodyweight upwards, bending the beam and feeling it creak from the wall. Splits formed in the plaster all along it and, suddenly, the beam tilted. It almost knocked her off, but she kept hold, scurrying across it just as the creatures had formed a tower of themselves to reach her. She kicked the gremlin at the top, knocking their entire hierarchy down to the ground before she heaved herself to temporary safety atop someone's house.

Galen had a minute to breathe. She had a second to rest. She sat on her haunches and saw Peep bursting from her home like an action hero from a film. Nothing seemed to terrify the cowgirl as she easily dodged a bolt of lightning, like she'd seen it coming, and scooped up Gil in her arms. There was nothing elegant or graceful about the way she threw Gil into her home, like a child would throw a teddy bear, and left him to close the door in front of him.

A smile erupted on Galen's face as she sprinted across the rooftops, casting a glance down to see the alleyway choked with zombie bodies. She'd confused them, at least. Those at the back didn't know where she'd gone, or what was happening, but those at the front were quick to catch on. A set of eyes saw her running and then jumping from house to house and, soon, the entire party was after her again.

Galen skipped from roof to roof before plummeting back to the ground in the town centre again. She could see Peep from where she was stood, and instantly headed for her. The torch was lit, and the flames were eager, but it was apparent that Eve had other plans.

As if the Dreamcatcher could see both Galen and Peep jumping towards one another, a bolt of lightning was sent out of the sky, striking the space just between them. A ball of powerful, unreserved energy coiled itself about Peep and Galen, vibrating and swelling before exploding and sending them flying in opposite directions.

Galen didn't need to see it, but she knew the torch had gone out. She rocketed through the air, colliding with a small wooden hut almost at the very front of the village and going straight through the wall of it. Her eyes closed as she felt wood bend under her weight, smacking into her again and again and again. When all the air was out of her lungs, her body dropped. She landed amongst a table and chairs, an arm twisted above her head and a leg surely popped out of its socket.

The pain wasn't enough to hide the pounding footsteps that were rushing towards Galen. Though her leg felt shattered, she still heaved herself to her feet. She stood almost timidly, too scared to put her weight on her left foot. Her arm was an easy fix. She'd popped that out of the socket many times and could do it as a party trick now. What had never grown on her was the sickening crack that followed her bone snapping back into place with her joint. She'd always hated it.

The door had been blown straight off and Galen could see outside. She ran for the exit, ducking as the hailstones swelled in size and were thrown down at her with much more strength behind them. Her eyes were only on the memorial that was, somehow, still alight. If she could reach that, then she was saved. All she had to do was dodge and thwart Eve's henchmen.

Grabbing at a stray board of wood, Galen jumped up onto the stony edging of the well and swung with all her might. She watched as a nail jutting from the end of the board stabbed straight through one of the creature's cheek. It was a sickening tear that followed as she yanked the wood back, splitting one side of its face in two. She swung again, smashing the board into the heads of three or four of the zombies before she darted off, leaving them to cry and whine over their new wounds.

A group still followed after her, persistent as ever. Galen danced and flitted amongst the hailstones, sliding like Peep had done out of the way of a lightning bolt. The minions behind her weren't so fortunate. A few of them fried in the electricity, writhing and jolting with the sheer energy that was coursing through their bodies. Still, somehow, there was a bunch that had kept their lives. They clambered after Galen like hungry dogs, following her every footstep. If she veered right, they would veer right with her. If she jumped, so did they. They were like circus performers, trained to put on a show.

Galen was so close she could feel the warmth of the fire lapping at the side of her cheek, but she knew she had to act fast. The lightning around her had become unbearable. She couldn't see in front of her anymore. The fire was almost invisible. She had become blinded by the constant and repetitive flashing right in front of her face, but still thrust the board into the warmth and held it there until she thought she could smell burning.

That's when everything stopped. The wind ceased. The hailstones stopped falling. The lightning bolts disappeared through the earth and never showed themselves again.

Galen rubbed at her eyes with her free hand, clearing her vision to see a crowd of minions ahead of her, gawking at the flames, and her board almost completely burnt through. Her heart skipped a beat, but the pity she had felt for these monsters evaporated. Her eyes became dead set on the creature closest to her, and then she pounced.

Never before had Galen experienced such energy. She flew into the crowd of zombies, hating how they still grabbed at her. They thought they had her in their grasps now, that they could still take her back to the Dreamcatcher, but they hadn't realised something. One by one, they were being picked off. Everything that the flames touched burst into nothingness, or into dust if they were lucky. Piles of ashes and soot littered the ground where Galen was dancing, but they were like moths to a flame. None of them showed that fear anymore. None of them screamed or shouted at the top of their lungs like monkeys. They'd either accepted defeat or were blindsided by how close Galen was to them. It was deathly silent as each of them erupted into dust, and even quieter still when Galen stood face to face with the last of them, panting.

It just stared at Galen, dead-eyed and unwilling to give up. Its chest rose and fell rapidly, its teeth bared still in a threat. There was no energy left inside the poor bastard. He tried to lift his arms in a challenge, but the sticks he had for limbs trembled at his sides. All he could manage was to lift his eyes as Galen tossed her burning torch at him, watching it soar through the air. Those eyes closed just before it smacked into his face and sent him to hell with the rest of his friends.

Galen collapsed onto her knees. She huffed and puffed and fought vigilantly to get her breath back, but all she could taste was the bitter flavour of smoke. A final crack of thunder rolled out above her head before the clouds parted, though it sounded more like a scream of outrage. It yowled like a threatened cat before it drifted off into nothing but an echo, as if it had never sounded before that.

"You're still alive," Gil's voice murmured tiredly from behind Galen. "That's good. That's better than what I could've hoped for."

Galen ignored his witty remark, staring at the sky as it returned to its pretty pastel colours and light, fluffy clouds. Had the Dreamcatcher given up? Surely not. It couldn't be. It couldn't be that easy.

"I thought both you and Peep were dead when that lightning strike got you," Gil grumbled remorsefully. "I didn't think you had the gall to actually do it. The thought seemed to sadden you."

"It's done now," Galen huffed. She sat back with her palms spread out behind her, running her tongue across her bottom lip. Why did everything have to taste like soot? "How many times have you fought them off?"

Gil took a moment to ponder. "I've never fought them this close to home," was his response. "There are only so many things in this world that I can keep track of and counting every single one of those things that I've murdered is not so important to me. What's more important is how the Dreamcatcher keeps making them. If she can make dreams come to life here, then the fight is over before it even started."

"It can't be that easy."

"Hmm?"

Galen turned and looked the bear in the eyes, her heart still thudding as if a threat was still looming over her. "Fighting her," she explained. "It can't be that easy. There has to be something more than that to it. She won't send those things after me every time."

"No, she won't." Gil mocked the way that Galen sat, though his podgy arms didn't keep him upright at all. He was almost lying in the mud. "She'll come herself sooner or later. Once she gets bored of seeing you defeat everything she sends after you, that is. She'll probably see a thrill in this, and it's probably fun for her. Expect the worst to come."

"Why is she the way she is?" Galen asked.

Gil just laughed. "Let's not ruin this moment with talk of her, shall we?" he proposed. "There's no better way than to end the day by watching the sun set. It calms the soul."

"Will you tell me eventually?"

A sigh escaped Gil, deflating him. "I'll tell you everything you want to know about her, just not now. The last thing I want is to think of her now, not when we've won a battle."

Galen conceded on her efforts. She turned back to the sunset, watching as the sun dipped lower behind the clouds. This first fight had already taken its toll on her. She could feel her leg throbbing with pain, but that was something she would keep to herself. Gil didn't need to know. He was already worried enough. Galen knew there was nothing else left in this world but to fight. There would be no moments to breathe, no seconds to take for herself. It would be a fight from start to end, but she was determined, no matter what, to end it with her own hands.

"You told me you'd tell me about her," Galen said gruffly. She stood behind Gil as he stared out across his ruin village and his burned memorials.

"Haven't I already?"

By his side, Galen observed the damage caused, and winced. "Not the full story. I want to know why she's here, how she got here, what she is. I want to know the things she was so desperate to keep from me."

Gil hesitated. "There's a reason she keeps things to herself. You should know better than to poke a bear like her, but still. If you're going to be here, you should be in the know." He gestured for Galen to take a seat on the bench behind him but didn't follow her. "What has she told you?"

"Excuses," Galen replied. "At least, that's what they sound like."

"What has she said?"

Galen winced at the sharpness of the bear's tone. "She said that I summoned her here with the strength of my dreams. She told me that her one priority is to keep me happy and that she would never cause me any harm. She wants to ensure that I believe in her."

"Of course, she does. She needs that. You know what will happen to her if you stop believing."

"Is anything she's told me true?" Galen blurted out. She was desperate to know. She felt like she had been left in the dark on purpose. The old bear was just as bad at answering questions as the Dreamcatcher was. "Have I been fed lies this entire time?"

Gil's shoulders lilted as he finally turned away from the edge of the cliff. "Well, who's to know? I'm sure she's so charming and effervescent with you. It'd be hard not to believe every word she said." He came plodding over to the bench and heaved himself up onto the end of it, letting his cane rest on the ground. "I believe it is true that you summoned her here, obviously not on purpose. It was an unwilling siren's song that you sung to her, and she listened. That's how she catches her prey."

"Someone else must've been stronger than me," Galen insisted. "There are billions of people in this world, and I was who she was drawn to?"

"Who's to say that there weren't other factors the lured her in?" Gil replied. "She has a type. You fit that type right down to the last strand of hair on your head. You're perfect for her, hence her relentlessness. As for why she's here…" he trailed off. He scratched at the back of his neck, at the tag that was still attached to him. It must've driven him nuts. "In layman's terms, my dear, she's here to kill you. She'll take one thing from you at a time until there's nothing left of you that yours anymore. She'll steal your heart from you, make you think you're in love with her, then she starts to suck away at your imagination. When you are weak enough, struggling, she'll start to sap your existence. I'm beginning to think that all she needs to be real now is you."

Galen's eyes widened. "What would that mean?"

"It would mean she'd be free of this place." Gil gestured all around him and chuckled wryly to himself, settling back down with a little shake of his head. "She would be free to roam your world, and not ours. She'd be as skin and bones as the next human, and you would take her place here, but you'd go to the place they all end up."

Galen hung her head, her breath shaking as she exhaled. "What is she?" she asked. She didn't want to hear about what would happen to her anymore. She didn't want to think about it. The Dreamcatcher was the target, and it was Galen's mission to find out every last little thing she could before the fight.

"Isn't that the question?" Gil chuckled to himself again.

"Was she a dream to begin with?" Galen pushed. "Did I create her? Did someone else dream her up?"

Gil's eyes stared straight through Galen's soul; his stitched mouth pulled taut into a frown. "Yes, someone else dreamt of her, created her," was his response.

He spoke so quietly, so slowly. This was a story he didn't tell often, and there had to be a reason. "It wasn't you. She was purposely created, but not with the intention of her becoming a monster. It's a long story—"

"We have time," Galen interrupted. "Tell me everything."

With a huff, Gil pushed himself off the bench and paced back and forth atop the cliff, kicking at the long grass with his paws held behind his back. "As I'm sure you're aware, time moves differently in dreams. To us, she's been here far longer than anyone else. She's outstayed her welcome. To you, it's probably been a hundred years or so since her inception."

A dream could survive for a century?

"I don't know the exact year, but there was a study that was taking place in a country called Georgia," Gil continued. "A group of scientists and sleep experts wanted to test the strength and the power that the brain can muster whilst dreaming. Their main focus was lucid dreaming—the ability to control ones dream whilst completely unconscious. One of their workers, a man called Stefan, had the ability to lucid dream, so he was inducted into the study as a subject. They made him keep a journal of everything that happened, every dream he ever had and everything he was able to do. If he manipulated the dream in any way, it was written down. If he was able to create something, it was written down."

Galen listened in like a child being told a bedtime story, truly fascinated and bewildered.

"There was hardly anything remarkable at the birth of this study," Gil lamented. He kicked at a patch of dirt laid bare by constant footsteps. "Stefan's dreams and his team's findings weren't all that spectacular. They faced having their study closed, until he awoke one night screaming and hollering about a woman." The bear looked towards Galen and sighed—he had to have been talking about Eve. "He had dreamt of her one night and she had come back to him the next. Then, suddenly, she was in every dream he had. She was always there, and she seemed both omnipresent and omnipotent. She had her own consciousness, her own thoughts, her own desires. She was every part the individual, and Stefan had created her using just the power of his mind."

"That's incredible," Galen murmured under her breath.

Gil's stitched mouth was pulled upward into a smug grin. "Incredible until that omnipresent, omnipotent person realised that she didn't truly exist," he remarked. "When Eve realised that she was just a test, a study, and not a real person, she began to sour. Her affections towards Stefan turned into aggressions.

She didn't trust him. She still went to him every time he dreamt, but she was unknowingly dragging him further and further into comas." Gil wandered up to Galen and tapped her knee with his paw. "That's what she's doing to you."

"What?"

"Stefan noted everything down in his journal," Gil continued, brushing straight over Galen's worry. "He was sleeping for days at a time, sometimes weeks. He was losing energy. He looked sickly, but he kept sleeping. He kept seeing her, and she kept doing him harm, albeit unknowingly. When his team had decided it was too dangerous to keep letting him sleep, they told him he needed to find a way to destroy her."

Galen gasped.

"He had created her, so it would be just as easy for him to get rid of her. That was their thought. Stefan agreed to it simply because he was so drained. He thought it would be nothing. The man was a fool," Gil spat. He let his anger take over him, slighted by the mistakes of the Dreamcatcher's creator. "He went to her, told her everything, ruined her perception of herself and of him, and then tried to kill her. Stefan did everything he could, but how can you kill a dream? Dreams can exist forever if there isn't a parasitic monster feeding off them. He was her first, though he made an excellent effort to save himself."

"What happened to him?"

Gil sighed deeply, so deeply that his whole body seemed to slump. "Stefan had one defence against Eve—voids."

"Voids?"

"Little spaces and gaps between dreams that he could hide in, places Eve couldn't see him in," Gil explained. "They're just darkness. You can see nothing but hear everything. He disappeared into one thinking he could stay there as Eve laid waste to his dreamland, but he was wrong."

Galen didn't understand. "How? Why?"

"Voids are dangerous. They help, but they are quick fixes. They aren't something you can commit yourself to." Gil moved away from the bench he'd been sat on, preferring to stand close to the edge of the cliff, where he had an eye on everything. "Time moves faster in dreams than it does in reality, and it moves even faster within voids. You have to time it right, or it crushes you. Stefan had a choice to face, though he didn't realise it. He could get killed by Eve or let the void absorb him and, before he could make that choice, the void collapsed, and he was destroyed along with it. The Dreamcatcher absorbed him, realising that she could become stronger and more powerful with every soul and every existence that she inherited. From that point on, she's hunted for people like you, for people like Stefan, and she has sworn that she won't stop until her existence is made a reality."

"There has to be a reason," Galen murmured quietly to herself.

Gil glared over his shoulder. "What?"

"There has to be a reason for this." Galen got to her feet and walked to him, twiddling her thumbs nervously. How could she be defending a person like Eve? There was nothing but pity and sympathy hanging heavy in her heart, and sadness plaguing her mood. "He just left her here? To do what?"

Gil's glare became accusing and angered. "She has no purpose here," he growled. "She wasn't created to have a purpose. She was created as a test. They had no intentions of ever getting rid of her, because they didn't feel like they would ever have to. She was just a dream. She was nothing to them."

"And look what they caused!"

"They would be over the moon if they knew what that bitch had become!" Gil roared. "She was a project for them! An accolade! They got rewarded for creating her, and we got lumped with dealing with what she became! There isn't an inch of you that should pity her!"

Galen hung her head in frustration. "How could you not pity her?" she asked. "How could you not feel the tiniest bit of sympathy for her? She just wants to be real."

"And she's killing all of us off to achieve that!" Gil marched up to Galen in a way that would've been threatening if he wasn't a tiny teddy bear. He even prodded Galen's shin with the end of his cane. "Which side are you on? Are you on her side? Should we ship you off to her before any of us get hurt?"

"I'm on your side," Galen growled through her gritted teeth. "I want her gone just as much as you do, but I still feel for her. I can't help that I'm a human that feels emotions. I can't help having a heart."

"Let me tell you something, kiddo—it would be a whole lot easier on us if you didn't have one."

Galen was taken aback. She fell away from her bear, keeping a few paces clear of him as her mouth fell open in awe. Had he meant that? The look on his face seemed repentant, but Galen couldn't be sure. She sealed her lips once more and pouted heavily, hurt.

"Don't feel for her," Gil warned. "It'll cost you everything."

"I can't help what I feel." Galen hung her head, regretting ever coming to the old bear. "I wouldn't wish what was done to her on anybody, and I wouldn't wish her on anyone. She was left hanging. How would you feel if you were created with no purpose?"

Gil held his arms out like a challenge. "What purpose could I possibly have?" he asked. "I'm just as useless as she is, yet I've accepted my fate. I've accepted that it is not reasonable or feasible to kill everything in sight and absorb it just to make me feel a little bit better. If it was just dreams, it would be less damning, but her claws have extended out to the real world. Think about that next time you tell me you feel sorry for her." He shoved past Galen and wandered off down the cliff, shoulders hunched. "You'll be needed at a meeting with us all soon, but before you come to that I suggest you rinse any talk of her out of your mouth. Make your allegiance known and make the right decision. If you choose her, I'm not coming to save you."

Galen didn't know how much time had passed since her last run in with Gil. She didn't sleep in her dreams. She didn't feel tired. There was nothing for her to base herself off, and she was beginning to feel lost. Though the sun rose and fell, Galen didn't know the concept of time anymore. How long had it been since she'd fallen asleep? Had her family noticed yet? All her questions were unanswered, and it was gnawing away at her sanity.

Galen sat at the back of the town hall that was filled with the residents. She was in awe to see all her childhood toys and all the little creatures that she'd ever dreamed of sitting in chairs, listening to Gil. They were so obedient, hanging off his every word as if their lives depended on it. In a way, they did depend on him. Gil was their saviour, their protector, and that was all that they had ever known.

"As you are aware, the Dreamcatcher has found this settlement," Gil announced. The whole room gasped and began to whisper, some of them crying out with fear. He raised a paw to silence them. "We cannot act surprised. This was always a possibility. What we have to do is simple—move."

Again, a thrum of gasps and whispers went up.

Galen scanned the room. She saw clusters of toy horses bunched together, frightened. There were other bears, bears she used to play with alongside Gil, sitting stoically like nothing ever bothered them. Ducky was by Gil's side, though his head was hung. Peep stood on the other side of the old bear, arms crossed, and face slightly scratched from the burst of lightning that had thrown her through someone's house. They were the three musketeers of the dreamland, here to save the day.

"We've discussed this all before in the past, so it should come as no shock to you," Gil sighed. He clung to his podium, withering away with every pair of eyes that weighed upon him. "I understand that you have families here, but to protect them and everyone else, we must relocate. We cannot risk all this work being lost in one fell swoop."

Though the room agreed, the anxious whispering and chattering still remained. Some eyes looked towards Galen, some happy to see her and some not so much. There were dreams here that feared her, choosing to stay as far from her as possible, whereas others had crowded around her just to feel safe.

"As I'm sure you've noticed, we've a guest among us."

Now, everyone's eyes were on Galen.

Gil gestured to her, trying his best to smile. "Our Galen, unfortunately, has fallen into the clutches of the Dreamcatcher. Before that witch could get her hands on her, she found her way to us. We must keep her as far from the Dreamcatcher as possible, to give ourselves time to find another foothold. We are at the disadvantage, but that won't be for much longer." Gil gestured to Ducky, who rolled forwards and let all the attention rest on him.

"A team will be sent out to scout locations for a new settlement," Ducky announced loudly. He silenced the whispers and the gasps in seconds, commanding all the power in the room. "Once found, we will begin to up our defences, and learn ways to hide ourselves better. Seeing how easily the Dreamcatcher's minions burst through our shield, it seems time to go out and find lost dreams to recruit them; dreams that still have their own power and wits about them."

"Who will be on the team?" a timid voice called out.

Ducky glanced to Gil who nodded his head deeply, giving him the reassurance that he needed to talk. "The team will be myself, Peep, Gil and Galen."

Galen perked up a little, surprised. They were going to take her with them? Gil had been so persistent that she stay at the village, and now he was taking her away? What could he possibly have planned for her? It made no sense in her mind, and the sets of eyes slowly burning into her skin made her only more anxious.

"Quiet!" Gil roared to soothe the crowd as they lost their minds. "Listen to the duck!"

Ducky gulped and grimaced, closing his eyes to shield himself against the shouting. "We won't be gone long, but we all need one another to complete this scouting mission successfully. Leaving behind any one of us would just slow us down."

"The Dreamcatcher will know!"

Gil, Ducky and Peep all froze. The bear was the one to step forward, eyes scrutinising the crowd and cane clutched firmly in his hand. He came to the edge of the stage he was up on, sliding in front of his podium so he was the only thing in sight.

"Who said that?" he growled.

There was an overwhelming silence that fell upon the crowd. Someone shifted. Galen could see them getting closer to the centre of the mob. She didn't recognise him. He was daring, and that's all she could say about him. The way he walked and held himself was bold and confident, arrogant even.

"I said it!" an arm was thrust into the air. The arm belonged to a young man with long, black hair and olive skin. He was dressed in finery that was unmistakeable from the renaissance, with boots that were clad right up to his thighs. He was one of the few humanlike dreams amongst the crowd and was glared at accordingly. "You expect to take the girl with you and not encounter the Dreamcatcher? She'll know the minute that giant steps foot outside of this threshold. She knew she was here all along! That's why she sent her minions."

Gil ran his tongue across his furry lips. "The Dreamcatcher's omnipresence is annoying, yes, but it is not always active. She has to sleep, too. There are times that we can move when she is not looking."

"And how will we know when she's not looking?" the handsome stranger argued. "We aren't all-knowing. We only go off the clues she gives to us. There is nothing that says she'll be asleep at any time."

"What we must be is resilient," Peep argued.

The stranger's attention turned to the cowgirl. "I mean no offense, Peep, but resilience will not further us in this situation. What we need to do is lay low, stay safe. There's no sense in thrusting Galen out into the open world where she can easily be snatched away from us."

“She won’t be snatched away from us,” Gil growled again. It was plain to see he was gravely annoyed. Had his cheeks not been fur, they would’ve turned bright red. “We’re not so keen to let her go, either.”

“It makes no sense, Gil. You’ve lost your touch.”

Peep stepped forwards again, intervening on behalf of the bear. “You will see that this is necessary!” she shouted. Her voice didn’t carry the same weight that Gil’s did. She wasn’t as frightening. “Don’t let fear cloud your minds. Don’t let the thought of the Dreamcatcher put you off. You would all see that there is logic in this decision. If we are hurt or thwarted, Galen has the power to protect us. Without her, we could all be killed, and you would know no better.”

“If she stayed here, Galen could protect us, too!” the handsome stranger argued. He had support behind him now, mainly from the other human dreams that were crowded about the room. “We see logic differently to you.”

“Enough!” Gil bellowed. His voice was enough to make Peep shrink back into line, and enough to make the very foundations of the town hall quake. “What we have decided will be what is done. I won’t hear any other opinions.”

The stranger shrunk back into line as Peep had done, but he wasn’t happy about it. He joined his fellow humans, murmuring something before casting a glance to Galen. They all stared her way eventually, their eyes curious and probing.

“We will leave immediately,” the bear announced. “There is no time to waste anymore. Things have become so dire so quickly. The longer we leave it, the more danger we put you all in.” He again slipped out from behind his podium and wandered off, as if to step down. “Whilst we are gone, you know what to do. It will be like the old times that we used to go scouting. Bury yourselves underground. The tunnels still remain. Hide yourselves in plain sight. Resist any unease in your mind. Stay loyal. Keep your allegiance. That is all that I can ask of you.”

Before Gil waddled off the stage, he glared at Galen. He didn’t believe in her allegiance to him. He had plenty reason not to, and he wasn’t yet willing to forgive her pity for his mortal enemy. He gave Galen a little nod of his head, summoning her to join his party, before the taps of his canes sounded towards the doorway.

Outside, Galen felt out of place. She stood with Peep, watching Gil and Ducky draw out a plan in the dirt. Her eyes followed the end of Gil’s cane as he drew line after line that meant something to him, but nothing to her.

"Where are we going?" Galen asked the cowgirl under her breath.

"West, it would appear."

Galen's brows came together. "Is there anything to the west?"

"I wouldn't know," replied Peep stiffly. She crossed her arms over her chest and stood with all her weight on one foot. "We've never been west. We've been here for years. We never thought it'd come to this."

"How do we know what we'll face if no one has ever been out there?"

"It's all down to chance," she revealed. "If the Dreamcatcher is asleep, we're all good. If she's awake…" Peep never finished her sentence.

"Let's be going," Gil announced. "There's no use in dillydallying. We'll only sign our death certificates if we do that."

Galen had been forced up the front with Gil. She hadn't spoken to him and hadn't looked at him. She was too busy admiring the scenery. It changed every time she blinked. New structures would arise from the ground. New flowers would blossom at her feet. The season would change. The weather would change. When they had started their trek, the sun had been high in the sky, shining for all to see. As soon as they were out of the threshold, it poured down with rain. Galen even thought she could feel the chill of snow starting to seep in, but she couldn't be sure.

"I should apologise for the way I spoke to you on the cliff," Gil said gruffly. "I don't like to admit that I was harsh or wrong, but I raised my voice when I didn't have to. I know you would never side with that monster."

"There is a difference between pitying someone, and committing yourself to them," Galen pointed out. She watched as the rain that fell on her froze before it hit the ground, crystallising into little beads of ice. The sky turned a yellowish grey, and snow could've only been imminent. "I can't deny that I feel for her, Gil. Her existence must be torture, but that is no excuse for what she's done."

Gil smiled. "I'm glad that we agree on that fact. I was beginning to worry for a minute that you thought she was justified in her actions."

"Never."

"That gives me hope."

Galen watched as the bleak; rainy day turned into a snow day within the blink of an eye. All the grass she could see weighed down by the heaviness of the raindrops was suddenly blanketed by thick layers of untouched, glistening snow. It was beautiful, but quick. Everything was devoured with a whiteness so bright it hurt the eyes. It looked exactly like the day Galen had to take off from school because her whole town was snowed in. That memory brought a smile to her face and a warmth to her heart, until she saw something drastically out of place.

A snake slithered alongside the path the gang walked down. It was unbothered by the cold on its belly, though lifted its head to glare up at Galen. Its tongue flickered out of its mouth, and Galen could've sworn that she saw it smile at her before it slunk underneath a pile of snow and didn't emerge out of the other side.

"I'm sorry for the mess I've caused at the village," Galen apologised slowly. She still watched for the snake, wondering if it would appear again out of nowhere. "Eve has a longer reach than I had first imagined."

"It isn't your fault," Gil sighed. "It's mine. I exposed you too quickly. I basically dangled you in front of her and expected her not to take the bait."

To Galen's surprise, she saw the snake slithering through the snow a couple of metres away from her. It pushed its way through the thick covers, gliding with ease and with elegance. Where had this creature come from?

"Gil?" Galen asked.

"Hmm?"

She watched the snake disappear again, like it knew it had been caught out. "The Dreamcatcher…can she take any form?"

Gil stopped the party in its tracks and looked up into Galen's eyes, confused. "What do you mean?"

"When she appears, is it always as herself?" Galen was frantically trying to spot the serpent again, but it had outsmarted her. She watched as all its tracks were filled in with snow and nothing remained of it. "Can she take the form of animals or creatures?"

"She's been known to appear as a snake," Ducky pointed out from the back of the group. He was struggling to keep up, the snow clogging his wheels. "Apparently, she likens herself to that kind of animal. That or a spider."

Galen felt her heart stop beating in her chest. She tried to speak, but her tongue was held in place. Her lips wouldn't even move, no matter how much strain she put on her muscles.

"That's just hearsay," Peep laughed. "She's too prideful to appear as anything but her human form."

Galen was frantically trying to talk, almost clawing at her mouth like there was a piece of food stuck under her tongue. No matter what she did, her mouth wouldn't move. Her lips were stuck, her jaw was tight, and her tongue was frozen in her mouth. She smacked her hand into Peep's shoulder, clinging to her, and staring her straight in the eye once the cowgirl turned her head.

"Galen?"

Staggering back, Galen couldn't be sure who had said her name. Her mouth had suddenly clamped shut, so she couldn't even make a single noise. She let her hand soar to her face, wrapping about her throat to peel off phantom fingers that were gradually choking her.

"Galen!"

Galen took another step back and froze to the spot when she felt breath at the back of her neck.

"It's good to see you again, Gil."

It was Eve's voice sounding in Galen's ear. It was so smooth and so crisp, so beautiful, but so haunting at the same time. It made Galen stand bolt upright, with her arms clad to her sides and her knees buckling from how straight her legs had become.

"Dreamcatcher." Somehow, Gil greeted Eve with some humility about him. Galen thought she almost saw him bow to her. "I'd say I'm surprised to see you, but this was to be expected."

"I don't like to be too predictable," the Dreamcatcher let out a small huff into Galen's ear, sighing with relief, "but this time there was something too precious on the line. I'm grateful you would be so kind as to deliver her to me."

Gil's face tightened. "You won't get what you want this time."

The Dreamcatcher laughed as Galen struggled at her side, refusing to pay her prey any sort of attention. "Oh, is that so? What are you going to do, old man? Take her away from me? Snatch her out of my grip?"

"It was a horrid thing of you to silence her," Gil snapped. "You should've let her talk. Are you afraid of a fight?"

"I've never been afraid of a toy duck, a doll and a teddy bear in my life, and I don't intend to start fearing such creatures." The Dreamcatcher moved away from Galen, but Galen was still frozen in place, unable to move. She sauntered closer to the party, crouching down, and sitting on her haunches to be face to face with Gil. "You're a bitter old dream who deserved to die a long, long time ago," she hissed at him venomously. "The only reason you are still alive is because of me."

"Is that what you believe?"

How did Gil have the gall to stand up to a woman like this? A villain like this?

"Gillette, my old friend. I have kept you alive all these years because you entertain me. Plus, you do good little deeds like this for me. I finally have my poppet back."

"You're not taking her."

The Dreamcatcher rose to her feet and, with a graceful swipe of her leg, kicked Gil over. "Do you see how easy it is to defeat you? You're a teddy bear, Gil. Literally. I'm a fully-realised human, and I am this close to turning you and your friends into a pile of dust just for the fun of it."

Peep was the one to pick Gil up off the floor and dust him off, whilst Ducky came rolling forwards with all the might that he could muster to slam himself into Eve's shin.

"You bitch!" Ducky yelled as he again and again rammed himself into the Dreamcatcher's bone. "You'll never win! We'll always fight!"

Eve just stood there and watched. "Aren't you fun?" She grabbed hold of the rope that acted as his lead, twisting it in her fingers. "Fight all you want, it's futile. I always like it when they fight back." She kicked Ducky away, sending him flying through the air and skidding across the layers of untouched snow before he plummeted into the cold.

"Duck!" Gil sprinted after his friend, turning his back just as Peep came forwards to launch an attack of her own against Eve.

Galen had to watch it all from where she stood, unable to talk and unable to move. She fought with all her might, tensing every single muscle in her body but to no avail. There seemed to be no wiggle room, no end to her torment. Still, her eyes remained burned into the Dreamcatcher. Pure fury blazed through her as she watched Eve just toss her friends around like the toys they were, unchallenged. The smile on the Dreamcatcher's face crawled its way deep beneath Galen's skin, setting her ablaze with rage.

And much to Galen's luck, that burning rage seemed to melt her muscles. She could twitch her fingers. Her arms would jerk and move just slightly, just barely. She thought she could feel her legs pushing forward against the pressure wrapped around her. Her feet slipped forwards in the snow, her lips tracing words painfully slowly, but still moving. She fought as hard as she could, forcing her limbs to move just as Eve snatched Peep up by her tiny, thin neck.

"What does this prove?" Peep managed to croak as the Dreamcatcher restricted her windpipe. She didn't bother fighting against Eve's hands, choosing to dangle from her grip rather than challenge her. "What does killing me and the rest of us prove to anyone? That you're a monster? That you're the exact thing they say you are?"

"Am I that much of a monster?" Eve crooned. "What makes me a monster, huh? Doing anything I have to so I can get what I want? Making sacrifices to make myself a better person? Giving myself a future?"

Peep finally struggled, wriggling unwillingly in the Dreamcatcher's hand. "Think of how you're doing those things. Is it all worth it? Killing us all off? Think of the blood on your hands."

Galen suddenly tripped forwards, landing face first into the snow but jumping hurriedly back up to her feet. She forced herself to run, her feet slipping in the snow but still propelling her towards the Dreamcatcher.

"There's no blood on my hands," Eve reasoned. "Dreams don't bleed."

Peep bared her teeth as defiantly as she could, proudly waving her insolence in the face of the Dreamcatcher. "You'll never win," she hissed so harshly that it was almost a whisper. "No matter what you do, no matter who you steal away from themselves, you'll never win."

"I always win," Eve countered. "It's as easy as crawling inside your head and taking over your consciousness."

Peep's mouth fell open, her horror clear to see.

"Did you forget I could do such a thing?" the Dreamcatcher laughed. "Honestly, so did I. It's easier than turning you into a pile of dust, and it's more fun. With you, especially. I know your kind." Eve tapped the tip of her finger against Peep's heart, only spreading the horror through the cowgirl's body. "Loyal until proven otherwise. Your intentions are different to Gillette's and that thing on wheels. You want a life of your own."

Eve brought Peep in close enough that no one else could hear the two. She let her lips brush gently over Peep's ear as she whispered something to her. Whatever it was she said was enough to frighten the cowgirl more than she already was. Her body began shaking, her eyes so wide that they didn't look to fit in their sockets anymore.

What had been said?

The Dreamcatcher was just about to snap Peep's neck but was quickly barrelled into from behind. Galen's feet smashed into Eve's back, kicking her forward and forcing her to drop Peep from her grasp. She landed elegantly, and popped up straight back to her feet, as if she had never fallen over in the first place.

Galen wasn't so quick. She hit a patch of black ice and went tumbling back to the ground, almost bowling into Eve's legs comically. She refused to let herself get that close. Galen instead clambered back up to stand face to face with the Dreamcatcher, squaring her shoulders and lifting her chin to stare up into Eve's stunning eyes.

"Poppet?" the Dreamcatcher questioned. At first, her curiosity and her shock sounded fake. The hurt that materialised in her eyes soon told the truth though—there was nothing fake about Eve. "These people want to hurt you, sweetheart. I'm only here to save you."

"You're not here to do anything but kidnap me and take me off somewhere that I can't escape."

Eve placed a hand over her chest to feign her hurt, her mouth hanging open though slightly lifted in a smile. "Well, then," she said simply, clamping her hands on her hips. "It looks like you've got me all sussed out, doesn't it? Do you think this halts me at all?" The Dreamcatcher slithered closer like the snake she was, holding herself tall and proud, high, and mighty. "You think this will stop me?"

Galen was forced back a few paces, until she was retracing her footsteps in reverse. "I don't think anything, or anyone will stop you. I know your game, and I know why you're doing it. There's surely a different way."

Eve's face fell suddenly. "You know my game?" she repeated. "As much as I like you, poppet, and as much as I find you endearing, you know nothing about me, and I intend to keep it that way. The less you know about me, the better. Don't let these people poison your mind, Galen. They are old dreams—jealous, forgotten memories clinging to the desperate hope that you might dream of them again."

Galen went back and back and back until she smacked into a tree, standing bolt upright with her hands pushed against the tree trunk behind her. Her chest rose and fell frighteningly fast, her heart thudding so hard against the inside of her chest she thought it might burst free.

"So long as I am here, and so long as you believe in me, you'll never see these cretins in the same way you used to. Your dreams won't be of them, but of me, and of the things that I can do for you." Pointing a jagged yet slightly angled finger in Galen's face, Eve bared her teeth. "One day, you will be grateful for me. You will appreciate what I can do. You will see me for me and not this…clone I've had to make."

"Why do you have to hide your true self?" Galen shouted back in the Dreamcatcher's face. "Nothing can be worse than the monster you're showing yourself to be now! The true you can't be this horrific. It's not possible."

The Dreamcatcher's facial features contorted for a split second. The movement was so fast, so quick, that Galen nearly missed it. Her lips tugged outward into a wide smile that stretched from ear to ear. The perfectly lined teeth in her gums elongated into spikes, but quickly shrunk once again. Her lips bounced back into place and the blackness in her eyes cleared as a sigh escaped her, deflating her lungs.

"I take great pride in myself," the Dreamcatcher growled. "I believe in myself—"

"And I believe in you too!" Galen burst. It wasn't until a few seconds after that she'd realised what she'd done and clamped her hand over her mouth to shut herself up.

Laughing, Eve's body began to contort. Her face clouded over with evil once more, her eyes choked with blackness. This time, the blackness leaked from her eye sockets and spilt onto her cheeks. It looked like she was crying ink. Her already thin face shrunk once more until her cheeks were entirely sucked into her face, revealing the sharp cheekbones that lay beneath. Her face was just a chasm riddled with holes and splits in her skin. Both her cheekbones and her jawbone were exposed as the rest of her face elongated and her eyes became that of a serpent's.

Galen managed to roll away from the Dreamcatcher just as her human torso stretched into a slithery, slippery, scaled body of snake. Top heavy, Eve tumbled against the ground and let the lower half of her body become overrun with bright emerald scales that glittered with gold ends. She was beautiful, but terrifying.

The gang all dove in front of Galen as the Dreamcatcher lurched towards her. Though they were all tiny, and just toys, they intended to protect Galen with their lives. The only one who seemed hesitant was Ducky. He turned his head and looked behind him, meeting Galen's gaze for a few seconds before he turned back towards the less-appealing monster that was lurking above him.

"Let me make something clear to all of you." Eve's voice was unrecognisable. She sounded like a demon that belonged in the depths of hell.

"If I wanted you dead, you would all be in your graves by now. A monster I may be, but what are all of you if not wastes of good energy and existence?"

"Begone!" Gil roared at Eve. He even thrusted his little cane at her as if it was a mighty sword that would pierce through her scales, but it bounced off them.

Eve didn't even look down at the assault. "You are a particularly annoying specimen, Gillette." She sighed deeply to herself and ruffled each of her scales. They moved in a rhythm that was mesmerising to watch, almost hypnotising. "You've been here a long time. Perhaps it's time you gave up that honourable fight. We both know it is one you'll lose."

"Did you not hear me, wench?" Gil snapped. He flailed his arms around like a frightening grizzly bear, ignoring the fact he was only two foot and stuffed. "Begone! Go back to your lair and stay there. We want no business with you!"

The serpent grinned, showing off each venomous, razor-sharp tooth hanging from her gums. "So be it, Gillette. I'll let you find a new place to set up your rundown little settlement, and leave you be, for now." Her attention turned to Galen, her smile turning a little less evil and aggressive. "You, my love, will not remain with this ragtag group forever. One day, and one day soon, you and I shall live the life we were always meant to."

"I will run from you as long as I have to," Galen replied calmly. Though her heart was thudding in her chest, she refused to show any fear in the face of the serpent. "You don't scare me, Eve. You never have. I pity you."

A wry scoff. "Keep that pity to yourself, poppet. I don't need it. For now, I will say goodbye. Think of me often, for you won't be leaving this place until I say so." She turned and slithered off, slowly and gradually shrinking in size until she was nothing more than a garden snake forcing its way through thick blankets of snow.

"What do we do now?" Peep asked timidly.

"We go west," Galen replied. "We carry on scouting out places for the settlement. We don't let her deter us."

Gil pushed ahead of the group, both paws clasped atop his cane. "She could've carried you off at any moment, yet you stood your ground. She really doesn't frighten you."

"No."

"Yet you empowered her."

Galen fought the urge to shrug her shoulders. "We should head west before she changes her mind. You should know better than us what she's like."

Gil nodded his head stiffly, cracking his jaw and gesturing for Galen to lead the way.

And lead the way she did. Galen took charge of the group, storming down the path they had been heading down with her eyes on the cobblestones. Everyone followed behind her, though Peep was right at the back of the group. It was almost as if the cowgirl was trying to keep her distance, and didn't want to engage, but Gil dropped back to her side and murmured something to her that caused Peep to sigh.

"It was nothing she hasn't already said to us all," replied Peep.

Ah. Galen guessed Gil had asked what the Dreamcatcher had said to Peep. She could tell the cowgirl was lying, though. It was something that Eve had never said and, whatever it was, had crawled its way under Peep's plastic skin and had burrowed itself away neatly.

"She can be stopped," Gil reassured.

Another sigh from Peep told Galen the cowgirl wasn't so sure anymore. "All monsters can be stopped, but something worse will always follow."

Chapter Five

There were no more pinks or purples or yellows in the sky. There were no brightly coloured flowers or pretty sights to be seen. There wasn't even that glistening blanket of snow that had haunted Galen and her gang down every road they'd taken. There was nothing.

Around them, the world was dying. The sky had become grey and heavy with dense, thick clouds that were choking out any and all light. It had stayed that way since the Dreamcatcher had slithered off. All grass and greenery had become black and gunky, like an oil slick that had covered the entirety of Galen's dreams. Anything that dared shine a little bit of colour was quickly stamped out, and anything that remotely stunk of life and existence was squashed beneath Eve's boot.

Galen led the charge up a twisting cobblestone road, leading to no place good. Ahead of her, sitting just on the miserable horizon, was a fenced-in plot of land that had storm clouds hanging tumultuously over it. The path led straight to it, though another option forked off to the right, down the slope and into a patch of gross, twisted, and gnarled rotting trees. Neither option was appealing. There was nothing alluring about either path, though Galen's feet were instinctually heading towards the iron fences and the towering, metal gates that pierced the sky and tore apart any clouds that breezed by.

"Stop," Gil suddenly called. Exhausted, he fought his way up to Galen and puffed as he reached her side, like an asthmatic that had just run a marathon. "Don't distract yourself by going up there. It's just another one of her demented attractions. It's not worth the pain it'll cause."

Pain? Now Galen was more intrigued.

She glanced down at the old bear with a frown heavy on her face. "What is it?"

"A graveyard," Peep perked up. She too pushed forward, leaving just an anxious Ducky to roll back and forth at the back of the pack. Her eyes fell upon the grand iron structure and her whole demeanour rippled with discomfort. "This is a place where good people get buried for all eternity. Dreams are laid to rest here against their will. Anything the Dreamcatcher had a remote connection to is kept here, where she knows it can never escape her."

Galen looked from the cowgirl back to the graveyard. She couldn't help but think she'd seen it before. It appeared like any other spooky graveyard did—heavy iron gates keeping visitors out, twisted metal ornaments adorning the fencing, a red, bleeding sky hanging over the top with storm clouds and lightning striking the graves, bats flying overhead. It was everything a horror fanatic would love, but to Galen it was saddening. She wondered if Gil and the gang knew anyone that was lain to rest there, or if she would recognise anyone's names. The curiosity only drove her forward, which prompted Gil to put a paw on her shin.

"Don't go up there, child," he warned. The seriousness in his beady eyes was almost enough to tempt Galen not to go against his word, but the gravesite was still calling her name. "It's not worth it. You'll see nothing you like up there."

"How long has this been here?" was all Galen asked. She barely paid the bear any mind, anxiously padding about the spot, eager to push open those gates.

Peep took Galen away from Gil, leading her slightly further up the path. "It's been here since Eve's creator was killed. She put up a little tombstone for him, to commemorate him, but she's added to her collection since his departure."

"Will you take me up there?"

Peep's face was covered in a wince. "I will, though I will tell you exactly what Gil has. There's nothing up there that waits for you but sorrow and pity. You'll realise that the Dreamcatcher is a monster but can at least pretend she has a heart." The cowgirl wandered off without Galen, stalking up the cobblestones as if she'd done it many times before. She glanced over her shoulder and gestured for Galen to follow with a nod of her head but stopped once she was within reach of the towering gates.

Galen rushed up to Peep's side, the gates spiralling up above her. They were oddly beautiful. The craftsmanship in the metal was extraordinary, like it had taken years to construct. Each bar was shaped and twisted into a vine, with little prickly thorns and leaves jutting from the branches. They wrapped about the centre of the gates in a tangled knot that lay home to a keyhole, though the lock was already undone. Galen reached out and, with just the tips of her fingers, pushed the gates open. They screeched and screamed bloody murder as they swung open, protesting the assault against them. Galen and Peep winced against the noise, covering their ears, and only peeling their hands away from their faces once the gates had come to a natural stop.

It didn't take long for Galen to head on in first. She was drawn in by the uniqueness of the tombstones, how they stood against the horizon. Each of them were so tall, so mighty, though one at the back was particularly drawing. It was a broad wall that stretched from end to end at the back of the cage-like structure. There was writing scrawled on the stone in such a tiny font that Galen thought it was just scribbling at first.

Her attention was quickly snagged by each individual headstone, and the names that were written boldly and brightly for all to see. Each gravesite had fresh flowers lain against the tombstone, and freshly turned earth. It was as if they had all just been buried, resting in the ground for a matter of days.

"Who are these people?"

"The headstones?" Peep replied. "The individual headstones are people that the Dreamcatcher managed to catch in her web—people like you."

Galen's breath hitched in her throat.

"Each one of them represents a time when she was unable to gain her own existence, but successful in the draining of their lives." Peep pushed past Galen once more, heading straight for the first tombstone that ready Gary Albright. She knelt in front of it, her plastic fingers running across the waxy petals of the lilies laid against the stone. "They are people from the real world that lost their lives because they lost the fight against that wench. Some of them think they made the conscious decision to stay here, unaware it would kill them. Others tried to fight her off but ran out of time. Then, a select few did the bravest thing a someone can do in the face of the Dreamcatcher."

"What's that?"

Peep let go of the flowers and stood upright, bowing her cowboy hat to the fallen Mr Albright. "They tell her they don't believe in her, to her face. They watch her lose everything that she's worked to steal. They may die, but they at least take away the power that she took from them, leaving her in the exact same place as when she started."

Galen didn't know that was possible. She stood with Peep until the cowgirl began to roam the isles of the headstones. All the names she read meant nothing to her, but she was sure they meant everything to the dreams here. It was saddening to see. So many people had lost their lives. Galen counted seventeen so far, though she found herself wondering if there were people unaccounted for.

"Would she have buried those that she didn't like here?" Galen asked as Peep stopped in front of another grave belonging to Eleanor Trevors. A petunia had been planted at the head of this grave, as if to symbolise something. There was even a little ice lolly stick poking out of the ground, with a message written on it in a foreign language.

"The Dreamcatcher has never particularly disliked anyone that she's trapped," Peep explained. "You can't be that fussy when your only means of survival are dreamers. She can pick and choose, but she bases that off the strength of your dreams, not on who you are. For that, she couldn't care less."

Galen couldn't help but be drawn in by the huge monument at the back of the graveyard. She drifted towards it, feeling the earth squelch beneath her shoe as she went. There were no paths, just mud. There were footsteps in the ground still, Eve's footsteps, that showed where she had been. Some graves were more popular than others. Some barely had any marking around them, but there was one path that was clear to see and led straight to the back of the sanctuary.

Stood in front of the wall, Galen didn't quite realise what she was looking at. It was like a war memorial with the soldiers' names lined up alphabetically. There was no more information other than that, just a name. Galen didn't know any of them. Her eyes were searching for a plaque or a nameplate, something to signify what the monument was showing. It was ancient history, from the looks of it. The first names carved into the crumbling stone were fading, in need of being redone. The last few looked like scribbles done by a toddler, etched it with a mere pick and nothing else.

"What's this?" Galen could hear Peep's footsteps coming up behind her and didn't flinch when a lightning bolt was sent from the heavens to pierce the ground beside her. "She's upset that I've found it."

"She's more than likely upset that the overall creepiness of this place didn't deter you," Peep replied calmly. "This is something a little closer to home. It's something I didn't think I'd ever lay eyes on, but now I've looked at it one too many times, and it makes me sick to my stomach."

Galen reached out and ran her fingers across the smooth, stone podium that was supposed to have bouquets of flowers resting upon it, but it was empty. "What does it signify? Why do the last entries look like that?"

"These are the dreams she's killed," Peep said gruffly. "The last few have been carved in less delicately because she stopped caring. Either that, or she's lost count and rushed it. It's a trophy to her, and a site of mourning for us."

"She lets you come here?"

Peep scoffed. "She can't stop us from coming here. There is nothing keeping us out. To me, she likes it when we come here because it causes us pain, and she hates us that much she wouldn't want to see us in anything other than great, unyielding pain."

Galen ran her fingers down the inscriptions and sighed. If she had known sooner, the list would've been much, much shorter. Though it did cross her mind; would she have been able to do anything at all? Would she end up here? Instinctually, Galen began looking for an empty site. Her eyes roamed the rows to see nothing that scared her, until she noticed a site sizzling—the site that had been struck by lightning.

There was a magnetic pull that led her towards it, almost moving her feet for her. Galen moved slowly and cautiously, dodging and weaving the Dreamcatcher's fallen victims until she reached the patch of earth that was singed and burning. She knelt, pushing a palm flat against the rising smoke to extinguish it, only to find it escaping around her hand. When she lifted it, she noticed a little seedling starting to grow. It was just a tiny flicker of green pushing out of the ground, and then a sprout. The head of it elongated and fell as it became weighted down, the stalk of the plant still growing and growing. It only stopped when a single petal had bloomed—a pink petal that had fallen right off a cherry blossom tree.

"We should go." The desperation in Peep's voice made it sound like a command, and not an idea. She took off her hat and held it over her heart. "This place isn't so welcoming anymore. We've seen what it holds. We should go."

"What is that?"

Another huff from Peep indicated her fear and her frustration. "It's an omen from the Dreamcatcher. As I've said, we should go before that omen becomes reality. We don't have much time left."

This time, Galen moved away with Peep when she felt the cowgirl tug on her trousers. Her eyes weren't willing to leave the plant that was shaking in the gentle breeze. It was the only thing that was alive. It hadn't wilted away yet, and it hadn't sprouted any more than one petal. That single petal flapped goodbye at Galen as she stepped outside of the graveyard and was trapped in as the gates slammed closed in a strop and groaned its last gripe.

"What omen was that?"

"That's where she'll bury you," Gil said. He hadn't seen a thing but knew exactly what Galen was talking about. "Thought she would've had a better place for you? Admittedly, I've never seen her so fond of her prey, but whether that's a good thing or not is still open to interpretation." He turned and wandered off, snatching up Ducky's rope and leading the panicked toy back down the path. "Come now," he ordered. "We must get back on the path we set out on, before this world turns into nothingness around us."

"We're in danger. We're in danger. We're all gonna die. We're going to be killed. We're gonna fry."

Ducky was infuriating to listen to. Ever since the run-in with the Dreamcatcher, the duck had been frantic. He'd been chanting to himself, and his eyes had been so wide that they were about to burst. He'd been wheeling himself back and forth in the same place, running himself so deep into muck that Galen had to keep plucking him back out. Now, he was being led along by his rope, unable to wander freely. It was a sad sight to see, though it was driving Galen mad.

"*What's wrong with him?*" Galen whispered to Peep.

The cowgirl seemed in pain, squinting, and wincing so hard that her entire face had changed. "He doesn't like being that close to Eve. He thinks that he can become possessed just by her touching him."

"Ah." Galen understood that, though a thought popped up in her brain suddenly. "Can he?"

"Beats me." Peep rubbed at her temple, making that part of her plastic flesh red and irritated. "I'm not sure what she's able to do anymore. She changes with every day that passes here."

That was something Galen hadn't thought about for a while. How long had she been asleep for? Had it been days? It was much longer than her last stint which cost her three days, so her family must've been panicked by now. Maybe they'd think it was the tablets she was given that had caused her prolonged slumber. Maybe they'd think she'd died. The thought made chills creep up and down her arms, though she refused to show the bumps and crossed her arms tightly over her chest.

"I'm not feeling so great," Peep finally said. She stumbled her last few steps before she stopped and clasped her head in both hands. Her plastic hair swooped into her face and her treasured hat fell from her head.

When she fell, Galen tried to catch her, but the doll slipped straight through Galen's grip. "Peep!" she cried. "Peep, are you okay?"

The cowgirl was writhing on the ground, legs brought up to her stomach and hands still pushed against each temple. She was perpetually wincing. One would've thought that was the expression she was made with. Her eyes were squeezed closed tightly and her lips would only part for a groan to escape.

Gil almost choked Ducky as he sprinted towards the other half of his group. He handed Galen Ducky's lead and knelt by Peep's side, putting his paw to her forehead. The panic on his face made Galen worry more. The bear had never been this startled before.

"We need to stop somewhere," Gil said abruptly. His eyes were searching for safe places that he could hide Peep in, but there were hardly any. They were out in a vast expanse of fields with few trees and little shelter. "Dream something," he ordered, glaring straight into Galen's soul. "Take us somewhere safe, somewhere she can recover."

Galen wanted to speak, but words wouldn't escape her lips.

"No, Gil," Peep protested. "We can't have her use any of her power. We'll need it to defeat the Dreamcatcher."

"That bitch can wait!" Gil roared. "This is a problem for now. Dream us a sanctuary, Galen, and do it now! We could be running out of time!"

Galen panicked. She dropped Ducky's lead and watched him roll around in wider circles, spurting out more enlightening phrases of how he expected to be killed in the most gruesome of ways. Her eyes couldn't concentrate on one thing, so she closed them. Even with her eyes closed, and blackness all around her, she could still see Ducky spinning and Gil tending to Peep. Images of the graveyard and the memorial and her undug grave flashed up at random, interspersed with vignettes of Eve's beautiful face. It was so loud she couldn't think, and she couldn't hear herself. No matter how hard she tried, she couldn't muster up anything. Nothing would appear in front of her but destruction and failure, so her eyes shot open just as she saw Ducky speeding off into the distance.

Enough was enough. Galen could see how much pain Peep was in, how much distress it had caused Gil. She squeezed her eyes shut once more, even pushing her hands into her eye sockets to darken the blackness. In her mind, she chanted to herself, village in the meadows, cottage in the village. Village in the meadows, cottage in the village.

We're in a village in the meadows, in a cottage in the village.

She imagined the houses, the rustic little bungalows with thatched roofs and Tudor exterior designs. She imagined the exposed wood and the beams that would run both inside and outside of the house. Galen could see the little stone wells and the massive watermill that fished out fresh water from the adjacent river. Trees and rolling hills popped up in the background to provide the village protection, and wild grasses shot up all over the village centre, adorned with wildflowers. She couldn't see any people but imagined a bustling community that was close knit and friendly. Those people manned the stalls in the marketplace, the loom in the fabric store, the kitchens in the bakery. They helped to stock the libraries and teach in the schools and decorate the town with pleasantly made, brightly coloured garlands as if to welcome their guests.

Oh, how Galen longed for it to be real and, upon smelling the luscious scent of freshly baked bread, she realised that she had willed it into existence all around her. She opened her eyes and saw the bustling society that she had made out of nowhere. It was the most normal thing she'd seen for a while now, and possibly the most beautiful.

Gil helped Peep up to her feet and watched in dismay as Ducky came rolling straight into him, a frown covering his furry face. "You, Duck, need to calm down," he warned. He went to point a thumb in Ducky's face, but just jabbed his entire paw at him upon realising he had no thumbs or fingers. "We're not dead yet, so there's no use fretting about it."

"It won't be long until she finds us," Ducky replied with a wry chuckle. "I'm telling you now. It's all downhill from here."

"I'm not sure I could get any worse," Peep interjected. She was barely hanging on to Gil. Her arm was slung over his shoulders but her other hand was still clamped against her head. She tried to reach both temples with one hand, but her fingers just wouldn't stretch.

Gil hushed her, to soothe her. "It'll be alright, Peep. We'll stay here until you feel better."

Galen was still in awe of what she'd created. She wandered slower than the others, peeling away from the group as they went to look for shelter. She was more interested in the wildlife, in the flora and the fauna that were clear for all to see.

Wild deer grazed on the tallgrasses that their fawns played it. They weren't at all startled by Galen and her gang. They took no notice of her as she padded about their town, ignoring her, and treating her as if she wasn't there. There were cats and dogs running around, being chased, or chasing children that were laughing with joy and glee. There had never been a happier image.

One by one, people started appearing. Townsfolk popped up behind their stalls and began calling out their goods to passers-by. Bakery windows opened to unleash the smell of bread and cakes and pies, and the bells above their doors began to ring incessantly. Families opened the doors to their homes, wishing their husbands and wives a good day at work and smiling as they watched their children play.

It wasn't at all what Galen was used to. She hadn't seen an inkling of this the entire time she'd been asleep. She'd never wanted this. How had this image popped into her head so clearly? She felt as if it had been planted there, though it felt so much like her own idea. Thinking about it made her head foggy.

"You there!"

Someone called to Galen, stopping her dead in her tracks. She held her breath and turned on her heels, watching a woman come running towards her. She expected to see someone clad in a dress of unremarkable colours heading for her, but instead saw a woman clad in a dark green tartan suit with a white undershirt that was billowing about her arms and loose across her chest. The sight made her stand even taller.

"What are you doing here?" the woman asked. "Where did you come from?"

Galen found her tongue tied up in her mouth. "My friend was hurt…"

The woman's brow arched. "That doesn't explain how you happened upon Eve's Bane. How did you get here? Which path did you take?" She was so brash and blunt that she forced Galen back with just her words.

"Actually, we didn't take a path…" Galen drifted off. She tried to mask both her intimidation and her adoration from her face by frowning, though it looked more like a pained mask of confusion. "I imagined this place, and suddenly we are here. We don't come to impose any sort of threat."

"I can't imagine someone like you would impose any sort of threat anywhere," the woman cursed. She glared at Galen, staring straight into her eyes and into her soul. Her eyes ran down the length of Galen's body and back up painfully slowly. It was as if she could see everything, inside and out. "And who are you, exactly?"

Galen gulped down her fear, tucking her chin in for fear of breathing in the stranger's face. "My name is Galen, and these are my dreams."

The woman backed off and eased up, her intensity instantly dialling back into nothingness.

"Who are you?" quizzed Galen. She walked circles around the stranger, taking in each and every remarkable detail. The way she was dressed was so prim and proper. This was no lord. This was quite obviously a lady, trying to make a statement. "I don't recall dreaming you up, but I must've. You wouldn't exist otherwise."

"My name is Alden," the woman proclaimed. The toughness in her voice was gone, but softness didn't replace it. "You dreamt of me a few times, and of this village, but I never expected you to actually come here."

Galen's shoulders lilted as she stood in front of Alden again, facing her. "I never expected to be here either, but one of my friends was struck down."

"Struck down by what?"

"I'm not sure, exactly."

Alden's smug grimace tightened. "You will have to forgive my harshness, but I am confused on how you managed to get here. No one has ever come here, not like that."

"You'll have to forgive my…" Galen couldn't remember the word, frowning heavily as she fought to evoke it, "uncertainty." Was that the word? It'd have to do for now. "I don't know what happened, but this place appeared in my mind, now we're here. That's all there is to the story."

"Let me meet your friends," Alden said gruffly. "I'd like to talk to them before word gets out around my village, and you start spreading panic."

Galen led Alden to the cottage that Gil and the gang had waddled off to, trying to figure out whether or not she liked the woman. She didn't remember dreaming of such a person. It had to have been so long ago. Either that or Eve had hidden that dream in the dark recesses of Galen's mind. That, Galen could understand. The Dreamcatcher was the jealous type, and Alden was most certainly Galen's type.

Gil confronted Alden in seconds, chest puffed out and arms held up by his sides as soon as she walked in the door. "Who is this?" he spoke to Galen.

"I live here," Alden answered for herself. "I keep this village from being attacked and tarnished by dreams that don't belong here. So, I might ask the same question of you. Who are you?"

Galen peered over Gil and saw Peep sitting in an armchair, still clutching at her head. She had a cup of water at her side and two cool pads pressed against her temples, though the pain didn't seem to be easing at all.

"My name is Gillette, and I've kept this dreamland safe for as long as it has existed," the old bear growled. "The cowgirl is Peep, and the duck is Ducky."

"Original."

"We're all going to die!" Ducky burst out again. He'd been quarantined to one end of the room, trapped in by furniture placed strategically all around him. He was a flight risk, still chanting of his and everyone else's imminent deaths.

Galen laughed nervously as she stepped between Alden and Gil, trying to separate the two. "Now, now. There's no need for hostility. We're all good dreams here," she tried to soothe. She put a hand on Alden's chest and pushed her away a few paces, surprised to see that the woman actually moved for her. "We won't be staying long. Perhaps just the night. We need time for our friend to heal. We can't carry on with our journey until she's okay."

Alden watched Peep. "What's wrong with her?"

"We don't know."

Alden went to step closer, but both Galen and Gil prevented her. Gil almost sprung on her like a wild grizzly bear, but just smacked into the back of Galen's leg like the teddy bear he was.

Galen stayed close to Alden, almost hugging her. "We don't want to worry her. Do you know what's wrong?"

"I've seen this kind of thing before and it's never had a good outcome," Alden hissed into Galen's ear. "I risk an awful lot letting you stay here."

"We've no other choice."

Alden's head whipped around so her eyes were on Galen's. "*And where does that leave us?*" she whispered, though her tone was anything but gentle and calm. "*You would rather put us all at risk than leave and find somewhere else to be your haven?*"

"No harm will come to you."

Alden stood bolt upright, her eyes slowly travelling from Galen down to Gil. "Do you know what kind of a place we are?"

"A place where you are rude to guests, I'd imagined," Gil replied.

"Not usually," Alden shot back. "We're non-believers, and we've been under attack these recent times. Your arrival here seems almost…too good to be true.

Having this place just magically pop into your head with no provocation is…" she waved her hand around in the air, trying to find the right word, "remarkable."

The tension in the room suddenly increased, and the atmosphere weighed heavier upon everyone's shoulders.

"Non-believers," Gil repeated. "Non-believers living so freely in a world dominated by the Dreamcatcher? I find that hard to believe. She would've wiped you out by now."

"She never knew where we were," Alden growled. "She never knew how to find us. Our location was always a mystery. She found us once, long ago, but was unable to do anything. She didn't have the power. She didn't have the host to possess."

Gil's cane was suddenly thrust forward into the limelight. "Not one of us here is possessed!" he shouted at the top of his lungs. It was almost as if he had forgotten Ducky. "We are all with our wits about us, even the duck. Grant us at least one night of impunity and then we'll be gone, out of your hair."

"One night can cost me a whole lifetime of work."

"No harm will befall you and your people, now go," Gil ordered. "I don't need you causing rifts between my people. We are already on edge enough. You planting seeds of possession and disbelief in our minds will only render us here for longer than we intend to be. Do you understand?"

Alden cracked her jaw. "So be it. A night is all you'll have." She turned on her heel and marched off, bursting out of the door, and slamming it shut behind her.

Galen was rather sad to see the fine woman go. "Non-believers?"

"Colonies like this still exist in some places, though they are far and few. They're scattered across the outskirts of your mind in places that the Dreamcatcher hasn't conquered yet. They don't believe in her existence, and they don't hide that fact either. They taunt her and they expect her to do nothing and, when she attacks, they act surprised and self-righteous. They get what they deserve, in my mind. Accusing us of being possessed is low of them, a move I haven't experienced yet, but a low blow nonetheless."

"Ducky can't be possessed, can he?"

Gil shrugged.

"Peep mentioned that he believes Eve can possess people just by touching them."

The old bear sat himself by Peep's side, watching her as she dozed off into a deep sleep. "I don't know anymore," he admitted with a deep sigh. "She's so hard to keep track of. That could be true, or it could be a lie. Anything to get into old Duck's head." He laughed to himself suddenly, as if remembering a joke that he found funny. "If she was going to possess anyone, you'd think it would be you. That makes the most sense."

"I think that would take too much of her strength to do," Galen combatted. "She'd have to go up against me, and if she lost then she'd have a hell of a lot of recovering to do."

"Don't you go underestimating her just because she has a soft spot for you," Gil warned. He wagged his paw at her and shook his head, his worry for Peep clear to see. "She may have spared you once, but I believe that to be because the thrill of the chase just wasn't grand enough. She's right when she says there's no fight. You saw how easily she breezed past me."

Galen sat herself down in a wicker chair, slumping until the back of her head rested against the top of it. "What will she do to these people?"

"Anything that happens to them is justified."

"You've told me countless times that her killing off dreams will never be justified," Galen countered, smiling smugly at the old bear. She grinned when he dropped his head, realising his hypocrisy. "Why are these people any different?"

Another sigh left Gil's body. "As I said, non-believers bring this on themselves. It's equal to shouting, 'kill me' in a serial killer's face and expecting them not to or smacking an angry bear in the face and expecting it not to attack." He covered Peep's hand as she napped peacefully in her chair, watching her face twitch. "Alden seems reasonable, however. She seems to have this place guarded as we had our settlement protected. She's not stupid."

"She's not fond of us being here."

"If I were her, and I believed as she did, I wouldn't want any outsiders here either." Gil finally clambered off his chair and pulled himself down a blanket from the vanity, setting himself up a little place to rest in the corner by Ducky. "She has every right not to trust us, though we mean her no harm. That doesn't mean to say the unintended won't happen. You bring trouble with you everywhere you go, whether you mean to or not, so this place won't remain untouched for much longer." He lay one blanket one the floor, ball up another as a pillow and then crept between a few more layers to keep himself warm. "It's not going to be fun for you, being here. Whilst we can sleep, you can't. You'll have to find a way to entertain yourself."

Galen smiled at Gil as he rested his cane just to the side of his makeshift bed, where he could reach it if any threat was inbound. She watched him flop onto his back and drag his blanket up to his chin, envying how peaceful the routine was. Her nightly routine used to be almost the same. She would peel herself from whatever she was doing, whether it be her art or her writing, and flop into bed and smother herself in her duvet. Galen missed that simple habit but knew what she had to do to get it back.

When everyone was asleep, Galen slipped outside. The night had fallen, and she was shrouded in darkness, barely able to see. There was a trail of fireflies lighting up a route to the middle of the town that she followed. The flies would dance about the air, bending one way and then another, almost leading Galen on a wild goose chase, until they stopped at the beginning of a slope.

The hill was vast. It stretched upwards for not too far, but the angle it rose at was intimidating. So steep and so unpredictable. There were footsteps in the muddy, well-trodden path, new footsteps—so fresh that the print of the boot could still be seen clearly. They led straight up, and then veered right to the overhang that dangled above Alden's house and stared out across the entirety of Eve's Bane.

Curious, Galen began to climb. She could feel the strain in her muscles within seconds, hating that she'd started the endeavour to begin with. As she climbed, she cursed herself over and over and over. Her lips traced swear words her mother would hate to hear and huffed and puffed, her face red and hot.

She got to the top in what felt like record time, but her body hated her for it. She was covered in sweat and doubled over as soon as the land began to flatten. Her hands found her knees as she bent her back and tried desperately to catch her breath. Never before had she looked so much like a fish out of water.

"Can you not sleep either, outsider?" Alden's voice asked.

Galen snapped bolt upright, straightening her spine with such force that her back cracked in two. "I don't think I can sleep," she mumbled through the pain. She hobbled herself over to where a shadow was cast across the ground but didn't sit on the bench that was a little too close to the edge for her liking. "What are you doing up here?"

"Watching," Alden replied simply. "Waiting. It's only a matter of time."

"You remind me a lot of a friend of mine," Galen said through hurried breaths. She picked her way along to the bench but slowed her pace as she grew closer and closer to the edge of the overhang. In her mind, she could see it not supporting her weight and snapping. That was a tumble she didn't want to take. "You're both stoic and brave, yet stubborn in your ways. All you want to do is defend your people against the evil that lurks here, yet you won't ask anyone for help."

Alden prickled at that remark. "Are you saying I should be asking for your help?"

"I don't think I'm much help here, so no," Galen refuted. "In fact, I seem to cause all the trouble that happens, so it'd be wise of you to stay away from me."

"Hence my apprehension to have you here."

Galen couldn't help but feel a little hurt. "You said I dreamt of you a few times, yet I don't remember you," she said suddenly in order to change the conversation. She wanted to see who Alden really was. The crabbiness was a mask, and Galen wanted to see underneath it. "I don't remember any dream with you or this place in it. Do you know why that would be?"

"You've forgotten me," was Alden's reply. She didn't say it in a way that indicated she was hurt, but she sounded down. "That's to be expected, however. You were fond of me. You would purposely think of me to dream of me. This place thrived because of it. You gave us so much power and strength, but the Dreamcatcher found a loophole."

Of course, Eve was responsible for this. Who else would it have been?

"She made you forget me. She got jealous, and jealousy is a rampant killer. There's nothing else to be expected."

"Is that why you're so harsh with me?"

Alden pursed her lips. "It's not your fault."

Galen made the brave move to dash forwards and steal a spot next to Alden on the bench, though her fears only worsened when she saw bits of dirt tumbling off the edge of the cliff.

"No one is to be blamed," Alden carried on. She sounded so wistful, so remorseful. "I have those dreams still, so at least one of us can still bask in them. A shame, my dear, that it can't be you."

Galen didn't respond. She stared in awe at the side of Alden's chiselled face. She couldn't help but notice the similarities between Alden and Eve. The high cheekbones. The sharp jaw. The bold eyes. It was all similar, but all different.

Alden was much softer. Though her cheekbones were high and mighty, they weren't as blunt against her skin. Her features were rounded, friendlier, smoother. There was nothing harsh about her face apart from her disapproving pout—an expression she'd undoubtedly learnt long ago.

Alden's hair was almost white against the moonlight, tied back on her head in a ponytail that was slicked to her scalp. Not a single strand of hair was out of place, and not a single braid or plait was imperfect. There wasn't a wrinkle in her clothing or a blemish on her face. No marks covered her at all, not even scars or freckles or beauty spots. There was nothing. Alden was a blank canvas with a beautiful face and a stony temperament, still with room to grow and develop.

"You're staring at me."

Ah! Caught!

Galen yanked her eyes away and blushed. "I stopped thinking for a minute there. I'm sorry. I got…lost in my thoughts."

There was the faintest hint of a smile tugging at one end of Alden's mouth. "What was it you were thinking of?"

"I was trying to remember your dream." That wasn't entirely true. She was actually thinking about how soft Alden's lips looked… "I don't like that I can be made to forget. It seems intrusive." Galen's eyes nervously flickered back, only to find that Alden was now looking at her. Her breath hitched in her throat as the bold eyes she had thought were a rich, deep brown were only black. She had no irises, no pupil, just blackness. The whites of her eyes were so bright in contrast to the darkness that lingered in the centre, a darkness with all the memories of a happy, living dream.

"You're staring again."

"You started it this time," Galen replied, barely moving her lips. At first, she wasn't sure if she'd said the words out loud. Had Alden heard her? Should she speak again? She knew by the smile that grew on Alden's face that she had indeed spoken, but her sheer astonishment of the woman had rendered her braindead. "Shouldn't you be on some sort of patrol?" were the words that came next. Galen didn't have control over her mouth anymore. She was just saying whatever came to mind.

Alden's brow arched. "A patrol? You want me to wander around my own town?"

"To make sure everyone is at home and safe."

"You make a good point." Alden stood, and held out her hand to help Galen to her feet. Her hand just dangled there for a while, glowing in the moonlight. How ethereal could one person be?

Galen stared at the hand and, if not for the muscles tightening in her jaw, her mouth would've fallen open by now. She took it, stifling the gasp that almost choked her as she touched skin as soft as silk. She was hauled to her feet with an ungodly strength, almost scooped up entirely in one arm, and then let go of to stand by herself. Standing alone wasn't fun, she decided quickly. She didn't like being so lonely.

"You and I can form a patrol party," Alden announced. She offered her arm for Galen to take, and only scoffed wryly when she was turned down. "For your one night here, I'll give you a tour, and then you will be seen straight off to bed."

"Where I will lay awake until the sun rises because I'm currently already asleep and trapped in my dreams for what appears to be an everlasting duration of time." Galen finished Alden's sentence for her, trying to sound as cheery and as happy as she could. In reality, saying those words aloud birthed a pit in her stomach. It hit her quickly. This was her reality now, her world.

Alden caught on to the dread. "This place is not as bad as it could be," she argued. "Where else would one wish to spend the rest of their time? And to be immortal? Isn't that most humans' wish?"

"I can't help but think of my family." Galen struggled down the hill, flailing all over the place next to a calm and composed Alden. How stupid she must've looked. Good thing everyone was asleep. "They'll miss me if I just…stay here. I'll die. I don't like to think of them as being sad and mourning for me."

"Alas that is a fear that I don't know how to soothe," Alden replied. "I don't have a family; at least not like you do. All dreams are supposed to be family, but the Dreamcatcher's presence has turned us all into a bitter, selfish bunch of nightmares. We're terrified of anything that moves, and our first thought is to quash that thing, so it can't hurt us."

Galen made it to the bottom of the hill without slipping, wishing she had taken Alden's arm. "I thought dreams were supposed to be pleasant, yet I've come to find they're extremely stressful."

"Only when a parasite is leaching off them."

Alden walked Galen around the entire town before leaving her on the porch of her hut, though she seemed hesitant to just walk away. "By morning, you'll be on your way to wherever it is you're heading. I hope that your friend is better by then."

"Because you couldn't possibly have us stay any longer," Galen finished. She smiled at Alden, her gratitude glistening in her eyes. "I understand, Alden. We'll be gone by morning, and not a second after."

"It'll be sad to watch you go," Alden confessed suddenly. She spoke so hurriedly that Galen wondered if she'd even meant to say those words at all. "Although, if you are unsuccessful in waking up…I would always have you here."

Was that a compliment?

"I know where to find you if I fail," Galen replied, somewhat stonily. She opened the door to the hut and gave Alden a little wave, her heart dipping slightly inside her chest. "Goodnight, Alden."

"Goodnight, outsider."

Dreams were incredibly boring. Several times, Galen tried to will time to go faster, or for the sun to rise in the sky. No matter what she did, nothing happened. Though the sun was rising, it was taking its time to do so. She found herself trying to conjure up little things to play with, like Eve had done. Her mind wasn't in it, though. Galen thought of Alden, of the sadness that had been in the atmosphere when the dream had wandered away. It was a sad sight to see, but hopefully not the last sight Galen got of Alden. Maybe when she woke up, she'd remember Alden's face and could dream of her again. That was if she ever woke up.

Galen was distracted from staring down at her hands by the sound of rushing footsteps coming up to her door. She perked up, hearing them pound at the earth. They sounded eerily similar to that of Eve's gremlins, which propelled Galen to her feet. She launched at the door, almost tearing it off its hinges and waking everyone inside the house up.

"What's going on?" Gil asked groggily. He reached for his cane and tried to stand himself up, but his legs failed beneath him. "What's happening?"

Galen didn't really know. She stared out of the door and saw Alden sprinting towards the hut, her cheeks emblazoned with redness. Had she run through the entire town? Galen trotted down the porch steps to meet Alden but was pushed out of the way.

"Are you okay?" Galen asked. She watched as Alden climbed the few steps and slammed the door shut, running a flat palm across the front of it. Her brow arched as Alden backed away again, relieved and with her head hung. "What's happened? What's gone on?"

"Everyone is gone," Alden growled through her gritted teeth. She kept her head low and clamped her hands on her hips, kicking up clouds of dirt. She gathered an audience about her as Gil and Peep came to the door, with Ducky not far behind them. "The houses have been marked with inverted crosses and there is no one here. They are all piles of ashes."

Peep gasped, and Galen thought she could feel her heart stopping in her chest. She said nothing, though. She could see the anger and the upset in Alden's eyes, and it was all directed at her. Her own head bowed as Alden marched up to her, standing just a few inches away, seething.

"Did I not say this would happen?" she barked.

"It isn't the girl's fault," Gil stepped in, his voice still groggy from sleep.

Alden whirled around on him. "Then who is to blame?" she yelled at him. Her voice was just like his, intimidating and hoarse. She commanded the attention of everyone around her, if there had been anyone around her. No wonder she was these people's leader. "My village has been slaughtered whilst they slept! This would not have happened if I hadn't welcomed you in!"

"There was no welcoming here for us," Gil refuted. He took a moment to just glare at Alden as he hobbled down the steps to face her. "You made it abundantly clear we were not welcome. You spoke this into existence. Did chanting your disbelief come around and bite you in the ass? Good. You got what you deserved."

"Hundreds of dreams have just been killed in one night," Alden hissed between gritted teeth. "Does that mean nothing to you, old bear? Do you not understand what the Dreamcatcher has just inherited?"

Gil's calmness was unmeasured. "And do you think that squawking about it is going to do anyone any good? Consider the fact she left you alive a blessing and make yourself scarce. Perhaps she forgot about you, or perhaps she has something else lined up for you. Take off before you find out what that something else is."

"You expect me to abandon my people?"

"What people?" There it was. Gil's temperament came back in full force, replacing his somewhat calm and demure display with nothing but anger. "You are by yourself now, Alden! Accept that! You did everything you could to keep this place safe but let's be honest with each other, we both know what happened here."

Alden stepped closer to the bear. "You got us all killed."

Gil waved away that accusation, disgusted by it. "You said it yourself that you found it suspicious our Galen knew exactly how to dream of this place, and exactly how to get to it—almost as if it wasn't her idea. You and I are smart enough to work out it was not her idea after all."

"What?" Galen perked up.

"My dear," Gil turned his attention to Galen, his features softening just a touch, "the Dreamcatcher planted a vision of this place in your mind. She told you what to picture and what to envision and knew exactly who would be waiting for her here. She never had the strength to get here without you, so she used you. This was not your doing. This was all her wicked magic."

Alden ran her fingers through her hair, pinning her snow-white hair back on her scalp. "I cannot just run away from this place as if it means nothing to me. Surely I should stand my ground and fight."

"Then stand your ground and fight." Gil was past talking to Alden. He sounded bored and tired and waved at Peep to gather up their belongings to leave. When his eyes finally found Alden's again, he huffed a little sigh. "What you do makes no impact on us. You aren't one of us, so you don't concern us. I've told you what you should do, and whether you listen or not is down to you."

"You do what this old man says?" Alden's words were directed at Galen. "This is the dream you're letting guide you about this place? You think he'll help you get to the Dreamcatcher?"

Galen backed off as Alden piled on the pressure, holding up her hands in surrender. "He was the first person I found here, the first person to welcome me in. I can't abandon the cause I've set out on now. I'm too far in." She only moved forwards again once Alden's hostility had dropped and put a hand on the dream's shoulder to comfort her. "Don't take this so personally, Alden. It wasn't your fault. This is a new opportunity for you now, though. You can go wherever you want to, start a new life over. You could start a new settlement over."

Alden stared holes through Galen. "I'd like for you all to leave now," was all she said. She spoke quietly, as if she was resolute in her ways. "You've done the damage I predicted, and now I want to be left alone."

"Don't kill yourself for your sorrows, Alden," Galen begged.

“Maybe I shall and maybe I shan’t. Maybe one day we’ll cross paths again and you’ll find out my fate. For now, I have to stay here.” Alden glimpsed at all the empty huts around her now, sighing deeply. Galen could tell how heavy her heart was hanging in her chest from the crystal tears forming in Alden’s lifeless eyes. “Please, just go. Get out of here.”

“We are already on our way,” Gil growled. He waddled off with Peep and Ducky in tow, only glancing back when he knew Galen wasn’t following. “She’s a lost dream now, Galen, and she’s chosen to stay here. We can’t do anything else for her.”

Galen felt like she could cry. “You won’t do anything stupid over this.”

“I’ll be here until somewhere else calls my name,” Alden replied. She didn’t smile. She didn’t light up. Her cheeks didn’t redden with blush. She just glared, accusingly. “You should be on your way.”

“I’m sorry, Alden.”

“Go.”

Galen hung her head in shame, like a scolded puppy, and followed after Gil. She didn’t look back because she knew Alden wouldn’t want to look at her. Her eyes trailed across the ground, watching the footsteps made by the bear and his companions. Her eyes filled with tears as she grew further and further away from her obviously beloved dream. If only she remembered Alden fully. If only she hadn’t caused so much hurt and pain.

Chapter Six

Peep was different. Ducky was also different, but he was just insane. Peep, however, was alarmingly different.

Everywhere they went, Peep would leave a trail of something behind her or say something completely unbecoming of her. She wasn't herself. Ever since she'd woken up at Eve's Bane, Peep had been a different person. There was this cheeriness about her that the cowgirl hadn't had to begin with, and it was starting to raise Galen's suspicions.

Finally happening upon a clearing in the west, Gil sat stoking a fire that everyone had built. Peep and Ducky were far off building lean-tos, but it was obvious that not even Ducky trusted the words coming out of Peep's mouth.

"What's wrong with her?" Galen asked Gil abruptly. She was snapping branches in half, feeding them to the fire whilst watching Peep act luridly and vulgarly. She was practically dancing around Ducky, gliding around in a way that was hauntingly familiar. "Why is she suddenly like this?"

"I don't know what you're talking about," Gil grumbled. He kept stoking the fire, stabbing at one log in particular until his stoker pierced straight through it. "She's perfectly fine. She's not complaining of any aches or pains, and she can walk. That's what we needed."

Galen scrutinised Peep's every move, a worry growing inside her. "She's not herself."

Gil finally threw a look to Peep, tilting his head to the side as he too watched her act the fool with Ducky. "I can agree with that, but what have you seen?"

"There's whatever that is," Galen said quickly, flapping her hand at Peep. "The way she's been talking is concerning. She sounds like she wants to be in charge of this party, choose where we go, what paths we take."

"That's concerning why?"

Galen's eyes found the bear. "Every suggestion she's had has been to lead us to a place where we can be easily picked off or segregated. It's like she's planning against us somehow. There's something in her brain that's just switched on."

Gil laughed at that. "Peep would never betray us like that. You think headaches cause mutiny? Maybe in your world, but not here. She's loyal to us and our cause."

"And I don't doubt that," Galen interjected. She knew how she came across. She knew how she sounded. Her paranoia was eating away at her, however. Had it really been her that had led the Dreamcatcher to Eve's Bane? Had Peep's headache been real? "What I doubt is that she's fully herself."

"If any one of us has that wench in our heads it's Ducky."

That wasn't the response Galen was expecting.

"I've seen him lose his marbles before but, this time, he's fully off his rocker." Gil found a new stick, a new stoker, to prod the burning logs with. What was he getting out of this? It was truly perplexing. "You've heard what he's chanting. Those are things the Dreamcatcher would say. Peep is just…Peep."

"We can agree to disagree, I suppose."

Gil suddenly pointed his lit stoker at Galen, not worried about the flame that was slowly crawling up the bark. "Until she proves otherwise, Peep is as right as rain. We'll mention nothing of it. We'll arouse no suspicion. If there's something dodgy going on, she'll out herself. Eve is not that discreet."

Galen raised her hands in defeat. She wouldn't argue anymore. She picked herself up off the fallen tree she'd been sat on and lay just in front of it, still garnering the heat of the fire. The only thing she was happy for was the discovery of new land. Gil had been so happy about it that he'd almost shed a tear. Galen was just happy she didn't have to walk anymore. Whilst Ducky and Peep built lean-tos, the old bear had claimed he was going to make a map. So far, he'd just prodded the fire like a sleeping lion. Galen had simply watched Peep after keeping her distance from the inauspicious cowgirl, and she'd liked not one thing of what she had seen.

"Will you two stop making that racket and come eat something?" Gil shouted in frustration suddenly.

Galen didn't bother opening her eyes. She wanted to rest. She could feel herself starting to drain of energy. Eve's magic was taking a hold of her, and all Galen wanted to do was lie down.

"You've been driving me nuts all day," Gil griped. "What's the matter with you two?"

"Peep isn't that great at building dens," Ducky reasoned. His wheels squeaked as he pulled up to the fire and reversed a few spaces, so he didn't catch alight. "She's more interested in—"

"In telling Ducky how great and benevolent this world is!"

The sheer cheeriness of Peep's sentence made Galen open her eyes. She stared through the fire at Peep who took a bowl from Gil and sat, but not how she normally did.

The cowgirl didn't just plop herself down on the fallen log like she did most nights. She instead lowered herself down gracefully, crossing one leg over the other and holding her bowl against her lap. The elegance of her movements was uncanny. Galen knew who she was watching, but she couldn't bring herself to believe it. It was just her paranoia. It was as Gil said, if Peep wasn't herself, she'd reveal it soon enough, so Galen closed her eyes once more and huffed.

"We don't need lean-tos and camps and settlements!" Peep went on. "We don't need to shield ourselves away. We should welcome all dreams, all beings. We need to stop shutting ourselves out or hiding ourselves. There's no danger in this world."

"You've perhaps forgotten Eve," Gil spoke up.

Now it was getting interesting. Galen's eyes flickered open again.

Peep scoffed, tutting. "That silly old woman?"

That wasn't at all something Peep would say.

"You put too much energy into fearing her," the cowgirl reasoned. "All she wants is love, friends; all the things normal people have. Is that so hard to understand?"

Gil sat up a little straighter. "It's not, albeit the Dreamcatcher isn't normal, and she isn't a person. After all, she is just a dream, like all of us."

One of Peep's eyes twitched, as if her demeanour was slipping. "She's not just a dream," scoffed the cowgirl. "She's much more powerful than we are. She can do a lot more than we can. Hell, she can create whatever she wants."

"Only because she killed her kin to do so."

Galen watched Ducky slowly roll away from the drama. She welcomed him over to her, and the two sat together just staring at Peep and Gil.

"*I don't trust her,*" Ducky whispered.

"*That makes two of us,*" Galen whispered back.

Peep stood up, placing her bowl to the side, and brushing all the creases in her clothes out so that they didn't exist anymore; a particular habit Galen had seen exhibited before in someone else. "I shouldn't be defending her, I know, but don't you envy her just a little?"

"No."

Again, Peep's face twitched. "Think of her power. Think of what kind of a leader she would be if dreams weren't so set in their ways. Every time a new dream pops up, they instantly know to hate her. Why does it have to be that way?"

"You instinctually detest what tries to kill you," reasoned Gil. "There is no defending Eve, or her actions. It's a pointless endeavour so I suggest you quieten down, eat your gruel and go to sleep like the rest of us."

Peep sat back down but threw a strop. "This wouldn't be happening if it wasn't for poppet."

Galen instantly sat up. "What did you say?"

Peep's mouth fell open. "I meant to say this wouldn't be happening if it wasn't for Galen, for you," she stammered, quickly trying to cover her tracks. "We're only in this position because of you. All she wants is you."

"Did you call me poppet?" Galen got to her feet and strode up to the fire. She wasn't angry, and she wasn't upset. All she felt was deep, dark worry that was starting to grow like a burning inferno inside of her. "No one calls me that but her."

"It was just a simple mistake," pleaded Peep.

Galen shook her head. "No." She glanced between both Gil and Peep, as if expecting back up from the old bear. When she got nothing, her attention fell upon Peep once more. "No, there is no such thing as a simple mistake in a dream." She marched forwards and fell to Peep's level, glaring deep within her eyes. When the cowgirl tried to look away, Galen held her face in place.

"Not too rough with her now, Galen," Gil cautioned. He too rose from his seat but did nothing to intervene between Galen and Peep. Instead, he kept Ducky far from the pair, and watched on like a benevolent father.

"Look at me," Galen demanded.

Peep's eyes were all over the place, but Galen could still see it lurking—the darkness.

"Look at me!"

Finally, Peep let out a sigh and looked into Galen's eyes. There they were. Clear as day. Eve's eyes staring back at her through Peep's. The Dreamcatcher had taken Peep over, was using her body as a vessel. Galen's heart smashed inside her chest.

She let go of Peep and staggered backwards, unsure of what she was supposed to do. "She's got her, Gil." Galen watched Gil near Peep, wandering cautiously and slowly. "She's got in her head."

The old bear scrutinised the cowgirl for himself, taking an extra minute to be sure before he retreated. "You're right," he surmised.

Both Galen and Ducky deflated, disappointed, and heartbroken.

"There's no getting her out of there, you know," Gil spoke. His voice wasn't directed at anyone in particular, but everyone listened to him. "You're stuck with her, Peep. I know you can hear me. I know you're still there. You know what we have to do." Gil summoned Galen forward, standing at a slant with his cane buried in the dirt. "She's got to go."

"*No…*" Galen whispered under her breath. She knew it to be true, but she just didn't want to admit it to herself. "No, there has to be something we can do."

Gil just shook his head. "Believe me when I say I've tried," was his response. "There is only one way. Ducky?"

"Yes, boss?"

"Get her before she runs off."

Ducky had never moved so quickly. In the blink of an eye he had charged forwards from where he was, scooted around the fire and managed to bind Peep's legs with his lead. A knot was tied tight so her legs were forced together, and she couldn't move. Every attempt at a run saw her face-plant into the ground.

"Here I was insistent that it was you, Duck," Gil chuckled wryly. He was sad too; he just didn't show it. The little beads he had for eyes were glistening with sorrow, but it was as he'd said. He'd put so many of his friends to death this surely couldn't bother him so much. To him, it was just a chore. "I knew one of us had to have picked up that parasite. It was impossible that we could've escaped freely. I didn't think it would be Peep."

"You don't have to do this, Gil!" Peep yelled. This time, Galen was sure that it was Peep who was speaking. The Dreamcatcher never begged, was never desperate. "You don't have to do this. I can just walk away. I can avoid you forever! I'll never lead her to you!"

Gil padded up to his old friend, staring down at her wistfully. "If only that was the case, my sweet," he cooed at her like a baby. "You've been by my side during these circumstances. These situations don't often end well if we don't end the problem straightaway. Letting you walk would be a grave mistake on my part, and I can't risk any harm coming to the rest of this place."

Peep was weeping, tears streamed down her plastic cheeks and stained her checked shirt. "It doesn't have to be this way this time. I'm different. I can prove to you that I'm different if you give me the chance to walk."

"And walk where, exactly?" Gil interrupted. "Your feet will lead you one way and one way only for the rest of your existence, and that way will always lead to Galen. So long as you live with that pest in your head, and so long as Galen is here, you are a problem and a threat. It's your time, Peep."

The cowgirl shuddered and sighed, resigned to her fate. Reluctantly, she nodded. She took the hat from her head and laid it in front of her, her bottom lip quivering all the while. Her chin crinkled as she sat bolt upright, facing her fate head on, though her eyes travelled slowly to Galen.

With a bent finger, Peep summoned Galen closer, and prompted her to lean in for a secret. "*Carve my name on the memorial,*" she whispered into Galen's ear. "*I don't want to be known as her slave. I want it known that she killed me.*" Abruptly, Peep held the back of Galen's head, knotting her fingers in her hair. "And I want it known that I'm every bit closer to getting my hands on you, poppet. I'm not far off. You won't evade me forever!"

Galen wrenched herself free of Peep's grip, tumbling through the dirt. She sat splayed resting on her palms, breathing as if the air had been forcefully pushed out of her lungs.

"Enough is enough." Gil took his stoker and set the end of it on fire but handed it over to Galen. When she didn't take it, he sighed his own sigh of frustration and forced her fingers around it. "I told you it'd be more than those gremlins you kill."

With the stoker in hand, Galen could only imagine what would happen to Peep. She sat herself up, crossing her legs beneath her and watching the flames climb closer to her hands. They were roaring, hungry, desperate to touch something or someone's skin. Galen straightened the stick and closed her eyes, turning her head away as she extended the stoker outward.

"I love you, poppet."

"No…"

Peep's sob could be heard. "You have to do this, Galen," spoke her real voice. "Do it for me and carve my name in that stone. Don't let me be remembered like this."

Galen couldn't listen to anymore. She thrust the stoker forward until she felt the end of it push against something. Her tears fell when she heard a little *poof,* like a candle being extinguished, but she knew that wasn't the case.

When she opened her eyes again, Galen saw the pile of ash that used to be Peep sitting before her. Just in front of the pile was Peep's hat, untouched but lonely. It didn't look right not being on her head. Galen dropped the stoker and pushed her hands against her face, sobbing uncontrollably. She felt Ducky and Gil move in around her to comfort her, but nothing did the trick. She'd just murdered her own friend. How could she ever say she was here to save dreams again? How could she ever say she wasn't the bad guy?

"It had to be done," Gil soothed. "You know it would've only escalated had we not done it sooner."

Galen wiped away her tears and stifled another wail, feeling it bundle up in her throat. "What do we do now? Eve knows where we are, where the new settlement will be."

"We'll stay here." Gil wandered away from Galen's side, taking up his seat in front of the fire again. The ash pile didn't seem to bother him, not even when it blew away with the wind. "I'll draw up a map, and we can start getting our people to their new homes."

"But we'll be under constant attack."

Gil glanced over his shoulder. "Not if we kill her before they get here."

That was the plan. The plan was to kill Eve before Gil's protected people arrived at the new settlement. It gave them not a lot of time, but the old bear was hopeful.

Galen wasn't.

She still felt torn. Her soul felt marked. She had killed her own friend. The Dreamcatcher had made her slaughter one of her own. Each and every heart string she had snapped one by one, leaving her heart dangling, and floating on its own. Gradually, it just sunk against her ribcage, dying and decaying.

Everyone was asleep but Galen. She couldn't rest. Even if sleep was an option, she wouldn't take it. The answer to all her problems had been brewing in her mind all night as she watched the stars pass overhead. Galen had to hand herself over. That was the only way.

She'd waited and waited for Ducky to finally go to sleep. It took no time at all for Gil, who lay bundled up closest to the now dead fire. Ducky, however, couldn't sleep. He'd parked himself next to Peep's hat and was constantly circling it. Every time Galen thought he'd drifted off, he'd move again, doing yet another lap of the site. This time, she was certain. His eyes were closed, and his head was hung, and he hadn't moved for what felt like a good half hour.

Slowly, Galen crept up to her feet. She didn't take a thing but kissed the top of Gil's and Ducky's head before she crept off into the wilderness.

Of course, they had to pick the only place that was surrounded by a thick forest. Galen didn't trust the sight of it when they'd first arrived, but now it brought peace to her. It was like her autumnal park, only withering and grey. She couldn't see much, but still wandered aimlessly through the trees trying to find a path.

Branches and twigs lashed at her face, one slicing against her skin so roughly that it split it open. Only a few drops of blood had leaked out so far, but it still stung. Galen kept her fingers pressed against the wound as she stumbled through a thicket of thistles, blooming beautifully in the moonlight. She had seen all these sights before. She'd wandered through many thickets and bushes and coppices. All the trees were the same and the birds and bats above never ceased. It was a loop, or at least felt like one. There was no end in sight, no end to Galen's walk and no end to her sudden act of heroism.

Suddenly, Galen stopped. She felt her bottom lip quiver again as Eve's name and face popped back into her mind. Her eyes lifted to the night sky; a sight that had always soothed her worries but now did nothing.

"I know you can hear me," she called out. She didn't shout or scream, neither did she whisper or murmur. Galen spoke as if the Dreamcatcher stood not three feet away. "I want to come with you. I've had enough. I want this to end."

Something shadowy crept closer and closer to Galen, appearing from out of nowhere. It was blanket of night sky, glistening with stars, or were they fireflies? Whatever it was, it moaned as it glided just above the ground.

"Take me wherever it is you want to take me and stop hurting all these dreams," Galen continued. From the corner of her eye, she watched the floating shadow draw closer. She was only disturbed by the sound that it made, wanting to get away as fast as she could. "You won't need them if you have me. Take me and let them all go. Let them live peacefully."

The shadow hovered just by Galen's side, and slowly began to unravel. Little by little, Galen could see more of what she was looking at. It started off as a bare leg, and then another, and worked upwards to reveal a midnight blue dress clad to a body that had perfect curves and sumptuous arcs, Eve's.

The Dreamcatcher appeared sleepy. Her eyes were heavy as she opened the cloak of stars that she wore to welcome Galen in. She didn't speak, but the look in her eyes was understanding. There was even a hint of regret, a hidden apology that would never be spoken into existence.

Galen took one step towards Eve and hesitated but was given no time to think. Before she even knew if this was the right thing to do or not, the Dreamcatcher's cloak leapt from her shoulders and coiled itself around Galen, squeezing and squeezing and squeezing until the world went black and Galen began to fall backwards into her own consciousness.

Galen didn't know where she was when her eyes opened. She didn't know what had happened to her. The trees that she had been stood in, the forest and the thickets, had all melted into nothingness. Her head was spinning, like she'd been sat on a merry-go-round for hours being spun at high speed. She could feel her pulse in her temple. Her vision failed her—all that she could see around her was outlined with a misty blackness that was slowly creeping inward. Was it possible to get a migraine whilst trapped in a dream?

"I wasn't sure how long you'd be out of it for," Eve's voice sounded from the doorway. She was just a figure against the doorframe, resting against it with her arms crossed, chewing on a fingernail nervously. "I wasn't sure if this was a trick, or if it was real."

Galen winced at every word the Dreamcatcher spoke. Though she wasn't shouting, Eve's words were echoing at twice the volume inside her head. She sat up from the soft, springy mattress she'd been lain on, still trying desperately to gather her surroundings. All she saw was a mix of grey hues blending together to make one awful colour. Her room was slightly circular, like that of a tower you might find a princess trapped in. Was it a castle? It could've been. If only her vision would clear up.

"You might feel woozy a little while longer," the Dreamcatcher advised. She came stalking into the room and, with her, brought the infernal sound of high heels colliding with polished floors. It was enough to drive Galen insane. "Your head will be heavy, and your eyes will feel weak. There's not much that can help it."

Ignoring every word Eve said, Galen tried to get to her feet. She felt them graze across the cold floors and pushed them flat, dropping all her weight onto her fragile and frail legs. At first, she wobbled. Her eyes were clear enough to see the Dreamcatcher dash forward to catch her, but no contact was made. For that, Galen was thankful. There was a bitter taste lying on her tongue. It could've been regret. It could've been hurt. It was more than likely anger.

Galen was enraged, but calm on the outside. Her demeanour was cool and collected as always, but on the inside she seethed. If her blood could boil, steam would be coming from her ears. Deep down, she knew this was the right thing to do. Still, it wasn't the ideal thing to do. She was alone now, in the Dreamcatcher's clutches with none of her friends to protect her.

"You should sit, poppet." Eve was like a frantic, worried mother. She padded closer and closer but would never touch Galen. Her arms would stretch out. Her fingers would be mere inches away, but no contact was ever made. "The last thing you need to do it hurt yourself."

"What do you care?" Galen grizzled. She ran her hands through her hair and pushed her fists into her eye sockets, desperate for her vision to clear a little. The throbbing in her temple was easing gradually, but not fast enough. This was the worst hangover she'd ever had. "You should just be happy I'm here now. You've finally gotten what you wanted."

The Dreamcatcher didn't refute that claim. "Whilst I can agree I'm happy you're with me, these aren't the circumstances I was expecting."

"Well," scoffed Galen, still wobbling about the place. "You know what they say. Expect the unexpected."

A little, delicate laugh filled the room. "And you are everything if not unpredictable." She plopped herself on the mattress where Galen had been lain, feet dangling just above the floor, and patted the space next to her for Galen to sit. "We've a little chat to have, I feel. Your sudden change of heart is slightly alarming to me. I'm not sure whether I should be worried or not."

"What is there to be worried about?" Galen did sit, but not because she was invited. She fell backwards, sitting down aggressively before flopping back to lay flat against the warm sheets. "Does it look like I can stage much of a retaliation? Much of anything? I can't see anything."

"That'll fade," the Dreamcatcher assured. She was twiddling her thumbs like a nervous schoolboy and daren't lift her eyes from her dangling feet. Something was off about her.

Galen propped herself up on her elbows and watched Eve closely. This was not the Dreamcatcher she knew. She wasn't dressed the same way. She didn't hold the same air about her. Her confidence was shattered. Where was all the glitz and the glamour? Where had her bravery gone? It didn't feel right.

"What's the matter with you?" Galen asked abruptly. "You're not yourself."

"I'm surprised you'd notice a feeble detail like that," was the Dreamcatcher's response. The mere mention of her not being herself shot life into her, and she shot to her feet to turn and face Galen with a gaze as heavy as normal. "Being with Gillette has made you like him. Stubborn. Blunt. I'm not sure we know one another like we used to."

Galen couldn't help but laugh. "Know each other?" she repeated. "When did we ever know one another, Eve? When was that? I must've missed it, because the only reason I know anything about you is due to literally anyone else apart from yourself. You told me nothing about you."

"You wouldn't have believed me even if I told you myself."

"That you wanted to kill me?" Galen blurted out. She saw the hurt instantly ripple in the Dreamcatcher's eyes. There was a hint of humanity there, though an overwhelming, dark anger was starting to cloud it. "You think I wouldn't have believed that if you didn't tell me?"

Eve's bottom lip quivered. "It has never been my intention to—"

"To cause me any harm," interjected Galen. "I know. I've listened to what you have said to me. You have hurt me, though. You've gone against everything you promised me."

"When?" the Dreamcatcher demanded to know.

Again, Galen could only laugh. "It's as if it hasn't been you this entire time. It's like you haven't been paying attention, and you've let someone else make my life torment. You crushed Gil's settlement, made me seem like the bad guy, tormented Ducky, possessed and then got Peep killed and you slaughtered hundreds of innocent dreams whilst they were resting because they didn't believe in you."

"They were killing me," Eve reasoned. "Those people were weakening me. They were draining me of everything I've ever had. I can't let some lowlifes take anything from me."

"And why did you have to do it through me? Why am I always the bad guy? Do you think if you turn everyone against me it'll push me into your arms?"

Eve's brow arched, and her lips pulled into a smug grin. "You're here now, aren't you?" She paced back and forth with her hands held behind her back, her long, blonde hair slung over one shoulder. The sheer elegance of the updo didn't match her pyjamas. The top half of her was ready for a ball. The bottom half was ready for bed. "What I did is done. I can't take it back. Do I understand why you're upset with me? Of course, I do. Do I owe you an explanation? More than likely. What I want to know, before I tell you anything, is why you gave yourself over to me so easily."

"You were hurting everyone around me because of me," Galen murmured gently to herself. "You were driving a wedge between Gil and his people. They shouldn't have to suffer for me. This was the easiest way out."

The Dreamcatcher stopped to peer out of a window. "Do you regret it?"

"No."

"Very well then," Eve conceded. She turned back to Galen, an uncertainty in her gaze. What could that have been for? "You've free roam of this place. I won't trap you in, though I will know if you try to leave me."

Galen nodded in agreement. She'd expected nothing less.

"I can give you a tour or you can wander around alone. It makes no difference to me." The Dreamcatcher edged closer and closer towards the door, her feet still making that hellish racket. "The people here have been advised to stay away from you, but I know your type. You're curious. You're going to want to talk to them. So be it."

"There are people here?"

Eve opened the door, throwing a glance over her shoulder. "Yes," was all she said. "Call for me any time, and I'll be there. For now, you should rest. It surprises me you haven't gone into a state of shock yet." She left after that. The door was closed but no lock sounded. It was surprisingly comforting to know she trusted Galen that much.

As soon as Eve disappeared, Galen's eyesight began to clear. She could see more and more around her, including the etchings in the wall that separated the grey hues into bricks. Her room was expansive, filled with oddities and antiquities. The bed was the biggest piece of furniture, boasting a super-king size bed with four posters and a canopy hanging down each side. It was almost romantic.

All the other furniture in the room looked rustic and chic. The wood was dark and distressed, some of it falling apart. The grand wardrobe had a wonky door but tons of character, towering above everything else in the room. Beneath the window was a trunk that belonged on the back of a pirate ship. Who knew what it was filled with? The rug stretched out on the floor was a deep blood red with emerald green spirals and gold embroidery to outline it all. By the door was a grandfather clock, ticking way, with the little door above the clock face just waiting to spring open.

There was only one window—a mere slit in the bricks just like castles had. Galen imagined that's where she was. If the Dreamcatcher was going to live anywhere, of course it would be a castle. Though, saying that, she'd seen outside of her room. The decoration didn't match Galen's room at all. It was gaudy. She could've been mistaken, had to be mistaken. When a few hours had passed, she'd investigate, but for now she needed to let Eve cool off.

What Galen noticed most was the massive portrait painting hanging on the wall. It was the only decoration apart from a few sconces to light the place. It sat in a heavy, ornate, golden frame that was straight from the renaissance period. The tones and hues were dark and melancholic, but it was clear to see who had been painted. Eve fit in with that time period, somehow. She was decked out in ladies' finery that included fur-lined cloaks and taut dresses that cinched in devastatingly painfully at the waist and flared out about the hips. That part couldn't be seen. The Dreamcatcher was sitting down, hands held in her lap and a fox sitting by her knees. She stared deadpan at the painter, no emotion on her face, no feeling in her eyes.

Galen stared up at the painting with her head cocked to the side, almost frowning. Her brows were knitted together, and her forehead was marked with creases. Who on earth could've painted this? There was no plaque, no card to state the artist. The piece wasn't even named. How strange.

"You would want to go outside, yes?"

Galen wasn't sure where the voice was coming from, but she hated it. It grated at her ears. She spun in circles trying to the find the person it belonged to, but now knew to look down. Meeting Ducky had taught her that. Her eyes fell to find a little dwarf with a beard longer than he was tall trailing behind him, glaring up at her.

"You would want to explore?"

The way he worded his sentences was confusing. His accent was even more off-putting. Galen found herself straining to understand him. She crouched, sitting on her haunches so their faces were level, her eyes roaming his tarnished, leathery skin.

"Miss Catcher said to go out is what you'd want."

"Why do you talk like that?" Galen murmured to herself. Oh, that was quite rude. She shook her head and dismissed her own comment, squeezing out an apologetic smile. "Miss Catcher, as you call her, offered me a tour. Has that invitation been revoked?"

The dwarf shifted his weight from foot to foot, wringing his hands together. "Miss Catcher said to be alone is what you need, but to go out is what you'd want. Corvid can ask again."

Corvid? Was that his name, or someone else? Galen had never been more confused in her life.

"Are you Corvid?"

"Corvid is what my name is, yes," he said happily. A little smile came to his chubby face, somehow lifting his mighty, bulbous cheeks. "Corvid will ask again. Miss Catcher would want to be asked."

Suddenly, with no provocation, the little dwarf burst into a cloud of black feathers that sent Galen reeling backwards. She tumbled over herself, landing on her front to watch as Corvid, the delightfully illiterate dwarf, flapped away as a beautiful, elegant raven. He squawked at her once and flew off down the corridors, chirping and singing to himself.

Galen decided this house was stranger than anything else she had ever encountered.

Corvid was gone for what felt like hours. Galen couldn't be sure. There were no working clocks in her dreams. She'd hoped the time on her grandfather clock would move, but the hands never went anywhere, and the little cuckoo bird never appeared once.

Enough was enough. Galen took exploring into her own hands.

There'd been no hints of squawking and no footsteps near her door. Galen had been left alone to wallow. Her sadness had built up the longer she'd been left to her own devices. She found herself missing Peep, missing Ducky, missing Gil. Her mind even wandered as far as Alden. That was a thought that stung her. She hoped so desperately that the forgotten dream had managed to survive. For Alden to die would've been an awful tragedy, and a massive loss.

The Dreamcatcher's lair was not the castle Galen had thought it was. Though her room was most definitely a tower, the rest of the house was not. It was huge, spiralling on forever. Some corridors led nowhere; others went into rooms that were completely unexplainable.

The corridor outside of Galen's room had an awful, gaudy 60s-style wallpaper lining it. Whilst there was no furniture, the place felt crowded by the equally as garish carpet lining the floor. Galen felt drunk stalking down it. What lay to the right of her room was still a mystery to her—she'd taken the left path, more entranced by the light glowing in the darkness. The light called to her, floating in the middle of oblivion that exploded to reveal an art deco stairwell with a spiral staircase leading down.

For such a small space, the decoration was beautiful. The stairs themselves were a sleek back, though the faces of them were white. Each wall was painted a dark grey, accented by an adjacent black wall, then a feature wall with the signature motifs of everything art deco. The strict geometrical designs were flawless. One wall was made up of just frames of the artwork, lit up from behind. Galen glided down them, running her hands down the squared banister rail, and ducking beneath the dangling chandelier whose teardrop crystals ran across the top of her scalp.

The illusion was gone once Galen stepped off the staircase. She stepped out of the 20s and into the modern era, with a minimalist lobby stretching out in front of her. Everything was white. The walls were white. The ceiling, although featuring crown moulding, was white. The curtains that hung either side of the white window frames were white. Every single piece of furniture was coated in a white varnish. The only saving grace was the wooden floors, though they were awfully pale.

Galen wandered through the lobby quickly, shielding her eyes. She thought for a second, she could feel her headache returning to her. God, how she hated things so bright and white. It reminded her of Dr Evergreen's office, and of how everyone had thought her to be crazy.

Her feet led her to a Mediterranean living room, where the Dreamcatcher was warming her hands by a grand, open pit fireplace. She didn't seem to notice Galen's arrival, either that or she was giving Galen time to admire the furniture and the artistry.

"Your house is strange," Galen announced after taking in the bright splashes of orange, yellow and red. It was all set against a creamy beige brick and a tan tiled floor that meshed beautifully together. It made Galen feel like a wealthy Contessa. "No room is the same."

"Do you like it?"

Galen wandered further in, slipping past low-set couches and an even lower coffee table adorned with books and trinkets. "I'm not sure what to think of it."

The Dreamcatcher didn't reply. She didn't turn. Warming her hands was on the top of her list of priorities. She had changed though. Her outfit wasn't the same. Her pyjamas were gone, replaced by that of slacks and a loose-fitting, billowy blouse that cut off at her mid-drift, showing off a muscly back and a toned stomach. Her slacks were orange in colour, with a belt that was leathery brown strapped so tightly it must've made her waist at least four inches smaller. On her feet were bright yellow shoes, and in her hair was a red flower. Galen couldn't tell which flower from how far away she was, but she could smell it.

"Your little..." Galen fought for words, trying to describe Corvid as nicely as possible, "friend, came for me. He never came back."

"You're talking about Corvid, I presume?"

Galen sat herself down in an armchair, her body sighing with relief at the comfort it provided. "I am. Strange little thing. He said that he would come back once speaking to you. He never did."

"He spoke with me."

"And?"

The Dreamcatcher threw a glance over her shoulder to reveal thick black eyeliner and a pop of a red lip. "And what? He was scolded for bothering you when he had been told not to. Sent off to his rooms where he couldn't disgust you any further."

"He didn't disgust me." Galen found herself defending the creature. She pitied him. She didn't want Eve to harm him in any way because of her actions. "He was..."

"Off-putting?"

"Unusual," Galen corrected, "but he didn't disgust me. I waited for him for what felt like hours. I got worried."

Dark, sultry laughter came from the Dreamcatcher. "Worried? For that thing? No, you shouldn't waste good energy on Corvid. No one else has or does. Why should you?" She finally moved away from the fire and strolled leisurely about the room, admiring the décor. "He did mention you were eager for me to give you a tour of this place."

"I did mention that, but there's no point now. I've seen it all."

"You've seen nowhere near what this place has to offer," the Dreamcatcher replied, feigning her offense. She sat in a chair opposite Galen, lounging across a sofa and propping her feet up on one of the armrests. "I'll tell you, poppet, that I'm surprised to see you out of your room. I thought for sure you'd avoid me at all costs. I've played the long game before, though this game I'm playing with you seems to have different rules."

Galen eased further into her chair. "I got sad."

"Sad?" Eve suddenly perked up. "Whyever were you sad? Can I help you at all? I can offer you a range of teas. The boys here know how to make all sorts. They're criminally underpaid for the services they supply."

Galen didn't like the sound of that. "I'll be fine without a cup of tea," she said somewhat sarcastically. "I wanted to see you because I want to talk with you."

"I love a good chat."

"You may not like this one."

Eve's hopeful, cheery smile fell.

Galen sat forwards, refusing to be sucked in by the comfort of the chair. "I want you to be honest with me." She watched the Dreamcatcher's eyes roll. "I know everything about you now, so you've nothing to hide from me. I just want you to be truthful with me. That's all I ask."

"That's all you ask?" Eve repeated, exasperated. "Do you understand how damaging the truth is? I'd rather not think of it."

"Talk to me, Eve."

The Dreamcatcher pouted like a child wanting to go home. "Fine," she spat. She sat herself up and shoved her feet against the ground. It was a miracle the heels of her shoes didn't impale either the floor or her feet. "You know, poppet, I thought you were a lot more fun when I met you."

Galen held up her hand, silencing Eve. "Enough of that," she commanded. "I want you to tell me your ambitions, your intentions. You keep telling me what you intend not to do, but I want to know what you do intend to do."

"Curious little thing, aren't you? Well, I suppose there's no harm in it now that you're here." Eve lounged back again, lifting a hand. As her hand rose, the lights in the room dimmed, and candles suddenly sat ablaze. The atmosphere became a lot more intense, a lot more intimate, a lot more romantic. "My intentions are clear, and they are simple; I want what was promised to me at my inception."

"Which was?"

"An existence."

Ah, so it was true. At least Gil hadn't lied to Galen about that part.

Eve shifted a little, leaning against the arm rest and playing with a strand of her hair that had come loose. "When I was created, I was under the impression I was as flesh and blood as any human. I thought I was real. I thought this world was real. It was amazing. Come to find out, none of it was true. My creator was a liar, a serial liar at that. I'm just a…experiment, with no existence, no heart, no real life at all."

Galen listened in eagerly. This was a story she'd heard, but not from the Dreamcatcher's lips.

"At first, my intention was to kill my creator, Stefan." Eve picked dirt out of her nails, completely disinterested. "After a while, I began to forgive him for what he'd done to me. I thought he'd stay with me, but he thought me a monster. He became frightened of me, like I'd do him harm. I didn't understand. I would follow him everywhere, beg for him to listen to me until…he just disappeared." The Dreamcatcher perked up a little, her eyes glassing over with confusion and with hurt. "He left me by myself. I didn't know where he'd gone. I didn't know what I'd done to drive him away, but he was gone. A few days later, I felt a rush come over me. I felt myself surge with power. I felt energised, renewed, real. Ash fell from the sky as if it had been just floating there the entire time, and that's when I realised that ash was him. The dream had crushed him."

She couldn't be blamed for her intentions, Galen kept telling herself. Eve wasn't to blame. After all, all she wanted was what was promised to her. That was the most human thing about her.

"Above all else, I want to be free of this world, be a part of your world," the Dreamcatcher sighed suddenly. She returned to her nails, this time running her fingertips across each one to change the colour of them with no varnish and no brush. "I want to be a real person. That's all I've ever cared about."

"I refuse to believe you were cold to others to begin with," Galen interrupted. "You had to have clung to some of the dreams here."

Eve's shoulders lilted. "At the beginning, they were very understanding. Every dream wants to be real, after all. I just didn't understand why they didn't do anything about it. To be honest, I didn't know how to do anything about it until Stefan died, and then it became glaringly obvious."

"So, you just thought to yourself that you'd slaughter your way through every dream to get what you wanted?"

"Not at first," Eve said again. "Killing someone or something was…unheard of to me. It was unspeakable. No matter what I was offered, back then, I thought I was righteous enough not to hurt a single thing." Her eyes became hazy, and her mouth fell in the corner. She was starting to live out her past, and it was haunting her. "After Stefan, it took a while for me to pluck up the courage to just end another dream here. I didn't how to. I found myself at a sanctuary for old, forgotten dreams that were decaying, and became attached to one person there. His name was Erik. I didn't know much about him except that he was dying, so I just waited. I figured I would stay in that place forever, absorbing all the old dreams' souls, however…"

Galen was right on the edge of her seat.

"The thing about forgotten dreams is that they're incredibly weak," the Dreamcatcher explained. "There's no power in them, and power is what I need. When Erik died, it did barely anything for me, and I realised there was no use in me staying at that place. I had to find a way to crush dreams and absorb them and, eventually, I did."

"How?"

Eve held up a finger and smirked a cheeky smile. "It's my turn to ask a question," she delightfully cheered. She mocked the way that Galen sat, right on the edge of her seat with her arms crossed over her lap. "What are your ambitions, poppet? What do you see for yourself?"

The question caught Galen off-guard. "My only ambition is to wake up."

"That can't be."

"I only want to wake up, and I know what I have to do in order to achieve my ambitions, not that I like it much." Galen pulled her eyes away from Eve. Despite all the horrid things the Dreamcatcher had done, Galen felt attached to her. Something connected her to Eve, and it was the last thing keeping her from hating the creature. "You have to go so I can wake up. You know that."

Eve smiled wryly. "I know that," she repeated softly. "You're a contender, you know. To think that I've had to jump from host to host just to match the power you have now is incredible. Years ago, I never would've been able to defeat you. You'd have flicked me from your mind like a bug off your arm."

Galen was flattered.

"Now, though, I think you'll struggle." Eve climbed to her feet and began to pace. She wandered through the cluttered furniture to the wall that was all windows, looking out upon an infinity pool glistening in the sun. "I'm not an easy fight. The people you are surrounded by are no match for me. I find it curious how you recruited a teddy bear and a toy duck to protect you. Why not real people?"

"I had a real person." Galen remembered Alden, and her calm demeanour started to sour. "You made sure to turn that one person against me and kill off all their friends."

The Dreamcatcher hung her head. "If I have to hear another word about Alden" she groaned.

"You know her?"

"Know her?" Eve laughed hysterically; a hand pushed against her chest. It wasn't real laughter. There was something so fake about it, something so sarcastic and bitter. Was this the jealousy that Alden had been talking about? "Galen, my sweet, Alden has been in my face since she was created! God, how I hate her. I had to sit by and watch every bloody dream she wormed herself into! It was torture! She was growing stronger and stronger whilst I had to sit by in the shadows, feeding off dreams from when you were a baby!" Exhausted from her outburst, the Dreamcatcher rested against the edge of the fireplace, conjuring up a glass of wine to cool her temper. "I don't know what you see in her, Galen. I don't like her. Not one bit."

That was a curious remark.

"Why did you spare her?" Galen asked. Should she have asked that? Maybe Eve didn't know that Alden wasn't dead. Although, there could've been a reason she was kept alive. "Why kill off everyone else but her?"

"As evil as I am, and as much as I hate her," Eve let go of a long sigh that she'd been holding in for a while, "I couldn't stand to hurt you like that. I knew how much she meant to you. You'd never come to me if Alden died. You'd never forgive me."

Galen was taken aback. Eve had some sort of sympathy in her. That was a miracle! Why couldn't she have shown that same care when it came to Peep? She glided around the edge of the coffee table, knocking off one of the trinkets. She watched with a little gasp as it jumped straight back up and fixed itself, sitting right back in the same spot that it had been in before.

"It's your turn to ask a question," the Dreamcatcher growled.

Standing by Eve's side, drinking in the same view, Galen sucked in her cheeks. "What's your purpose?"

The Dreamcatcher began to laugh a deep, hoarse, throaty laugh. "You've definitely been spending too much time with Gillette." She turned for a minute, eyes burning deep into Galen's soul. "Next question."

Galen held her hands up in defeat. "What is something you want, but have never had?"

"Love."

That was a quick answer.

"I want to be loved, like other dreams are," Eve replied. "Somehow, they manage to find love amongst themselves. Two dreams can fall in love and live as close a life to the humans as possible. Yet, somehow, I haven't found anyone for me."

"You could surely create someone for yourself."

Once more, the Dreamcatcher's shoulders lilted. "Where is the fun in that? There should be someone already here, waiting for me, but there isn't. Also, you've seen what happens to the people I create. You saw Corvid with your own eyes. They feel nothing, and they're illiterate. The two worst sins someone can commit."

Galen couldn't help but chuckle slightly. "He does speak strange."

"There's always a flaw with them!" the Dreamcatcher suddenly burst. Galen seemed to have caught her out on a topic she was passionate about—herself. "Some of them can't talk right. Others are deaf or blind or dumb. Some don't have arms or legs, or have wings, or weird ears and teeth. I'm the most powerful dream in this world and yet I can't make a person be normal." She sat herself down on the sofa again, raking her hands through her hair. "How could I make someone normal when I'm not normal?" she muttered to herself.

Though the words were quiet, Galen still picked up on them. "You're not normal?" She followed the Dreamcatcher's footprints almost step for step, until only the coffee table separated them. "What do you mean?"

"I was created with a flaw. A massive flaw that eats away at me constantly because it's such a normal habit, an instinct, that I'm not able to perform."

"What are you talking about?"

Eve was about to explode. "I've never been touched!" she roared. She threw herself to her feet, tossing the coffee table to the other side of the room by just flicking it with the tips of her fingers. "No one has ever touched me! I haven't been hugged! I've never had someone hold my hand! I've never felt someone's fingers through my hair! None of it! I've never had any of it!"

"That's why…" Galen recalled all the times Eve had gone to touch her but had become so deathly scared of doing so. "That's why you've been so scared of touching me. That's why you always pull your hand away."

"I don't know what to expect." Eve stared up at Galen, looking her weakest. "I don't know if it'll hurt, or if it'll work at all. The little minions I've created tend to just…reach right through me. I don't know who or what the problem is, and I'm too scared to find out."

Galen's mind began to whir. "I can help you with that."

Eve scoffed.

"I'm serious," Galen insisted. She trotted past the Dreamcatcher's legs and sat next to her, staring up at her. "I can help with that. I can assure you it doesn't hurt unless I punch you in the face."

The Dreamcatcher's eyes hardened, her lips peeling back from her gums just a touch. "Why would you help me?"

"A deal for a deal."

"Ah, of course." Eve shook her head. "I'm starting to wonder if that sounds worth it."

Galen felt like she was losing the Dreamcatcher. "I do you a favour, you do me a favour. It's an honest transaction."

"You'll ask me to let you go," Eve surmised. "Or you'll ask me to wake you up and leave your mind. I'm not that stupid. I've done these deals before and have them backfire into my face."

"I don't want that."

The Dreamcatcher's brow lifted. "Then what?"

Galen thought on it. She could ask for anything. Figuring out what was the hard part. The Dreamcatcher was the most powerful dream, as she kept boasting, and was able to conjure up whatever she wanted, but so was Galen. They were completely matched up, so there was nothing truly that Galen could ask for to achieve the advantage. One thing sprung to mind, however. It kept repeating until Galen listened to it, and felt the words weigh down her tongue before she spoke.

"No more possessing people," Galen instructed. "And no more…putting ideas into my head. It's creepy and it's invasive."

Eve took a moment to think, simply shrugging it off. "Done. Only that in exchange for some affection?"

"There's nothing else I can ask for." Galen ran her hands down the front of her jeans and stared deeply into Eve's topaz eyes. She wondered what Eve's skin would feel like. It looked soft, like velvet, but imagined it would be as cold as ice. "Are you ready?"

"As ready as I can be," replied the Dreamcatcher. She shifted her body, so she too faced Galen, though there was still a space between them. The atoms that separated them trembled and vibrated with both excitement and fear. They became squeezed closer and closer together and Galen leant in, extending an arm forwards and letting her open palm hover next to Eve's cheek.

Galen hesitated, but only because she watched the Dreamcatcher flinch. She knew a wince when she saw one. Her fingers trembled, her fingertips accidentally stirring some strands of Eve's hair, but nothing more. With a deep breath in, and then a slow exhale, Galen tensed her muscles and moved her hand closer. Just lightly did the surface of the Dreamcatcher's cheek graze against Galen's palm. It was barely a touch, but Galen felt it. She wondered if Eve had also. There was no reaction on the Dreamcatcher's face so, with a hand that now shook, Galen placed her palm against Eve's face and swiped her thumb across her cheek to a chorus of sighs.

She was right. The Dreamcatcher's skin was deathly cold, but still soft. She could feel the powder that Eve had dusted on her face come away with her fingers. Galen even caught a tear. Eve was crying. The look in her eyes was one of love, one of gratitude, one of adoration. She even lifted her own hand to cover Galen's, intertwining her fingers slowly as if she didn't know how to do it.

Galen didn't know what to say. The connection she felt to Eve only strengthened as she swiped away more and more tears. She couldn't bring herself to glance away but didn't have to.

Though it felt like an eternity had passed, Eve wrenched away from Galen's hand after a few seconds. She threw herself to her feet, backing away and tripping over furniture. Her face had turned a bright shade of red, and a golden aura had begun to surround her being. When she was at the doors, the Dreamcatcher glanced at Galen for a split second before throwing the door open and bellowing down it.

"Corvid!"

"Are you alright?" Galen got to her feet and tried to move but was frozen to the spot as the Dreamcatcher threw out a hand directed at her. She was held in place, unable to move and unable to talk. Great. Not this again.

"Corvid!"

"Miss Catcher would like to talk to Corvid?" the little dwarf appeared, still shaking off a few feathers. It was very evident he'd flown in from his coop, either that or he'd just woken up from slumber.

Eve flapped her hand in Galen's direction, obviously flustered. "Take her back to her room."

Corvid glanced at Galen, and then at Eve. "Miss Catcher would like to have tea?"

"Just take her back!" Eve roared.

Those were the last words Galen heard. The next thing she knew, Corvid had burst into feathers again and was soaring towards her, massive wings elongated at his sides. They were much larger than that of a raven's, and encased her as he collided with her, dropping her back into her room, and then disappearing again without even so much as a goodbye.

Chapter Seven

Galen's chess game with Corvid was disrupted rudely by the thudding of sudden loud music. Her king piece fell, toppling to the ground much to the delight of the strange little dwarf.

"You have relinquished the win to Corvid!" he cheered, throwing his stubby arms up in the air.

Galen wasn't about to take his victory away from him. "How you keep beating me is beyond me."

"Smart is what Corvid is, yes?" he replied happily. His bulbous cheeks turned bright pink with pure delight as he picked up the pieces and reorganised them. "You would want to learn to hide your plays, Miss Poppet."

He'd taken to calling Galen that. He must've heard Eve use that name with her. Not once had he called her by her name in the times that he'd come to play chess. It was always Miss Poppet, nothing different. Saying that, he always referred to Eve as Miss Catcher. Did he think that was her last name? Maybe it was. Galen had never thought to ask.

"Is Eve throwing a party tonight?" Galen asked the dwarf. She got up and wandered away from the chessboard on the floor, opening her door and peering out of it. Though she was free to leave, she felt banished to her tower by the Dreamcatcher. "It sounds like she has guests over."

"Miss Catcher would like you to go see her, Miss Poppet."

Galen met the dwarf's eyes as she glanced over her shoulder. "She wants to see me?"

"Miss Catcher wouldn't like to feel awkward after the previous meeting. Miss Catcher would want to make things better." He stood up abruptly, dusting himself off as if Galen's floor was incredibly dirty. A little black aura began to vibrate and thrum around him, a sign he was about to burst into feathers. "Relay Miss Catcher's invitation is what Corvid should have done but enticed by chess Corvid was." He burst into feathers abruptly but, as soon as the feathers began to float in the air, he reappeared with a bundle of clothes in his short arms and laid them to rest on the end of Galen's bed. "Miss Catcher would want you to wear this garment. Miss Poppet wouldn't want to stand out in the ball."

A ball?

"The ballroom is where Miss Poppet would need to be once changed, yes?" he asked, or did he ask? The way he spoke messed with Galen's head. Half of the reason she played chess with him so much was to understand his dialect, but it hadn't been any help. "Looking forward to seeing Miss Poppet there is what Corvid is feeling." Again, he burst into feathers, this time disappearing for good. He left a little pile of black feathers on Galen's floor, but that was all that remained of him.

Confused, Galen shut her door and wandered to the clothes that Corvid had lain out for her, that Eve had picked out for her. She was half expecting to find a dress. That was her worst nightmare. If a dress lay before her, she'd hide herself away in her tower and refuse to come out. Only her mother would try to force her into dresses, and it never went well. Though, saying that, the last thing Galen wanted to do was offend or insult the Dreamcatcher.

To her surprise, it was a pantsuit. It looked almost identical to the one that Alden had been wearing. Galen scooped it up in her hands and held the trousers in front of her, admiring the beauty of the fabric. She'd expected there to be silk or lace adorning it, but it was made from the softest velvet. It was a light grey in colour, Galen's favourite, with little flecks of white and black adorned in the fabric. The shirt she had was just plain white, with golden buttons that reflected in the dimmest of light. The sleeves fell to Galen's elbows, and the bodice was tight to her ribcage.

A mask tumbled out from the bundle too, that of the top half of a fox's face. It was bright orange with white stripes along the sides of its snout, and a small, black button nose to round it off. Its ears stood up tall, alert, listening. Galen started to see now what kind of ball this was.

Galen put it all on, if not to amuse herself. She turned back and forth in the mirror, admiring how she looked. How had the Dreamcatcher gotten her exact measurements? She'd never fit into clothes like this. They hugged her tight, but not too tightly. They fit perfectly. Even the shoes had glided onto her feet with ease and didn't squeeze her feet no matter how hard she pulled on the laces.

The jewellery she had—a gold necklace, three gold rings and bracelets of rose gold and yellow gold—tied the whole thing together. The Dreamcatcher knew exactly her tastes and what she would want. The fox mask, however, was confusing. Was that how Eve saw her? She put in on anyway, placing it over her eyes and staring at her reflection. Galen didn't know the person staring back at her. She didn't recognise herself at all. This was the person that she had once wanted to be, and secretly still yearned to be. The elegance and the glamour of it all was thrilling. It made Galen feel like a different person.

It distracted her.

Galen did as Corvid had told her to. She wandered throughout the hallways, down those beautiful art deco stairs and past the Mediterranean lounge where the Dreamcatcher had seen her last. The music called to her, leading her down the winding corridors and past rooms that caught her eyes, beckoning her closer to the ballroom. It thrummed. Whether it was the beating of drums or the pounding of footsteps, Galen was enthralled by it. A smile had crept across her face, a secret happiness blooming within her. So, this was what an apology was supposed to be. Galen could get used to this.

Throwing open the massive doors to the hall, Galen lost her breath once her eyes lay on the scene playing out in front of her. The room was dark, eerily so, only lit up by that of hundreds upon thousands of burning candles placed in clusters all about the hall. They sat in the alcoves, had been piled upon tables, and littered the top of the grandest fireplace that Galen had even seen. A fire roared within its mouth, with no guard to keep it contained. Elegant ladies wandered by it with no fear that the tails of their dresses would catch fire.

On every wall and plastered across the ceiling were renaissance-style paintings—a common trend throughout Eve's lairs. That was the only constant about the entire house. They were decadent, but still dark. They depicted great lords and ladies drinking and dancing and lusting after one another, much like what was happening in front of Galen's eyes. All the guests had been painted down in infamy, though no one else but her seemed to notice.

Opposite her, at the far back of the hall, was a grand staircase leading up to balconies that looked over the entirety of the floor below. Pillars of gold stretched upwards against the wall either side of the crimson carpeted marble steps, etched with cream details of filigree and latticework. An archway separated the stairs from the balconies, and almost hid another staircase off to the left-hand side. Where did that lead to?

Galen stepped foot onto the swirling marble floor but felt out of place. Everyone around her wore dresses that she only saw appear on red carpet events or worn on catwalks and runways. They were so fashionable, so beautiful. The one thing Galen couldn't get out of her mind was where they'd come from. Where could they have all been hiding? Were they figments of her imagination? Had she dreamt of them? Were they the people to the last party the Dreamcatcher had thrown?

Once inside, Galen's eyes roamed for that man that had warned her about Eve. She didn't really expect to see him. The Dreamcatcher surely wouldn't have kept him around after his betrayal. If she had, she must've forgotten about him. Galen kept looking for him anyway, snagging a flute of blood-red wine from a passing waiter's tray and holding it with just the tips of her fingers.

She was trapped amongst of sea of animals. It was like a jungle spreading out around her. The people, though elegantly dressed, took after the mask of their choice. Most people eyed her fox mask with intrigue, though others were quick to shoo her away. In some people's eyes, she was a beautiful creature, stunning and wild. In others, she was vermin, a scavenger, an opportunist. Those that frowned at her weren't much better off. They wore masks of vultures, of hyenas, of rats. She saw one boy with the mask of a praying mantis shuffling by, trying to keep himself hidden.

The people that wanted to stand out were lions and tigers and panthers. Men as tall as trees with rippling muscles and huge arms were decorated as the beasts that they truly were. They were as arrogant and as mighty as the high and proud lions of the Savannah. The women on their arms were lionesses in their own right, beautiful and graceful—more powerful than their male counterparts.

There were monkeys, parrots, elephants, eagles, dogs, crocodiles, bears, deer, antelope all alike. Galen spotted giraffes and coyotes, zebras and badgers, bison and kingfishers, seals, and elks. Only a handful of people wore the same kind of mask, and those people never once separated. She'd stayed away from the clans of lions, not liking the arrogance that radiated off them. The group of flamingos had been eager to call her over, desperately wanting to chat and to gossip. She'd gone to them, but they'd not said a word. Their faces expressed their happiness and their glee as they huddled around her and protected her, suddenly transporting her across the hall, keeping her safe amongst their ranks.

Jaguars watched her closely, their eyes scrutinising and hungry. A koala looked on unbothered. They gave her a glance but were too keen on finishing their salad to pay her any mind. A lemur laughed as she passed by, scared off by the male lynx that came to lay claim to the female puma just minding her own business.

Before Galen knew it, she was thrust from the flock of flamingos and left by herself by the steps leading upwards. Should she have been climbing them? Whatever lay up there frightened Galen. There weren't as many candles—they'd probably run out. The sheer amount clustered up on the sides of the steps was more than Galen had ever seen. She just stood and waited, sipping from her wine, and admiring the crowds as they bustled together, coexisting just for one night.

"You look more dashing in that than I had previously imagined." Eve's voice carried through the air like sweet nectar.

Galen turned her head and stared back up the staircase, seeing the Dreamcatcher, decked out in a suit almost the same as Galen's and a wolf's mask, standing at the very top. She said nothing, but eyed Eve blatantly. There was no helping it. Every time Eve dressed up; she outdid herself. Her clothes were the same as Galen's, but much more feminine. Everything flowed much more softly and wasn't so tight or restricting. She wore no waistcoat, but had a thick belt strapped about her waist to keep her billowing blouse about her body. On her feet were not smart shoes like Galen's, but heels. Those dreaded heels, higher than Galen had seen before. Every time they got higher and higher by an inch or two. It was a wonder she was able to walk at all.

Still, the Dreamcatcher glided down the staircase with ease, running a hand down the polished handrail. "Do you like the mask I picked out for you?"

"I, uhm," Galen stuttered. She backed up a few paces as the Dreamcatcher descended the steps and stood by her side, still in awe. The cat had truly caught her tongue. "I didn't understand it at first."

"You're cunning," Eve replied quickly. She caught a waiter passing by and snatched a champagne flute from his tray, sending him away with a little flicker of her fingers. Galen had never seen someone run so fast before. "You're swift, quick-witted and opportunistic."

Galen cocked her head at an angle. "I'm not sure whether I should be offended or not."

"I mean no offense!" the Dreamcatcher laughed sultrily. She put a hand on Galen's shoulder, touching her for the first time ever. There was no reaction, though. Could she not feel it through her thick, heavy gloves? "Take it as a compliment, my sweet. I would never do you wrong. If I wanted to offend you, I would've given you the mask of a dung beetle, or something else just as ridiculous." She took Galen's arm, despite it not being offered, and led her through the sea of people. Unsurprisingly, they all parted for her without knowing it, moving both unwillingly and unknowingly out of her way.

"You gave yourself a wolf," Galen pointed out. "Any particular reason for that?"

The Dreamcatcher lilted her shoulders. "I didn't think a spider, or a snake was as pretty to look at. Plus, you and I make a nice little pair this way. We're both hunters one way or another."

"You banished me to my tower a few days ago, only now to talk to me as if nothing ever happened." Galen watched Eve's cheery disposition fall away from her to reveal a sour and embarrassed one. "Now, you touch me freely and take my arm and charm me half to death. The sudden switch in you is alarming."

"Consider this my apology for my outburst those days ago," said the Dreamcatcher slowly. She picked her words carefully and washed them back down her throat with a hearty sip of her wine. "I don't like to leave things awkwardly or have unspoken feelings hanging in the air. And as for touching you…" There was a moment when Eve didn't say anything. She stared across her hall, across the sea of people, and winced just slightly, words tumbling around her brain. "It seems that I underestimated my flaw. I can't feel you, poppet. Only when you touch me does that…rush hit me, and it hit me like a ton of bricks. I couldn't deal with it. I didn't know what to do with all that emotion, and it's something I would rather not experience again for the meantime. I already have a plateful of distractions in front of me, I don't need a main course."

Ah, so it was a distraction. Galen couldn't help but smirk. She kept that tidbit of information smuggled away in the back of her mind, sliding her arm free of the Dreamcatcher.

"I'm happy you joined in the fun." Eve was quick to change the subject, quick to divert back to her cheeriness and her happiness. The rosiness reappeared in her cheeks, but there was still something unsaid lingering in her eyes. "I wouldn't have wanted this all to go to waste."

"Who are these people?" Galen was watching the crowd move as one, like a wave in the sea, bobbing and falling together. They all danced around each other. Her eyes were set on a jackal and a red panda as they danced together, spinning one another around to the beat of the music. "What gives you both the power and the right to conjure up partygoers whenever you please to?"

The Dreamcatcher's face became taut with smugness. "These are my people," she explained. She leant against the wall by the fireplace, letting the heat of the flames warm her. "These are the people that have sense, that believe in me, truly. They are the reason I'm still alive."

Her people?

"To them, I'm a monarch—royalty, if you will," the Dreamcatcher went on. "They want to be real too. They share my passion for taking what is rightfully mine."

"They serve you?"

Eve nodded gleefully. "They live under me. There is a whole kingdom where they are allowed to live unchallenged and free in their ways. They want to believe in me, they want to fuel me so that, in time, I can give them the life they have always wanted."

Galen's heart dropped to her feet. So, this was what this was all about? Gil had never mentioned Eve's own kingdom. Perhaps the bear didn't know. He needed to know, though. This was something that couldn't be glossed over. If the rest of the dreams were unaware that the Dreamcatcher had her own army, they were walking into a fight that would be like slaughtering fish in a barrel.

"Come now, poppet," Eve soothed, running a finger across Galen's jawline. She just hated that Galen wasn't looking at her, favouring her guests over her. "They're nothing to be afraid of. They'd never hurt you. They celebrate you being here."

"When did this happen?" murmured Galen under her breath.

The Dreamcatcher pushed off the wall. "What do you mean, my sweet?"

"This is…does anyone know?"

"Know what?"

Galen faced the Dreamcatcher, a knot of fear building in her throat. "Does anyone know that all these people are here?"

Eve's eyes were once more cast out into the ocean of her minions, but she just shrugged. "No one has thought to ask, poppet. They're too concerned with themselves. The one thing you'll find out very quickly about dreams is that they are self-centred. They don't want to know about you, or about me. They just want to know about themselves, and what concerns them."

"Gil has to have figured this out by now."

"Gillette," the Dreamcatcher took a swig of her drink, "is the worst offender of them all. There's not been a single minute that he's been alive where he has cared for anyone more than himself. That old bear is not in your best interests, Galen."

Galen wrenched away from Eve. "But you are?"

Annoyed, the Dreamcatcher rolled her eyes. "Compare the two of us for a second, if you would," she grizzled. She emptied the rest of her flute and discarded it on a passing tray that didn't even look to be attached to anyone's hand. "Do you think that we both care for you the same amount? Do you think that he wants to give you a life you can live and be truly happy within? What has he told you will happen to you if you fail in your mission to oust me? What has he promised you?"

"He hasn't promised me anything."

"And what do you think I would give you?"

Galen's brows furrowed. "You'd kill me."

"You would still be here, poppet! You wouldn't go anywhere! Maybe outside of this world you would die, but here you would thrive. You could be whatever you wanted. Be the opportunist I know that you are, Galen. Don't let old, tired dreams weigh you down."

"Are you not just that?"

Eve stiffened. "What?" she said under her breath.

Galen knew she'd made a mistake as soon as she'd opened her mouth. "Are you not a tired, old dream?" She began to back away instinctually. The music that had been playing cut suddenly, but it wasn't silent in the hall. All the people around her began to talk, to chatter amongst themselves. They turned on her.

"I may be an old dream, Galen," the Dreamcatcher followed Galen, taking a step forwards for every one that Galen took backwards, "but I am not tired. You think that Gillette and I share any sort of similarities? You think that we hold any of the same values? Open your eyes, Galen! See what is really stood in front of you! You know, deep down, that saving him was not the only reason you came to me."

"Did I strike a nerve with you, Eve?" Galen chuckled nervously to herself. She found herself in the centre of the ballroom with the guests lined up around the sides. The flock of flamingos that had escorted her to the Dreamcatcher were behind her, looking worried, breathing heavily. "I didn't mean to upset you."

The Dreamcatcher scoffed. "Well, you did. It's like you don't see what I do for you."

"You want to kill me, Eve. I don't see that as something good."

"He has put that picture in your head!" the Dreamcatcher roared. Her voice had never been so loud. Some of the guests flinched, and others ducked down for their lives. "He has poisoned your mind! He's turned you against me with every minute he's had with you!" She came forwards, putting one, long leg in front of the other and gliding across the marble floors, stalking her prey. "If you'd have seen sense at the beginning; if you had only opened your eyes you would've known he was no good for you! If you'd had just come with me, you would've seen!"

In pure anger, the Dreamcatcher summoned one of her waiters forward. She was doing her best to calm herself, though couldn't do it without a drink. Ordering him to stay still whilst she snatched flute after flute from his tray, Eve chugged the wine relentlessly. She didn't care that he was shaking in his boots. She didn't care that tears were visibly streaming from his eyes. All she wanted was the drink.

When the tray was empty, the Dreamcatcher let out a sigh that was sharp and curt. "I don't want to kill you, Galen," was what she said. Her tone was so dull, so monotonous. All that anger and rage had suddenly dissipated. "I don't want this to end in death. I never have. That has never been my intention." She clapped her hands together and, instantly, the party started up again. Music filled the hall, and the people began to dance, uncaring that their leader had almost just bitten all their heads off. "I spoke with Gillette many years ago, you know. He orchestrated a sort of sit-down between us, and I agreed to show my face. We talked about this very occasion, these circumstances."

"He never told me that."

"Why would he?" Eve chuckled. She put her hand on the small of Galen's back and led her away. Her eyes first burned into the encroaching flamingos. She said nothing to them but shot them a look that sent them scattering. "He wouldn't want you knowing that we agreed to peace." The Dreamcatcher led Galen to the staircase again and began to climb them. Galen followed suit. "Before all this happened, I was living in your mind peaceably. I didn't show myself in your dreams, and you didn't know I was here. To him, I was encroaching on his land, his territory. He knew who I was, apparently, and he wasn't having any of it. So, he arranged a sit-down, and attempted to have me killed."

At the top of the stairs, Galen hesitated to go any further. "He would've told me all of this. He wouldn't have hidden this from me."

The Dreamcatcher took Galen's hand and led her to one of the balconies, where an overly stuffed chaise longue awaited them. "He wouldn't want you knowing, poppet. He knows that it is not only his gravest mistake, but his biggest failure." Eve sat herself down, and practically dragged Galen down with her. "The terms that he agreed to were real. He signed a document to say so. I had his word."

"His word for what?"

"That if you were to ever see me in your dreams, he would let you come with me," the Dreamcatcher sighed. She hung her head, her elegant up-do swinging into her face to shield her true emotions. "Gillette agreed to not intervene. I told him you would not be harmed. You'd never experience an ounce of pain or upset whilst you were with me. You'd only ever be happy and cared for, but he couldn't let that be. He couldn't let you go."

Was that true? Galen hadn't felt conflict like this for a while. She could feel her heart thudding inside of her. Had she put her trust in the wrong person? It couldn't be. Gil was sweet and caring, and only wanted the best for all the dreams that were still alive.

"I wasn't a monster before you got here," Eve carried on. "At least, not like people think I am now. I didn't mercilessly pick off every dream I saw. I picked off his people. I picked off the people that he sent to me, to kill me, to get you. Every dream I have ever wiped out has been his follower. He is just as big a tyrant as me, if not worse."

Galen couldn't believe her ears. She thought the music in the hall had gotten increasingly louder, but she wasn't sure. The ballroom was spinning about her. Her stomach churned, and she could feel the wine she'd finished crawling little by little up her throat.

"That settlement that he had, that you stumbled across, was a terrible place, poppet." The Dreamcatcher covered Galen's hand with her own, staring into her eyes pleadingly. "I need you to believe me. It's a lot to take in, but that little bear is a dictator. Dreams think they're safe going to him. They think that the place they're going to is a sanctuary to keep them protected, but it isn't. It's a camp. They're never free again once they're there."

Galen stood up. "I would like to go back to my room."

Eve followed her up, taking her hands in hers. "I'm not a bad person, Galen. I'm not. You'll see for yourself in time. I promise you that I am the perfect choice, and that my word means everything to me. I would never lie, not just to protect my own hind."

A commotion in the crowd was the only thing that kept Galen from passing out. She heard a crash and the breaking of glass. One of the windows was shattered. A rope was dangling against the window frames. Her eyes travelled downwards to see Gil, carrying Ducky, fighting his way through the legs of the guests.

The Dreamcatcher saw it too. "Seize them!" she bellowed, pointing down to Gil. A spotlight was instantly set on the old bear as he dodged and weaved between people's feet. Surprisingly, he wasn't kicked or trapped. "Seize the bear!"

A frenzy began. Every guest became the animal that they wore, becoming predators and hunters alike. They did their best to snatch at Gil, but the bear was surprisingly nimble. He had the attribute of being absolutely tiny compared to everyone else on his side. People jumped atop him, but he still slipped free of them. He kicked away masks, revealing people's true faces, and slid across the marble floors on his belly like a penguin through the legs of three lions. Not all these people could be so stupid, surely. It was quite funny to watch. The only person infuriated by the show was the Dreamcatcher, who grunted and muttered something incoherent under her breath.

As Galen watched Gil near the steps, she was dragged away. Eve grabbed hold of her wrist and pulled her away from the balcony, hauling her up the steps that Galen had been so curious about. The further up they went, the more submerged in darkness they became. Galen couldn't see a thing as she was whisked this way and that, flung down corridors until she was barrelled into a room that was tiny and confined.

"I don't mean to startle you." Somehow, the Dreamcatcher was still calm. She was looking for something, scurrying about the room searching all the bookcases and drawers she could find. "It's a lot to take in, I know, but I can't have you leave me now. There's too much at risk, Galen. You won't understand at first but, in time, I can make you understand."

Galen could hear Gil progressing through the crowd, beating the masked minions with ease. She said nothing back to the Dreamcatcher but watched her withdraw a small vial that had the glistening night sky trapped within it. The liquid was intoxicating to watch slosh back and forth. Little stars glittered in the bottle, caught in the light as Eve turned it back and forth.

"You have to take this," she implored. "There's no other way. If he gets his hands on you then this world will be torn apart and more hurt will be inflicted upon you when it doesn't need to be."

"What is it?" Galen asked as she palmed it. It was warm, like the liquid inside was burning hot. It only continued to heat up as it remained in her grip.

The Dreamcatcher curled Galen's fingers around the vial for her. "You just have to take it, Galen. Do you promise me?"

"But I," stuttered Galen. "I don't know what it is. Will it hurt me?"

"It will protect you," Eve rushed. She was speaking so fast that Galen could barely keep up with her. She had to have heard Gil progressing closer too and was panicking. "It will send you back to me, like the cloak did. You drink this, and it'll bring you here. My people will come for you. You'll be safe from him."

Galen didn't know what to say. "I don't understand…"

"It's a lot, I know." Eve wrapped her arms around Galen in a warm embrace. Pity that she didn't feel any of it. Galen had never felt safer. It was like a drug. "You have to put your faith and your trust in me, not him. You can ask him if you must. He'll have to tell you. He can't lie to you now."

There was pounding on the door. "Open this door, Eve!" Gil yelled at the top of his lungs. If Galen didn't know any better, she would've said that a tall, gruff stranger was coming to rescue her. "Open the door! Hand her over, now!"

"They're coming, Gil," Ducky murmured nervously. "They're gonna get us at any second."

Galen was torn. She kept glancing between the door and the Dreamcatcher. This was a whole new side to Eve. Why hadn't she said all this to begin with? It had to be a power play. She must've made it up to mess with Galen's head. The way she spoke was so convincing, though. The emotion in her eyes was so real and so raw, there was no mistaking it.

"I beg you to stay with me, poppet," Eve pleaded. She cupped the sides of Galen's face as her breathing quickened. Her heart must've been pounding out of control. "I'm pleading with you. Don't let this all fall to ruins because of him."

"Open the door!" Gil shouted again.

"I don't know…" Galen whimpered.

There was a sudden rush of footsteps. Hundreds of people swarmed outside, charging up the corridor and slamming into the walls. They rushed so fast that the door was flung open, bursting into splinters upon impact. Again, they tried to grab Gil. The bear evaded them at every cost, grabbing hold of Galen and dragging her towards freedom.

She didn't want to go, but she wanted to go. Galen wanted to stay, but she wanted to leave. Galen believed the Dreamcatcher, but she had trust in Gil. Her heart was split in two. It separated inside her chest, pulled apart and only held together by a few strands of muscle.

As Galen was dragged from Eve's clutches, she reached towards her. Her fingertips just barely grazed over the Dreamcatcher's cheek but, upon contact, Eve fell to the ground clutching her face. Galen could only watch Eve bask in that gentle touch before she was again whisked away, forced to sprint down the corridor away from a rabid pack of wild animals.

"What do you call this?" Galen asked, shouting. She had to wrench herself free of a few hands that grabbed onto her, smacking them away and snarling down at Gil. "You think this was the wisest thing to do?"

"What would you call abandoning us in the middle of the night?" Gil shouted back at her. "I wouldn't be here if you hadn't made one of the most self-centred decisions I've ever seen!"

Galen almost stopped in her tracks. "What else would you have had me do? Everyone was dying because of me! It was only a matter of time before you would've died too!"

The pair veered to the right as the hallway came to a dead-end, barrelling into a spare bedroom that was abstract and hard to look at. They came to a skidding halt, hearts racing and chests pounding, looking for a way out. Galen only saw one. Gil saw it too and headed for it instantly—the window.

"I thought she had stolen you away, but no. You decided to leave on your own accord. I told you that this wouldn't be easy. I told you that you'd see more death than you would want." Gil grumbled as he searched for something to break the glass with.

There wasn't enough time for that.

Galen grabbed hold of the teddy bear, holding him to her chest as she dove feet first at the window. Her eyes closed, but she could feel the glass bend against her feet before shattering completely. She soared through the window, blades of glass scraping against her skin and leaving her with hundreds of marks. Her flying quickly turned to falling. Her body tumbled into the roofs of the house, colliding with every obstacle possible until she splatted upon the roof of a porch.

She thought her bones were all broken as she let Gil wriggle free of her grasp, laying still and only lifting her forearms.

"You could've gotten us all killed, Galen," Gil cursed. "What were you thinking? How could you do that to us? Ducky and I were…" Gil suddenly stopped. He turned around him, doing a full rotation until he glared back at Galen with dread smothered across his features. "We left Ducky," he announced.

Galen peeled herself from the porch roof. "What?"

"They have Ducky." Gil paced back and forth and ran his paw across his scalp. "We have to go back."

Galen heard hounds barking and shook her head. "There's no time." She grabbed Gil again, though this time he fought against her grip. She paid him no mind as she stood on the edge of the roof, glancing down to the ground. It wasn't that bad of a fall, but it would still suck. Still, there was no other way. It was this or be eaten alive by hungry dogs.

"We have to go back for—"

Not letting Gil finish his sentence, Galen jumped. This time, she kept her eyes open. It provoked a scream from deep within her as she glided through the air towards the front grass. That scream only stopped when she tucked into a roll to save her poor, achy bones from any more harm. She still hit the ground with a force that knocked the wind from her, though. Her lungs were like empty plastic bags as she hobbled back up to her feet, Gil still coiled in her arms.

She hadn't seen the front of Eve's house before. Outside, it looked like a huge mansion, almost like Versailles. Galen was sprinting across the front lawn that stretched on for well over a hundred metres. If she didn't move quick enough, the hounds would have her. She could still hear them, though their footsteps hadn't quite reached her yet.

The gate was getting closer and closer and closer. Galen could smell the outside world. She barrelled towards it despite the aching in her muscles, the strain in her legs. At any second, she'd tumble to the ground. She knew it. Exhaustion was starting to set in. She just had to make it forty more metres, then she'd be free.

Thirty more metres.

Her thighs were beginning to cramp up, her calves stiffening.

Twenty more metres.

Her feet slowed, her hamstrings ready to pull and snap if she went any faster.

Ten more metres.

Were the gates slowly moving away from her?

Five metres…

Galen sprinted towards them, one arm extended to push them open but, when she thought she'd collide with them, she and the old bear just glided straight through the bars. The gates were a mirage. Galen wandered through them as if she was a ghost and rolled out the other side relatively scot-free. She didn't recognise her surroundings, but this wasn't Eve's turf anymore. This was Gil's turf, and Gil had a hell of a lot of explaining to do.

Palming the vial of starlight, Galen couldn't help but watch Gil distrustfully. The old bear hadn't said two words since they'd broken free of Eve's estate. He would glare at her sometimes, but that was all. Nothing was ever said. He hadn't even realised she held onto something—that's how little he cared.

"Eve had a lot to say for herself," Galen perked up. She admired the little hiding spot that they'd managed to escape to, a cave not far from the gates of the Dreamcatcher's lair. "Working out which parts were true and which parts were lies is going to be tough."

"I imagine it was all lies," Gil growled back at her. He'd chosen to keep his distance. He sat himself down in the mouth of the cave, staring out at the rainfall that pounded the earth. "I imagine she told you whatever she felt like she had to just so you'd stay there. You're smarter than that."

"She had a lot to say about you, Gil."

The bear glared over his shoulder, the moonlight reflecting in his eyes.

"You tried to have her killed," Galen continued. She sat in the very back of the cave, shoulder blades pressed against the harsh stone, vial betwixt her fingers. Not once had she stopped looking at the old bear. Not once had she trusted him. "Back before this all began, you summoned her for a treaty."

A sigh escaped Gil. He didn't refute those claims, which was awfully suspicious.

"The Dreamcatcher was happy to make peace. You tried to slay her."

"The terms were too high."

"You agreed to them willingly."

Gil laughed as he picked himself up and faced Galen, tufts of fluff missing from his face. "Is that what she told you?" he asked wryly. "Let me guess. She painted me to be the big, bad bear whilst she was this coy and innocent monster in the making. Am I right?"

"If she's lying, tell me what really happened."

"What would be the point?" Gil threw his arms in the air, defeated. His snarl had never been more prominent, more defined. "You believe her, don't you? You believe what she told you."

Galen shot to her feet, pain instantly crawling all throughout her body. "You're not giving me much reason to believe otherwise, Gil! Defend yourself! Tell me what happened if her story is a fake."

There was a pause from Gil that only made him seem that much more guilty. "What would be the point?" he repeated. Tiredly, Gil faced the rain and sat himself down in the exact same spot he'd been in for hours. "I tried to kill her. I'll admit that to you. I lured her in with the prospect of peace, agreed to whatever she wanted and then tried to burn her alive. It didn't work."

Galen listened carefully, gripping the vial with so much strength that it almost shattered in her palm.

"I'd heard of her before she stared causing any sort of nuisance here," Gil continued. His words were washed away by the thrumming of the rainfall, so Galen paced closer to listen better. "I didn't believe her story—that her creator had abandoned her and empowered her after his death. I only knew she was a monster, and monsters weren't welcome in my world."

"What made it your world to begin with, Gil?" Galen asked softly. Though she was fuming, she didn't want to shout or raise her voice. She wanted the full truth from the bear, and nothing less than the truth.

Gil glowered over his shoulder once more, though this time it wasn't moonlight that enriched his eyes; it was hatred and anger. "It was mine because I protected it. I was its saviour, its guardian. To me, I had let her waltz in like she owned the place. She was getting too close, too cocky. I knew her game, and I wasn't about to let her play it in my world."

This was a side to the old bear that Galen had never seen, had never dreamt of. This wasn't something she'd created for him, but something he'd developed by himself.

"You signed a document," said Galen abruptly, to a chorus of scoffs, sighs, and grumbles. "You gave her your word. You have always been true to your word, Gil. Why did you break it?"

"That document was a trap," Gil snapped. "I signed it before I realised the grave error I'd be making if I let her act on that signature, on my word. She wanted me to just let you go off with her once she appeared to you, to let her kill you. How could I have done that?"

Galen was all out of words.

"I may have agreed to terms, Galen, but I didn't understand them. I didn't support them. I gave her my word because I knew that's what she wanted to hear."

"These sound like excuses, Gil." Galen sat herself next to him. She let her fingers snatch up tiny little fragments of glass that were stuck in her trousers, flicking them away and into a nearby puddle. "She never killed anyone until you started sending people after her. She only ever killed your minions, people you'd sent with the intent to kill her."

To that, Gil didn't respond. His silence was incredibly infuriating. It prompted Galen to raise her voice just a touch with him.

"She called you a tyrant, and I tried to defend you," she insisted, though it still felt as if he wasn't listening to her anymore. Galen dug one hand into the mud, pushing her fingers as far in and squeezing out all the rage in her body. "What was the settlement like before I came here?"

Still, nothing.

"Was it a camp?" Galen shouted. "Did you force dreams to stay, even if they didn't want to? Did you drag them back with you and enslave them there in the fight against her? Did anyone there have a choice?"

"No one should have a choice if the decision between being killed and killing isn't glaringly obvious!" Gil shouted back at her. He stood—if not for him being a teddy bear, he would've towered over Galen intimidatingly. "I did what I had to! I was the only one willing to put up a fight against her whilst everyone else went about their business as if she wasn't here! What am I meant to do? Let her roam freely? Poison people's minds?"

Galen stared at him in shock. It was true. It was all true. It hadn't been a game. The Dreamcatcher had told Galen what Gil had failed to mention, and now it weighed heavily on Galen's mind. She had to pick between two candidates, just as terrible as each other. One was revered as a monster and a murderer, whilst the other was just as bad but shrouded in secrecy. Gil had let the past hide his actions, whereas he constantly dragged Eve's into broad daylight, where everyone could persecute her.

"I may have made mistakes, but so has she," Gil growled through his teeth. He still stood with his chest puffed out, casting the tiniest of shadows over Galen's lap. "I'm not a monster. I didn't do anything out of spite or pettiness or personal gain. I did what had to be done to keep you alive."

"I'm hurt, Gil," Galen admitted dully. She released her hand from the dirt, flicking clumps of it away. It had buried itself beneath her fingernails, and stained the colour of her skin, marking her. "Why wouldn't you tell me any of this?"

Gil wandered off. "You didn't need to know." He sat somewhere else, somewhere in the shadows that Galen couldn't seem him. "It's because of you that Ducky is still stuck there. She has him now. She's probably killed him."

Galen swallowed her guilt. "You never had to come and rescue me."

"I'm starting to wish I hadn't."

That hurt. Galen got to her feet, shoving the vial of starlight into her pocket, and waltzed straight out of the cave. She didn't look back, not even when she heard the bear stirring. His footsteps reverberated in her ears as he reached the mouth of the cave, not willing to take another step closer.

"Where are you going now?" he called to her.

Galen didn't respond. She wandered out into the wilderness, hands buried in her pockets and hair slicked down to her head. She left behind one of her most beloved toys and the fox mask she'd been given, though didn't care about either one anymore. Her feet took her further and further into the forests, leading her away from Gil and aware from his bad energy. Galen couldn't stand him. She wanted to be alone with her thoughts for a while, so she could process it all. The last thing she needed was someone else whispering in her ear. Ahead of her she saw a tidy little cove, a place she could hide. She strode up to it confidently, muscles about to burst inside of her and a scream developing in the middle of her throat when the ground suddenly disappeared beneath her.

Galen walked straight off the side of a cliff, tumbling down into a ravine that had no end.

Chapter Eight

Waking up with a jolt, all Galen could hear was the manic, frantic beeping of machines all around her. She gripped whatever was closest to her, which happened to be the frames on the side of a bed to keep her from tumbling out. Her eyes were wide open but blurry. Galen had no clue where she was, but she could see white all around her. There were people too, rushing into the room to soothe the beeping, to assure the machines that all was well, but the beeping just kept getting faster and faster and faster.

"She's awake!" one man shouted.

"Get her stabilised! She'll go into shock!"

Galen had no clue what was going on around her. She could feel tubes resting against her face and her chest, and an ungodly breeze that swept across her legs. What was she wearing? She pawed at herself, tugging on the tubes only to gag as they tickled the back of her throat and the inside of her nose.

"Get her hands down!"

In seconds, there were hands snatching at Galen's forearms and wrists. They pinned her hands down to the soft mattress beneath her, but she only panicked more. Her writhing was satiated by more hands holding her down against the bed, keeping her in one place as a liquid was injected into the tubes and forced down her throat.

The wooziness that overcame Galen was like a great wall of water washing into her and shooting up her nostrils and down her throat. She felt choked by it. Still, she relaxed. Her urge to fight back was subdued. The muscles in her arms and legs went as lax as rubber bands. She just lay there, staring up at the ceiling, drooling.

"She'll be okay," someone cooed. "She just needs time to rest. We don't really understand how she's woken up so suddenly. She was in an extremely developed and extensive coma, so this is as much of a shock to us as it is to you."

"She doesn't need any more medicine?"

Was that her mother's voice? Galen almost came round, trying to move her head but failing. She was forced to stare up at the white, yellowing ceiling, watching the fan spin round and round.

"We'll keep her on a mild sedative just so she stays relaxed. What she needs more than anything is sleep."

"Thank you."

That was her mother's voice. Galen let her head flop to the side, a movement that was so small yet required so much effort. She felt as if she'd just taken a beating by the time her cheek hit the pillow. Still, there was no one Galen was gladder to see than her mother. Her vision cleared just a touch in the centre, so she could make out Nessa's worried, gaunt face. A smile crept onto Galen's face, though it took too much energy and strain to hold, so it fell shortly after.

"You're awake," Nessa soothed. Did she usually speak that quietly or was it just Galen? She put a hand on the rails that Galen had been clinging to life to but moved it quickly to cover her daughter's. "I didn't think I'd ever get to look into your eyes again. I thought you'd left me."

"Where am I?" Galen asked groggily. That was still the question at hand. She remembered falling from a cliff, storming away from Gil the teddy bear after a furious argument. Was she still in her dreams? "What happened? Did I survive the fall?"

Nessa's brows furrowed. "Fall? What fall, honey? You've not taken a fall."

"I fell off a cliff," Galen explained. She squinted as the harsh lights around her grew brighter, as if someone had cranked them up to full power. "Am I in hospital? Did I break my leg?"

"No, Galen," Nessa sighed deeply. "You didn't fall off a cliff. You went into a coma."

"What?"

Galen's mother gripped her hand for dear life, afraid to let go of it. "You went to sleep after your trip to the doctors and you didn't wake up again. You weren't breathing properly. You were as pale as a ghost…" The whole ordeal had been evidently traumatising for Nessa. She'd lost so much weight. Her face was so thin and skeletal. She looked like a mere shadow of herself. This wasn't the mother that Galen recognised. "You've been here for some time, my sweet. Your brother and I have been by your side every day, watching over you. We've been waiting for a sign of recovery, but we never got one…until now."

Galen was in a hospital, hooked up to life support machines with tubes that fed her and pumped medicine into her routinely. This was a circumstance she'd never experienced before. She glanced at the monitors either side of her, watching her heart rate on one of them and a bunch of random numbers change on the other. Her hands were littered with countless needles and tubes shoved into her veins, taped into place. Those tubes ran up her body, diving into the veins in the bends of her arms, up her nose and even down her throat. She wanted them out. Now.

"A coma?" Galen stuttered. How long had it been? The doctor's visit didn't feel like that long ago. It couldn't have been. The state of her mother indicated otherwise. No one could lose that amount of weight in only a week or so. "How long have I been here?"

"It's been a couple of months, sweetheart."

Months? Galen's heart rate monitor began beeping incessantly. She could feel her breath hitching in her throat, either that or a tube had come loose. Her body ached and groaned as she tried to sit herself upwards, but her mother put a stop to that instantly.

"No, no, Galen," she soothed. She helped to ease her daughter back down, fluffing up her pillows so she was sitting a little more upright. Nessa's hands were so caring and so gentle, it was as if she was frightened of hurting or breaking Galen. "You can't get up. You're incredibly weak. You have to rest, bub."

"Where's Cress?" Galen demanded to know. "You said Cress was here. Where is he?"

Nessa stared at the open doorway. "He went to go get some food. He should be back soon."

"I want to talk to him."

Cress would believe her. He'd believe anything she had to say. He always liked listening to her stories whenever she read them out to him, but this would be different. This one actually happened. He had to know what happened, what threat lay in wait for her. Someone had to know that, if she died, it was because of the war waging in her dreams.

"I want to talk to him! Where is he?"

"He's coming, sweetheart." Nessa was beside herself. She was blinking back tears that formed on her eyelashes, trying not to let her daughter see them. "I'm so happy you're awake. Any longer and your father would have shown up…I didn't want that for you. I didn't want you to have to lay there and be ogled at by that man."

Cress swaggered into the room whistling, holding a packet of crisps and endless amounts of chocolate bars. He moved as if he didn't know his sister was in a coma, or that she was awake. His usual boyish happiness and charm was still fully radiating about him. Nothing seemed to affect him. Not even the prospect of his sister dying tarnished his cheeriness in any way.

"Ah, you're awake," he said somewhat unimpressed. He cocked his head to the side, staring at Galen as if to make sure the sight he was seeing was real. His eyes then flickered over to his mother. "When did this happen? Why didn't you come and get me?"

"It was so sudden," Nessa explained. She flapped her hand at the chair by Galen's side, desperately trying to get her son to sit. "She wants to talk to you. She was calling for you."

Cress sat himself down and began to bounce his leg within seconds. "What's the problem?" he asked with that cheery smile plastered across his face. "What did you want to talk to me about?"

"You have to believe me," Galen growled under her breath. She tried to lean over to him, but it took her some time to move. She flopped rather ungracefully onto her side and reached out to him with the hand her mother had been holding, which had become clammy and hot. "If something happens to me, Cress, it's not because I'm insane. It's nothing medical. There is a parasite in my mind that is draining my existence from me and killing me."

"The woman from your dreams?" he asked.

Galen had forgotten she'd mentioned Eve before. "Yes! Yes, her. If I fall back into a coma, you have to know it's because of her. I'm not insane. I'm not mental. I'm being slowly murdered."

"I believe you."

"I have to try and stop her, but I can't do that if I'm awake." Galen peered over her shoulder at her mother, who had never been paler before. She knew she'd made a mistake spurting this all out, but someone had to know. "I don't know how much time I have left. I don't know how long I'm going to be able to stay awake for, but I need you to do something for me."

Cress pulled a face. "I've never been good at things."

"You'll be great at this," Galen reassured. "I need you to go to a library or turn to the internet or do something, but just look up the name Stefan and find out everything you can about sleep studies conducted in Georgia."

"That's a lot to remember."

Galen huffed in frustration. "Stefan. Georgia. Sleep studies. Got it?"

"Got it," Cress said confidently. The smile he wore suddenly fell into a look of confusion. "Why?"

"If I have any chance of beating the Dreamcatcher, I need to know everything possible. Stefan was the man that created her, and he partook in a sleep study where he noted everything down in a journal. I need that journal. If you can find it for me, I'll do your chores for the rest of your life."

Cress nearly jumped out of his chair with eagerness. "I'll go get that for you now, then." He dashed off, sprinting out of the room, and flying down the corridor. Somehow, that wasn't even the most excited Galen had ever seen him.

"Galen…" Nessa's voice trailed off.

Rolling onto her back and grimacing from pain, Galen strained to meet her mother's anxious gaze. "Yes?"

"Are you okay?"

The words were blunt. They cut through Galen like little daggers. Her mother thought she was insane. Galen knew that's how she came across, it had to be. If she'd heard the story she'd just told Cress, she would be equally as confused and worried. This was her mother, though. Nessa had to understand too. She couldn't be left in the dark—not this time.

"I'm fine," Galen replied with a smile. "I'm fine. I'm still having…nightmares."

"What happened to you?" Nessa had to choke back a sob to stop herself from crying, though the tears still slipped down her cheeks. "How did this happen to you? Was it the tablets? I read through the leaflet Dr Evergreen gave me about them, but it didn't say anything about them causing comas and I just…" She let out a huge sigh that deflated her, causing her to slump in her chair. "I thought you were dead."

Galen knew she would be soon. "If I tell you what happened, will you promise not to think I'm insane?"

Nessa nodded her head enthusiastically. "I'll listen." That wasn't the promise that Galen wanted to hear.

With a deep breath in, Galen took her mother's hand in hers and squeezed it tight. "That woman that I dreamt of, the reason we went to the doctors, is incredibly dangerous," she started off, choosing to ease her mother lightly into the tale. "She's a parasite of sorts who feeds off people's dreams and absorbs their energy and their existence. If she is successful in doing this, the person dies in real life. They stay trapped in their dreams forever, and their family loses them."

Nessa wasn't following. The sheer horror in her eyes wasn't because she believed her daughter, but because she worried about her. She wasn't squeezing Galen's hand back anymore but was holding onto it limply.

"I will die if I don't stop her, Mum. I have to fall asleep again. I have to finish this."

Nessa pursed her lips into a thin line. She made a small noise under her breath as she picked herself up from her chair and leant over the bed. Softly, Nessa kissed Galen's forehead three times. Some of her tears fell onto her daughter's cheek. When she backed away, she gulped down another sob and stayed standing, frequently looking towards the door.

"You don't believe me, do you?" Galen asked, defeated.

"I'm worried about you, Galen," Nessa replied. She shook her head and brought her hand up to her mouth, chewing on her thumbnail nervously. "Something isn't right. You're not yourself."

Galen tore her eyes away from her mother. "I need to rest," was all she said. She glared at the white wall ahead of her, waiting for Nessa to take her things and go. "I'm tired."

"I'm going to talk to the doctors. I won't be long. I'll be here when you wake up."

Galen didn't know if she would wake up. She snuggled down deeper into her bed and brought the covers up to her chin, letting tears bubble in her eyes. They only fell when Nessa disappeared. She didn't want to her mother to see her so sad. It'd only break her heart more.

Nessa never did come back. Galen guessed it was because visiting hours were over. She hadn't seen a soul walk by the window into her room for hours now. She didn't fully trust herself, though. Her eyes had begun to hurt and ache a long time ago, and her vision was blurred immaculately.

Galen had told herself that she wouldn't sleep. She couldn't drift off now. She had to stay up for Cress. Her brother was reliable. He wouldn't let her down.

Galen needed whatever research he could find to take back with her into her dreams. The Dreamcatcher would be defeated one way or another, and Stefan's journals would be a major step towards beating her. That was if those journals actually existed.

Just as Galen found herself slipping away, she heard footsteps smacking into the floors outside. Someone was running? She gathered it would be a nurse—this was a hospital after all. The more she listened, the more she was inclined to believe otherwise. Why would just one nurse be running? Who else was in a hospital at three in the morning? She angled her head so she could see the window, recognising the fuzz of hair that whizzed by suddenly and laying eyes on a red-faced Cress as he burst into her room.

"So," he announced, breathing heavily. Had he run all the way from home? It sounded like it from his heavy breathing. At any second, he was going to pass out, Galen told herself. "I've found things. I've drunk so much coffee that I think my heart is going to fail, so let's get into this."

Galen heaved herself up, so she was sitting upright, and let her eyes run across the mass amount of papers that Cress threw into her lap. "This is everything you found?"

"I've been doing this a long time so don't be surprised if some of these notes are repeated three or four times." Cress organised all the sheets together, forming a timeline and fussing over his work so that it was perfect. "There was a lot to find out and I am only a little bit traumatised and scared of sleeping now, so thank you. What I did find was that Stefan died during this sleep study, and it was closed down by the rest of his buddies who all then fled Georgia and changed their names."

"Why would they do that?"

Cress pointed to a specific sheet of paper. "They didn't want to be tied down to this study because their government would've been able to rule Stefan's death as a murder and no one wants to be a murderer," he rushed. How did he manage to get so many words out in so little time? "I couldn't find anything on them other than the fact that they maybe wanted to shift the intention of study towards that of some sort of torture for prisoners of war?" Cress stopped for a minute to gather his thoughts, sucking in as much air as his lungs would hold. "I don't think that ever happened but what did happen was that they buried this entire study and tried to burn down their lab and all of Stefan's research with it, which they were successful in doing."

Galen's heart sunk in her chest.

"The building burnt down and all remnants of Stefan and his work and this dream woman was gone, but," Stefan suddenly lowered, bringing up his satchel and plonking it on the bed by Galen's leg, "they didn't manage to get everything of his, because not all of it was at the lab."

Galen's hopes rose again.

"Because no one reported Stefan's death, the police began to snoop around after a missing person's report was filed by his wife." Cress flapped another piece of paper under Galen's nose, which she read as quickly as she could before he started to yap again. "They ruled that he'd been killed in the fire and *blah blah blah* and obtained a warrant to search his home, where they found this." Cress placed the holy grail of holy grails in Galen's lap—Stefan's journal.

"Is this real?" Galen gasped. She ran her fingers over the leatherbound tome, afraid that if she picked it up it would crumble into nothingness. It had to have been so old. How did they find this? "Where did you get this?"

Cress was still trying to catch up on his breathing. "At the library."

"You found this at the library?" Galen was in disbelief. "Cress, this isn't something you find at a library. This is something that belongs to a museum! Do you know what secrets this could hold in it?"

"I've read it," he revealed. "It's great. I mean, I don't understand it but it's great. The librarian told me that it had been donated in like the seventies and she just filed it on the shelf and didn't understand what it was. I'm guessing relatives or descendants of Stefan were going through his stuff and throwing it away, and they saw a book he'd wrote and decided to turn it over to the library. It was in the history section. I hate it there. It smells."

Galen ignored his comments and flipped the tome over, getting a face full of dust in the process. She flipped through the pages, seeing Eve's name jotted down here and there. There was no mention of a Dreamcatcher, though. That made sense. She hadn't obtained that moniker yet. He noted everything down to the very exact detail. He'd listed her appearance and the way she liked to dress. He had put down her interests, her likes and her dislikes, everything that made her happy and sad. Stefan had made a meticulous note of things that she created in his dreams, and how that was a remarkable development in his study. He was so proud of Eve, until a few pages towards the back indicated otherwise.

There, four pages to the back of the book, Galen found the page marked as 'voids'. It was long and expansive, written in beautiful cursive handwriting. It showed the instructions on how to create them but failed to mention how dangerous they were. Obviously, he'd not escaped Eve in time to update that part of the manual. They were described as pockets of nothingness within the mind, a purgatory that could be created and then dissipated whenever needed. The first creation of a void didn't appear to go too well from Stefan's notes. He didn't know how to escape them at first and wondered if he'd be trapped forever within them. Little did he know that they'd kill him eventually. His own discovery would bite back, and he'd be consumed by his life's work.

Shutting the book, Galen let out a little sigh of relief. "*I don't know how to thank you for this,*" she whispered to her brother.

"Well, you can start by cleaning my room when we get you home."

Galen laughed heartily. "I would do so with glee if I manage to take her down."

Taking up a seat, Cress finally caught his breath. "Why did this happen to you? How did she get from Stefan's dead brain to you? Are you dead too?" He suddenly gasped, his eyes widening. "Are you a ghost?"

"I wish," scoffed Galen. "That'd make things easier. No, I don't know how this happened. She feeds off powerful imaginations and strong wills, and I was calling out to her, so she snagged her opportunity."

"Could she come for me?"

Galen weighed that up in her mind before lilting her shoulders in a shrug. "If I die, she could. You've got an overactive brain. Although, I'm not too sure she'd like what she'd find in there. You're a strange one."

"So, my off-putting thoughts would put her off?"

"Cress, hearing you talk puts just about everyone off you, let alone your thoughts." Galen hugged Stefan's journal to her chest and sighed deeply again, feeling like she could finally get some rest. "Did you know mum thinks I'm crazy?"

Cress nodded his head. "I did," he replied sadly. "She came home crying. The doctors here said they were going to do a bunch of scans and stuff on your brain, study your psychological state."

"What are they saying about me?"

"That you're insane." Cress suddenly caught himself, gasping in so deeply that he made himself choke on air. He smacked a fist into his chest as if to cough the air back up, choking and turning red in the face once again. "Not insane! Traumatised! That's the word they used. They wonder if you might need to be evaluated and sent to a mental institution once you recover from whatever this is." Cress gestured vaguely at his sister, flapping his hand at her. "They want to put you on a series of tablets which I researched at home because I was in research mode and apparently, they turn you into mush."

Galen arched a brow. "Mush?"

"They make you a vegetable."

Ah, that didn't sound too fun.

"I don't like vegetables that much," Galen replied quietly. So, the hospital was conspiring against her. How lovely. She couldn't blame her mother for telling them her worries. She was suffering. Her brain was suffering. Her mental state was non-existent now, and she would be insane if she came out of this battle alive.

"I don't want you to be a vegetable," Cress sighed to himself, pouting heavily like a child. "Dad's already threatened to come storming up in here and take you to one of those fancy hospitals in the Maldives or something. He thinks mum isn't caring enough for you."

Galen turned her nose up at the mention of her father. "He's not taking me anywhere. If I go back under, mum will fight tooth and nail to keep me here. She'd kill him if he touched me."

"I don't want you to go back under." Cress was suddenly forlorn. He stared down into his hands, twiddling his thumbs, and picking at his nails. "I don't want to run the risk of losing you. As much as I love our mother, I don't want it to be just me and her at home. It'd feel empty."

"You know why I have to go back to sleep, don't you?" Galen asked. She put the journal to the side of her and reached over to grab Cress's sweaty hand. From the sheer clamminess of it, Galen almost found herself regretting that move. "You know I'm not making this up. You realise that if I don't do this, then the fight is futile."

Cress hung his head, swiping his thumb over the back of Galen's palm. "I know."

"I'm glad you understand, Cress."

Lifting his eyes, Cress let out a final sigh as he got up to his feet. "I should probably leave," he said quietly. "I pretty much broke into this place just to give you all of this. They won't be too happy if they find me here."

"Why can't you just be a normal person?" Galen laughed to herself.

"Normal people are boring," was Cress's reasoning. "You wouldn't like me nearly as much if I was normal."

Galen tucked herself up under her covers. "Bold of you to assume that I like you, Cress."

"Go to sleep," he commanded, walking towards the door. "Kill that bitch and then wake up. I've got no one to play video games with."

"Goodnight, Cress."

Another tiny sigh filled the room. "Goodnight, sis."

Though her eyes were closed, and she lay buried amongst mass amounts of pillows, Galen didn't rest. She kept her eyes closed out of spite, playing the part of the sleeping patient as nurses and doctors all bustled by her room. The last thing Galen needed was them coming in to check on her, though sometimes they did. A man kept popping in and out to check the beeping machines at her sides, and if he saw that she was awake, he'd ruin her night by injecting morphine into her veins and making her woozy.

Are you ever going to come back?

Galen nearly jumped out of her skin. She thrust herself upwards, sitting bolt upright resting on sweaty palms. Her eyes shot open at that sound of the Dreamcatcher's voice reverberating inside her head. She had mere seconds to look around herself, fearful that Eve had somehow materialised in her room, before she lay herself back down and squeezed her eyes shut again as the man came back to tap at her heart rate monitor.

Are you going to avoid me forever? You can't leave me here with them, not now that you know what Gillette is. You have business here.

Galen checked over her shoulder to see the man slip out of her bedroom again and shut the door behind him. "*You shouldn't be here,*" she hissed, whispering. "*They think I'm insane. You put me in a coma for months!*"

Sometimes, there are things we have to sacrifice, and the opinions that others hold of us are precisely those things. Why do you care what people think of you?

"*If I get you out of my head, and I escape this alive, they'll lock me up in a crazy house because all I can talk about is you!*" snapped Galen again. She kept her voice hushed in a whisper, her eye constantly watching the window and the door. "No one believes you're real out here. Every time I mention you, I'm drugged up to my eyeballs because they think I'm hallucinating."

Come back and fix the mess that's been made.

Suddenly, Galen could hear the shouts and the screams of someone that she recognised. She brought her brows together, frowning heavily as the screams grew louder and more prominent. As they continued, turning into wails, Galen recognised Ducky's accent screaming for her help. Her heart sunk in her chest, the muscles tightening until they were pulsing and ready to snap.

Don't you feel bad for leaving him behind?

"*You can't guilt me into this,*" Galen whispered. She almost pleaded with the Dreamcatcher. Had she not changed at all? Had the person she'd shown herself to be at ball not truly existed? "*He is of no worth to you. Let him go. He's not the one you want.*"

No, he isn't, but he'll bring back the one that I want. You better come back too, or I'll kill him just for the fun of it. Does that help you make your mind up?

There was no other choice for Galen to make, so she sighed in frustration and closed her eyes once more. "Drag me back, then," she growled. She could feel a fogginess wafting through her mind, clouding her consciousness and weighing her down to her bed. Galen let it float over her gracefully, refusing to let it frighten her. "Why did you have to go back to being a monster?" she yawned, barely staying awake. She buried her face into her pillow, letting it puff up about her head, and let out another heavy exhale. "Why couldn't you be the person you were at the ball?"

I can be, once this is all over. Come and finish this, once and for all. I'm sick of this playing out. End this, so we can be happy.

Chapter Nine

The Dreamcatcher's rot had begun to infect the world. Galen could see how Eve was killing her. She was watching it happen before her very eyes as she zipped all throughout her dreams. Her destination was Eve's little fortress, her kingdom, but she couldn't remember it clear enough. With her memory patchy, the places that Galen dreamt up were just faux castles and knock-off manor houses that were nothing like that of what the Dreamcatcher resided in.

Appearing in a foggy field attached to a far-off Victorian mansion, Galen let out a sigh of frustration. She was dumped inelegantly amongst the mud, tripping over her own feet and landing in a puddle that instantly drenched her clothes. Somehow, miraculously, she still wore the clothes Eve had picked out for her at the ball. She looked a shadow of her former self, though. Galen had been so graceful and so refined, handsome even. Now, she was covered in muck and filth with her temperament boiling over.

"Where are you, then?" she shouted out into the abyss. The cold night that surrounded her didn't answer her. The stars blinked and the moon hid behind a thicket of clouds as if to avoid her question, but there was no response. "Are you hiding from me? Are you scared?" Taunting the Dreamcatcher wasn't the best option, but Galen found herself running out of them quickly. She also found her patience running painfully and dreadfully thin. This was not like her at all.

A crash of thunder rolled overhead as soon as Galen dared to take her feet from the mud that was slowly swallowing her shoes. It froze her in place as it growled and rumbled, grumbling to itself like a grumpy old man. When she moved again, a flash of lighting struck the spot her foot would've landed in, edging Galen back to her muddy puddle where she belonged.

"You're back here."

A voice from behind her prompted Galen to whirl around. She didn't recognise it, and she didn't recognise the face that she was presented with. Her head cocked to the side as she stared a young boy straight in the eyes, her teeth half-bared.

"Of course, I'm back here. She dragged me back here," Galen growled through her teeth. She balled her hands up into fists as the gang the boy was with began to disperse. Two of them slipped to her right, whereas one glided around to her left as if to trap her in. "Who are you? Are you some of her followers? Did she send you to come get me?"

"You could say we were followers," the boy replied. He had no intonation in his voice, no feeling. His eyes were full of emotion, however. He was worried, that much was clear to see. "As for coming to get you…we had no idea you'd be here, and nor did she."

What? Galen frowned heavily, bringing her brows together in a thick line. "She brought me here," she repeated slower. "What don't you understand about that?"

"She would've been waiting for you if she'd brought you here," the boy replied. This time, his upper lip curled back in a snarl. It was the most emotion he'd shown all conversation. "What are you back here for? To cause more chaos? To plunge our way of living deeper into uncertainty?"

Galen chose not to respond to that.

The boy scoffed at her. "I don't know how you've pulled this off, but the Dreamcatcher isn't going to be too pleased about it. You made her think she had full control over you. For her to realise that she doesn't is going to cause problems, for us and for you."

"Why do you think I care what happens to you?"

The individual to Galen's left charged forwards all of a sudden as if to rush her, but she simply took a step back and watched him slip and fall in the mud. She recognised something about him. His clothes were oddly familiar. Everyone that surrounded her were dressed in all black, like those going to a funeral, and had incredibly pale skin. If Galen didn't have her wits about her, she would've thought them to be vampires. Their icy skin was almost see-through—she could see every single vein that ran throughout their body, but they were void and empty of blood and substance. They were as dead as the Dreamcatcher.

The clothes she recognised from Eve's ball, but Galen's mind was crowded with so many faces and so many masks that she couldn't put her finger on it. She looked from the man on the ground to the two women at her right, then back at the young boy that led the troupe with an aggravating amount of self-confidence.

"You're starting to recognise us," he presumed. He flattened the lapels on his blazer and met the eyes of his female compatriots, his worry only growing. "You were so fun and carefree at the ball. I'm starting to wonder if you're the same person."

"Did I see you at the ball?"

The young boy cracked a smile that almost tore the skin on his cheeks. "You were one of us for a short amount of time. We felt your energy. You felt comfortable amongst us."

The flamingos. This had to be them. There was the same amount of them, all dressed in their classy suits. All that was missing were their vibrant pink masks that hid their ugly, unsaturated faces. No wonder they'd chosen a mask that consumed most of their skin. Galen would've done the same thing.

Taking a step back, Galen sighed heavily to herself. "You were much more welcoming at the ball. Of course, I wouldn't recognise you now. You've made yourself out to be something you're not."

"And what's that?"

"Intimidating," Galen snapped. She wouldn't let this arrogant bastard intimidate her. He was just a boy after all. "If you're going to take me to her, then do so. I'm tired of waiting."

The young boy faltered. He held up a hand to stop his encroaching friends from moving any closer. They glared at him, shocked and confused, waiting for his signal, but he never gave it. His eyes were on Galen, his worry turning into something much harder to read.

"I'm not turning you in," he said after a while. It seemed he'd lost himself deep in thought. Had that what he'd been contemplating? Whether to hand her over or not? "There isn't a reward in it for us." His gang receded, though they were evidently not happy about it. Even the one in the mud huffed a sigh as he picked himself back up. "You should make yourself scarce. Once she realises that you're here, she's not going to be as easy-going as she has been. As much as she wants you to love her, she grows more impatient every time you evade her."

"You're letting me go?" Galen couldn't believe what was happening.

The boy nodded. "Yes, and I'm going to do more than just that." He waved his hand in the air suddenly, jerking his whole arm in the sweeping motion. As his fingers lowered, each of his friends disappeared. They turned into puffs of pink feathers, just like Corvid would when he disappeared, and were gone within the blink of an eye. "I'm going to take you somewhere that she can't see you. I'm going to take you to someone who would like to talk to you." He wrapped an arm around Galen's shoulders, producing a hug that she quickly tried to shrug out of, but his grip was relentless.

As soon as he touched her, the muddy field and the Victorian mansion turned to blackness. He whisked her through hundreds upon thousands of places and dreams, until they both came to a screeching halt. Galen felt as if she'd been dragged through a bush backwards. Never before had such a wind flown past her, threatening to blow the skin off her bones. She'd clung to the stranger, gripping his silk shirt with one hand and pushing him away once her feet were on solid ground.

Galen hit the floor. She landed heavily on her ass on a dryer earth, making no attempt to catch herself whatsoever. The motion sickness was intense. When she was a child, she'd avoided going on roundabouts for this exact reason. Dizziness was the bane of her life. It was the one feeling in the world she hated more than anything, and this bout of vertigo just wouldn't go away.

"It shows that you've not been here long," the boy remarked. He glanced all around himself, again flattening the creases in his finery and flicking off flecks of mud. His eyes fell to Galen, his lips curling up in disgust. "You should be safe here, for now. She won't recognise your presence until you make it glaringly obvious you've returned."

Galen was listening to him, but she didn't care to respond. She was fighting to get herself up on her feet, but her head wouldn't stop spinning. Her palms were flat against the ground, as were the soles of her feet, but she just didn't have the strength to get herself stood upright, so she stayed in her awkward yoga position as her guide wandered away from her.

"Ms Elzbieta!" the boy called. His voice was so gruff and hoarse. It was as if he was ageing the longer time went on. His voice had dropped an octave or so just since he'd met Galen. What a strange young man.

Galen stood to see a frail, old woman approaching her guide. Her eyesight suddenly cleared, and her head stopped so abruptly that she almost tumbled again, but she kept herself up. With her arms spread out to the sides, Galen found her balance. She watched the old woman fondly embrace the young boy with a loving smile on her face. Galen felt as if she was watching a mother hug her son. That couldn't be, though. She was far too old, and he far too young.

Slow approaching, Galen could hear mumbling amongst the two, and instantly attracted the attention of the elderly woman. She was shown no such smile or love. Everything was wiped clean of the woman's face, and she glared stonily at Galen with no remorse and an ironclad chin.

"Ms Elzbieta," the young boy cleared his throat roughly and vaguely gestured to Galen. "This is Galen. She's the Dreamer."

"I know who she is, Anders." The old woman pushed the boy away from her and stood alone, all four foot of her standing tall and mighty.

Anders. What a stupid name. Galen stifled a giggle.

"Why have you brought her to me?" Ms Elzbieta asked. She hobbled closer to Galen and observed her dirty clothes. Her hand crept forward as if to touch the fabric, but she yanked it away again in pure disgust. "She reeks of Eve. Why have you stunk up my farm with her presence?"

Anders put his hand on Ms Elzbieta's shoulder to calm the tiny yet frantic woman. "*Miss Catcher doesn't know she's here,*" he whispered to her, just loud enough that even Galen could hear his deepening voice.

Elzbieta's eyes lit up. "Oh, how interesting."

"Why is that interesting, exactly?" Galen asked, perking up for the first time. She watched with her own eyes as Elzbieta's repulsion became intrigue and curiosity, and a smile replaced her snarl. "Who are you?"

"My name is Ms Elzbieta," the old woman responded as if Galen didn't already know that for a fact. "I'm the only dream here older than Eve. I'm the only one who truly knows her, and I know that you could do with my help."

Galen's eyes travelled to Anders. "You said I'd be safe here."

Anders's shoulders lilted, his uncaring demeanour starting to become infuriating. "You're as safe as someone can possibly be. You should have a little trust in me."

Galen scoffed. "Once you've given me a reason, Anders," she sneered mockingly, "then I'll start trusting you."

"Come, come!" Elzbieta said. She hobbled up to Galen and put her hand on the small of her back, pushing Galen forward with remarkable strength. "I won't have this childish arguing. You and I have things to talk about."

Galen looked over her shoulder as she was pushed away and sneered at Anders once more. She absolutely hated the little wave he gave her. She wanted to punch his face in.

Ms Elzbieta had pushed Galen all the way into her little farmhouse where she sat her down at a table and was busy bustling about making tea. She was humming to herself as she worked, going up and down stepladders and up onto stools to reach everything.

"If you need help, I can—"

"I've never needed a dream to help me," Elzbieta interjected, "and I especially do not need help from the Dreamer. I've been here long enough to get on with my life gleefully by myself. You being here makes no difference to that."

Galen had been sharply put in her place, so she shut her mouth and kept her lips sealed until Elzbieta told her to unseal them.

"You being here without Eve knowing is an awfully large achievement, Dreamer," Elzbieta remarked. She finally clambered down her steps and brought over a teapot, though struggled to put it on the table. As she hauled herself into her chair, the old woman grunted and groaned like her muscles and bones were on the verge of giving out. "That hasn't been achieved before you, so you should be proud. This is the furthest anyone has ever been, and more than likely the furthest anyone will ever go."

"What do you mean?"

Ms Elzbieta poured a cup of violet tea into the tiniest of teacups and pushed it as close to Galen as she could manage without tearing her arm out of her socket. "You're starting to diminish some of her powers," the old woman revealed. "You're leeching off her, just as she's leeching off you."

"How could that be?"

Elzbieta wasn't one for talking quickly, Galen learnt as the old woman faffed with her own cup of tea. "Well, it's because of one thing and one thing only."

"That thing being?"

"Feelings."

Feelings? Galen wished that her dreams weren't so complicated and confusing. She huffed a sigh of frustration and palmed the tiny teacup, delighted that it fit so perfectly amongst her fingers.

"Now, now," Elzbieta chided. "Don't grow impatient with me. I'm old! You shouldn't expect too much of an old woman, not one as peaceful and as…unwilling to participate as me."

"I wasn't aware that dreams were given the choice to participate in this…feud. I thought it was something that happened without anyone knowing. You're either on one side or the other. Either way, it'll get you killed."

Elzbieta's smile was alarmingly filled with amusement. "The way you think, Dreamer, is very black and white, isn't it? I suppose that is down to the company you have decided to keep. Neither Gillette nor Eve herself would explain this world for what it was. Not on their lives," she said almost reminiscently. This was a talk she'd given before—at least, that was the vibe she gave off. "This world isn't black and white; I can assure you. Everything here is very grey. You have the advantage over all of us. You see it through rose-tinted glasses, but we have the best knowledge of what happens here, of what we all are."

"You said that we had things to talk about."

"That we do."

Elzbieta's penchant for interrupting grated mightily on Galen's nerves. "What do you have to say to me?" she asked, tired. This was the hundredth story she'd be told; she knew it. It'd be a differing version, something completely different to what she'd already been told. "Is it about her? Is there anything else I can possibly learn about her?"

"The woman is a mystery—was, a mystery," Elzbieta begun. She sipped her tea, letting it warm her from the inside out and boasting a smile that was created from pure happiness and content. "I was here when she turned up and let me tell you…" the woman trailed off chuckling to herself, shaking her head as she remembered far into the past, "it was never like this. Eve never intended it to be like this. You are the latest in a long line of attempts to find what she really wants in life, what she really desires."

"An existence." Galen finished the sentence for Elzbieta, sighing deeply with irritation. "I know all this. I've been told by Gil and by Eve. I don't need to hear it again."

"If you would listen for a moment and shut that trap of yours," Elzbieta pointed a crooked, weary finger at Galen and let her smile drop, replacing it with a glare, "you would come to find this is not the same story."

Like a chided grandchild, Galen bowed her head and kept her gaze to herself.

Elzbieta settled back into her chair and grumbled her discontent, naming Galen a petulant child and an impatient brute. "Eve wants to exist, yes, that is true. There isn't a dream here that doesn't know that. There's something else, however."

Galen perked up.

"There will always be something else." Elzbieta again drank from her tea, this time emptying it. She filled it up again, though this time the tea came out pink instead of violet. "You see, the thing with villains is that they claim to put it all on the table. You know what they want the minute that you meet them. That's supposed to be their game. They hide nothing from you. Well, let me tell you, Dreamer." Elzbieta shuffled in closer and giggled to herself like an excited child. "*She's hiding everything under the sun from you,*" she whispered.

"Like what?" Galen pleaded to know. "She's been incredibly upfront and verbose. She tends to dance around the things I ask her, yes, but she talks to me nonetheless."

"What is it you ask her?"

Galen wet her bottom lip with a quick flick of her tongue. "Who she is, what she wants, and why she has to do this."

"I can give you my answers to those questions, if you could bring yourself to sit through another different batch," Elzbieta proposed.

Not inclined to turn the adorable old lady down, Galen gestured for her to continue and sat back against her chair with her arms folded neatly over her chest.

Elzbieta emptied her cup of pink tea, filling it up again with a liquid that was orange and vibrant. "She is a lost dream—lost in the sense that she doesn't know herself and doesn't know where to begin looking for herself. What she wants…is love."

Galen felt her heart suddenly jolt in her chest.

"Above all else, she wants love." Elzbieta's eyes were tinged with a sadness that was like no other. The atmosphere changed, weighing heavy around the two as they still sat crammed against the table. "She wants to love someone, be loved, and fall in love. That is what she treasures the absolute most, no matter if she says differently."

That was indeed different to what Eve always preached. Galen had heard the Dreamcatcher speak of love. It came out of her mouth often. Galen had never thought Eve knew the meaning of the word. The way she threw it around was so loose and so lax that it never struck a chord with Galen, until she heard it out of the old woman's mouth. The Dreamcatcher was beginning to look a whole lot different under this lighting.

"All the people that she's been through, including you, have been her hoping that she would fall in love at the same time as achieving her existence," Elzbieta continued. "Of course, there came the problem that those two things couldn't intertwine. If she loved this person, she couldn't have them because she'd kill them. She couldn't be with them because she would take their place. She could only dream of them, and that wouldn't be enough."

"Then what will she do with me?" Galen asked. The confusion that weighed on her mind was like no other. She could feel a migraine coming on. "She's expressed her desire to exist, to drain me completely until I am nothing more than a hollow shell of a person. If she wants to be with me," Galen shuddered midsentence, the thought conflicting with her, "then she can't go through with killing me. What will she do?"

Elzbieta tipped her head to Galen, recognising her confliction. "And here we are, at the crossroads that Miss Catcher sits at too. Eventually, she'll come to an answer, and so will you."

"Me?"

"Everyone must have an answer to that question," replied Elzbieta calmly. She drunk her tea, once more emptying it, but neglected to fill it up again. "What will we all do, Dreamer? What will we do once a decision is made, an answer declared? The fate of all dreams lies with you and with her, and that's quite frightening, really."

Galen couldn't decide like that. There was no way she could choose. Both options were so permanent. If she chose to live, she would miss Eve. She could at least admit that to herself. She would miss gallivanting about in her dreams with no consequence, reminiscing over old dreams that she had no previous recollection of. If she chose to stay, she would miss her family. She would miss Cress and her mother. She'd miss living, having a heart that beat inside her chest, having blood in her veins. The pressure was crushing her.

"There will come a time when you face her, and you have to make a decision." Elzbieta's voice woke Galen from her daydream, booming out proudly and strongly. "You must choose the right path, Dreamer. It'll be hard, but there are lives to consider. She chose you for a reason. She'll fight for you. There is a benevolence in her that only prevails because of you, Dreamer. Remember that."

"I don't mean to upset you, Ms Elzbieta," Galen drifted off for a moment, fighting off the urge to throw up all over Elzbieta's lovely, handmade tablecloth, "but you have made things incredibly harder for me now."

Elzbieta just smiled. "Life is hard no matter where you are. The choices we make are what define us, and I can see so many bright and lustrous things in your future. I know you're going to make me and the rest of this world proud."

"How?"

Reaching across the table, Elzbieta covered Galen's hand with her own. "You just are."

Galen stared in awe at Elzbieta's hand. It felt like her mother's hand. It felt like she was in the hospital again, and Nessa had just realised she hadn't lost her daughter. The sheer warmth from Ms Elzbieta's palm was enough to make tears bubble in Galen's eyes. When they fell, Elzbieta caught one on her thumb.

"This is not the time to cry," she soothed, "but the time to rejoice. You're going to be reborn, one way or another, no matter the choice you make. I trust you with the fate and future of this world, and I know Anders would too, though he'd never admit that."

"Is he your son?"

Elzbieta's head shook. "No. There is no blood relation, but I knew his mother. She was one of Miss Catcher's most devoted believers, but she perished crossing over from Eve's last victim to you. I took care of Anders whilst he was determining his beliefs, and I believe that he'll be coming back to me ever so soon."

"He doesn't believe in her?" asked Galen. A part of her already knew that answer. He'd brought her here, hadn't he? He'd had the perfect opportunity to throw her at the Dreamcatcher's feet, and he hadn't. Anders had gone against earning the highest praise and reward possible all so that Galen could meet Elzbieta. "I suppose I knew that already. The defeat in his eyes is hard not to notice. Even at the ball he was…distant."

"Anders is a reasonable boy, and he thinks too much." Climbing to her feet, Elzbieta gestured for Galen to do the same.

Quickly, Galen chugged her tea and placed the teacup back down, rushing up to her feet and following Elzbieta to the door.

"Because he thinks too much, he keeps himself in this permanent state of uncertainty. He's unsure if he believes in Eve because he doesn't like some of her qualities. He recognises that she's a bad person but can also see the good in her." Elzbieta held the door open for Galen, revealing a night sky instead of an early morning. Had the time moved that fast? Had they been talking that long? She had been making tea for a while. "He believes she deserves love but believes she should be crucified for the blood already on her hands. He believes that her mission to truly exist is courageous, but believes her methods are barbaric. Do you see his conundrum?"

"I can see that," Galen agreed. She walked back up the path to the stoop of the hill, where she saw Anders gallantly waiting for her. His auburn hair had been slicked back, but there was a cut on his cheek that even Galen could see from how far away she was. "That wasn't there when he dropped me off here. It wasn't there when I first met him, either."

Elzbieta could only sigh in defeat. She said nothing of it, choosing to ignore Galen's statements as she handed her back over to Anders. The old woman held her hands in front of her apron and bowed her head to Anders, trying to smile at him and not see the deep gauge on his cheek.

"Where am I taking her?" Anders refused to even look at Galen. He refused to acknowledge that she was there. His full concentration was on Elzbieta.

"You know where she needs to go," replied Elzbieta. "Whilst you're at it, you can give Miss Catcher a piece of my mind about cutting that perfectly good face of yours."

Anders lifted his hand to cover the mark. "If I take her there, she runs the risk of being detected."

"She's not stupid, Anders."

"I beg to differ," he muttered under his breath. His eyes travelled to Galen, his fingertips still lingering on the cut. "So, you want to go back to the lair?" he asked tiredly. He rolled his eyes when Galen nodded and cracked his jaw, shaking his head despondently. "I was doing you a favour when I brought you here. She's been preoccupied and wouldn't have noticed you for days."

Galen smacked her lips together. "The longer I stay here, the quicker I die. That's not something I want for myself."

"Suit yourself," Ander grunted. He went to wrap his arm around her waist this time, not her shoulders, but he hesitated. His arm still lingered about Galen, but he didn't touch her. Staring off into the distance, he flared his nostrils and mumbled something under his breath. "What are you going back for?"

Galen was confused. "To end this. To save my friends. To save Ducky."

"The duck?" Anders scoffed. "You're going back for the duck?"

"Not just the duck," snapped Galen. "There's so much more to it that you wouldn't understand, so I won't waste my breath explaining it to you."

Anders shook his head. "Whatever." He threw a final glance to Elzbieta and grabbed hold of Galen's waist, giving her no time to prepare.

Galen managed the briefest of waves to Ms Elzbieta and mouthed her thanks before she was yanked back through thousands of dreams. The dizziness hit her like a sack of bricks, colliding with her with such force that she had to wrap her arms around Anders's neck. Though he didn't stop her, he scoffed in her ear, which caused Galen to smack her fist into his chest. As soon as her fist hit him, the wind and the dizziness stopped. He wheezed as he hit the steps to Eve's castle first and coughed up a lung when Galen landed atop him.

At least it was a smoother landing than last time.

Galen popped up to her feet in seconds, putting as much distance between herself and Anders as she could. "Is there no better way to travel?" she asked, exasperated. "Isn't there a train I can just hop on and make my life so much easier with?"

"I don't know." Anders rose slowly and brushed the dirt and grit from his suit, even picking a kernel of concrete from between his teeth. "You tell me, Dreamer. You created this shithole." He glanced up at the massive structure towering above him and tutted, as fond of it as Galen was. "I got you this far, you can do the rest by yourself. It'll be bad enough if she catches you, but if I'm with you and she sees that…" He didn't bother to finish that sentence. "Whatever you plan on doing, do it fast. Don't be stupid about it either."

"Your lack of faith in me is extremely concerning."

Again, Anders could only scoff. "I've seen more promise in that duck she's got strapped up in there." He turned on his heel and began to descend the large staircase down to the front gardens, refusing to look back. "I hope I never see you again, Dreamer. You're not quite the person I was hoping you were." Before he could reach the bottom of the stairs, Anders evaporated into the night. He didn't turn into a cloud of pink or black feathers, but a cloud of fog that was there for only a millisecond before it was blown away.

Galen turned her attention back to the doors. "What a dick," she murmured to herself, trying to work out how she could get in.

It took Galen what felt like a lifetime to devise a plan. She still didn't really have one. Her mind was whirring as she scurried up the nearest drainpipe to sit atop the porch roof, where she'd been resting with Gil. It didn't bring back fond memories, but it was the ledge closest to a window. In her back pocket, weighing her down just a touch, was the biggest rock Galen could find. It was only the size of her palm, but it'd do. It'd break glass, she determined, and that was good enough for her.

Crouching outside of the windows, with her feet resting against slippery, slanted tiles, Galen fished the rock from her back pocket and cradled it. She peered through the window first, staring into a room she didn't recognise. It was brightly coloured and garish, belonging to the seventies, but empty. That was a good sign.

Hitting the glass as hard as she could, Galen winced and cursed under her breath when it shattered. She felt shards of it slice against her forearm, cutting her open so easily. Was she made of paper in her dreams? It sure felt like it as she shimmied her way through the broken glass and tumbled onto the floor below the windowsill, landing somehow on her shoulders. She flipped over and stopped her heels from smacking too loudly into the wooden floorboards, letting her legs just hover over the floor.

In her mind, Galen tried to map the layout of the castle. She knew it was an impossible feat. Her chances of finding Ducky were slim to none, but she was determined to rescue him. She would just have to check every room, every corridor and every crevice without the Dreamcatcher realising she was asleep.

That was virtually impossible.

Galen snuck from the garish room and entered a corridor she thought she recognised. She closed the door quietly behind her and veered right, heading towards sound. There was music playing, but she couldn't tell where it was coming from. It got louder and louder as she got to a staircase, but not because she was any closer. Someone was cranking up the volume. Someone was trying to hide something else, drown something else out.

Rushing as fast as she could, Galen climbed the staircase and hid at the very top of the stairwell as a flock of people went wandering by.

"He just let her go, like that," a voice said. It was a female talking, scoffing after every word that left her lips. The person she was talking to was ignoring her vehemently, standing at the doors to an elevator, repeatedly pressing the button. "He didn't even think to tell Miss Catcher."

"Did you tell Miss Catcher?" the other person asked.

There was a falter. "Well, no. Why would I do that? I don't want her to kill me."

"Then you better shut up talking about it before she kills us both."

The doors to the elevator pinged and the two people flooded in. Luckily, no one came out. The doors swept shut and a little *bing* let Galen knew it was time for her to make her move.

The music was loudest up here. It was flowing down the remarkably wide corridor, heading straight for her. Galen didn't let its volume deter her. Though it hurt her ears, Galen pushed forwards. She could see the hallway fanning out at the end, opening up into what looked to be a French balcony. The massive chandelier that illuminated the hall below was dangling at the centre of it all, beckoning her in closer. It eliminated all shadows, and, for that, Galen hated it.

Rolling up to the balcony, Galen peered over the edge and down into a second ballroom. This wasn't the one that the masquerade ball had been held in—it was much too small. It was still dimly lit and still a brooding place to be, but there was something unfinished about it. The walls weren't as beautifully decorated, the furnishing wasn't the same either. It had appeared out of nowhere and was like it had been created just for one purpose—imprisoning dreams.

Below, Galen saw Ducky tied to a post in the corner of the hall. He wasn't the only dream she saw. She saw everyone else from the settlement too, including Gil. The poor bear had been tied by the neck to a stake in the very centre of the hall, lit up by a spotlight. He had his head down and his hopes even lower. Everyone around him was tied to chain links or cuffed together in one big daisy chain. They too wallowed in their own misery. Were they the last of the dreams Eve needed to round up before the whole world was hers? Surely not. There were only twenty or so people, and not one of them looked strong enough to pose a threat against the Dreamcatcher.

Speaking of her, Galen watched Eve burst into the room with a fire lit under her ass, as furious as ever.

"So, it comes to this," Eve started off saying. She flounced about the hall, dancing between the different clusters of dreams. She patted some of their heads, glancing down at them almost sympathetically. "You ruin my perfectly innocent evening, make off with someone who is rightly mine, and then make a pathetic attempt to cover up how Galen could've possibly woken up."

Everyone kept their mouths shut. The Dreamcatcher was talking to one person and one person only, but his attention was on the polished floor beneath his feet.

"She fell off a cliff," the Dreamcatcher said mockingly. She put on a voice, standing opposite Gil with her hands on her hips and her face a bright shade of red. Something looked different about her, Galen realised. Eve looked tired. "How would she have just fallen off a cliff, Gillette?" she roared.

"How would I have pushed her?" Gil replied dejectedly. He was so tired. The bear was so defeated.

Eve was practically pulling her hair out. "She can't have just fallen!"

"I'm telling you that's what happened." Gil was starting to snap. He didn't lift his head, but it was evident he'd met Eve's eyes. "We got into an argument and she stormed off. The next thing I knew, I saw her tumbling down the ravine. There wasn't anything I could do."

"You let her get away from you!"

Gil spat at the Dreamcatcher's feet. "The further away from you she is, the better!" the bear shouted back. This time, he did lift his head, and so did all the other dreams around him. "If she's awake, that means you can't get to her!"

"You pushed her." Eve knelt in front of Gil and grabbed the chain that kept him bound against the stake. She began to wind it around her hand, wrapping it tight about her knuckles and pulling it taut so it choked him. "Tell me the truth, Gillette. You pushed her off because she was finally beginning to see sense." How did the sound of Gil choking not startle Eve? How could she sit through that comfortably?

Galen had to roll away. She lay on her back staring up at the ceiling wondering how she could save them all. The Dreamcatcher was a hard person to trick. Eve knew everything. She knew everything that went on around her, but she still hadn't picked up on Galen's arrival. Why was that? Was she too enraged? Too distracted? She had to get down there, and she had to do it fast.

The sound of chains smacking against the floor accentuated the Dreamcatcher's footsteps away from Gil. "I grow tired of this. I grow weary. I need to rest, Gillette. Why do you plague me like this?"

"I do to you what you have done to us," was the bear's fiery response. "You can keep us all in chains, but you will never survive our burden. We will weigh on you until you can't stand anymore. We will—"

Galen accidentally made a noise. She had flopped onto her front, but her wrist had smacked into the floorboards. The bracelets she'd been wearing at the ball, the god-forsaken, chunky, thick metal bracelets, ricocheted into the wood creating a thud like no other. She might as well have called Eve's name.

Gritting her teeth, Galen hoped that Eve would look past it. She squeezed her eyes shut as the Dreamcatcher's footsteps sounded again. Galen knew they were Eve's because they were the deafening sound of high heels. The Dreamcatcher was never without her signature high heels.

"Who's up there?" Eve's voice called.

Galen didn't respond.

"Anders?"

Why would she have called Anders?

"Have you got news for me?"

Galen held her hand over her mouth to keep herself silent but opened her eyes. She managed to wriggle her way back to the balcony again, hoping to keep herself out of sight. Flipping onto her side, she peered curiously down into the hall where Eve was staring upwards. Somehow, the pairs' eyes never met. Galen watched the Dreamcatcher pacing back and forth, knowing she'd given herself away so easily. How could she be so stupid? It'd be a matter of time until someone came for her, so Galen knew she had to move.

As she watched the Dreamcatcher summon Corvid, who burst onto the scene in his usual ball of feathers, Galen began undoing her bracelets. She worked at the clasps and didn't stop until all of them were off her. The rings on her fingers came off too, just as a precaution. She couldn't afford to give herself away again.

"You know what you have to do," Eve sung to Corvid. She cooed at him as if he was an old lover, soothing him with a sirens' song that was incredibly hard to ignore.

"You would like Corvid to search the whole house?"

"The whole kingdom," Eve corrected. "Something is out of place. Fix it."

Corvid squawked as he erupted again, leaving Eve alone to deal with Gil and his friends.

Galen had to pull her eyes away as she crept along the wall, avoiding the balcony. She couldn't see anything from where she was. Popping up onto her feet, Galen clung to the metal jewellery that was piled high in her hands. As she crept, she left some of it behind. She left a pile sitting randomly on the floor, hoping that whoever found it would be confused enough to leave it be. Galen kept hold of one bracelet, though. She clung to it as she slipped against the wall and stood looking down upon the Dreamcatcher, who had her back turned to her.

"What do I do with you, Gillette?" Eve asked.

Gil didn't see Galen either. "Do what you like," he responded gruffly. What a tough, macho man. "You'll never get what you want. She's too quick, too evasive. Seems you made a mistake when you picked a victim so much smarter than the others."

"Well, I can attest that she's smart," Eve agreed. "The others were infatuated with me because of my looks, but Galen is different. My poppet is…well, she cares for me deeper than any of them did."

"She doesn't care for you, Eve. She wants you gone."

Galen crept closer and closer until she was face to face with the balcony. She had the bracelet dangling from her hand, ready. All she had to do was pick the right moment. She fed her arm through the gaps in the bannisters, moving so slowly. If she caught any attention, it was game over. She just wanted one person's attention, and this was the way to do it.

"She wants the version of me you created gone," the Dreamcatcher spat. "You turned her against me the second you had hold of her. You promised her to me, Gillette! Does your word mean nothing to you?"

"You think I'd be so happy as to let you have the Dreamer? That isn't how games are played, Eve!"

Galen strained every muscle in her body as, suddenly, almost involuntarily, she let go of her bracelet. She watched in both fear and an adrenaline-fuelled excitement as it fell gracefully through the air. It'd land perfectly. Galen grinned from ear to ear as the bracelet smashed into the polished floor just between the Dreamcatcher and Gil. It bounced, tumbling onto its side, and spinning round and round and round, until Eve bent over to pick it up.

It took her a second. In that second, Galen began to run. She didn't care that the sound of her footsteps alerted every single person in the house that she was back. This was all part of her plan.

"Galen?" the Dreamcatcher called.

Galen ignored her. She ran for her life, back down the hallway she'd scurried up and to the top of the stairwell. A little *whoosh* stopped her in her tracks. Her hand was on the banister, her foot on the first step, but her eyes were on the Dreamcatcher, watching as Eve levitated up from the hall and landed on the corridor.

As the pairs' eyes met, Eve gasped. She dropped the bracelet and faltered for a moment, buffering like a villain in a videogame. Once she came to her senses, her entire demeanour changed. Desperation clouded her like a plague, sticking to her, as she opened her mouth and yelled as loud as possibly could.

"Get her! She's here!"

Galen just laughed as she sprinted down the steps joyously and flung herself out into a lobby. It was an open room filled with people she'd seen before. They were all enjoying cups of coffee and glasses of wine and plates of cheese until they saw Galen sprinting at them.

With no time to react, Galen knocked through clusters of them and slipped beneath arms that were thrusted so suddenly into her face. She slid across the floor and dodged and weaved her way through people she'd seen dressed up as animals at the balls. She knew exactly who these people were. The lions and the tigers couldn't grab hold of her as she danced amongst them. Some of them didn't even try to grab her. They just let her go, watching her in awe as she burst out of the back door.

"Gil!" Galen called. She was desperate to find the hall before the Dreamcatcher found her. She turned every which way, hoping to hear someone's voice call back to her. "Gil! Ducky!"

"In here!"

It was so quiet, but Galen heard Ducky shout back at her. She sprinted for him, avoiding doors that flew open at random and objects that were flung at her. Eve had poltergeists? No, of course not. Galen laughed that thought away as she knew the Dreamcatcher was throwing everything that she could in her path to stop her.

Feeling unstoppable, Galen skipped and hopped and jumped over it all, except for one thing. An ornate vase that was almost as big as she was flew into her. It collided with her chest, knocking the wind out of her. It halted her, stopping Galen just outside of the doors to the hall. She could hear the dreams inside calling to her, but she couldn't call back. Her hand flew to her chest as it seized up, her lungs refusing to expand despite how hard Galen sucked in.

Fighting through it, Galen rose to her wobbly feet. Her knees knocked together as she pushed the doors open and slammed them shut again behind her. She took a few steps back, falling to her knees out of weakness. Her eyes closed, and she imagined a steel bar being threaded through the door handles and bent, so the doors could no longer open.

When she opened her eyes, Galen saw the bar in place. She let out a sigh of relief and closed her eyes again. This time, she imagined an impregnable steel cage that covered the top of the balcony. She imagined it sealing the hall up so no one could get in, and she imagined the steel melting together to become one thick sheet.

The darkness that fell over her soothed her soul. She opened her eyes and saw herself trapped in the hall. Now, there was no way out. She was alone with the dreams, though she found herself wondering if her defences could keep the likes of the Dreamcatcher at bay.

"You're back," Gil panted.

Galen decided she'd free him last, going around everyone else and breaking their chains. "Did you think I would be able to stay awake forever?" she asked him. She tried not to snap, but she couldn't help but still be angry at him. "I thought she dragged me back here, but apparently I was wrong. She was preoccupied with you, so I guess I'll thank you for that."

"How do you expect us to escape?"

Galen broke the last of the chains and stood still, huffing. She felt her lungs twitch and jerk inside her. Something was definitely wrong in there. Using all her strength was wearing on her, but there was just one more thing she had to do.

Staring at the side wall, Galen imagined a portal. She imagined it swirling with blues, greys, and purples, leading to the settlement that had yet to be built. In her mind, she created it. She created buildings and houses and homes for the dreams, with roofs made from hay and walls made from brick. There were flowers littering the floor and trees barricading the place in. The sun was always in the sky, shining as fiercely as ever, and the sky would always be blue.

Galen could hear the whirring and the gasping. Her eyes opened, and she watched the portal as it stretched against the wall. It was just as she had imagined. She only hoped it worked as she imagined.

"Go, go!" Galen ushered, hurrying people towards the portal. She guided every dream she could to it, watching them glide through it. Once they'd entered it, Galen could no longer hear them. They were gone in seconds. At least they were free of this place.

Pounding on the metal sheet above almost frightened Galen out of her skin. She pushed the last of the dreams through the portal and closed it, quickly dashing to Ducky's side. Her hands worked quickly against his binds as the pounding quickened and the sound of Eve screaming in desperation pierced through it.

"Galen! Galen, you can't do this to me!" the Dreamcatcher roared, her voice distorted.

"What's your plan now?" Gil asked her as Galen freed Ducky.

She kept the duck close to her as she came to Gil's aid, peering up at the sky as Eve's talons pierced through the steel. Of course, that had to happen. Her heart sank in her chest as she tried again and again to break Gil's chains, but they were much stronger than the others.

“I found Stefan’s journals,” Galen explained quickly. Her words were so breathy it was a miracle anyone could understand her. “I’ve read through them. I know how to evade her. You just have to put your trust in me.”

“The last few times I’ve done that, you’ve let me down.”

Galen broke Gil’s chains as Eve tore a small hole in the metal sheet and began frantically clawing at it. “Well, it’s a chance you’re just going to have to take. We don’t have any other options.” She held onto Gil under one arm and had Ducky under the other as she closed her eyes and imagined nothing. She cleared her brain of everything, thinking of absolute darkness and total silence.

It was slightly distracting that Eve was scraping her nails across metal above Galen’s head, but she persevered. She knew the Dreamcatcher was close to coming in. She knew that Eve had made a bigger hole. It didn’t matter. Galen focused on nothingness, on blackness, on darkness, until the tiniest speck of white appeared. Her eyes latched onto it, making it swell and grow until a ball of energy burst all around her.

Opening her eyes, Galen rushed towards the void before she even knew if she’d done it right. It was just a big black orb floating in the middle of the hall, with nothing entirely discerning about it. She collided with it, falling inside of it, and floating like she was trapped in a bubble. It felt like she’d passed through a wall of jelly as she landed softly on the other side, hearing the defeated cry of the Dreamcatcher just as the wall sealed up behind her.

She was safe, and she’d successfully rescued every dream, including Ducky and Gil. How could the bear hate her now?

Panting, Galen lay herself out on the floor. She didn’t mind the everlasting nothingness that was surrounding her, though it quite obviously bothered both Ducky and Gil. They were busy trying to find a way out, whilst Galen took the time to collect herself, to rest her chest, to refill her lungs with fresh air.

“What do we do now?” Ducky asked, panicked. “We can’t stay in here. It’ll kill us. It’ll crush us.”

“I’m sure our mighty saviour has a plan for our escape,” Gil growled through gritted teeth.

Galen rolled her eyes, cheek still pressed up against the floor. “Even when I risk my own life to come and get you two, you can’t help but take a dig at me. Have I really upset you that much? Do you hate my guts that much?”

“I hate that you don’t prepare for anything,” Gil replied, surprisingly calm. He was running his paw along the edge of the void, observing it, feeling it for any inconsistencies or breaks. “Thank you for saving us, Galen. We wouldn’t have survived if you didn’t come for us. I’m thankful for what you did for our people, but where did you send them?”

“I sent them to a new settlement far away, where Eve won’t be interested in hunting them down,” replied Galen, who peeled herself from the bottom of the void and stood. “They’re safe, and you will be too eventually. I just have to figure out how we can…escape out of the other side of this.”

Ducky was rolling back and forth, keeping himself unusually quiet. “You know she’s not going to be too fond of you because of this. This isn’t going to end well for you, Galen.”

“She doesn’t scare me.”

“That isn’t the point.”

Both Gil and Galen turned to look down at Ducky, scrutinising him. The way he moved was suspicious. He drew attention to himself and checked over his shoulder repeatedly as if someone could see him. Maybe it was because he was trapped, unable to leave. Maybe he was hiding something.

“What did she do to you when it was just you and her?” Galen asked. She pushed forwards, hiding Gil behind her, and crouching down to stare into Ducky’s eyes. “Did she torture you? Did she make you spill everything to her? Did she put poison in your mind?”

“She didn’t do anything.”

Galen tipped her head off to the side, feeling the void shrink around her—she was running out of time. “She just kept you here for no reason? If that was the case, wouldn’t she have let you go? She would’ve had no use for you.”

“She didn’t do anything,” Ducky said again, this time more aggressively. He growled the words through his teeth, backing up a few paces so he no longer cowered underneath Galen. “Will you drop it? I don’t want to talk about it.”

“Leave him be, Galen,” Gil snapped. He tapped on the wall of the void and watched it wobble. “We need to get out of here. This thing is collapsing. We’re all going to die.” He turned and faced Galen, his face unforgiving and stony. “Get us out of here. Take us to the settlement.”

Galen did everything that Stefan’s journals told her to do. She had taken them at face value, hoping that they would work. She closed her eyes and kept them closed as she imagined a split forming in the void. It worked like a bubble, slowing ripping apart until the entire outside of it popped completely. She quickly had to imagine the settlement spreading out around her, with everyone that she'd sent that ready to greet her. One by one, the people popped up in her mind. Galen saw everyone, recognising their smiling faces. She went to step out, to free herself and her friends but, just as she thought she could escape, the void snatched her back in and tightened even more, groaning.

"*We're stuck,*" Galen whispered to herself. She fell to her knees, pressing her hands against the cold interior of the void. Her heart dropped in her chest. So, this was how she'd go after all. It wouldn't be the Dreamcatcher. It wouldn't be a coma. It'd be her own stupidity.

Oh, how ironic this all was. How Eve would laugh at her.

Chapter Ten

"We have to think of something, and we have to think of something fast," Galen deduced. The walls of her void were closing in all around her, limiting the amount of space she had to move. "If we panic, we die. We'll lose focus if we let this get to us."

"We are being swallowed by a void!" Ducky cried. "What do you mean we shouldn't panic? Aren't you scared?"

Galen's eyes shot to the little toy duck. "Of course, I'm scared! I'm trying to keep my wits about me so that we can get out of this sooner rather than later." A sigh left her body, her lungs deflating inside of her. Only just had the pain inside her chest subsided. "I don't want to be crushed inside this place. I read the journals. They told me what to do. All I have to do is try again."

"You realise that Stefan was unsuccessful in at least fifty percent of all his voids," Gil spoke up. It was the first time in a while that the bear had made his voice known. He sat away from everyone, despondent and tired. The void was draining him. "Anything that was written in that journal is probably untrustworthy. Voids killed that man, and they'll kill us too."

"You're so fun to be around," Galen commented. "You're the life of the party. If you start telling yourself we're going to die, we will. That's how fate works. You attract what you put out, and the energy you're putting out is toxic."

Gil went to speak again, his lips peeling away from his gums to snap, but he was stopped as Galen threw herself up to her feet.

"I don't want to hear it," she snapped at him instead. "If either of you don't have anything useful to say, then I don't want to hear either of you talk. Is that understood?" Galen glanced at Ducky who nodded and wheeled away from her, and then at Gil who glared back at her hatefully. She took a step towards her old friend, teeth bared. "Is that understood?"

"Fine," Gil grizzled.

Galen let out a tiny sigh of relief. That must've been the first time they listened to her. She stood facing the wall of the void that kept shrinking with every passing minute, her heart racing in her chest. Her hands stayed down at her sides as she closed her eyes and again envisioned the wall splitting. When the image didn't appear, Galen pushed her hands against the wobbly wall and dug her fingers into it to give it that extra helping hand.

She didn't imagine anywhere specific. All Galen wanted to see was the wall opening for her. She wanted to be able to breathe in fresh air, feel the coolness of the wind at her skin. She wanted the sun to be shining down on her, bathing her in a beautiful glow.

Gradually, she could see the sun's rays piercing through the void. There was the tiniest little opening of light, a little sliver that penetrated through the jelly. Galen pushed towards it. She rushed, knowing there was no time to waste anymore. In a few minutes, she'd be crushed, dead. There'd be no turning back. This wasn't a game, and Galen's life depended on this tiny hole in an immaculate forcefield.

Gritting her teeth, Galen sank all her energy into the void. She could hear stirring going on behind her, a scuffle perhaps. Were Ducky and Gil fighting? Gil had slithered off from where he'd been sat once Galen had shut him down, but the two had been dead silent since that. The urge to break her concentration and look behind her was intense, but she fought against it. She could feel her muscles straining in her arms as she physically and mentally tore that hole wider and wider. The sun was hot against her face as it split open and ripped, leaving behind strips and thin strings of jelly.

Abruptly, the void began to tremble. The semi-solid ground underneath Galen's feet began to vibrate, bouncing her around as if she was a kid in a bouncy castle. Was this a ploy to break her concentration?

Out of spite, Galen kept her eyes shut. She forced more of her energy into her hands, into breaking down the void, as the destruction continued around her. It was hard not to pay it any mind. It was difficult not to listen to the wet tearing coming from the opposite side of the void, and to the little spin of wooden wheels. Ducky? Had Ducky fallen out? He hadn't made a noise. There wasn't any screaming.

"Galen!" Gil shouted at her suddenly.

Galen ignored him, arms buckling, and mind almost completely diminished of strength. She was using all her energy, all her might. This couldn't have been good for her. It was draining her quicker than the Dreamcatcher ever could, but that only made her more desperate to escape.

"Galen, she's got Ducky!"

What? How could that be?

This time, Galen opened her eyes. She glanced back over her shoulder to see Gil standing behind her leg and no one else in the void. The sun from outside had lit up the back of the inky void to reveal absolute nothingness. The duck was gone, but how? How could that be?

Galen fell.

All of a sudden, the void opened up underneath her and spat both her and Gil out as if they were a bad taste. She went soaring through the air, a sensation she was uncomfortably familiar with now, and hit the ground like a sack of potatoes. She landed on her shoulder, momentarily forcing it out of its socket before she flipped around on herself and popped it back in when she landed on it.

The consciousness flowed back to Galen in a steady stream, leaving her dizzy and otherwise incapacitated. She held a hand to her forehead, opening her eyes slowly but seeing nothing but a haze. Everything was blurry. This was common, too. Galen felt like an alcoholic in a constant state of hangover all the time, never being able to see what was in front of her clearly. These surroundings, however, were so familiar that she couldn't mistake them for anywhere else.

Galen was at home, in her room.

Shooting up to her feet, Galen rubbed at her eyes and searched her bedroom for Gil. "Gil?" she hissed under her breath. Though the sun was shining outside, Galen refused to believe that anyone would be awake. How had the void brought her home? Was she awake? "Gil, are you here?" The lack of a reply led Galen to believe she'd woken up. She held out her arms. There were no marks where her tubes had been at the hospital, no prick marks from needles or cannulas.

This had to be a dream.

Hurriedly, Galen began tossing things around, trashing her room in an attempt to find the grizzly old bear. "Where are you? Where did you land?" she hummed to herself. Her eyes searched every corner, under her bed, atop her surfaces, even atop her bookcase, but she couldn't find Gil anywhere. "How did I lose you so quickly?"

"You've not lost me." Gil's voice was groggy and weak. He was scaling the back side of Galen's bed, where it didn't quite meet the wall. That tiny gap had been the producer of many of Galen's nightmares, and now Gil was struggling to clamber out of it. "That thing had some force behind it," he coughed and wheezed. Was that laughter? If it was, it sounded pained. "Is this freedom?" he asked, hauling himself up the last inch of Galen's duvet. When he glanced around himself, his mouth fell open. "This…this cannot be. How are we here?"

Galen just shook her head. "Your guess is as good as mine," she replied darkly. She kept her guard up. This was one of Eve's ploys. She could tell. The Dreamcatcher had brought her here once before, to make her feel safe, but this time Galen knew better than to let her naivety run wild. "Don't believe everything you see. I don't think this is real. We're not safe here."

Gil was already looking around. He'd pretty much tumbled off the bed and hit the ground with a soft *poof,* instantly hunting for the things that he had once lived amongst. There was a sort of childlike innocence about him as he moved, gazing over everything that littered Galen's room.

"It's all changed so much," he remarked under his breath.

"I'm not a child anymore," said Galen. She wandered to the window and peered into the back garden, gasping when she saw her mother standing at the washing line. Something was wrong. Nessa wasn't acting her usual self. Never before had Galen seen any human struggle the way her mother was struggling to pin up a single sock. "Whatever this place is, it's not right. We came here for a reason, but we've yet to find out why."

Gil huffed to himself as he recognised none of Galen's belongings, sitting himself down on her circular rug. "I don't think we have anything to fear from this place. What we must take into mind is how Ducky was yanked from a void. It must've been her."

"It can't have been her," Galen shot back. "She can't see voids. They're the one thing that she has no control over."

"Then how did he just fall out the back end of a void?"

Galen again could only shake her head. "I must've…made the void with flaws. It must've been flimsy."

"That's not how it works, Galen," Gil reminded her.

Staring out of the window still, Galen was worried as she watched her mother repeatedly try to hang up the same sock, only to see her drop it every time. "We'll find him again, don't worry. He can't have gone far. We need to hurry up and get out of this place first, though. It's giving me the creeps."

Galen held Gil in her arms the way she used to when she was a child. Together, they'd probed all of the upstairs of the house. Cress hadn't been in his room, and Galen already knew her mother was outside. She found herself wondering where her brother could've gone to. In this world, he could've been anywhere. It was the finding him that scared her. She didn't know what to expect, or what she might come across in the process.

Stood in the doorway of the back door looking over the garden, Gil and Galen watched Nessa faff with the sock.

"That's the sixth time she's dropped that," chuckled Gil. "You'd think she'd give up by now."

"*I don't think she knows any better,*" whispered Galen. It had hit her like a ton of bricks when she realised Nessa wasn't really herself. The actions that she was doing, the movements and the motions, were all involuntary. This was all she knew how to do or, at least, it seemed that way. "Doesn't she remind you of Eve's little goblin things? The way she's acting?"

Gil paused for a moment. "She's certainly acting enchanted or possessed."

"You stay here." Galen put Gil on the ground and stepped out into the garden, holding her shirt tighter around her body. How any of her clothes had remained intact was a mystery to her.

Galen waded through the tallgrass of her back garden until she stood a few metres away from Nessa. Her mother hadn't noticed her coming, and still didn't know she was there. Nessa was consigned to her sock and nothing else, but Galen wanted that to change.

Daring to take one more step closer, Galen swallowed down fear. "Mum?" she called to Nessa, expecting an immediate response. What she got was a slow turn of the head, like a zombie would do once it picked up on a human scent. She watched as her mother's head lolled backwards, as if there was no strength in her neck, and her arms dropped loosely to her sides. "Mum, are you okay?"

Nessa definitely wasn't okay. There was nothing okay about her. Her muscles and limbs were loose and slack, unable to undergo much strain or work. It seemed like it was a job and a half just to keep her head lifted. Her eyes were the most different thing about her. Their usual colour was gone, completely. All that remained was a foggy sheet of white that covered the entire eye. She looked blind. Could she see through that fog? Had the Dreamcatcher taken her sight? There were so many unknowns.

"Mum, what's happened to you?" Galen could've cried. She took the tiniest shuffle backwards as Nessa dropped the washing that had been sitting on her hip and extended her lifeless arms towards her daughter. Her mouth opened, but all that came out was a groan. "Mum?"

"Galen!" Gil shouted from the kitchen. "We have a problem!"

Checking behind her, Galen watched Gil running for his life away from Cress, who moved just as lazily and lifelessly as Nessa. His eyes were the same too. They were foggy, clouded over like frosted glass. Cress could see, though. He could clearly see where Gil was heading, which led Galen to make the devastating realisation that her family had been possessed.

"Run, Gil!" Galen shouted to the bear. She stifled a last look at her mother, whose face had turned into a horrific snarl. Nessa was even moving a little quicker, but she couldn't keep up with her daughter as Galen turned on her heel and sprinted after the old bear.

Galen caught up to Gil in seconds. She dodged the manic grabbing of Cress's hands and scooped Gil into her arms again, cradling him. Where she was heading, she had no idea, but she ran like the wind. No matter how fast she went, her family always caught her. It was comical. It was as if the ground underneath Galen's feet was moving so that every step she took forwards, it brought her back towards her family.

"How did this happen?" Gil asked as Galen ran. His words were muffled as he was pressed into Galen's chest, almost unable to breathe. "This makes no sense, Galen!"

"Why are you asking me?" Galen laughed hysterically. She burst from her front garden into the road that her house sat on, finding that there were no cars and no people all around. Even the houses that were scattered everywhere were gone. There were just empty front gardens with no homes and no owners. "I've got no idea what's happened here. I don't know why the void dumped us here, and I don't know how the Dreamcatcher got her fangs into those two so quickly. I don't know anything."

Gil climbed up so that he was clinging onto Galen's shoulders, but quickly gasped. "What I know is that we should start moving again, and fast," he urged.

Galen checked behind her and screamed as Cress lunged towards her. She ducked underneath his arm and brought out a leg of her own, tripping her brother. She'd done it many times as a child when they'd play together. Cress never saw it coming, and neither did this version of him. Galen didn't bother to watch him fall. He hit the ground and Galen took off, running through her neighbours' yards until the dream ended abruptly.

There was no more land. There was nothingness. Galen stood at the edge of this dream, staring off into the purgatory of her mind. Only a blank sheet of white was spread out ahead of her. There were only a few blades of grass separating her from a never-ending fall through limbo, where there was nothing to harm her, where there was nothing at all.

Looking behind her, Galen noticed her mother tending to her fallen brother. They hadn't regained their own consciousness, still moving like zombies, but Nessa still cared. It broke Galen's heart to see her mother pick Cress up off the ground and brush him off, constantly glancing down at the leg she'd kicked. They groaned at one another in a language they both understood, eventually embracing, and turning to glare at the outcast. Their lips peeled back from their gums as they hissed and yowled hatefully at Galen, more than likely cursing her out, before they turned and hobbled back up to their house, back up to safety.

Galen set Gil down on the ground with a sigh, eventually sitting down herself. She let her legs hang off the edge of the dream, dangling them into nothingness. Somehow, a faint breeze made her feet swish. How amusing. All there was in purgatory was a light wind.

"Are we safe here?" Gil asked. The tone of his voice was tired and defeated. This old bear had given up a long time ago, and now he had to endure his least favourite company. "Can we finally stop running?"

"I have no idea," Galen admitted, defeated. She combed her fingers through her hair and redid the ponytail that had been hanging from the back of her head. Fishing in all the strands that had fallen out, Galen met Gil's eyes. "I suppose it isn't over until we get Ducky back. We just have to figure out where he could be first."

Gil hung his head as he cosied up to Galen's side. "He could be anywhere. This place is vast and unforgiving. My bet is on Eve."

"As it always is."

"Who else could've done this?" Gil questioned. "Dreams can't penetrate voids. She has to have found a way to work around them."

Galen stared into the limbo beneath her, wondering what it would feel like to fall through it endlessly. "Why would she take Ducky?" were the words out of her mouth. "That doesn't make any sense. She doesn't want Ducky, she wants me. I was there. Surely, she would've taken me and let the void close up around you and Duck."

"You're standing up for her."

"I'm telling you that not everything that goes wrong here is down to her," Galen snapped gently. She didn't let her frustrations fully take over her, but her blood was starting to burn a little hotter. "This had to have been something else."

Gil suddenly stood up and brushed himself off, stretching out each of his limbs. "I'm going to check around, make sure that he didn't just…prematurely fall out somewhere nearby."

"Don't go near the house," Galen warned.

The bear held up his paws in surrender. "I won't. They may not be able to catch you, but they'll catch me in no time. I'm not a runner." He turned on his heel quickly, eager to get away, but called a few words over his shoulder. "You stay right there where I can find you, okay? I've had enough of losing you every time it's just us. One of these days, I might lose you forever."

Those words sunk Galen's heart. She closed her eyes and fell into herself, trying not to cry. She was so tired. It wasn't even the lack of sleep that was getting to her, but the constant hurt that she was causing. All this strife for nothing. Her mind kept gnawing at her, all her thoughts picking away at her. It was Elzbieta's words that burned the hottest. The choice that she had to face eventually was looming ahead of her, and Galen was picking the most tumultuous path to the end. When would she have to choose? She didn't know, and she didn't want to know. She didn't need to know.

"Wherever you are, Duck," Galen yawned, rubbing at her eyes, and slapping her cheeks to wake herself up, "I hope we find you quickly. The last thing I need is to leave you behind. You mean too much to this group."

Suddenly, Galen watched the purgatory ahead of her ripple slightly. It cracked and boomed, sending shockwaves through the earth she sat on, almost knocking her into limbo. She scattered away and watched as part of the whiteness peeled away to reveal what was almost a floating television in the sky. Upon it was nothing, yet. The picture hadn't appeared but flicked on once Galen sat herself back down a little further away.

Galen saw Ducky in the Dreamcatcher's home, in the ballroom that Galen herself had been in not too long ago. She gasped as she watched him roll up to Eve's side, who sat on the balcony overlooking the floor.

"You saved me," Ducky said gently, staring up at the Dreamcatcher in awe. "I didn't expect you to do that."

"Where is she?" was all Eve responded with. She was drinking something—wine, from the looks of it. The goblet dangled from her fingertips, filled to the very brim, almost spilling in the Dreamcatcher's lap.

Ducky gulped down his fear. "The void spat her out somewhere near Purgatory," he said shakily. "She and Gil were dumped out in her home. Both your minions were alerted, though."

"Did they grab her?"

"No."

The Dreamcatcher made a little noise in the back of her throat. "Does she know you're not on her side anymore?"

Ducky refused to answer that one.

Galen couldn't believe what she was watching. Slowly, she pushed herself onto her feet. She wanted to run away but couldn't take her eyes away from the screen. Was this real? This had to be another trick. Ducky wouldn't turn his back on her, would he? Galen stayed to watch, keeping herself on her toes so that she could flee any second it went awry.

"I'm thankful for your help, Ducky, but I can't help but fear how our poppet is going to take this when she finds out that you're a backstabbing traitor." It sounded like Eve was pleased by the fact she'd corrupted one of the gang. It brought her pleasure to know that Ducky no longer believed in Galen's cause.

Ducky wasn't so thrilled. "I can't die for her. You said if I brought her back to you, or told you where she was at all times, I'd get to live."

"Of course, you would. For when I take her existence, you'll remain immortal, and she'll remain here."

Galen thought she was about to throw up. Or was she about to cry? Was it a mix of the two? She had no idea what she was feeling. Her heart was in knots inside of her chest, causing so much pain that Galen had to push her hand against her chest to soothe it. It did nothing, though.

So, this was what heartbreak felt like.

"Well," Eve said simply, pushing herself up to her feet. For the first time, the Dreamcatcher faced Galen and the audience. There was a twinkle in her eye that told Galen she knew that she was watching. "I have no more need for you today, Ducky. Go with the others and rest. It shouldn't be long now until you get what you deserve."

With a gleeful smile, Ducky rolled away. He was escorted by Anders and another suited boy who didn't say a word, but Anders whispered something to the Dreamcatcher. Ducky watched as his guide did this but wasn't at all fazed by it. He'd put his full trust in Eve, and in Anders—something that he should've known never to do.

Left alone, Eve stared straight at Galen and even tapped the screen, her smile perverse and hungry. "Are you still watching, poppet?" she asked.

Galen had no idea if Eve could see her or hear her, but all she could muster was the tiniest of nods as streams of tears rolled down her cheeks.

"Oh, come now," the Dreamcatcher soothed, cooing to Galen as if she were a baby. "There's no need to be so sad. Betrayals happen all the time! How could you have not seen this one coming?"

"*I didn't think...*" Galen trailed off, her words barely louder than a whisper. "I didn't think he'd do this to me."

Eve's eyes were filled with something akin to sympathy. "His intentions were never to keep you safe, my sweet. He's a very self-centred thing indeed. I don't like him all that much, but he's provided me with information that I didn't feel like seeking out by myself."

"You did this to him," Galen accused.

"No, no, darling! He did this to himself! He did this of his own free will!" Eve paced back and forth. Her smile dimmed in the corners, the dimples she had in her cheeks disappearing. "You see, when I snagged him the first time, I had every intention of putting him out of his misery. I can't stand his accent, and I can't stand his attitude, but...like the weasel he is, he offered his services to me. How could I refuse?"

Galen wiped at her eyes, but the tears kept flowing. "You could've turned him down! Sent him away! You didn't have to poison his mind!" she sobbed, sitting back on the grass with her head buried between her legs.

"I didn't poison him, poppet." Eve's voice turned stern, cold, and unforgiving. She tapped on the glass again to get Galen's attention and offered her the smallest of beams once their eyes met. "He was already poisoned before you came here. He despised you the second you arrived, and he despised Gillette the second he enslaved him in his colony. He wanted a way out and he knew the only way to get that was to come to me. I've never heard a dream beg and plead the way he does. It's quite amusing, really."

"What will you do now?"

The Dreamcatcher's shoulders shrugged. "Well, I know exactly where you are. I could come and get you."

“What are you going to do with him?” Galen rephrased, spitting the words out of her mouth.

“Ah, well…” Eve trailed off, wincing as she pondered it a moment. “I hadn’t quite thought that far ahead. What would you want me to do with him? You’re the one he’s betrayed, so surely it’s only fair that you get to decide his fate.”

Galen’s head shook—her sadness was starting to turn into anger. “You said you’d give him what he deserved. What did you promise him?”

“Was I not clear enough for you, Galen?” the Dreamcatcher chuckled. “He’ll get what he deserves in due course. You shouldn’t worry about him anymore. He’s made it abundantly clear that he is your foe in this fight, not your friend.”

“And what are you?” Galen felt like she could hurl rocks at the screen, though there were none around her. She wasn’t even sure what that would achieve. “Are you my friend, Eve? Are you here to keep me safe and protect me?”

The Dreamcatcher’s eyes went wide. “I could be,” was all she murmured. She waved that away quickly. “Don’t you see what kind of a point I was trying to make with this? I showed you this betrayal so you would know not to trust everyone so easily. Few people here have your best interests at heart. Do you know how many dreams would hand you over to me in order to gain something stupid? Something material or something monetary? They would trade you in and bargain for something they feel is better for them, something that won’t get them killed.”

Almost pulling her hair out, Galen let out a scream that rocked the very earth she stood on. She forced it out of her body and didn’t stop until she went woozy. Dizzy, Galen climbed to her feet and flung her limbs around. She looked like she was fighting the air. She stopped only when her muscles failed her, and her dizziness took over. Her head spun and Galen fell back to her knees facing away from the screen, away from the Dreamcatcher.

“I believe Gillette told you that you’d experience more than doing harm to a few dreams,” Eve started up again. Her voice was soft and wrapped around Galen like a tight hug. “You know what you have to do. You did it to Peep.”

“Because of you,” Galen wailed.

The Dreamcatcher sighed. “So, this should be easier, no? I can feel the hatred coming off you, my love. There’s a dark side in you, a side that doesn’t like to be crossed, and that’s exactly what’s happened. You and I are programmed the same way. We thrive off revenge. Come and have yours.”

Galen shook her head, tumbling forwards until she was bundled up in a ball with her face pressed against the grass. She said nothing else. How could this have happened? What else could possibly go wrong? The sadness she had felt at first was gone now. Her heart, still broken, was stinging with hatred.

After everything she had done in order to protect Ducky and the rest of the dreams, he'd turned his back on her the second things looked rough. He had no faith in her, no love for her. Galen could only scoff to herself as she sat herself back up, digging her hands into her thighs and staring at Gil who was slowly plodding back over to her. How could she have not seen this coming?

"You know what to do, poppet," Eve said again. "Call for me when you're ready. I'll be there to come and get you."

"Thanks, I guess," Galen replied with a scoff.

A bright light pierced the sky behind Galen, repairing the damage to limbo. She didn't watch it happen, keeping her teary eyes focused on Gil. She wondered if the old bear knew anything about this. Was it brought up whilst she was gone? From the look of worry on Gil's face, he was innocent of this crime.

"What happened? Was that the Dreamcatcher?" he asked, rushing up to Galen. "What's wrong, Galen?"

"We've been ratted out," Galen whimpered softly to herself. Her bottom lip trembled as she spoke those dreaded words. "Ducky betrayed us. He turned to Eve's side when he was kidnapped. It took nothing for him to tell her everything. She's onto us now. We can't escape her."

Gil's mouth was wide open, his beady eyes filled with sorrow and disbelief. He kept trying to talk, kept mouthing words, but never fully formed them. His head would shake and then stop, his brows furrowed and then relaxed. The bear wet his lips and peered back up at Galen, his eyes asking her what the next move was.

"There's only one thing I can do," Galen murmured. She brushed the grass stains off her knees and cracked her jaw, sniffing in. Oh, what a state she was in. "I have to go back there. You have to let me go this time. This has to be the end of it."

Gil didn't reply straight away but pursed his lips together. "You'll kill him," he realised.

"He hated us, Gil!" Galen burst. She got to her feet and paced back and forth; hands run through her hair again. That ponytail she'd worked so hard to fix was ruined once more, sliding down the back of her head. In agitation, she yanked the hairband out of her hair and threw it to the ground. "He hated me! He hated you! He only thought of himself! He thinks Eve's going to give him the world! He thinks he's saved himself because he's no longer affiliated with me! If I don't kill him, she will!"

"Does that make you any better than her?"

Galen couldn't believe what she was hearing. "He's a traitor!" she roared at the top of her lungs. "If we fail, he is partly to blame! She wouldn't have found us if not for him! We had a chance to put distance between us, but now she knows exactly where to find us no matter where we go!"

"You can take me with you."

"I can't do that." Tired, Galen doubled over. She wrapped her arms across her stomach and bent at the waist, so all the blood rushed to her head. "I can't do that. I can't have you die as well. One of us has to survive."

The old bear was resigned to his silence. "I understand," he said painfully quietly. He gulped, waddled over to Galen, and hugged her shin. "I'm sorry I couldn't have done more for you."

"I'm sorry I've done this to you."

"None of this was your fault," the bear chuckled wryly. He smacked Galen's shin playfully, letting out a small huff that was supposed to be another laugh. It came out like a pained sigh. "I never want you to think that you brought this on yourself. This wasn't your fault. Only one person is to blame, and it's me."

Galen lifted her head. "Why? Why is it you?"

"Because I broke my promise, and I went back on my word," Gil admitted. "If I had just…stuck to what I'd agreed to, none of us would be in this mess. Peep would still be alive, and Ducky wouldn't be a traitor. We wouldn't know each other, and maybe that would be for the better."

"You'll see me again," Galen growled, determined. Her hands curled into fists by her sides, squeezed up so tight that each finger eventually cracked. "This isn't our last meeting. I refuse to have this be our goodbye."

Gil smiled. "Well, just in case it is, I'd like a hug." He opened his arms wide and grinned even wider when Galen scooped him off the floor.

Galen hugged the bear like she used to when she was a child. She held him against her shoulder where he snuggled against the side of her neck and squeezed as tightly as she could. He still smelt like her childhood. She didn't let him go for a while, crying a few more tears onto him before he began to push against her to be freed.

“Alright now,” he laughed. “Before you crush me, could you send me to the others?”

Galen put him down with a sigh and closed her eyes to imagine the portal that had sent every other dream home. It appeared to her left, whooshing in from nowhere and shining brighter and stronger than the other. The veil between here and there opened up and Galen could see the settlement thriving.

It was beautiful.

The dreams were about their work, improving what Galen had given them and laughing and playing as families. If only Galen could go back too, but that wasn’t what fate had in store for her.

“You keep your wits about you!” Gil called to her. “Don’t you let her in your head. She’s persuasive, but you’ll always be stronger than her. Remember that.” He playfully punched Galen’s shin, a hit that Galen barely felt, and toddled off towards the portal. Before he climbed through it, he looked back at Galen. “Beat the shit out of her, for me,” he asked.

With a smile, Galen could only chuckle. “I’ll do my best.”

Nodding, Gil stepped through the portal with a smile on his face. He landed in the settlement instantaneously. The rest of the dreams were so happy to see him. They came running up to him, hugging him and crying over him. He had never appeared to be so happy in his life. The smile on his face was contagious. Galen ended up wearing it herself as she watched him wander to where his people had built him a home. How could this bear be a villain? How could he be such a bad guy?

Galen shut the portal and dropped her smile within seconds, remembering the treachery that had been done to her. “I’m ready for you,” she called into the abyss. She shuffled her feet in the mud and pushed her fallen sleeves back up to her elbows, lifting her head to stare forwards. “Come and get me. I’m all by myself.”

“So I can see.” The Dreamcatcher whooshed in behind Galen, appearing from a veil of starlight. She didn’t wear the cape this time. Her face was laden with a grin as happy as can be as she looked over Galen. “Are you ready to go home?”

“I’m not ready to call it that yet,” replied Galen. She didn’t step towards the arms that were open for her. Her feet were as heavy as lead and didn’t want to move. “You couldn’t let me have anything here, could you? You had to take everything I have and leave me with nothing.”

The Dreamcatcher's brows came together in a frown. "Are you blaming me for your apparent friend's unfaithfulness? You think that I made him turn on you?" She swept ever closer, bringing that mist of starlight along with her. It coiled about her shoulders and drifted down her arms as she held Galen by the biceps, hands smothered with her patented gloves. "I wouldn't do that to you. I'm not a monster, as you know."

"You wouldn't do that to me, but you would wilfully agree to his betrayal," Galen surmised. "Sounds just like you, honestly. I can't say I expected you to act any differently."

"You should always stay true to who you are," Eve replied. She lifted her chin and glared down her nose into Galen's eyes, a single brow arched high. "Shall we go?"

Galen had no other option. "I suppose we should." She took in a deep breath and wrapped her arms around Eve's waist as the Dreamcatcher pressed her tightly to her.

The very second that Galen touched Eve; the Dreamcatcher burst into starlight with a little sigh of relief. She took Galen with her, and the two appeared in the centre of the ballroom where mere memories of the masquerade ball lay.

Stepping back, the Dreamcatcher took a moment to gather herself. "You should get used to this place, poppet. It'll become your home soon enough. You'll be here with me all the time."

Galen could think of nothing worse.

"You loved it the first time you were here."

"I didn't realise it was a prison the first time around," rebuffed Galen. She paced about a little bit, remembering the huge throng of people that had surrounded her at the party. How could they live with themselves, supporting such a distasteful asshole?

Eve's cackling filled the room, though it was cut short by the sound of metal clamping down tight.

Galen suddenly couldn't move her hands from behind her back. She'd been caught, again. She rolled her eyes and let out a deep sigh of frustration, cursing herself. For the love of god, she thought. How many times would the Dreamcatcher play these stupid games?

"Anders?" the Dreamcatcher called. Eve had already lost interest. It hurt to see her swagger up the steps to the balconies, not even bothering to watch her minion arrive.

Bursting onto the scene in a puff of feathers, Anders stood with his hands behind his back too, but his weren't chained. "Yes, Miss Catcher? You called?"

"Take her to her room, lock her in and post guards on her door at all times," Eve ordered. "If she escapes, I'm going to personally see to it that each of your limbs are torn off and you are beaten to death with them."

Ouch.

Anders gulped, his Adam's apple bouncing in his throat. "Of course, Miss Catcher." He took hold of Galen's chains and led her from the ballroom, tutting when she wouldn't walk peaceably. He had no time for that, no patience for nonsense. Anders hauled Galen off her feet and kept her over his shoulder as he strolled leisurely through the corridors, parading her around as if she was prey from a hunt.

"Do you enjoy this line of work?" Galen asked.

"Prisoners don't often make small talk," Anders replied. "I, for one, am sick of seeing you back here. How do you keep managing to get caught? I don't see how it is possible for you to be that stupid."

Galen swept her tongue over her lips, forgetting how charming this boy was. "This time is different."

"Different how? Have you finally seen the light? Do you love Miss Catcher now?"

"No," Galen said stiffly. "It's just different. This was done on purpose."

Anders laughed heartily. "You think you're going to be able to target her from the inside? This is where she's strongest, you idiot. You won't be able to do shit to her here."

"What makes you think I want to do anything to her?"

Anders put Galen down in the doorway of a room that she recognised straight away. It was the same room she'd been in before, but it looked bleaker. Moss and algae grew on the walls. The window was fogged up and marred with blood and dirt. The floors were hideous, covered in rot and fungus. The only thing barely salvageable was her bed.

Galen knew she deserved this.

Anders unlocked Galen's cuffs and pushed her into the room, hovering his hand over the doorway. As he wiggled his fingers, a little forcefield appeared, patching itself together with twinkles and shining lights. As pretty as it was, there was no getting through it.

Galen pressed her hands up against it and pushed, but it didn't budge. "Is all of this really necessary? Does she think I'm going to escape again?"

"She knows you'll try your hand at something," Anders replied. He shoved his hands back into his pockets and rolled his eyes, bored. "I can't believe you're back here. I don't understand either the attraction or the fascination you have with this place."

"It calls to me." Galen backed away and climbed up onto her bed, pushing her legs underneath the covers. There was nothing for her to do but rest, lay in bed and let her body heal. She couldn't sleep, but she'd lay in spite with her eyes closed for however long if she had to. "You should probably go. She wouldn't like to see you hanging around me. She'll beat you with your limbs."

Anders scoffed. "You're exactly where you deserve to be."

"Goodbye, Anders."

There was never a reply. Galen was left in the dark with her own thoughts. She didn't mind that so much. She let her eyes stare through the brick wall opposite her. Her anger had subsided, but her thoughts had reignited it. All she could think of was the hurt she'd been through, the struggle, how Ducky had only caused her more pain. She wanted to get her hands on him, talk to him, strangle him, but it was all just a matter of time. Galen had to play the waiting game now. She had to play Eve's game.

Luckily, she knew exactly what she had to do for that.

Chapter Eleven

Hell.

This was hell.

It had to be hell, or some version of it.

Galen sat at the foot of her bed throwing a stone against the wall. Sometimes, she caught it when it came back to her. Other times, it hit her. She'd tried to imagine more fun things to do, tried to conjure up something to occupy her, but none of that worked here. All she had was her stone, but even that was starting to fall apart.

"Have you learnt any lessons yet?"

Anders's voice was the only voice Galen seemed to hear these days. Only God and the Dreamcatcher knew how long it had been. He was still just as tired and bored of her as ever, if not more. Sometimes, he'd come to her door just to taunt her. He'd leave once he grew impatient and tired of her ignoring him, but this time, Galen faced him.

"Why do you keep coming back?"

"Miss Catcher has something for you," Anders explained. He wrung his hands together and nodded to the two people that had been stood watch ever since he'd sealed Galen in. His eyes watched them walk away, only coming back to Galen once they were gone. "You should know that she's in tatters."

Galen arched her brow as she stared Anders down. "Eve is in tatters?" she repeated. "Forgive me, but I don't understand. The woman has feelings? Is that what you're trying to tell me?"

Anders pulled a face. "Very funny," he jeered. "Now, get up. She wants you down in the dungeons."

"Sounds like a fun place." Galen didn't move. She stayed where she was, goading Anders to come and get her. A smile crept onto her face once she saw he'd realised that she wasn't going to come out without a fight.

"You know, you piss me off more than anyone else alive, and I'm a pretty easy person to annoy," Anders commented. He swept his hand through the forcefield in the door and broke it, stepping through without any consequence. "It's a remarkable talent you have," he grunted as he lifted Galen forcefully off the floor and carried her on his shoulder. "You're truly blessed with the ability to creep underneath anyone's skin and infuriate them. Just your face does it for me."

Galen could only laugh. "I'm glad I do something for you, Anders. I'm glad we have a bond."

Scoffing in disgust, Anders made sure to bounce Galen's forehead off the doorframe as he walked through it. "Shut your mouth," he commanded. "You're not supposed to be so cheery. You're supposed to be a prisoner."

"Oh, I'm a prisoner, alright," Galen laughed wryly into Anders ear. She kept trying to bite him, giggling every time he had to wrench his neck to move his head away in time. "I don't get fed, I've forgotten what sunlight is, I've been playing with a rock for what feels like years and I stink. What more could you want from me?"

"For you to shut your mouth," Anders growled through gritted teeth, yowling as Galen sunk her teeth into his earlobe. He dropped her, on purpose of course, dumping her on the ground as hard as he possibly could.

Galen was almost knocked unconscious. Her head bounced off the floor again, this time harder. It knocked her vision into a complete blur and made a stream of nonsense flow out of her mouth. She could only just see Anders's face as he crouched over her and grabbed hold of her face.

"Simple, really. Just shut up, and you won't get hurt," he snarled at her. He scooped her up and, this time, carried her in his arms. "It's always me who gets the shitty jobs," he grumbled to himself. "Never the others. Always me."

Galen was too dizzy for a quick-witted reply. She just laughed hysterically at him instead. That got under his skin just as much, it seemed. He would've dumped her on the ground again, but he hesitated. Galen wondered why. She glanced around herself, noticing the occasional flickering light mounted on the walls and the embalming table in the centre of the room. That woke her up from her daze pretty quickly.

Stood on her feet, Galen saw the Dreamcatcher faffing with something behind the table. She took a small step back, but she felt Anders hand on the small of her back prompting her to stay in place. Whatever was happening, Galen hated it, and she wanted to go back to her room.

"I have her, Miss Catcher," Anders announced. His voice ricocheted off the walls and prompted the Dreamcatcher to turn around, glancing over her shoulder. "She's a little dizzy."

"Dizzy?" Eve replied. Hurriedly, the Dreamcatcher rushed around the table and stood as close to Galen as she could get, pinching her chin. She tilted Galen's head back and looked her over, staring all too deeply into Galen's eyes. "Why is she dizzy?"

Anders gulped. "I found her this way."

"He dropped me on my head," Galen said quickly. She glared at her guide over her shoulder and turned her nose up at him, snarling almost. "He also bounced my head off the doorframe."

The Dreamcatcher was livid. She moved so quickly, like a flash of light, and snagged Anders up in her grip. The two flew backwards into the wall, with Eve's hand curled about Anders's neck. She held him up against the wall, several feet off the ground, choking the life out of him.

"Is this true?" she roared into his face.

Anders tried to pry the Dreamcatcher's fingers off his Adam's apple. "She bit me!" he choked. He let out a little yelp as Eve dropped him to the ground. He fell much like Galen had done. His head hit the floor, but he didn't get back up again. His head had bounced off stone. Ouch.

Galen winced as she watched the Dreamcatcher stalk away from Anders's body, following the perfume trail that Eve left behind. She found her eyes on the embalming table soon enough, wondering what the hell it could've been used for.

"I have two rules here," Eve announced, clearly annoyed. She positioned herself behind the table again and spread her hands out atop it, leaning all her weight on it. "Don't be a nuisance, and don't bite my staff," she growled. "I presume you know why I've brought you down here."

"I don't," Galen admitted. She pointed at the table. "That threw me off. I thought I knew, but now I don't. I'd like to go back to my room."

The Dreamcatcher's signature smile illuminated her face. "Go back? Before you've spoken to Ducky? I didn't think that of you. You were so upset when you watched him spit in your face."

Ducky. Of course.

Galen stood upright, lifting her head high as if to peer over the edge of the table. "Is he here?"

Eve replied with dark, evil laughter. She swept to one side, holding out an arm and gesturing to the cage at the back of the dungeon.

Ducky was stuck in a cell that was barely big enough for him to move. He was constantly wheeling back and forth, doing the best he could to escape, but there was only one way out. There was a hatch on the roof of the cage, one he couldn't get to, and that had the key still sitting in the lock.

Ducky's frantic eyes fell onto Galen, and he gasped. "What? What is she doing here?" he asked Eve, though he got no response from her. "Did you catch her? You did, didn't you? That means this is all over. You can let me go now."

"No, Duck, I don't think I can," the Dreamcatcher whined. "You see, Galen here saw everything. She heard everything. She knows what you did to her." Eve clicked her fingers together and, suddenly, Ducky's cage was hauled off the ground. It floated towards the embalming table and rested in the middle of it, where Eve could rest a hand against it. "As you would imagine, she's not all that pleased with you. She considered you a friend, a close one at that, and you twisted that dagger so deep into her back it's a wonder it didn't come through her chest."

Ducky again glared at Galen, the bottom half of his beak quivering. "Galen, I did what I had to do. You can understand that, surely? You know why I did it."

The Dreamcatcher gestured to Galen and, slowly, Galen came forwards. She took Eve's hand and was led up the few steps to the table, eventually standing in front of Ducky. Her hands fell to the edge of the table which she gripped for dear life, emotions burning through her like fire.

"*I don't know why you did it,*" she whispered to her old friend. Her bottom lip was trembling—she was going to cry again. The tears bubbled in her eyes, but Galen blinked them away in anger. "All this time I thought you were on *my* side. I thought you wanted to live, to win."

"I want to live!" Ducky exclaimed. "That's all I want! I don't care how I win; I just want to live! I don't want to die because of you, or for you. I'm not Gil! I'm not stupid enough to throw my life away for you—someone who won't stick around if they win this war. You'll never be back, and you'll never dream of us again."

Galen felt her heart break even more. It sent shudders all through her. If not for the table in front of her, Galen would've fallen. She bowed her head and let loose strands of her hair fall into her face, doing the utmost not to burst into tears. A hand on her back soothed her, but Galen couldn't bring herself to look at Ducky anymore. She stared at her feet instead.

"You're selfish," Galen hissed through gritted teeth. "I trusted you, and you repay me with selfishness."

"You would've killed me."

Galen's head lifted, and her eyes burned with sheer fury. "What do you think is going to happen now?" she roared at him, so loud that he rolled back until he hit the back of his cage. "What do you think is going to happen to you? Do you think that she's going to let you go free?" The hand on her back slipped down to her waist, hugging her almost. For once, Galen was thankful for the embrace. "You'll die either way," she huffed, letting her lungs fully deflate. "It's obvious you thought I could never save you, but why you think Eve would've is beyond me."

"She's not wrong, Duck," Eve piped up. She kept her arm around Galen and rested her chin on Galen's shoulder. Though she spoke to her prisoner, her eyes were burning into Galen's cheek. "I can't let you go free."

"What?" Ducky squealed, exasperated. "You said you'd let me live if I gave her up!"

"I said you'd get what you deserved," the Dreamcatcher growled. She let go of Galen and grasped Ducky's cage, shaking it in anger. "This is all you deserve! To be imprisoned your whole life! Dreams like you should've never been allowed to exist. You think of no one but yourself, and you have no care for this world. You are vermin, and I never needed you from the start."

The duck began to cry in fear. "No, please! Please, you can't do this to me. I was trying to do the right thing for me!"

"Sometimes, the right thing is to admit defeat." Eve wandered away, and Galen watched her go.

The Dreamcatcher was sauntering up to a burning fire where a red-hot poker was sticking out of a pile of coals. She grabbed hold of it, yanking it out of the embers and wandering painfully slowly back to the embalming table to the symphony of Ducky's fearful shrieks.

Galen felt her heart sink to her feet. "I don't think I can do this…"

"This is what he deserves. This is what all traitors deserve."

Galen remembered how Peep had burst into ashes once fire had touched her and backed away. She shook her head and held her hands up in defeat, wandering further and further away from the table.

The Dreamcatcher watched curiously; head tilted to the side. "Don't tell me you're getting cold feet."

"I can't do this," Galen pleaded with Eve, staring straight into her eyes. She hoped that she'd reached Eve's soul with her pleas but started to wonder if the Dreamcatcher even had one to begin with. "We should spare him."

"Spare him?" Eve repeated slowly, spelling out each word. Did she not know what that meant? "Why would we do that?"

Galen was shaking with fear. "We can banish him somewhere," she said quickly, forcing the words out of her mouth. "You can banish him somewhere! You're powerful enough. You don't have to kill him, just send him away. How happy can his life be if he's all by himself?"

Eve pondered it for a moment.

"Please, Eve," Galen begged. "I can't see another dream die."

"Listen to her, Eve," Ducky piped up. That, surely, was a mistake. "Don't let the rest of the dreams out there think you have no mercy."

The Dreamcatcher whirled around on Ducky. "You, shut up!" she ordered. She turned back to Galen and strolled up to her, burning hot poker still in hand. "This isn't at all like you," she murmured under her breath, almost groaning. She was so close to laying the poker against Galen's cheek. The smoke was beginning to sting Galen's eyes. "Why the sudden change of heart? Tell me what you feel for him."

"Pity," Galen sighed. "I pity him. I'm not a killer."

"You killed Peep."

Another sigh left Galen, this one followed by a few tears. "Because I had to. It was the only way for her to be at peace. You…" Galen presumed Eve knew what she'd done to the cowgirl and chose not to bring it back up. "I wouldn't beg for anything, but I can't stomach to watch another dream I know turn to ash."

Eve dropped the poker by her side, not letting it go but letting it rest low. With hunched shoulders, the Dreamcatcher hummed as she wandered around. She was truly considering it! This had to be a breakthrough of some kind. Galen had gotten through to Eve! The Dreamcatcher was sauntering around, racking her brain for the right thing to do. Her feet led her behind the embalming table where Ducky was huddled in his cage, breathing heavily. She let her eyes drift to Galen's, and showed her a true, loving smile.

Suddenly, that all changed.

"I don't think I will," Eve said. With no warning, the Dreamcatcher lifted the poker and jammed it through the bars, running Ducky straight through. He evaporated into ash with a cut-off scream, still burning when Eve withdrew the poker.

Galen covered her mouth with her hands and choked back a sob. She fell to her knees, staring at the pile of ash that had once been her friend. Though she despised him for what he'd done, she cried for him. Her heart broke, this time out of sorrow. She bowed her head and closed her eyes, though that did nothing to stop the flow of tears.

"Come now," Eve shouted, tossing away the poker and storming back down the steps. "You cannot be upset over the loss of a traitor! Do you think kings and queens weep every time one of their mutineers are beheaded? No!"

Galen could barely hear what the Dreamcatcher had to say. A high-pitched hissing had begun in her ears, drowning out everything else around her. She tumbled backwards, landing heavily on her ass, and sat defeated in the dungeon. Her lips moved, but no words fell from her tongue. She had nothing left to say. She just wanted to be alone.

Galen zoned out. She had no idea what was happening around her. The Dreamcatcher was talking to her, singing at her, but Galen couldn't hear a single thing she said. The hissing in her ears drowned everything out, even Eve's probably harsh words. She stared vacantly out ahead of her at Ducky, at the pile of ashes that remained of him. How could she have been so stupid to think the Dreamcatcher would spare him? She should've stepped in. She should've spared him herself. She should've given the traitor some mercy.

There was a hand on Galen's shoulder, Eve's hand, squeezing tightly. Galen turned her head and looked up into the Dreamcatcher's eyes through a wall of tears. She noted the worry that was plastered across Eve's face, but she didn't really care. Her heart and her chest were void of all emotion and feeling. She was numb and felt nothing as the Dreamcatcher pulled her in and rested her head on her shoulder. Embraced in a tight, loving hug, Galen still felt nothing. She let out a deep sigh and closed her eyes, melding into Eve and letting the tears stream freely down her cheeks.

"Anders?"

Galen could hear Eve's voice clearly now, ringing loud and proud in her ears. She lifted her head and watched the Dreamcatcher reanimate Anders. Her mouth fell open in awe as Eve's magic picked Anders off the ground with a few flicks of her fingers and stood him on his own feet. Still, the boy didn't wake up, which prompted the Dreamcatcher to sigh heavily and peel herself away from Galen.

"You stay right here. Don't you move," she instructed. Eve strolled away to her minion and sized him up. The Dreamcatcher first clamped her hands on her hips, standing at a slant as Anders just snored in her face. She scoffed lightly once more and took one of her hands off her hip, slapping him the face roughly and backing off again.

Anders jolted awake. "Yes, Miss Catcher! Of course, Miss Catcher!" he blurted out. He shook his head and ran his hands over his face, his fingers lingering on the red mark on his cheek. "What happened…"

"You fell asleep on the job, my boy," Eve sung lightly. She again looped an arm around Galen's waist and pressed her face against the side of Galen's head. Was she going to kiss her? That hadn't happened yet. The kiss Galen expected never came, but the Dreamcatcher stayed as close as she possibly could. "I need you to take her back to her room. Poor poppet has seen a few things that have messed with her mind. I think she needs some alone time, some rest."

"Yes, Miss Catcher," Anders replied wheezily. He shook his head again and blinked rapidly, as if to clear his vision. Gradually, he began to pace up to Galen. One eye was facing one way and the other was facing the other way as he grabbed hold of Galen's bicep and hauled her away from Eve.

Never before had the Dreamcatcher moved so fast in her life. She suddenly sprinted forwards and weaved her way in front of Anders, once more slapping him in the face. Was this how she treated all of her staff? Eve beat Anders back to the floor and stood over him, breathing heavily.

"How dare you treat her like a common prisoner?" the Dreamcatcher roared at Anders.

Anders scurried away like a beetle and rose to his feet only when he was behind Galen. He used her as a human shield, clinging to her shoulders and pushing her forwards as the Dreamcatcher seethed and raged at him.

"You will guide her back to her room and you will take good care of her, do you understand me?" Eve growled through her gritted teeth. She stepped forward and tenderly cupped Galen's cheek, staring lovingly into her eyes. "She's precious to me, Anders. I hope you realise that sooner or later, or those limbs are definitely going to come off."

Galen was suddenly scooped up into Anders's arms, yelping as her feet flew from the floor. She tried to fight, pushing her hands against Anders's chest, and wriggling in his grip. Surprisingly, the boy was strong. She couldn't get free of him, so lay still staring up at the ceiling with her limbs going dead and limp. Her eyes closed and her heart went still inside of her as Eve's hand fell away from her. This surely felt like the end.

"Be gentle with her," Eve pleaded.

"Of course, Miss Catcher." Anders bowed to Eve and wandered past her with Galen still in his arms. He didn't have sort of witty remark or retort this time, no comeback that would sting one's ego. Anders, for once, said absolutely nothing. He kept his mouth shut as he carried Galen up the stairs and back up into civilisation, where a sigh escaped his lips. "You truly are precious to her." To hear him speak was quite surprising, but Galen wasn't really listening. "I see it now. I envy you." Anders glanced down at Galen and let out another sigh, almost huffing to himself. "Ignoring me, I see. That's fair. You get your rest. You'll be feeling a lot worse very soon."

That was threatening. Galen paid it no mind. She kept her eyes closed and wriggled away from Anders as he lowered her into her bed. Galen turned her back instantly, bundling herself up under the covers and wishing that a sweet sleep would wash over her. Knowing it never would, Galen let out a sigh as she felt her mattress warp behind her.

"Are you okay?" Anders asked. For once, it sounded like he actually cared.

Galen scoffed to herself and squeezed out a few more tears, burrowing deeper into her bed. "Go away, Anders," she whimpered. "I don't want to talk to you."

"Things are about to get a lot worse, Galen. You should listen to me."

"Go, Anders." Galen threw her arm backwards and pointed to the door, refusing to watch him go. She let out a sigh of relief when the mattress sprung back to its normal level, bringing the covers up over her head. Through the fabric, she could hear the door shut. As soon as it locked, Galen began to sob. The tears flowed freely down her face, stinging her eyes, and the sobs that she had tried to keep silent became loud and throaty. She hadn't cried so loud before, or so hard. Her heart was truly broken, fully broken. None of her heartstrings remained intact. Her heart just floated in her chest, hanging there limply with a massive crack down the centre of it. Would it ever repair itself?

The crying had stopped a while ago, but Galen's face was incredibly sore. The muscles in her cheeks were taut and strained, her eyes dry and cracking. She sat cross-legged on her bed, atop the covers, staring up at the full moon that shone over Eve's province. There were people outside. Some sort of party was being held. Galen had watched the Dreamcatcher boss people about to set it all up, propping up tables that were then laden with elegant foods and drinks. A makeshift floor had been laid down atop the front stretch of lawn, and little tents, pagodas and gazebos had been erected for cover. All the guests had arrived, collecting plates of foods that Galen didn't recognise. At one point, she'd wondered why she hadn't been invited, but then she found herself realising that she didn't care.

One thing that Galen did notice was that Eve wasn't at her own party. The Dreamcatcher had made herself known when she'd been bossing everyone around but, as soon as everything was ready, she had disappeared. What else could Eve be doing? There looked to be important people down there, bustling about, socialising with one another. Though they kept to their cliques, a few people mingled. Galen watched them closer. There was one man who was going from group to group, introducing himself to the ladies before moving on to the gentlemen.

"It's a thriving kingdom," Eve's voice sounded from the doorway. She let light flood into the room that almost blinded Galen but was quick to shut it behind her. "It's a party to envy, for sure. I wouldn't want to miss it for the world."

Galen sniffed in, running her hand underneath her nose. "Why are you not down there?" she asked. She watched the Dreamcatcher over her shoulder, but instantly yanked her eyes away once Eve tried to meet her eye. "I watched you set it all up. Why would you exert all of that energy for nothing? Was it just a distraction so that no one would interrupt you?"

"Interrupt me from doing what, my sweet?" Eve cooed. "What do you think I've come up here to do?"

"I'm not entirely sure I want to know."

Eve sat herself on the side of the bed, kicking off her high heels and pulling up her legs to cross beneath her. "How do you feel, Galen?" she questioned suddenly. "Is your head heavy? Are your eyes tired? Do you feel…off?"

"Why do you care?"

The Dreamcatcher's eyes hardened and flickered away. "You'll be upset with me, Galen, I know you will, but I need you to listen to me. I need you to hear me out."

Galen turned around, pushing her back against the window and glaring at the Dreamcatcher. "What do you have to say?"

"It's become apparent to me that you're coming into your own whilst you're here, which is both delightfully pleasing but problematic." Eve wriggled around until she faced Galen, reaching out with a hand to draw a circle on Galen's knee with her gloved finger. "You're gaining power, becoming stronger, giving me a run for my money. You can surely understand why I can't let this happen. You're weakening me, poppet. I know you don't mean to, and I know you're not doing it on purpose, but I can't let this continue."

Swallowing her pride, Galen brought her legs back to her and tried to wriggle away from Eve. She suddenly felt uncomfortable. Her skin was crawling with dread as the Dreamcatcher followed her. Galen tucked herself into the corner and grabbed hold of her pillow to thrust in front of her, as if that would protect her.

"I can't let you out of this room," Eve said sharply, suddenly. She climbed off the bed, standing tall and proud and flattening the creases in her glittery dress. It was a dark, midnight blue in colour with sparkles that were yellow and white. "This is where you have to stay until this is all done with, until this has ended."

Oh, that was what this was about.

Galen relaxed her grip on the pillow and let it tumble away from her. That's why Eve had been asking all those questions. The Dreamcatcher was draining Galen's existence and, this time, Galen could feel it happening.

"Won't you talk to me?" the Dreamcatcher begged. "Don't you have something to say? I know how you must be feeling…Trust me, poppet, this isn't how I wanted this to go. This isn't how I wanted you to feel about me."

"I don't feel anything," Galen replied with no intonation. She met Eve's eyes, giving out a sigh that deflated her lungs. "I know what you're doing, and I don't think I have enough energy to do anything about it. So, what happens now?"

Eve took a moment to herself. "We both know what happens now, Galen. No point talking about it."

"I'm going to die, aren't I?" Galen chuckled to herself, forcing out a smile. She'd known it for a while now. "This really is the end. You've won this fight. I don't understand how I went so wrong. I'm going to be trapped here forever."

The Dreamcatcher came scurrying back to Galen's bedside. "Now, now. You shouldn't think like this," she soothed. She sat herself down again and reached out to cover Galen's hand with her own, squeezing it lightly. "Once I have your power, once this is all over, you'll be free to roam the dreamland. I had plans for us, actually. There were things that I wanted to do with you at my side."

"How would that happen, Eve?" Galen shouted. "You'll kill me! You'll live out there, in the real world, where I should be. I'll have to watch on whilst you live the perfect life you've always dreamt of whilst I'm stuck here, rotting away, existing only as a dream."

"Doesn't sound like an ideal fate, does it?" Eve replied with a little attitude. She caught herself suddenly, realising her harshness. "I didn't mean to snap at you, my love. I can understand your sourness. I've been meaning to have a talk with you and, whilst now seems like the perfect time to have said talk, I'll spare you of it."

Galen's brows came together. "What do you mean?"

Eve just shook her head. "Plans have changed, Galen. Keep that in mind. I have…other intentions at heart. What you should know now is that you and I are destined for one another. You'll love it here eventually. I know you will." She got up, sliding her feet back into her high heels and heading straight for the door. "I'll be seeing you every night, poppet. I want to make sure nothing goes awry, and I want you to know the real me. I want you to know I'm not a monster. I have big things planned for you, Galen. If only you knew…" She stood in the doorway with one hand around the door handle and her eyes on her prisoner. She stared longingly at Galen with nothing but true love in her gaze. It was devastating to see. The woman was truly losing her mind. "Get some rest, sweetheart. I'll be back."

"What are you here for?"

Anders had been hesitating in the doorway for around ten minutes but hadn't said a word. He'd been just looking at Galen, staring at her in horror before tearing his eyes away to look elsewhere. His hands were deep within his pockets, his auburn hair falling into his eyes, his eyes filled with disgust.

"What are you here for?" Galen repeated, glaring over her shoulder. She'd taken to sitting with her back to the door. Looking out of it brought her too much pain. It made her dream of an escape. Instead, she always sat in front of the window, watching whatever the gardeners or the staff or Eve's devoted slaves were doing.

“Miss Catcher asked me to come,” Anders explained, clearing his throat. Still, he didn’t step into the room. What was keeping him from coming any closer? “She asked me to keep you company until she arrived. She’s gone out for the day.”

Galen knew that already. “I watched her go.”

“Right…” Anders drifted off.

Pacing back and forth in the thin doorway, Anders fought for conversation. His eyes were piercing straight through Galen’s back—she could feel them. He looked at her the same way everyone else did, with horror in their eyes. There was something they were seeing that she wasn’t.

Galen just wanted to know what that was.

“You don’t have to stay here,” Galen mumbled to herself. Curious, she peeled herself from her bed and extended her legs out, so they were flat. Her bones creaked and groaned as she stretched them, cracking as she stood and hobbled her way to her mirror. “I can see how much it pains you to stand there and look at me. It pains everyone. They’re always so eager to leave.”

“I’m not eager to leave,” Anders defended, pushing his vascular hand through his pretty red locks. “You and I aren’t the best of friends, is all. I don’t understand why she keeps sending me up here.”

Galen stifled a smile and a laugh. “Maybe she wants us to get to know each better so we can all get along and be friends. Her intentions these days are extremely unclear.”

“You’ve heard she’s shifted her beliefs.” Anders pondered that for a moment, his face rife with confusion. Galen was staring at him through the mirror, watching his eyes cloud with confliction. “I suppose that’s good. I suppose that means she’s told you.”

“Told me what?”

That was just the thing. Eve had visited her many times since the elegant party that had been thrown out front, but never had she told Galen her new intentions. There had been whispers through the corridors, mumblings through the walls, but Galen was still left in the dark. Maybe Anders would let it slip. Maybe she’d finally find out.

Anders ran his tongue across his bottom lip. “From your eagerness, I’d say she hasn’t told you. That’s…her job. I’m not going to do it for her. She’s already threatened to kill me about four times today, I don’t need her to actually go through with it.”

Galen turned back to herself in the mirror. She pulled at her baggy clothes. They just hung around her body, like they were hung on a coat hanger. Nothing she wore flattered her anymore. Was this what everyone was so horrified by? Her fashion sense? She couldn't help that. With a shake of her head, Galen dismissed those thoughts.

Deep down, she knew what was driving everyone away. The gauntness of her face said it all. Her eyes had once had life in them, but now they were just listless, dull, and colourless. Though she'd had high cheekbones before, the skin of her face was hanging off them. They jutted out against her flesh, pulling it so taut that every single teeny tiny vein could be seen struggling to pump blood. Galen pulled at her face, though nothing really moved. She ran her fingers over her blunt jawline, down her yellowing neck and across her chest. Had her collarbones always been so prominent? She lifted her shirt and stared at her torso. Were her ribs supposed to be this apparent? Her stomach fell in as her ribs ended, becoming sallow and empty. She'd eaten plenty, the Dreamcatcher made sure of that. Still, she was wasting away. There was nothing she could do but watch and be everyone's oddity to ogle at.

"It shouldn't be long now."

Anders's voice woke Galen up from her daydream, prompting her to move away from her horrid reflection. She knew what he was talking about. She'd be dead soon. Galen had known that a long time ago. The time she'd spent dwelling on it was time she'd never get back, so she dismissed it with a flap of her hand.

"It won't hurt, if you're worried about that," Anders went on. There was a slam of the front door that frightened him out of his skin and made him that much more eager to leave. He began to stare down the corridor, eagerly awaiting the arrival of his boss. "You won't feel a thing. It'll be like nothing ever changed. You'll go to sleep, finally." He cracked a smile at Galen as she sat herself on the edge of her bed, one leg crossed over the other. When she didn't smile back, Anders chuckled wryly and dropped his grin. "You'll go to sleep feeling and looking like utter shit and wake up looking and feeling immortal and untouchable. It's quite the trade."

"Despite your efforts, you've not made me feel any better about dying," Galen told him.

His head hung again. "I'm not the person for this. She knows that. It would be better if she just left you to your own thoughts."

Galen held up a single finger as if to scold Anders. "Ah, but she doesn't like that. She thinks I'm unhealthy and destructive. She thinks I need someone around me at all times to make sure I'm not going to hurt myself."

"What damage could you possibly do to yourself?"

"The number of things I can think of and have thought of would shock you," Galen replied. She could hear the footsteps approaching. Those cursed high heels. It had felt like years that she'd been trapped within Eve's province but still she wasn't used to that infernal racket. "Is that her?"

Anders didn't even have to look. He nodded his head and bowed out of the way as a tall shadow fell over him. His eyes bore into Eve, not looking into her eyes but glaring at her. Galen could tell he still didn't believe in her. In fact, from the way he glowered at her, it seemed like he had learned to hate her even more.

The Dreamcatcher dumped her fur coat in Anders's arms and dismissed him with a little flap of her hand, not saying a single word to him. She didn't even wait to see if he'd left before she swept into the room and slammed the door shut behind her. Eve was furious. It was written all over her face. She'd gone out to achieve something, and it hadn't gone her way.

Notorious for her hissy fits, it took every muscle in Eve's body not to throw the biggest tantrum of all time. She did her best to calm herself, running her fingers through her hair and holding it back on her scalp, breathing in a slow, soothing rhythm.

None of it worked.

"Bad day?" Galen remarked. She felt like she and Eve had become an old married couple. This nightly visit was a routine that she both loved and hated. The Dreamcatcher was one of the only people who didn't stare at her like she was a freak. Though she came to suck more of Galen's life from her, it didn't matter anymore. She was nice about it, at least. That's what Galen kept telling herself.

"You wouldn't believe what I have had to deal with," Eve growled through gritted teeth. This would not be one of the good nightly visits—the cosy ones where the Dreamcatcher would light a fire and hold Galen close to her. "You've caused me a lot of strife today, poppet, and this is the first time I'm seeing you."

Galen had no idea what she possibly could've done.

"That settlement you made for Gillette?" Eve recalled, laughing. "He's weaponised it. He is dragging any dream that gets close enough, kicking and screaming, into that colony and keeping them there. He's building an army. Why is he building an army?"

"Gil never expressed any intention of fighting when I last saw him."

Again, the Dreamcatcher just laughed. "Why would he tell you? He has no faith in you now. You're one of my belongings, at least, that's what he thinks." She threw herself on the end of the bed, lying flat on her back with her hands knotted over her stomach. "The one time that I open myself up to pity the bear, the one time I try to make a deal with him, he spits in my face."

"What happened?" Galen twisted her body, so she looked down into Eve's eyes, seeing the hurt on the Dreamcatcher's face.

It was hard not to be attached to her. It was hard not to develop feelings. For however long she'd been trapped, Galen had tried to keep herself distanced from Eve. The Dreamcatcher was a mixed batch of eggs, some rotten and some fresh. Was she a horrible person? No. Did she do horrible things? Yes. Did those things make her a horrible person?

Well, it was hard to say.

Galen found herself pitying Eve at first, but that pity had soon snowballed into an affection like no other. The more physical Eve grew with her, the more confident, the more she found herself leaning into the Dreamcatcher, asking for hugs, holding her hand, soothing her when she was upset. Galen knew she had to stop, that it would only make things worse for her, but she couldn't help herself. Eve was a person worthy of love, and it was difficult not to give her that love.

"I tried to reason with the old bear," Eve explained with a sigh. She sat herself up, pushing her hair from her face and rubbing at her eyes fiercely. The Dreamcatcher was getting tired. "I told him that I didn't want to hurt you anymore. I told him…" she drifted off, running her tongue over her teeth.

Leaning in, Galen put a hand on the Dreamcatcher's knee and received only a shudder as a reply—it was clear that Eve still wasn't used to receiving her touch. "You can tell me."

"I told him that I had other plans for us, for me," she finally went on. She wouldn't meet Galen's eyes, choosing to stare dead ahead of her at the door. "He said that he'd had someone on the inside this entire time, someone that was feeding him information. He said he saw you in this state." This time, Eve did turn to Galen. She ran her gloved hand across Galen's gaunt face and let out a different kind of shudder. "To make things short, he didn't want to accept any sort of deal I laid out in front of him, no matter if it would spare his life later down the line."

"Why have your intentions changed?" Galen asked suddenly. She gripped the Dreamcatcher's knee tighter and begged her to meet her eye. "Why does everyone keep asking me if you've told me something? Anders said your beliefs had shifted, and the rest of your staff keep telling me that you've made grand changes to your plan. What's going on, and why won't you tell me?"

The Dreamcatcher's jaw cracked so loud it sounded as if it had snapped in two. "My staff should know better than to run their mouths," she growled. She eyed Galen up, taking Galen's chin in her hand then pushing her away again. "My beliefs have shifted; I'll freely tell you that much." She got to her feet, slipping her heels off and kicking them towards the door. "It took me a little while to realise that nothing in the real world really waits for me. I'll have no power there and, eventually, I'll die. I don't want that."

Galen already didn't like where this was going.

"I want a world that I can rule, that I can still be all-powerful in, and the real world just isn't that world." The Dreamcatcher hugged her arms around her and sauntered to the fireplace, flicking her fingers towards it, and setting the kindling and the coal inside it ablaze. "This world needs me, and I need what is in this world. I wouldn't dare step foot anywhere without you and, if I were to become real…I would kill you."

Galen sat on the edge of her bed, her heart pounding in her chest. "So, what is this all for? Why are you still draining me of my existence if that's not what you want anymore?"

"Who said I was draining your existence?"

Galen's world rocked. She found that her head started to spin, and her vision became encircled with blackness. Sprawling backwards, she scurried into the corner so that the walls would keep her upright. Her eyes focused on Eve as the Dreamcatcher came wandering back to her bedside, her bottom lip quivering.

"Things have changed, poppet. You're not going anywhere, and neither am I." She grinned evilly at Galen, showing off her perverse colours. It made Galen's skin crawl. "As for the likes of Gillette and all those other miserable dreams, well…we're just going to have to find a way to make them submit."

"S-s-submit?" Galen stuttered. "I don't understand…"

A little, ditzy sigh left Eve's lungs. "You won't," she whined. "Not for a while, but don't you worry. By the time this is all over—" The Dreamcatcher reached forwards and ran her fingers down Galen's face, staring at her both lustfully and lovingly. "By the time I'm reenergised with your strength and power, I'll have fixed everything for us. Then, you'll understand everything."

What could she be planning? Galen didn't even have the strength or the focus or the concentration to decipher the Dreamcatcher's plans anymore. She kept flip-flopping. One moment, she desperately wanted to be set free and let loose amongst the real world. Now, that didn't seem ideal to her. What could've possibly changed her mind? What plan could've replaced her old one?

Galen would've pushed for an answer. There were nights that she'd spent arguing with Eve until she'd heard what she'd wanted from the Dreamcatcher's mouth, but she was just too tired. Her mind was barely working. Stringing together a sentence was too much work. All Galen could do was sit tight and hope for the best, hope that Eve's monstrous habits weren't preceding her.

"I need one last thing from you tonight, poppet." The Dreamcatcher was the door, with her high heels dangling from her fingers.

Galen's heart fell in her chest as she clumsily rushed forwards, falling off the bed. "You're not staying with me?" She picked herself up, though her arms barely had the strength to push her up. It took her several attempts to get to and stay on her feet, and even longer to struggle over to where Eve was stood. "Why are you leaving so soon? You usually stay with me."

The look in the Dreamcatcher's eye was one of pity. "Oh, my sweet." Eve combed her fingers through Galen's matted hair and hid a wince, or a grimace of disgust. "I can't stay tonight. I have things to do."

"But—"

"There is something that I need from you though, Galen," Eve spoke over Galen. Something else had happened with Gil. There was a fury burning like no other in the Dreamcatcher's eyes. Did she think she could just hide it? "I need you to tell me you believe in me still."

Galen's jaw went slack. How could she possibly ask for this? Galen had half a mind to tell her that she didn't believe anymore, though she had been privy to what happened to non-believers. Becoming a pile of ash wasn't on her bucket list, funnily enough.

"I need to hear it, my love," Eve crooned. Her voice was so alluring, so convincing. She could sell ice to an Eskimo. In another life, the Dreamcatcher could've very well been a siren. "Something in you wains, and I don't want to believe it's because you've lost faith in me. I'm still the same person. You believe I'm real, don't you?"

Knowing that she shouldn't say it, Galen fought with herself internally. She gulped down her fear and her pride, though it stuck in a ball in her throat. Her hands pushed against the Dreamcatcher's chest, her touch sending enough energy and electricity through Eve to jolt her away. Separated, Galen felt like she stood on her own two feet again. She opened her mouth to talk, the word 'no' sitting at the tip of her tongue, when Eve rushed in and fiercely pressed her lips against Galen's.

There was no other feeling like it. Galen had no idea what to do. Should she pull away? No, she couldn't. Deep down, this was what she had wanted. There was so much tension between the two. She couldn't kiss Eve, though. Eve was the bad guy! The villain! Still, Galen found herself instinctually melting against the Dreamcatcher. Her body fell into Eve's. Her eyes closed. She gently, timidly, kissed Eve back, moving her lips only slightly.

Just as Galen wanted to throw herself at the Dreamcatcher, Eve pulled away.

"*Do you believe?*" Eve whispered, looping her arms around Galen's waist.

It was a trick. It was all a trick. Galen pulled away from the kiss feeling more drained, more tired. The last of her life had to have been gone. That had to have been it. Her energy and her strength were completely depleted. Her knees began to shake beneath her. She couldn't keep herself up by herself anymore. Her body slumped into the hug that the Dreamcatcher gave her, her arms flopping over Eve's shoulder. There was only one way to feel better.

"*Yes,*" Galen whispered back shakily. She fell to the ground, hitting her knees into the floorboards and almost slumping forwards. Luckily, Eve didn't just leave her. She was scooped back up, hoisted from her feet and into Eve's arms. If she was any more awake, she would've found the gesture romantic. Instead, Galen was barely clinging to life. She could hear rapid beeping in her ears, like the sound of her heart rate monitor from the hospital.

She had to have been dying.

Is this what dying felt like? If so, Galen rather welcomed it.

Chapter Twelve

Galen wasn't dead.

Out of her room, wandering around the gardens all by herself, Galen breathed in the fresh air around Eve's kingdom. It was the first time that the Dreamcatcher had let her out in a long time, though Eve had been dubious about letting her go alone.

"You'll need someone to show you round, won't you?" the Dreamcatcher had proposed.

Galen just shook her head. "I'll find my way."

And found a way, she had. Where she was, Galen didn't really know. It felt like she'd been walking for days. It was a miracle her legs were still working. After her last encounter with Eve, Galen had barely been able to move. The more belief she put into the Dreamcatcher, the less of herself remained. She was donating her energy to Eve. The Dreamcatcher was ever so insistent on letting her know that all her energy and strength would return to her but, for now, she'd be a little sore and a little slow.

Galen caught on to the sound of a second set of footsteps. For a while now she'd been suspecting someone following her. She hadn't been sure at first, but she also hadn't been surprised. There were two names in her mind of who the culprit could be. The first was obviously Eve. The Dreamcatcher had insisted on a guide and must've chosen to follow in Galen's footsteps once she was rejected. The second was Anders. No matter where Galen was, Anders was also always there.

She leant towards it being Anders. There weren't any high heels sounding in her ears. Galen didn't have a blinding headache because of the incessant tapping. No, it sounded like boots squishing the gravel down into the path. Whoever wore them walked hastily, too. Anders was always rushing to places.

It had to be him.

In the distance, Galen could see a stone bridge that connected to floating pieces of land. A gushing river stormed underneath it, tumbling downwards into a waterfall once it had passed beneath it. That was where she was headed. No one else stood over there. No one else was remotely near there. They all stuck near the house and whispered behind their hands as Galen veered down the path towards it.

When she got to the middle, Galen turned abruptly and walked straight into Anders's chest. She'd been right. All she could muster was a cheeky grin and a little wag of her finger which she prodded Anders with, jeering at him.

"I knew it was you," she snapped, chuckling to herself. Galen mustered the strength to push him a few paces away from her, but it took almost everything she had. "Why are you following me now? Are you in love with me?" Galen found that comment made her stomach churn. "If you are, I politely do not reciprocate."

Anders rolled his eyes. "There isn't a polite way to tell me you don't love me," he remarked, flicking Galen's hand away from him, "and no. I don't love you. I've found that you're the only company I can keep without being insulted or maimed in some way."

"You think I have the strength to hurt you?" Galen couldn't help by hysterically laugh. If she was up to it, she would've doubled over and slapped her knee. "Have you seen me? You could snap me like a twig."

"I could snap you like a twig even when you are your normal self." Anders adjusted his blazer, his usual black suit still smothering his body, and let his hands sink to his pockets. What did he have in there that was so interesting? His hands never left his sides. "I'm disgusted that she'd take it this far with you. She has more than enough power, she can't need anything else."

Galen scoffed. "Unluckily for her, I don't think I have anything else to give. I'm like an empty Capri Sun packet. All I have left is my will to live."

"Can't say I've noticed you had one of those."

"Yeah, not so much these days." Galen hung her head and continued wandering across the bridge, taking her time to pick her steps. Her legs couldn't stretch that far ahead of her anymore. She found herself shuffling much like Ms Elzbieta had done. Oh, how that old woman would laugh at her now. "She finally told me that she had something else planned, that she didn't want to be real anymore."

"Did she tell you what she had planned?"

"No."

Anders scoffed.

"We're getting there!" Galen reasoned. She huffed to herself and stopped at the nearest bench, struggling to sit herself down. It was embarrassing going for a walk and only managing a few metres before collapsing in exhaustion. She felt like everyone around was laughing at her, including and especially Anders. "This has started to become normal to me. Feeling like this. It's as if I've aged about fifty years overnight. I'm barely able to keep my eyes open."

"Well," Anders stretched his back and took the vacant seat on the bench next to Galen, sitting slovenly like a school kid. He still kept his hands in his pockets as he watched everyone on the other side of the bridge bustle and work. Some of them weren't doing much of anything but pretended to once his eye landed on them. "You know what that means then."

Galen rolled her eyes—here came more of his morbidity. "The end is in sight," Galen repeated mockingly. How many times did she have to hear that? She shook her head and let out a sigh of frustration that flared her nostrils wide. "Why does it have to take so long? I thought she'd done it last night, but apparently, I was mistaken. I wasn't expecting to wake up and still look like a skeleton."

"Why's that?"

Galen hesitated. "Well, she…" she drifted off, awkwardly scratching at the nape of her neck. The topic made her blush. She remembered last night well. She'd spent the whole time she'd been left alone thinking about it. Thinking about it now only made her want to do it again, but she shook away those temptations and did her best to forget they existed. "She kissed me."

Anders went silent and rigid, stiff as a board.

"I don't think she meant anything by it," Galen quickly explained. She was stumbling over her own words, not able to string together a tangible sentence. "I think it was a trick. She was frightened I'd tell her that I didn't believe in her anymore."

"And kissing you would make you change that opinion?" Anders repeated. "She must be draining your common sense as well as your power because you've become as dumb as a rock all of a sudden. Either that, or you've started to develop the same feelings as she has."

Galen glared at him. "Same feelings?"

"You're in love with her, you idiot."

"I'm not!" Galen insisted. She didn't mean for that to come out so harsh, but even she was taken aback by her firmness. For a split second, Galen gathered herself. Why couldn't Anders just be a nice person for once? "I don't think I am. I would know, wouldn't I? If I was?"

Anders shrugged. "I'm not sure why you're asking me."

"I thought you'd know."

He brought his brows together. "Why on earth would I know? I don't know about all that stuff. All I know is that as soon as Eve has love, she'll stop being so…uptight." He flipped his auburn hair out of his eyes like a member of a boyband trying to get girls to swoon for him. His face annoyed Galen. "I was hoping that you'd wise up to her advances a little quicker than you did, but you disappointed me."

"Good."

"Why she can't just snap your neck and be done with it, I don't know," Anders snarled. He didn't hear the footsteps leading up behind him, the high heels tapping against the brick bridge. He also didn't see the Dreamcatcher looming behind him, grimacing at him.

"I happen to treasure the girl, Anders."

Galen had never seen a man jump out of his skin quite the way Anders did. He curled into himself, almost wrapping himself up into a little ball. His body flew from the bench, his legs and arms flailing around him as he landed like a frightened cat a few feet away from the bench. It took everything Galen had not to laugh at him.

The Dreamcatcher was less impressed. "Why is it that whenever I find you, you're always with Galen?" she asked him. She held her head to the side and stared holes through him, gradually prowling up to him. "Is there something you want to tell me, Anders? Have you warmed up to her company?"

"No, Miss Catcher," Anders said quickly. It was painful for him to keep eye contact, Galen could tell. There was nothing else he wanted more than to be able to look away from her. "I'm not awfully fond of Galen. She's not the company I would choose to keep if there were other options in the house."

"It's a grand house, Anders," replied the Dreamcatcher. "The rest of your flock would quite like to welcome you back. They've missed you."

Anders's brows furrowed with confusion. "My-m-my flock?" he stammered. "I don't understand, Miss Catcher."

Eve towered over him. "There's a reason you were given the mask you were," she snarled at him. Ah, the masquerade masks. Anders resembled nothing of a flamingo, though. "You were all put into groups for a reason. Go back to your flock."

Dread filled Anders. "Yes, Miss Catcher. Of course." He slunk away like a scolded child, head bowed, and hands still pushed deep within his pockets. His feet walked him quickly back to the house where he promptly disappeared. Galen knew he wouldn't go looking for the rest of the flamingos. He hated them. No, he'd go somewhere else and hide.

He'd pretend.

"You are getting that boy into an awful lot of trouble," Eve reprimanded, wagging a finger at Galen. "Is this your way of acting out, poppet? Is it your way of getting my attention?"

"There are a lot of easier ways to get your attention that I can think of," said Galen, who slowly pushed herself up to her feet. She was thankful for the hand that coiled about her bicep and picked her up, though she never mentioned her gratitude. "No, it seems he is just fond of keeping me company wherever I go. His excuse is always that you send him."

The Dreamcatcher scoffed as she extended her arm for Galen to take. "I don't know who that boy thinks he is, but he has a very high and mighty opinion of himself."

"Why do you keep him around if you don't like him?" Galen took Eve's arm wilfully, eagerly. The Dreamcatcher would make sure she was always kept upright. Plus, being this close to Eve fed some of her energy to Galen. She felt stronger, more alive.

"It isn't that I don't like him," Eve refuted. "I know he doesn't like me. I can see it in his eyes. He makes me curious, is all. There's something shifty about him, like he's hiding something."

Galen glanced back at the house that was slowly growing more and more out of sight, a nervousness overcoming her. "Where are we going?" she asked timidly.

"You and I are going to spend some time together alone," explained the Dreamcatcher. She held her hand in front of her and let her fingers wag, wiping away everything that was in front of her.

Just like that, the beautiful scenery of her gardens disappeared. She stood side by side with Galen in limbo, a place that Galen had hated being the first time around. The blinding whiteness was too much for her, so she buried her face in Eve's arm to hide from the brightness. It prompted a little giggle from Eve, who simply ran her fingers through Galen's hair and kissed the top of her head.

"Look up, poppet," the Dreamcatcher commanded after a few seconds.

Galen could hear water. Still, she was reluctant to look up. She turned her head just a touch, so she could peek out through the corner of her eye. Much to her surprise, limbo was gone. The Dreamcatcher had replaced it. She'd conjured up a place like no other, a place that truly did require so much strength and power. Galen would've never been able to produce such a dream. It would've crushed her.

Staggering away from Eve, Galen admired the vast castle that was stretched out in front of her. It was huge. Built symmetrically so that ever corner matched, the castle towered high into the sky with a towering cathedral bursting from the very centre of it. On either end were two huge towers that were big enough to be houses or mansions just by themselves. They were topped with cone roofs decorated with windows overlooking the limitless lawns and the deep, bubbling lake that was the centrepiece of the front gardens.

There were endless archways and dormer windows and pillars spiralling up the brickwork of the palace. No place like this would ever exist in reality, Galen knew. The two massive towers that sat closest to the entrance, framing it neatly, were topped with gothic-style windows and roofing that towered on high up into the clouds, piercing them. Huge windows took up most of the front of the castle, decorated with stained-glass windowpanes depicting images that Galen couldn't make out from this distance.

Galen was stood with Eve on the grainy path leading up to the serpentine front steps. The Dreamcatcher didn't expect her to walk up those, surely? She couldn't manage it. The childlike part of Galen wanted to dash around manically and explore everything, but her feet wouldn't move. She was frozen in awe, only able to move once the Dreamcatcher pushed her hand against the small of Galen's back.

"Wonderful, isn't it?" Eve asked. The smile on her face was like no other. She was always beautiful when she smiled but, this time, she was truly happy. It shone in her eyes and blossomed in her cheeks. The Dreamcatcher was home. "I've been having it built over the past however long. It must be centuries now. I never thought that I'd find someone who could help me escape the dreamland, so I built this place in case I had to stay here. Turns out, my backup plan has become my main plan, and my immigration to reality has fallen apart."

"*How could you...*" Galen whispered to herself, stammering. She still couldn't get over the sheer size of this place. She thought of the gardens behind it and what they must look like. Oh, the gardens! The land! The everything! Galen could've swooned. "I don't understand how you did this. Wouldn't this drain you?"

Eve nodded. "That's why it took so long," she reasoned. She looped her arm around Galen and walked her up the grainy path. "I had to use my energy wisely. When I didn't have a steady home, I worked on this place. When I found you…it went stale for a while. I was unsure about you. Now, though, it's nearly ready. I knew from the minute you told me you believed that we would live here, together."

"Together?" Galen gulped.

"This will be our home, and we'll never be wont for anything again."

Galen could feel a knot in her stomach. This wasn't a place she could turn down, but she refused to just accept death. This was Eve's way of poisoning her mind, and it was working. Was there a way Galen could just laugh this off? Surely not. Not with a structure like this looming over her. She would've loved it to be her home. It was a place she knew she'd take to, but there was something evil about it. The atmosphere was dark and unruly. What could the Dreamcatcher's intentions be with this place? Just to live? It couldn't be. There was something else.

Eve was always hiding something else.

"Isn't this what you want?" Eve asked. She faced Galen, sliding in front of her and smiling down at her. That damned smile. It made it so hard to focus on the evil and the darkness that lay behind it. "You could have all this. You could have anything you want! You'll be as powerful as I am, if not more. The people will love you. You'll—"

"I don't understand where this has all come from," Galen said suddenly, treading on the Dreamcatcher's toes. "Why would we, or you, ever need a place like this?"

The Dreamcatcher's grin widened. "You and I are going to rule," she crooned. She held Galen's shoulders, her eyes burning with passion and determination. This was her new plan, it seemed. "We'll be royalty, King and

Queen. There wouldn't be a single dream here that could stop us. We'll rule this world and everyone in it!"

"You still want me to stay here," she realised.

Eve's smile fell in the corners. "Why would I ever want you to go?"

"I didn't think…" Galen drifted off. She didn't think that Eve would still want to kill her. Did the Dreamcatcher not care about that? Was she so selfish? Withdrawn, Galen gulped and uneasily met Eve's eyes again. "Your shift in beliefs…is because you can't rule in reality?"

"What I want the most is you," Eve replied quickly, harshly. "I have been ruling since I was created. I am a born king. These people bow to me, I have my own kingdom. To overthrow the rest of it is my only desire now, and I want you to rule as my queen."

Galen couldn't believe her ears. "You'd kill me for this?" She thought Eve had lost her mind. "Don't you see what hurt it'd cause my family?"

Already, the Dreamcatcher was tiring of the conversation. "I would be your family, Galen. The rest of the people here would be your family. You'd learn to accept it. It would be like nothing had ever changed for you."

"But I'd never see my family again."

The world around Galen was beginning to rot. She could see it happening behind Eve. All the grass that has been so lovely and fresh and green was turning black and rotting away before her very eyes. Some of it spiralled out of control, growing into huge black spikes that formed a forest around the Dreamcatcher and Galen. Through the tendrils, Galen could still see the castle crumbling like it was made from biscuit. It hit the ground and sent cracks splitting through the earth, rocketing towards the huge body of water that pooled behind Galen. She'd surely drown.

"I don't understand your attachment to them," Eve said sternly. "Am I not enough for you? Have I not made my love and my affection clear enough for you?"

"It's not that!" Galen cried, staggering backwards. She had to stop when her back met the wall overlooking the moat, but first peered over the ledge.

The water beneath was now murky and green, spiralling round and round like a little whirlpool. It was gradually growing in height and would eventually reach her. Trapped within the waves were rotting bodies and souls that reached out to her, as if to grab her. Their faces were warped and falling apart, being ripped to shreds by the current.

"Eve, please!" Galen begged. She couldn't stomach the sight of the tormented souls anymore and cowered against the barrier with her knees tucked under her chin.

The Dreamcatcher loomed over her, as fearsome as ever. "What is it then, Galen? What isn't enough for you here? What else could I possibly have to do?"

"This isn't what I want! I don't want you to be evil!"

There was a pause in Eve's scowl. "What?"

"Can't you just listen to me for a minute without getting defensive?" Galen asked. "All I want is for you to understand why I'm so upset! Wouldn't you be? Imagine being ripped away from the only people that have ever cared about you!"

The Dreamcatcher stood straight, staring at Galen as if she was speaking a different language. It was very clear she didn't understand at all. She should've done. Stefan had done the same thing to her that she was trying to do to Galen.

"Imagine them suffering, Eve. How would you feel if you were waiting on the other side for me? If it was you sitting by my hospital bed, waiting for me to wake up from my coma and realising that I never will? That I'm dead?"

"I…"

"You'd be heartbroken, and I know you would be!" Galen shouted. She found the strength to pick herself back up. The Dreamcatcher didn't scare her, but what Eve could muster did. "You'd be devastated realising that I'm gone forever, that your last words to me were that you'd see me at home, that you expected me to survive. Would you do that to my family?"

Eve hung her head and fought off a snarl. "Your family mean nothing to me," she hissed. "The only person who means anything to me is you, and I will do anything I have to so that you are always by my side."

"Don't be the monster that everyone thinks you are," Galen growled back at her. She found her confidence, balling her hands up into fists at her sides and tearing her lips back from her teeth. "I care about you, Eve. I do. I find myself missing you when you leave me by myself. I want to be around you. I don't care for this side of you, though."

The Dreamcatcher couldn't help but gasp. How could she really be surprised?

"Look what you've done." Galen gestured all around her, at the perfect world that had been torn apart in seconds. "This place was so serene, and you tore it up over nothing. How could you expect me to just wilfully leave my family behind?"

"I thought I was enough for you."

Galen huffed her displeasure. "I'd still come back! I'd still dream! You'd see so much of me that you'd tire of me!"

"That isn't enough."

"Nothing is ever enough for you," Galen remarked under her breath.

That one comment was enough to refuel Eve's ire. "No, Galen. Nothing is ever enough for me." The world resumed its rotting, the thick black spikes only thickening and growing taller. They melded together to form a thicket that was almost impenetrable. "Don't you understand everything I've been through? I've been alone this entire time, and the one chance I have at company is you! You are my last hope, my last chance, and this is how you repay me for all I've done?"

"You're killing me!"

"If that is what I must do to keep you here then so be it!"

The world around Eve fell apart, like a school play set. The castle fell backwards and the walls either side of Galen tumbled back too. What was revealed was Eve's home, as if they'd never left. The house still stood proudly, untouched by the Dreamcatcher's darkness, and the gardens Galen had found her peace in were still flowering. The people in the gardens were no longer there—in fact, almost everyone had miraculously disappeared.

The Dreamcatcher grabbed hold of Galen and held her in place, face still stretched in a snarl. "Understand that everything I do; I do for you! I do everything I can to make sure I give you a life that makes up for the tragedy I'd put your family through, but you don't see that! You're too selfish to see that! I only want to give you my love, Galen. Why won't you let me?"

"You threaten to wrench everything I hold close out of my hands and toss it in a fire where it'll burn to cinders!" Galen roared back. "You can kill me, but you can't make me forget what you've done! Kill me, Eve, and I'll never forgive you for it!" Galen freed herself, tugging her arms from Eve's grip and storming off. She used far too much strength too quickly but kept her pace up. She wouldn't let Eve win this fight.

"Get back here!" the Dreamcatcher screeched.

Galen ignored her, instead heading for the front gardens where a commotion was stirring. She thought she could hear the distant sounds of a battle pounding on. That couldn't be. Her feet picked up the pace, going only the slightest bit faster. She would've burst into a run if she could've, but there was nothing left in the tank.

Galen rounded the corner and pushed her way through the heavy iron gate, bursting onto the front lawns with a gasp. There, at the gates, were Gil and all his dreams. There were thousands of them fighting their way into the Dreamcatcher's province with no one on the other side to stop them. They were dressed in armour, holding weapons that had to have been forged at the new settlement. Each one of them had an axe or a sword or a spear. Funny how Gil had taken the medieval route. Galen didn't take him for that kind of person.

What Galen did notice were hundreds upon thousands of lit torches. Fire. It was everywhere. Gil meant to cause harm on this day and was well prepared for it. He had the army for it, too. This was exactly what Eve had been fearing.

"Galen!" Eve called again, sounding like a mother reprimanding her child. Her footsteps pounded the earth, her high heels stabbing into the ground with each step she took.

Galen saw her approaching quickly and took off. She gave it her best shot, running for as long as she could across the lawns before she fell. Eve was closer to her than Gil was, but the Dreamcatcher hadn't noticed the army outside her gates. In her rage, she was hyper-focused on only Galen, and didn't watch as Galen threw her arm out and flicked the last bit of strength, she could into undoing the locks of the gate with her mind.

They scraped open slowly, painfully so. Galen could only watch as Gil and his army rammed themselves into the gates to force them open, praying that they'd get through. Her head suddenly jerked around as she watched Eve stand over her, reaching down with her hand. Her neck was constricted as the Dreamcatcher picked her off the ground by her throat and let her dangle in mid-air.

"I don't like to hurt you," Eve huffed and puffed, out of breath. Still, she hadn't noticed Gil and his gang. "I want what's best for you. You're making this much, much harder than it has…to…be…"

Finally, the Dreamcatcher saw them. She heard the gates pop off their hinges and fall to the ground, clattering loudly. Eve heard the battle cry that came from Gil's army, and the thousands of footsteps that came rushing for her. She dropped Galen and let out a battle-cry of her own; a deafening, bloodcurdling screech hat came from deep within her stomach. It was a signal to all of her own people, who began to flit onto the scene from out of nowhere.

They arrived in clouds of fog and feathers, gradually lining up on the frontlines to meet Gil head on. Eve herself levitated a few feet above the ground as huge, black wings burst from her back. Twisting black horns erupted from her forehead as she beat her wings against Gil's charging army. A few of them were knocked back, blown away by the gust of wind but the majority stayed upright and pushed through it, which only wrench another cry from the beast that the Dreamcatcher had become.

Galen didn't know where to go or what to do. She was stuck amongst the Dreamcatcher's throng, trapped in by bodies that were way too close to her. What she needed to do was get to Gil, and she needed to do it fast.

Her feet began to work in the dirt. She scuttled across the ground like a bug as the two armies collided with one another. Galen did her best to drown out the screams and the cries of terror. She could hear sloshing and slashing through flesh and bone. Huge waves were running rampant across the lawn, staining it an awful shade of black.

"Gil!" Galen called. She thrust herself onto her feet and ducked beneath a sweeping arm that wasn't targeted at her. Her hand pushed against the elbow, forcing whoever's fist it was to collide with their face. She staggered around, legs weak, trying to locate the tiny purple bear. "Gil, where are you?"

No one responded to her. She'd have to find him the hard way.

Galen plucked a spear and a torch from a dead dream's hands, watching them as they gradually turned into a pile of ash. Before they did, Galen looked away. She couldn't stomach seeing that happen again.

At the sight of fire, Eve's army turned on Galen. They hissed at her and spat at her, some of them charging right at her. One man came forwards with no weapon, but his arms spread wide. He had long, sharp fangs hanging from his gums. Every single one of his teeth were as sharp as a blade. Even the fingernails on his hands had been fashioned into metal spikes, sharp enough to slice through skin.

Galen squared up with him. Every time he lunged towards her, she slashed at him with her spear. He'd just laugh at her, though. This was no way to kill a dream. It would hurt him, stun him momentarily, but it would never kill him. Suddenly, Galen remembered. She glanced at the fire burning on her torch and gasped to herself. That was it! This had to work. It just had to.

When the man lunged forwards again, Galen met him and stabbed her torch into his chest. It took all of three seconds for the man to realise what had happened, gasp, and then explode into a cloud of glittery, black dust. A green light was revealed from within the ash pile, though. It floated towards Galen and surrounded her, forcing itself down her throat. The light burst from within her, spreading across her body and rejuvenating her bones and her muscles. She felt the littlest bit stronger again, able to stand on her own two feet.

No. It couldn't be.

Galen had become a dreamcatcher all of her own.

She had no time to dwell on it. The sight of their fallen brother brought forward more and more fighters. In their anger, they didn't see the fire that Galen held in her hand. They never saw it coming. Galen struck them all with the torch, skewering two of them on her spear whilst pushing the flames of her torch into the side of another's face. As she danced with them, more and more green lights floated towards her. Each one she killed fuelled her, drove her to act faster and harder. Though she grew stronger, she grew angrier. Every burst of energy she got only made her kill in worse ways. Her spear was stained right to where she held it, her torch blunted and almost extinguished. Both her arms were smothered with black, inky gunk right up to the elbows. Her chest was painted black and her face was splattered with someone else's life. This wasn't her at all.

Out of breath, Galen stopped for a second. There was a clearing around her, covered in ash. The last of the green lights floated towards her and seeped through her skin, making the aching in her hands go away. Galen could feel those souls crawling around inside her, restoring her muscle to her. They filled out her face and her stomach, stopped all the aching inside her bones, fuelled her heart with fury.

It was almost enough for her to see why Eve was so obsessed with this feeling.

Galen had fought her way through a handful of Eve's army but couldn't see the Dreamcatcher anywhere. She could hear the beating of wings and the roar of what sounded like a dragon. Her eyes went upwards, to the sky, where she saw Eve holding her own against a dragon her own size. They tore shreds off each other, but the Dreamcatcher was winning.

Eve clapped her wings against either side of the dragon's head and lunged forwards so quickly that no one saw it coming. She tore out the dragon's jugular, dropping the chunks of flesh to the floor and roaring in victory as the dragon's carcass fell to the ground and crushed a small battalion of Gil's army.

Suddenly, Galen watched as Eve began to suck up all the souls of the fallen around her. They had been just floating aimlessly against the ground with no place to go. A few of them had bumped into Galen, thinking she was their new home, but they had been wrong. They all soared through the air in one beam of colour, colliding with Eve and emblazoning her in a bright ball of green energy. That shield around the Dreamcatcher soon sunk into her skin and all her damage was repaired. She was strong once more, unbeatable it seemed.

"Galen!"

Gil's voice brought Galen's eyes down from the sky.

"Gil! There you are!" Galen fell to her knees and hugged the bear tight to her, panting in his ear. She was so thankful to see him. She pulled away from him and slashed through the legs of one of Eve's followers, rendering him unable to move on the ground. "I thought maybe she'd gotten you." She put out the torch on the poor man's writhing body, extinguishing it for good. Quickly, her eyes began to search for another. "How did you get here? How did you get this many people to fight for you?"

"I met up with an old friend who was more than happy to help."

"Who?"

Gil smiled up at Galen and scoffed lightly, shaking his head as he watched her impale yet another minion. "I believe you know her. Ms Elzbieta."

That crafty old woman.

Galen snatched another torch from the ground and blew against the flames, creating a huge gust of fire that enveloped a wall of minions that had come running for her. They didn't even have time to scream as the fire touched them. Each of them dissipated, and their souls came rushing for Galen, eager to bury themselves within her heart and her spirit.

"Time to kill this bitch," Gil roared. The rest of his army cheered with him, though they were thinning in numbers. That didn't stop them. As Gil charged forwards, so did everyone else, pushing back Eve's wave of minions and forcing them up against the front of the house.

Galen stood watch, weapons drooping by her side and mouth agape. She'd never seen the old bear in his element before, but it was apparent this was it. Her eyes were fixated on him as he charged through the opposition's leg, stabbing them with torches and running the end of his sword through them. He would throw his head back and roar as he ripped the souls from their chests and flung them towards Galen, sending them on their way. They all came gleefully, entangling themselves with Galen—wrapping themselves about her arms and her legs and sinking deep within her pores.

"We need to trap her!" Galen shouted towards Gil. She didn't know the names of the other dreams and couldn't call on them. They did look towards her as she parted the sea of minions for them, slashing her way through as many people as her spear could muster. She worked her way up by Gil's side, piercing the heart of one attacker and watching him fall at her feet. "We need to get Eve under control, trap her if we can. She'll kill us all if we give her the chance. We can't let that happen!"

"How do you intend on trapping her?" Gil asked. He took a moment and glanced up at the sky to see Eve soaring around, wings spread wide for all to see. "She's a bloody dragon! We're not going to be able to get her down from there!"

Galen pondered it a moment. "Would fire kill her?"

"I would doubt it," Gil replied, shouting over the screams of the minion he swiftly put to death. He blew the ash pile away and kicked the soul towards Galen, almost handing it to her. "You'd need a whole lot of fire to burn her alive. A flimsy little torch would do nothing but stun her."

Stun her? That could work. Galen searched the ground, scurrying around groping the mud with her palms open. She drove her spear through the heart of one minion, one of the flamingos. She recognised his face and expected him to talk, but he couldn't manage it. Ooze dripped from his mouth and onto her face as she held him dangling in the air above her. Galen dropped him again, letting him fall further down the spear and leaving him for dead. She rushed by him, snatching a torch that had been dropped and spotting a bow not too far from where she was. To reach it was tricky. Tens of people fought atop it, treading on it, almost shattering it. Galen had no other option.

She dove into the crowd for it, wildly swinging her torch around and extinguishing meaningless minions around her. They didn't even see it coming, didn't even notice her moving amongst them. One of them turned roughly, swinging their arm towards her, and catching her in the chest. Galen was knocked down but made sure to keep a tight grip of the torch. She clung to it for dear life, bringing it with her as she rolled beneath the end of a sword and jumped up to kick her attacker into the mud. Galen shoved the torch against his rear and turned him to ash, absorbing his soul and making a dive for the bow.

Snatching up the bow, Galen knew she had one shot, and only one shot, to bring Eve back down to the ground. She pulled back the drawstring, notching the torch where the arrow should sit and aimed up to the clouds. In her mind, she cursed the Dreamcatcher for moving so fast.

"Hold still," Galen hissed under her breath. She closed one eye and focused on Eve's chest that had elongated and broadened, toughened with scales. This was not the person Galen recognised—she was barely a person anymore.

When the Dreamcatcher perched atop the arched roofing of her house, Galen fired her shot. The head of the torch was aimed square for Eve's chest, where it would strike her in the sternum. It flew towards her, untouched by any of the other debris flying through the air. The flames erupted from it as it collided with Eve, knocking her off-balance and bringing her down to the front steps.

The Dreamcatcher landed in a heap. Her wings folded around her and her tail, which Galen hadn't even noticed, was folded up behind her. She roared in either pain or anger, or maybe both. The sound startled each one of her minions. For a split second, they stopped fighting.

Gil's army took the opportunity they were given.

All at once, hundreds of Eve's men were slaughtered where they stood. Their souls soared high into the air, collecting into one massive, pulsating orb of green light that shot towards Galen as she made a run for the Dreamcatcher.

Galen focused on nothing else. Even as the giant orb of souls collided with her, Galen didn't stop moving. She kept her bow clutched in her hand and sprinted through the barrage of people. Gil's army parted for her, the dreams that were fighting for her let her through and stopped all who tried to stand in her way. They forged a sea of souls that followed Galen like a trail of fireflies, not intertwining with her, but sitting about her shoulders like a glistening cape of power and strength.

Almost face to face with Eve, Galen fell to her knees and reached out. She dropped her bow by her side, staring at the Dreamcatcher. Her breathing was heavy, and her eyes were closed, but Galen knew Eve was still alive. Though she was struggling, the Dreamcatcher would inevitably be back for more.

"Eve?" Galen asked quietly.

Everyone around her ceased their fighting. Eve's minions threw their arms up in defeat, dropping their weapons and falling to their knees. They surrendered. They saw their leader in tatters, lying injured on the steps of her own abode.

"Eve?" Galen said again. She could see the Dreamcatcher's wings receding into her back and watched her tail slither up behind her and disappear. When

Eve's face became normal, Galen pushed a few strands of matted hair from her cheek.

"Is the bitch dead?" Gil stood behind Galen, covered in gunk and muck with his sword dug in against the ground. He was panting. The bear had fought harder than anyone else here. He deserved a little rest. "Is that really all it took?"

Galen's head shook. "She's still breathing."

"Shame."

Galen threw Gil a scathing sneer but was quick to turn her attention back to the fallen Dreamcatcher. This was a state she'd never seen Eve in before. This was how she'd imagined the Dreamcatcher would be when weakened. All the strength and power she'd had was gone now, floating away from her. Galen had sapped most of it from her, but it was for her own good. She'd understand when she came to, she had to.

"I say finish the job," Gil growled. He lunged forwards as if to stab Eve in the throat, but Galen knocked him back viciously.

Sweeping her arm out with all her renewed strength, Galen sent Gil flying down the steps. She gasped to herself gently. She hadn't meant to hit him that hard. It was unusual having this much power. Galen observed her own hands and her veins and how they glowed a bright, iridescent green. Part of her understood Eve's obsession with the power now, but she knew it wouldn't get to her head. She'd never let it get to her head.

Gil padded back up the steps, no sword or shield in hand. "You've got quite the swing on you, girl," he remarked, falling to his haunches by Galen's side. Surprisingly, he wasn't unhappy about being launched. He mentioned nothing else of it. "You've got her at your knees now, Galen. This is the time to make the choice, to end this all."

Galen stared at Eve's peaceful face, shaking her head. "I can't just kill her," she murmured under her breath. "I wasn't expecting…I didn't think…it was only one torch…"

"I was surprised too," Gil said. He put his paw on Galen's shoulder and stared down at his mortal enemy, sneering. He was all too happy that she had fallen. If it was him, he would've run her through by now. "If you can't do it, you know I am more than happy to. I would drag that bitch's death out for all to see, parade her severed head about all the dreamland."

"You'll leave her be," Galen growled under her breath. "For all you know, we could need her. You could need her. You must forget what she's capable of."

Gil was taken aback—that paw he put on Galen's shoulder slid off. "I think it is you who has forgotten what she's capable of. Do you know how many people died today just because of her? This was all because of her, and here you are defending her."

Galen pushed Gil's voice out of her mind. This was not the time to argue. She had questions, and the only person who could answer them was dead at her feet. Her eyes had caught on to Eve's still chest, and how she didn't breathe anymore. There were tears in her eyes, bubbling and brewing, ready to fall. She reached out with a tentative hand, frightened to touch the Dreamcatcher's cold skin. Her hand just hovered over Eve, until she couldn't take it anymore. Galen lowered her palm and cupped the side of Eve's cheek, swiping her thumb just under the Dreamcatcher's eye sockets.

It took all a matter of maybe five or six seconds—the Dreamcatcher moved fast.

As soon as Galen's skin touched hers, Eve's eyes burst open and she sucked in a deep breath of air. Once her lungs were filled, she batted Galen away, much like Galen had done to Gil, and staggered up to her feet. She groaned and growled as she stood, laying eyes on Gil, and letting out yet another bloodcurdling scream. Her minions screamed back with her, but their voices were cut short as they all began to choke and gasp for their lives. The Dreamcatcher tilted her head back and held out her arms, tensing every single muscle in her beaten body. She closed her eyes and roared to the skies and, as her voice carried, every single one of her followers' souls were sucked from their chests, through their throats and out of their mouths.

Galen tried to get up. She tried to stand, but her legs wouldn't hold her. Pushing her hands flat against the ground, she managed to prop herself up to see a sea of corpses standing on their feet with their souls levitating just above them. It was horrifying. Their faces were still mangled with terror and with fear. Some were still on their knees, clasping at their throats or pushing their hands against their chests. There wasn't a person clad in black clothing who had kept their lives. Eve had taken them all.

The Dreamcatcher began to chant in a language that Galen didn't understand. Her mouth moved quickly, tracing the words of a prayer that she yelled up at the sky above her. The quicker she spoke, the higher into the air she began to hover. All the veins in her body were pressed up against the surface of her skin as she kept her muscles tensed and ready to burst. Some had even begun to snap. They lashed against her flesh, warping the shape of her arms and her legs, but it didn't bother her none. Eve was transfixed with her chanting, shouting louder and louder with more passion as the prayer went on.

Galen knew it meant trouble. She clambered to her feet desperately, running like a new-born deer across the battlefield and towards Gil. There was no saving anyone else.

Eve's army were already dead, and those that came to support Gil were goners. They'd started to run the other way, towards the gate, but were trapped in when the iron doors swung shut and sealed themselves. The metal twisted about itself, warping and forming tight knots that ran from one gate to another. Some of the dreams had begun to scale the walls but, at the very top, they just burst into flames. They died slowly. They felt the pain of the fire that was dancing across their skin. Each of them fell from the top of the walls, patting rapidly at the fire that clung to them, desperate to put it out. After a minute or two of them fighting it off, the flames would claim them. They'd turn to sludge, not ash, and melt into the grass beneath them.

Galen sobbed as she sprinted for Gil who, unsurprisingly, ran towards the Dreamcatcher. There was nothing he could do to stop her now. He was just a stuffed bear. Galen intersected him as he made a leap for Eve's feet, grabbing him in her arms and getting launched from one end of the lawns to the other as the Dreamcatcher exploded into a green ball of pure, unrestrained energy.

She felt like she'd spent a lifetime in the air. Galen soared so fast that her skin and her face dislodged from her skull. At one point, she feared her face would tear straight off.

Just as her eyes began to bulge in their sockets, Galen smashed into the brick wall and fell into the bushes below. She still had Gil clamped in her grip, but he wasn't moving. Galen wasn't moving either. She opened her eyes but couldn't see a thing around her. She tried to breathe in, tried to replace the wind that had been knocked so senselessly from her lungs, but her windpipe was closed.

It was no good. She'd lost her fight. Her arms wouldn't move, as they were snapped in two different places. Her forearm bent one way, but her wrist bent the other. Beneath her, her legs had crumpled up like paper, bending and contorting unnaturally as she'd landed.

Each part of her was broken and warped. She wondered how this would be fixed as she lay face-down against the ground. Her wheezing and her groaning were the only sign of life coming from her, but the same couldn't be said for Gil.

Chapter Thirteen

Galen pried herself from the bushes. She tumbled from them, dragging Gil along with her. She lay Gil peacefully beside her, putting her hand on his chest and sighing with relief when she still felt it rise and fall.

"*I'm glad you're still with me,*" Galen whispered to him. She cupped his cheek and picked out a few tufts of fluff, grit, and bush. A smile crossed her face, though it didn't stay long. It was too painful to uphold. "*I don't know how you do it, but you're one tough little bear.*"

A roar at the other end of the front lawns tore Galen's attention away from Gil. She panicked. Her heart quickened instantly inside her chest as she saw the Dreamcatcher striding towards her. There was no way she could escape, not in the state she was in. Her eyes ran over the huge wings that had resurfaced from Eve's back, doubled in size and in strength.

Eve was renewed. As she wandered through the battlefield of corpses, she sucked up the souls of her people who she had killed and snatched those that didn't believe in her. Her eyes were dead set on Galen, and she refused to take them off her prey.

Galen wouldn't go down so easy. She tensed the muscles in her arms and winced instantly, the pain surging through her veins. Luckily, one wrist was perfectly fine. She grabbed hold of her broken one and sucked in three quick breaths through gritted teeth before she snapped it into place. The pain sent her reeling backwards. Galen cried out in agony, tears streaming from her eyes as she clutched her fragile bones.

There was no time to delay—she had no time to waste. Her hand moved upwards to her elbow—she could feel each individual bone sliding around out of place beneath her skin, but she could fix that. A quick yank forced those bones back into place, but that quick yank sent a wash of blackness over Galen. The pain was so strong that it blinded her for a moment, rendering her unable to see three feet ahead of her.

Woozy but not defeated, Galen turned her attention to her legs. Now this would be hard to fix. She grabbed hold of her shin and pulled upwards, reconnecting her knee to the bottom of her leg. The pain wasn't getting any better. Wave after wave of darkness smacked into her face as Eve took stride after stride closer to her.

Galen snapped her other ankle back into place and pushed that knee back into its socket from the side of her leg, almost throwing up from the cracks and the crunches. She hobbled up to her feet, one leg fixed but one leg not.

Something was wrong. Though she stood straight, her right foot was facing sideward. She tensed up her hips and pelvis and grimaced, breathing in and out rapidly. She knew what she had to do but feared how it would hurt.

It couldn't be any worse than what the Dreamcatcher was about to do to her, though.

Just before Eve could reach her, Galen rapidly twisted her upper body and felt her entire right leg pop back into its socket. Finally, it faced forwards. The pain that rose from the bottom of her foot and flashed up the side of her ribs sent Galen to the ground. She fell straight backwards, her eyes rolling back in her head and her throat burning with bile. At any second, she'd pass out or throw up.

Fortunately, or unfortunately, Galen was never given that chance.

Picked up off the ground by her throat, Galen found herself dangling from Eve's warped hand. The Dreamcatcher's fingers had elongated and were coiled all the way around Galen's neck, giving her absolutely no room to wriggle. She could barely see Eve through the wall of pain that blackened her vision. Her head lolled back and forth no matter who hard Galen fought to keep it still. All her pain only brought a scoff forth from Eve.

"You're stronger than I thought you were," the Dreamcatcher growled, spitting a glob of black gunk onto the grass. "I'll give you that. You put up a good fight."

Galen stretched her arms out, groping randomly trying to touch Eve's face. She felt her hands get batted away and winced from the pain that rapped against her knuckles. Like a scared child, Galen brought her hands back to her, hugging them to her chest.

"I don't know about you, but I could fight for as long as I have to," Eve growled. She lowered Galen but didn't let go of her neck. The Dreamcatcher stepped forwards; her body pressed against Galen's. "If this is the route that I have to take, I will. I will kill every last dream until it is just you and me. Do you understand me?"

"Yes," Galen gasped. She pried at the fingers around her neck, blinking repeatedly until her vision finally cleared.

It was as if Eve hadn't fought for a second. Her skin was perfectly clear of all cuts or scratches or wounds. There were no blemishes on her at all. Her back was the only thing that oozed, but her huge wings had torn at her flesh and ripped it open, almost exposing the bones underneath her skin. What Galen did notice was the Dreamcatcher's emboldened eyes. They were brighter and more beautiful than ever. A shame that it had taken absorbing so many lives for that to happen.

"Tell me you felt that rush, that thrill," Eve sung to her. She let go of Galen's neck and laughed when Galen toppled over again. The Dreamcatcher didn't bother to scoop up her prey. She stood over Galen, beating her wings once against the breeze. "It's invigorating, isn't it? To take someone's life, absorb their soul?"

Galen didn't know how to respond.

With her head cocked at an angle, Eve scoffed and smirked. "What, did you think I hadn't seen that? How could I have missed it? You were practically glowing the entire time you fought! I've not seen anything quite like it."

Wheezing, Galen tried to sit herself up to talk. Just as her vertebrae began to creak like old wood, Galen was thrust back to the ground by a boot placed on her sternum. That hurt more than anything in the world. Galen had just snapped her broken bones into place, but nothing hurt worse than this.

She gasped and wheezed and choked as the precious air that she'd sucked in was pushed out of her like she was a squeaky dog toy. The noise she made was ungodly. Nothing deterred the Dreamcatcher though. No amount of pain could satiate Eve's fury.

"Don't you just hate not getting your own way?" the Dreamcatcher asked. She stared down at Galen's struggling, pleasure erupting in her eyes. Was this doing something for her? The woman truly was sick. She crouched, boot still on Galen's chest. "Think of where you could be if you had just taken my hand and not asked any questions. Think of where you could be if that damn bear didn't poison your way of thinking."

As if on cue, Gil threw himself at Eve's shin and bit and clawed his way through her flesh. He was tearing chunks of her skin away from her bone, but the

Dreamcatcher just watched him do it. She gave him a laugh and shoved him away as she rose to her full height, unbothered by the ooze pouring from her.

"You," she hissed. "You did all of this." Eve gestured around her at the waste and the mountainous piles of ash that were being blown over by the wind. "Are you proud of yourself now, Gillette? Is this what had to happen before you would finally back down?"

"I'll never back down!" Gil roared. He charged forwards, but Eve just punted him back. Flipping over himself three times, Gil finally landed on his front and pushed himself heroically back to his feet. "This should've happened a long, long time ago," he huffed. Were his lungs collapsing? It sounded like it. "You should've been driven out a long, long time ago!"

This time, Gil snatched up a sword that was too heavy for him to carry and ran at Eve. He bellowed at her as he charged, running at not even a mile an hour, and swinging the sword with all his might. His beady, glass eyes filled with terror as the blade ricocheted off the Dreamcatcher, not even leaving a dent behind. Gil dropped it and sunk to his knees, well and truly defeated.

The Dreamcatcher let out a hearty laugh that echoed around the empty courtyard. "Is that all you've got, Gillette?"

Galen flipped onto her front and heaved herself through the mud and the filth, desperate to get to her feet. She wanted to reach Gil in time before Eve killed him.

She wanted to intervene.

"You've every opportunity to kill me, and that's all you've got left?" Eve picked Gil up, holding him under his pits and dangling him in the air. She stared at him for a minute. This was her nemesis. The Dreamcatcher tutted as she surveyed him, running her eyes over every fibre of her being. "To think that I let you torment me for all this time. You, a stuffed bear. Out of every single dream living here, it was you that gave me the most trouble. Do you know how many people I've met capable of ending my life with a simple snap of their fingers?"

Pushing her feet flat against the mud, Galen desperately tried to use the rest of her strength to pick herself up. She was so close to standing, so close to making a lunge for Gil, but her feet slipped against the mud and sent her sprawling forwards. Her chin clattered into the ground, her teeth jutting upwards into her top lip. Would this suffering ever end?

"I'm going to kill you slowly," Eve growled at Gil, though the bear was so despondent it was a marvel that he was even listening. She shook a little bit of life into him, gritting her teeth and tightening her grip about his small arms. "I'm going to make sure that you pay for every little inconvenience that you've caused me. You're going to feel every bit of pain that I cause you, because I want you to feel how I did when you wrenched my poppet away from me!"

Galen heaved herself up again. She dug her toes into the mud and clambered upwards. At first, she stood, but swayed drunkenly around the place. Her body bent again, her fingers scraping through the stained grass to pick up a sword. She let her other arm swing down to snatch the nearest shield, strapping it to her throbbing arm and letting out a deep exhale.

Was this the right thing to do? Would Eve ever forgive her? It was now or never. Galen knew what she had to do. She had to save Gil and banish Eve from her dreams if she ever wanted to see her family again. This was the only option left—force the Dreamcatcher into a fight, give her an ultimatum, give her the hardest fight of her life.

Just as Galen began running for the Dreamcatcher, she watched Eve drop Gil. He didn't fall for long, as Eve brought up a leg and punted him far across the stretch of grass. Galen didn't even see where he landed. She watched the Dreamcatcher's feet shuffle forwards and took her chance, holding her shield up to her chest and barrelling into Eve's back at full speed.

Together, they fell as one. Eve didn't even see it coming. She was the last one up to her feet. Galen beat her to it, jumping up and whirling around on her to push her boot against Eve's throat. Somehow, it was invigorating. Galen pointed her sword down at the Dreamcatcher's jugular but took more pleasure in watching Eve struggle. Fuelled by the anger that burned like a blazing fire within her, Galen refused to back down now. This was a fight to the end.

The Dreamcatcher shoved Galen's boot off her and went to sweep Galen's leg, but she missed. She flew back up, giving Galen no space to breathe as she snatched up a weapon of her own. Was that the spear that Galen had dropped? It could've been. Eve wielded it with incredibly skill and power, thrusting it forwards before spinning it through her hands and sweeping it against Galen's legs.

Hopping over the spear, Galen just about landed cleanly on her feet. She swayed about, catching her balance as quickly as she could before she parried another blow from the spear. Galen caught her own reflection in the blade of it as Eve tried to slice it into her shoulder. She stared into her own eyes, felt her heartbeat throb in her temple, and hauled the Dreamcatcher away from her. Her mouth opened as she let out scream after scream of frustration, each shout growing more impassioned with every strike she landed.

Galen began to drive Eve back. She ducked beneath another sweep and smashed her shield against the Dreamcatcher's face when she got too cocky. Her sword swung around and stuck against the wooden shaft of the spear that Eve lifted to block the blow. The blade snagged in the wood, but Galen wrenched it free, spun around and connected her boot with Eve's exposed stomach, kicking her with all the strength she could muster.

It was quite amusing to watch another human being slide through mud like a bowling ball. Galen followed the track that the Dreamcatcher made, standing over her and pointing her sword down at Eve's face again. The tip of it nicked the end of Eve's nose, drawing up a single droplet of black ooze that slid down her nostril and onto her cheek.

Breathing heavily, Eve writhed and wriggled, trying to get her spear free. She tried to turn it so the tip would face Galen but, as she moved, Galen sliced through the shaft and cut it in two. Eve's eyes had never been filled with so much fear and shock before.

Galen wrenched the front half of the spear from Eve's hand and pierced it deep into the ground. She covered her face with her shield as the Dreamcatcher beat against it with the lower end of her weapon, furiously denting the metal. Dropping to the ground, Galen wormed her way between Eve's legs, pressed down against her with her shield and forced one arm out to the side. She jammed her sword into the dirt and bent the metal, screeching as she wrapped her hand about the blade and cut through her own skin just to trap the Dreamcatcher's limb.

Bleeding profusely, Galen felt the Dreamcatcher land a blow on her skull, causing her brain to rattle inside her skull. She gritted her teeth and pushed through it, remembering all the pain Eve had caused her. She sat atop Eve's waist, still clutching her shield and grabbed the last part of the spear. The Dreamcatcher's fingers slid off it and Galen tossed it like she was throwing a stick for a dog, but this was one stick she didn't want to see brought back.

With one more shot to the face with her shield, Galen subdued Eve beneath her. She threw the battered shield away and leant over, pinning the Dreamcatcher's other arm down with her forearm and panting heavily into Eve's shield.

"Where…" the Dreamcatcher rasped, a smile somehow smirched across her ruined face. "Where did you learn…to fight…like that…"

"You're predictable," Galen huffed. She squeezed her knees against Eve's ribs and pushed her forehead against the Dreamcatcher's chest, arm still pressing down against Eve's bicep. "You've got to stop."

Eve let out what could've been a laugh. "I'll never…stop…"

A huge sigh left Galen. "I can't let you do this. I'm sick of this. I don't want this anymore." She could hear wet footsteps approaching her but refused to sit up. Galen cuddled herself against Eve, feeding off the Dreamcatcher's warmth. The rhythm of Eve's breathing was soothing her, keeping her calm and collected. "I don't want to fight you anymore. I don't want to hurt you. I don't want anyone to get hurt."

The Dreamcatcher had no response. She tilted her head back and stared up at the cloudy sky ahead of her, her breathing still strained. A little whistling noise emanated from her every time she exhaled. This was the calmest she'd been for a while. There was no more fight in her, no matter what she said. The Dreamcatcher was only so strong—Galen was impressed she'd made it this far.

"Kill her," Gil's weak voice sounded. He limped up to Galen's side and collapsed, pushing a dagger into her hand. Too weak to thrust it himself, the bear curled Galen's fingers around it and pushed down against her knuckles. "End this now. Kill her. Be done with it. Wake up and go home."

"I can't kill her," Galen sobbed into Eve's shoulder. She gritted her teeth and tried to fight back a scream that was rumbling from deep within her, but she couldn't keep it in anymore. Her back straightened and her head fell back as she let out a screech from deep within her. Every muscle tensed, every vein throbbed, every wound bled. Galen was done harming anyone else. Eve was no different.

Galen tumbled off Eve. She lay on her back in the dirt, letting the blood and the grit seep into her skin. How had it all come to this? Galen had single-handedly ripped apart her own dreams, and for what? She felt as if she owed it to all the dreams that had died to stay and rebuild what she had broken, but her family…If she died now, would she die forever? Was it true what they said? If you die in your dreams, you die in real life. Would it shock her awake if she perished? Would she be free of it all? Part of her didn't want to be free. Part of her felt she didn't deserve to be free. This was all on her.

Gil took the dagger for himself. He staggered up to Eve and went to plunge it in her chest, but the Dreamcatcher caught it.

Eve held the dagger by the blade and tugged it from Gil's grip, swiping at him viciously. She sat herself up and knelt, swishing, and swiping all she could. Not once did she hit him. It was as if she wasn't even trying.

Exhausted, the three lay together on the grass, staring up at the sky. A symphony of wheezy breathing was all that could be heard. Galen could hear her own heartbeat thrumming in her ears above everything else. She could feel it, too. It vibrated in her skull. She didn't know what was worse, snapping her own bones into place or this.

"This could've been over with," Gil reminisced. "We were so close to the end, and you let her get to you. You've gone soft on her, you've gotten weak."

The world was starting to rot and fall apart. Part of the sky had fallen. The clouds were tumbling down to the ground and exploding into seas of fog that rippled about the fallen. The grass was just sludge and muck, enveloping the ash that rested upon it. Just like at the castle, parts of the grass grew into unyielding spikes that dripped black gunk, forming thick forests that were dangerous and impregnable. The patches that circled around Galen, Eve and Gil had climbed high and leant to the side, intertwining, and weaving together to form a thick wall. No one could get in. No one could get out.

"Look what she's doing to your mind," Gil spat. He doubled over and coughed up globs of gunk and fluff, wheezing and groaning as he sat himself up. "Why is this not easy for you to do? Why can't you see that she's a leech! She's a bad person, Galen! That'll never change. Not for you, not for anyone."

"I have never..." Eve perked up, still struggling for air. "I have never poisoned anyone...I have never manipulated their minds."

Galen sat up, turning to watch the Dreamcatcher struggle to speak. She was amazed there was still life in Eve. Not only was she amazed, but she was also thankful. It brought tears to her eyes to see what she'd done to Eve. The pity within her grew. Was it still pity? Galen wasn't sure anymore. It could've been pity, it could've been sympathy, or it could've been the very first seedlings of love.

"All I have ever done..." the Dreamcatcher continued. Her sentence was interrupted by a fit of coughs that brought up alarming amounts of filth. She flipped herself onto her side, back facing Galen, and spat out mouthful after mouthful of precious black gunk, hissing inward and clutching her ribs.

Galen scurried over to her. She took Eve in her arms and cradled her as the Dreamcatcher spat up the last glob of ink, one bigger than the rest. Her fingers worked to pull strands of Eve's hair from her face and hold it against her scalp. Her urge to look after Eve was immaculate. It was all she could focus on.

"All I have ever done…" Eve repeated, "is what I know to be right…I never wanted…to hurt anyone, but my hand…was forced…" The Dreamcatcher tried to sit up, but she just tumbled into Galen's lap and glared angrily at Gil. "You…" she hissed. She lunged for him but came back willingly as Galen held onto her and kept her from moving. "You caused this."

"I wanted you gone," Gil growled as he clambered up to his feet. He swaggered around before finding his balance, picking up his dagger just to protect himself. The bear kept it pointed at Eve always, refusing to even let it sag. "I wanted my world to return to normal. I wanted my way of life to return to normal. Everything was perfect the way it was."

Galen closed her eyes and nuzzled her face against Eve's neck, her connection to the Dreamcatcher stronger than ever. She said not a word. She couldn't bear the ferocity she'd receive from Gil. Galen was already sure he knew her feelings. She could feel his listless eyes burning into her as she hugged Eve. Most of her didn't care, but a tiny, teeny part of her felt incredibly guilty.

"Is this what you choose for yourself?" Gil asked, defeated. "Death? You show her love now, but she'll never show you the same kindness. She's not capable of it. There's no heart in that chest."

"And there's no heart in yours!" Galen roared. She lashed out, turning to face Gil, and showing him the volume of tears that were streaming from her bloodshot eyes. Her temper took over her, her fury only restrained due to her exhaustion. If she'd had the strength, she would've beat sense into him. "You two are one in the same, but you can't see eye to eye because you're cut from two different cloths," she sighed to herself. Galen peeled away from the Dreamcatcher and rose shakily to her feet. When she walked, her kneecaps slid from their proper place, but Galen had to pace. She had to burn off some steam. "Why do you pretend to care about me, Gil? Why do you pretend to show so much worry and fear? Is it because my actions impact your world, as you call it? When did this place become yours?"

Gil, offended, lifted the dagger to Galen. "You aren't thinking rationally because of her," he grunted, gesturing to Eve with a little nod of his head. "She's put lies in your head and you're believing them. Kill her now and it's over."

"It'll never be over!" Galen shouted at the top of her lungs. She frightened the crows away with how loud she yelled. "Don't you see, Gil? I've done everything I can! You can't kill what isn't real! She'll always be here!" Galen dropped to her knees at Eve's side, hands hovering just over the Dreamcatcher's chest. "I pity her…I pity the bones of her. Seeing her this way, so tormented and hurt by me, breaks my heart…"

"You love her," Gil realised. The tone he spoke in was so despondent, so hopeless. He dropped his dagger and hung his head, his breathing only just starting to steady. "I led those dreams to their deaths because I had hope you would do the right thing."

Galen cried over the Dreamcatcher's body, gasping gently when Eve's hand clasped her cheeks. "I don't love her, but I don't hate her. I can't hate her. I can't…"

"You'll doom us all."

"Let me say…my piece" Eve pleaded. Gradually, the Dreamcatcher recovered her strength. A faint, green aura began to appear around her as her breathing steadied and her wheezing ceased. In seconds, she was renewed, back to her usual, selfish self. "You will never be able to kill me, Gillette. Not by yourself. It's already obvious that poppet won't hurt me ever again." Eve stared into Galen's eyes and cupped her chin, wiping away the tears that fell. "I can strike a deal."

Gil scoffed. "To hell with you and to hell with your deals! They will never work! They never have!"

"You have broken each and every deal I have ever made because they never suit you!" the Dreamcatcher shouted back at him. "I have but one thing to say to you, poppet." Her eyes still bore deep within Galen's, filled with exhaustion and hope. "Leave me, and I'll kill everything that remains alive and then I'll kill you. Stay with me, and this world will resume order. Everything will go back to normal. You'll stay alive."

Galen's heart sunk. "Eve"

"That is the deal. It is your choice."

"Kill her, Galen! Can't you see she's no good for you?"

The Dreamcatcher laughed at that. "And you're much better, are you? She may banish me, or at least try to, but this world will then fall into your hands. Are you much better than I am? I think not."

"I don't kill for the sake of killing."

"I only killed your stupid little non-believers! And I did so to stay alive. That is reason enough to me."

Galen clamped her hands over her ears to block out their arguing, but she could still hear every word repeating over and over in her head.

"She should've taken your head from your shoulders the second she had the chance to!"

"You never took the time to get to know her, did you?" Eve accused. She crouched in front of the bear, flinching only slightly when he spat in her face. As calm as the Dreamcatcher could be, she wiped the spit away with the back of her hand and grimaced. "You don't know a thing about her. All you know is that so long as Galen is alive, you have power here. You can force dreams into your little internment camps, and no one will say a word against you."

Gil bared his teeth. "I have never enslaved a thing."

"You're a dictator, through and through," Eve dismissed. "You're worse than I am, Gillette. Face it. You were the cause of this struggle. If you'd have kept your word, you wouldn't be here now."

Galen couldn't bear another word of it. This had to end. She wanted it so desperately to end. There were no pros, no cons. Nothing. It was a simple choice made hard by feelings and consciences. Galen damned herself for caring so much. They were both monsters! They both deserved to die.

Still, Galen had to choose between them. Not only that, but she also had her family to consider. She could see their faces in her mind, staring down at her as she lay in a coma. Galen could hear her mother crying and her brother telling her all about his day, thinking she could hear him. She only cried harder.

"If I had as much power as you said I did, wouldn't I have killed you by now?" Gil asked, somewhat sarcastically. "I'm an old dream, an old bear. You talk of me as I'm this grand, unbeatable leader."

"You've painted yourself to be that grand, unbeatable leader! The tales of you slaughtering any dream that wouldn't commit to your cause are not just tales, Gillette! I know them to be true. I saw you on that battlefield. I saw how easy it was for you to rip souls from dreams like taking candy from a baby!"

Galen urged them to stop.

"I'm no monster!"

Galen gritted her teeth so hard she thought they may crack and break.

"You deserve to perish along with all your other little enslaved dreams!" the Dreamcatcher bellowed. "You should've never been allowed to live after what you did!"

"Stop!" Galen shouted at the top of her lungs. This was it. This was the time to make a choice. With her family's faces still burning in her mind, Galen rose to her feet. She stopped her crying, her tears drying on her face as she stood between Gil and Eve. She daren't look at either one of them. "*You're both terrible, awful people,*" she whispered, watching the black, twisted forest writhe around her. Some of the blades had died. Galen could see the end in sight. "I can't find someone to blame for this, because it's me who has caused all this." She glanced down at Gil. "If you had kept your word, you would've been much better off. You had no reason to care about me. If I was dead or alive, you would've remained the same."

Gil bowed his head in shame, his eyes closing and his features falling.

Galen glanced at Eve. "You are…something else entirely," she cursed. "I damn you for being who you are, for being the way you are. If someone had only shown you kindness and mercy…" she lost her train of thought, drifting off for a split second before returning, "you wouldn't be this way." Galen hung her head and felt her entire body drain of energy. This time, it wasn't Eve that was lynching from her. She felt it was her time to go. Breathing in, Galen steadied her racing heart and closed her eyes. "I can't…bring myself to leave this place now, not after what I have done."

There was a stillness in the air. The whole world stopped.

Galen gulped down her fear, curled her hands into fists and squeezed. "I have to stay here." Her eyes found the Dreamcatcher's, tears leaking from them once more. Her bottom lip quivered, but Galen kept a stone heart and as stony a face as she could muster. "*I choose you,*" she whispered. "*I'll stay with you.*"

The blackness and the rot that the world had been encased in suddenly reversed. It moved quickly. Above them, the sky shone a brilliant shade of blue with not a cloud in sight. The sun burst back onto the scene, illuminating everything that had once been covered in muck. The blades of grass that had erupted into spikes shrunk, slowly regaining their emerald greenness. The lawn levelled off at a perfect length with not a drop of blood or pile of ash atop it. Wildlife flittered through the skies—birds sung beautifully to one another, dancing with each other through the trees that lined the edges of the province. All remnants of war vanished, drifting away into the atmosphere, sparkling, and glittering out of sight. The last thing to change were the gates. Bit by bit, the metal unfolded, screeching, and screaming in protest as the ornate bars were forced back into shape and the gates swung open.

"You've damned us all, Galen," Gil murmured with no emotion. He kept his eyes low, throwing his dagger to the ground before it evaporated and running his paws across his head. "You'll never get this place back to how it was, no matter how hard you try. You know exactly what's killing it, and you're keeping it here."

"If I left," Galen started, swallowing past the lump in her throat, "I would spend the rest of my days fearing what had happened to this world. I left it in ruins, and I will fix it. Only then will I be able to leave peaceably." She met the Dreamcatcher's eyes as she felt fingers intertwine with hers, not smiling but not snarling either. Her face was void of emotion as she watched Eve smile lightly. "You will keep me alive," she growled. She saw the Dreamcatcher's smile drop. "Keep me in a coma. Give my family hope that I'll come back. Don't you dare kill me."

Eve bowed her head. "Whatever it takes to keep you with me."

Galen closed her eyes and took in a final calming breath. Was this the right choice? It was done now. She had a different fight to win, a different cause to spread. This world would thrive one day but, until then, Galen would remain prisoner for as long as she had to.

Feeling taps at her shin, Galen crouched to meet face to face with Gil. She could see the hurt in his eyes. The betrayal had damaged him severely. Was it hurt or was it evil? The bear was glaring at her. If he still had his dagger, Galen had no doubts that he would've run her through with it.

"I will never forgive you for this," he told her bluntly. He pointed at her accusingly with the fat end of his paw, turning his lips back from his gums. "You will rue the day that you turned your back on us."

"I'm sorry, Gil."

The bear held up his paw and stopped Galen in her tracks. "Save it, I don't want to hear it. I don't need an apology from a traitor." He sized her up one last time and scoffed at her before he took off, wandering away with his spirits smashed. "I had hoped you were different, Galen. Now I see that you're just like her. The two of you will be at my feet when I'm done with you. I'll mount your heads on pikes and the rest of this dreamscape will know who their true saviour is."

Galen watched him go, feeling choked by her own guilt. She had betrayed him. There was no denying it. A traitor was what she was now. She'd just have to get used to being called that.

Arms slipped about Galen's waist, and a kiss was placed on her cheek. It was so tender and so delicate that Galen couldn't help but shed a few more tears. Her head turned to meet Eve's eyes, so loving and so endless. There wasn't a single muscle in her body or face that could muster even the faintest sign of a smile.

"Shall we go home?" the Dreamcatcher asked.

Once again, Galen felt her heart break in her chest. She hung her head as Eve held out a hand for her to take. If she took that, she'd be led down a path she'd never recover from. This had to be her fate. Galen imagined what lay ahead of her and hated it.

No.

She wouldn't let herself become a monster. If Eve wanted to rule with her, then Galen would rule. She'd put this world to right, and she'd put the Dreamcatcher in her place. Galen would become stronger, more powerful, more loved. She'd do anything to fix the damage that she had done unto a world completely undeserving.

Galen took Eve's hand, and never once let it go again.

Epilogue

The wars were endless. Gil's attacks were relentless. He still revelled in his fury and his rage, disgusted with his creator, bent on revenge.

Galen couldn't blame him.

She watched on as the battle waged below, just outside of the castle walls. They'd never break through. They never had. This was a sport now—a simple game to see how long it took to slaughter tens of thousands of dreams. Where they were all coming from, Galen didn't know. Since choosing the Dreamcatcher over her own reality, Galen found her dreamscape drastically expanded. She was privy to every single dream alive, from every single human being on Earth. These dreams had been rallied by Gil in a pointless fight they'd never win. He always seemed to forget to tell them they'd all be killed. How he kept winning them over to his side in the first place, Galen would never know.

Sipping on her wineglass, Galen stared down at the battle waging outside of her province. She silently congratulated Gil on getting this far. This was the closest she'd seen him in years. Still, it wasn't quite close enough.

The drawbridge was undone and, as soon as the bridge was lowered, Anders galloped out into the battlefield on his black stallion, wielding a sceptre that held an ungodly amount of power within it. It was rumoured that the Dreamcatcher's own soul was what powered it. It apparently floated about freely in the glass orb at the head of the sceptre and was the light that all dreams were attracted to.

Galen knew that had to be bullshit.

Anders held the sceptre high, creating a stream of dreams behind him that followed him wherever he went. They paced after him like zombies, like moths drawn to a lamp, their want for the precious green light unbreakable.

Leading them away, Anders turned his horse about face and slashed the sceptre in front of him. Just like that, hundreds of dreams vanished into ash. Caught in the breeze, Galen could barely see the endless amounts of souls that were sucked into the sceptre through the fog.

Was that it? Was it over? This was usually how it ended.

No, not this time.

Cocking her head to the side curiously, Galen watched as Anders made a beeline for Gil. The two were both on horseback, both striding towards one another. She couldn't help but feel her heartbeat quicken as they prepared to clash. This couldn't be how Gil met his end, could it?

She took a step closer to the window, placing one hand on the windowsill and watching close. Her eyes never once moved from the purple teddy bear. An excellent fighter he was, but he was no magician. He couldn't magically disappear. Anders was heading straight for him, sceptre pointed forwards and mouth open.

Just as Galen thought Anders would strike Gil dead, the bear leapt from his horse and called the retreat. He stood defiantly staring Anders down as the Dreamcatcher's champion turned around in confusion. The smile on his face was one of pride and of smugness. What an arrogant little bear he was. Galen couldn't help but scoff too as he was snatched back up onto horseback by a fleeing dream and whisked off to safety for what felt like the millionth time.

It was getting tiresome. Galen felt useless. In the years she'd spent in the dreamscape, she had aged horridly. Though her appearance stayed the same, perfect, and pristine, if not better, her mind grew weary and tired of the battles. The arguments it caused were endless. Galen had learnt how to hold her own, how to be her own person, how not to shrivel up in the Dreamcatcher's shadow, but she'd also learnt how to hold her tongue. The scars on her face and her neck were proof of that alone. She ran her fingers across the raised marks and sighed to herself, reminiscing over the misery that had been those first two years.

It was better now, though. At least it was better now.

Galen emptied her wineglass and left it standing in the windowsill, turning away from it, having had enough of the fight. She got only mere paces away until she heard something *whoosh* towards her at a frightening speed and smash through it. Her upper body twisted rapidly, and her hand came up to catch an arrow mid-flight, her eyes wide. The tip of the arrow was just inches away from the space between her eyes. What a perfect shot.

Letting out a shaky breath, Galen paced back to the window. She kept hold of the arrow as she glared outside and saw Alden with a bow in her hand.

Ah, this pretty creature again.

Rage filled Galen's body. She held up the arrow for Alden to see it and broke it in her fist. The shaft snapped in two, and Galen crushed it until it was just dust that floated off her palm. She blew on it, sending it back down to Alden who only sneered in response.

"How you could turn your back on me now, I don't know," Galen said. She knew Alden didn't hear her. Alden never heard her. The amount of insults she'd spat out of this window for them to fall on deaf ears was remarkable, but still, she persisted. "Why you would side with him, I also don't know."

Alden hopped onto the back of a horse and only looked away from Galen once she was nearing the brow of the hill. Her eyes were full of both sorrow and fury. What a beautiful blend of emotions. She wore it so well across her face that it had become carved deep into her features. Alden felt nothing else but a furious ball of sadness and untamed rage. What a nightmare she must be for Gil to deal with.

Galen thought nothing else of it. An attempt on her life was a daily occurrence. There wasn't a single dream alive that loved her like they used to. Her own people were besotted with her, but that was to be expected.

For those that loved her, Galen showered in both luxury and praise. There wasn't a dream living an uncomfortable life under her rule. Outside of her province, however, was a different story. She daren't lift a finger for them.

Those that would scale her walls and come to her court, pleading with her, insisting she believe they had turned their back on Gil, were mercilessly executed in front of her. What had once been a scarring and traumatic thing to witness was now almost a pastime. Galen was convinced that a permanent layer of ash was smothered over her skin at all times. It had to be.

Wandering out of her tower, Galen strolled through her thriving palace with her head held high. She met no one's eye. They had all filed in from the war, beaten and tarnished. Some had appendages hanging on by mere fibres of tissue and muscle. Others were fine. There was one person that Galen wanted to speak with, and one person only. Only then would she talk.

Outside, Galen watched Anders trot back across the drawbridge and leap down from his stallion. It rode off without him towards the stable, so well-trained and obedient. Anders himself spotted Galen waiting for him and approached, sinking to a hesitant knee in front of her with his helm tucked under his arm.

“Your Grace,” he growled through gritted teeth. It had been a long time since Galen had become queen, but still Anders couldn’t bring himself to speak to her with respect. “I’m surprised you’ve been let outside.”

“I’m not a dog,” Galen replied with a taut, cautionary smile. She held her hands in front of her as the drawbridge was slammed closed, and the locks shoved back into place. “I go where I please whenever I please. You should know this.”

Anders simply dipped his head.

“What did the bear have to say this time?” asked Galen.

This was another one of her almost monthly routines. Each attack, Gil had both a different motive and a different game plan. Galen honestly tired of hearing them but made sure to keep a note so that, one day, when she had Gil at her feet, she could bore him to death by reading the list back to him.

“Same as usual,” Anders said stiffly. He shrugged his shoulders and let his squires undo his armour, standing with one arm stretched out to the side. Why he had to wear such heavy metal was beyond Galen. He never got hurt, or even scratched. “He demands revenge. He wants to dethrone you, kill you, parade your head around on a pike.”

Galen rolled her eyes. “It’s getting tedious to hear these things repeated back to me every time. Doesn’t he have any imagination? You’d think, being the product of an overactive imagination, that he would come up with something new each time.”

“So you would think.”

“And Alden?”

Anders eyes focused tightly on Galen at the mention of that name. He had his own vendetta with Alden. He never spoke of it, never liked to, never wanted to, but Anders hated her with a fury that may have been fiercer than Galen’s.

The makeshift knight dropped his arm and lifted the other, swiping his tongue so hard against his teeth they almost snapped in two. “Alden never says a word.”

“Still resigned to her silence, I suppose.”

“That’s the only thing I could ask of her,” Anders spat. He waved away his squires once his gauntlets were freed from him. His shoulders rolled as his breastplate fell forwards and was unbuckled from around his waist, leaving only the bottom half of his suit of armour intact. “As long as she keeps her mouth shut when we fight, I’ll have no complaints.”

Galen mustered a smile; a rare sight to see from the queen. "You must tell me the story of you and her one day. It can't be as bad as you make it out to seem." She gestured for Anders to follow her back into the castle, which he did so stubbornly and sulkily, stomping his feet against the floors. "The king will want to hear of the result of this battle. I'm sure she's sitting patiently in the throne room for just such news."

"You haven't told her yourself? Are you fighting again?" The smile on Anders' face was infuriating. He glowered down at Galen as he grinned, his white teeth glistening in the light. How proud of himself, he was. Galen should've beaten the wits out of him long ago. "That doesn't surprise me."

"We aren't fighting," Galen growled. She led Anders down through the main hall until they stood outside of the grand oak doors to the throne room. She turned to him, staring up into his damaged eyes and preying on each and every insecurity. "I don't see much of her these days. There's been something on her mind, something she's planning. For one reason or another, she doesn't think to tell me."

"Maybe she tires of you."

Galen's brow arched. "Just as I tire of you?" She muscled in closer to Anders and fixed his undershirt for him, tying the threads of his tunic tighter and tighter. "If you weren't such a grand champion, you would've been one of the first dreams to go. I don't hold you in such a fond light, Anders. If I tire of you, I can make the king tire of you. It doesn't take much."

Anders let his eyes harden into sparkling, rage-filled glass. "I've heard how you whore yourself to her just to manipulate her mind. Are you scared of letting her think for herself?" He yanked himself away from his queen and sneered at her, turning his nose up like he smelt something rotten. "I'm impressed by how much you've grown and how you've learnt so quickly, but I'm not a mere flamingo anymore."

"What do you think you are now?" Galen laughed at him. She nodded to the guards, the real knights, who drew open the towering doors for her and her guest. Once the sunlight hit the two of them, Galen began to saunter towards her throne, leaving Anders behind. "Tell me, do you think you're a lion, or a tiger? Is that how far you think you've climbed up the food chain?"

Anders jogged to catch up with Galen, trying his best to hide his resent for her in the presence of the king. "Do you not see my prowess on the battlefield?"

"I see you waving around a glittery stick."

"That glittery stick happens to hold more power than you ever will," he hissed under his breath at her, straight into her ear. Just the movement alone was enough to draw whispers from the Dreamcatcher's court. All eyes were on him now. He must correct his horrid behaviour. "Maybe the next thing you should plant into Miss Catcher's head is you riding out onto that battlefield by my side, so you can see first-hand it isn't as easy as it appears from your tower."

Galen pulled a face to mock a damsel in distress, pouting and staring desperately up into Anders's eyes. "Oh, but I'm just a little queen. I'm too fragile to fight. My arms are too weak to hold a sword and my owner would never let me off my lead." She snarled at him viciously, frightening him off a few paces just before she reached the dais her throne sat upon. "Wise up, Anders, before you get yourself into a lot of trouble. Just because my king likes you, doesn't mean I do. Opinions change very quickly."

"You fit the role of a villainous queen right down to a tee," Anders spat back.

Galen flipped him off as she climbed the dainty steps up to her throne. She didn't sit straight away but leant over the arm of the Dreamcatcher's throne and placed a kiss upon her cheek. Her smile beamed across her face as she finally took her seat and watched Anders sink to his knees, head bowed.

Everyone took their seats as the Court General pounded his staff against the polished floors. There was no more whispering, no more talking, no more gossiping. They fell silent, watching as their king, the Dreamcatcher, got to her feet and stood over her disciples.

"Anders!" she cheered, her dulcet tones blossoming throughout the room. God, how it was so easy to fall in love with her. "I'm always glad to see you back unharmed. It brings me confidence. Our army is unbeatable."

Anders lifted his head a touch. "We lost a handful of good men to minor mistakes. Some of them grow too bold. They think that Gillette is too old to be smart and sneaky."

"Overconfidence is better than fear, Anders," the Dreamcatcher replied. "So, tell me. How long did it take to drive them back?"

"They reached the castle after a four-day march and remained on our soil for a matter of hours."

Eve threw her head back and laughed.

Galen watched from her throne. She always just watched. Her eyes were stuck on Eve, watching as her beloved paced back and forth. The words that she said faded out into silence as Galen stared and drew in the Dreamcatcher's beauty and aura. She knew how she'd been so enticed by this woman. The pull she gave out, the allure that she possessed, was unreasonable. It was unfair, almost. No one had a chance, especially not Galen.

Over the years, the Dreamcatcher had started to change, much as Galen had. She always wore her hair up, braided, ready for war. Eve never once let her guard down. If her hair was down, she claimed, she wouldn't be able to slip on her helmet as easy. Her snatched-back locks gave her thin, chiselled features a chance to shine. Those high cheekbones and devastatingly strong jawline were on display for all to see, as well as her rare, but still existent, dimples.

When Galen had first met the Dreamcatcher, not a single mark had tarnished her skin. Now, the king, as she was so determined to be called, fought regularly. Her flesh was littered with the scars and the markings of war and battle. There was a chip out of the bridge of her nose, a few gouges in her cheeks, and raised, bumpy lines through her eyebrows and her lip. Galen always told her it made her look rugged and wild, and she wasn't at all wrong.

Decorated in dark purple finery, the Dreamcatcher lavished herself in gold jewellery, fit for a king. Atop her head was her prized possession—her crown. It sat so beautiful atop her golden locks. It glimmered everywhere she went, even if there was no light. The jewels that were set within the golden metal were alive with trapped souls and shining monsters, creatures only the darkest of minds could muster. Little, thin chains dangled against her forehead, handcrafted with such delicacy and love. She never went anywhere without it, nor was she ever without the matching rings and bracelets and bangles, or mass number of necklaces stacked high about her throat. If she were to be thrown into the ocean, she would surely drown.

Waking herself up from her daydream, Galen saw Eve stood right in front of Anders, her hand on his shoulder.

"You've always done me proud, my boy," the Dreamcatcher praised. "You're my champion for a reason! You've never once let me down. I know that I can count on you to win my wars in my absence, though now…now we are going to fight side by side."

Panic flushed through Galen at the thought of Eve going back out onto the battlefield. She almost said something, but her king knew she would interrupt, and gave her absolutely no time to muster any sort of sentence.

"For too long I've been stuck inside this castle, planning and plotting, unable to get my hands dirty," the Dreamcatcher boomed. She wandered about until her feet were planted still in the centre of the hall, staring out at her court. "It's time that bear learns who his king is."

Uproarious cheers went up as everyone flung themselves from their seats and showered their monarch in applause. There wasn't a single person still sat down. There wasn't a single person refusing to give a hand to their king. Their faces were smothered with glee and excitement. This was the end of an era, and the years to come would be doused in oceans of blood and souls.

Eve came wandering back to her throne and spared a second to glance lovingly down at her beloved. "My queen," she murmured, though still loud enough that her voice ricocheted off the walls. Her words silenced the crowd. They all waited with bated breaths on the edge of their seats for the king's next words. "My beautiful, decisive queen. I've been away from you for too long, poppet, but no more. You and I are going to go on a conquest."

A conquest? Galen couldn't think of something worse. She still smiled when Eve took her hand, though that smile wavered when she caught sight of the ring sitting about her ring finger. Her mind flashed back to her wedding, that unhappy night, that tumultuous fight.

"Soon, you and I are going to rule the entire dreamscape, with no challengers threatening our throne!"

Cheers went up once more.

"Those that dare to stand up against us will pay the ultimate price for it!"

Another loud cheer washed over Galen.

"Their souls will turn the sky green and their bodies will pave the roads we tread, for there isn't going to be a single stretch of land we leave unconquered. This world is ours for the taking, and there is no one strong enough to stop us now!"

Galen had never heard clapping or cheering so loud. The people were delirious, besides themselves with excitement and anticipation. They were all evil bastards. Each and every one of them had done dastardly things. That's how they'd all gotten to this court. Lords and their ladies who had killed in Eve's name, in Galen's name, just to gain a seat closer to the Dreamcatcher. Galen didn't like nor trust any of them, but still rose to her feet when Eve tugged on her arm.

"*You seem worried,*" the Dreamcatcher whispered to her.

"Alden was back."

A pause from the king indicated her displeasure. "I thought she was dead."

"She is not."

"What did she have to say?"

Galen put on a brave face and smiled at the crowd, feeling each individual muscle in her face pull taut. "Nothing, as always."

"Nothing…"

"She did send this my way, though." Galen held out her hand and, slowly, the arrow that Alden had shot at her materialised in her palm. She held on to it tenderly, letting it roll back and forth up her fingers.

The Dreamcatcher was incensed. "She shot at you?"

"Again, as always."

Eve glared deep within Galen's eyes and swallowed her fury. Her nose still twitched as she leant in and kissed Galen delicately and passionately. When she pulled away, the king kept her forehead resting against Galen's and let out the shakiest breath.

"*I will see my boot rest on her head by the time this war is done,*" the Dreamcatcher whispered to Galen.

"*I've no doubts,*" Galen whispered back.

Taking in a calming inhale, Eve turned outwards so she faced her crowd. She grinned from ear to ear, the news of Alden only driving her forwards. Intertwining her fingers with Galen's, she lifted their knotted hands together in the air to the sound of uproarious applause.

Letting that inhale out, the Dreamcatcher eyed Galen with a lusty, hungry glare and grinned at her dirtily. "Shall we?"

Galen couldn't help but smile back. "Let's go," she said simply. "We have a world to conquer."

CPSIA information can be obtained
at www.ICGtesting.com
Printed in the USA
BVHW041042200423
662718BV00011B/418

9 781398 459748